Pandora's Inner Goddess

Marmeduke M Gibbons is a playwright, poet and novelist. Born in London, England he now lives in Rome, Italy. His daily eccentric and extravagant exploits are chronicled at:

www.facebook.com/marmeduke.gibbons

M M Gibbons

Pandora's Inner Goddess

MMX Press

Published by MMXEP, 2012
Copyright © MMXEP Ltd., 2012

First published in Great Britain and on-line by

MMXEP
Fazeley Studios
191 Fazeley Street
Birmingham, B5 5SE

www.pandorasinnergoddess.com
facebook: www.facebook.com/pandorasinnergoddess

Published by MMX EP Ltd. Reg. No. 7530483

ISBN 978-0-9546514-3-5

Book design by Karl Binder
Cover design by Karl Binder
Cover image © Richard Battye, 2012

For Millad and his Merry Men

ACKNOWLEDGMENTS

I am indebted to the following people for their help and support:

To Mistress Nicole for planting the seed; to Mistress Mary for watering it, and to Mistress Jacqui for her nurturing of the emerging foliage.

To the Mysterious Patsy.

To Richard Battye, ace photographer.

To Karl Binder for creative and technical brilliance.

To the real Millad, Sparky, Dean and Jamie for invaluable research and insight.

To my tabby cat Fyodor, my familiar and confidante.

To Antonio and Theresa for their physical love.

CHAPTER ONE

I scowl with frustration at myself in the mirror. I have been trying for over half an hour to sculpt the peaked side-crop (that my sister Naz cut for me) into a stand-up hairdo with radical texturizing fibre glue gel. But it keeps flopping over - like I've been out in the rain. And I will be out in the rain in fifteen minutes; it hasn't stopped hammering it down all summer. The last sunny day was in May and now July is midway through. When I was woken up at half seven by my iPhone alarm tone (featuring *Biggie*, the *Notorious B-I-G*), I thought it was Friday, so I was a bit disappointed to remember when I reached the bathroom, that it was only Thursday. I put on the same blue-striped shirt I wore on Monday, Tuesday and Wednesday, hook round my neck the red tie I always carefully slide off after work so I don't have to bother re-doing the knot the following day, and try to find my shoes. One is generally under the bed, the other one could be anywhere. Today it happens to be on top of the wardrobe. I don't remember putting it there. As I leave my bedroom and close the door behind me, I'm in the main room of the flat I share with Sparky.

Sparky is my best mate and he is down with some random illness, as ever. He's eating *Cheerios* on the sofa and watching breakfast TV.

"Morning, loser," he yawns.

"Morning, tosser," I reply, putting the kettle on. "Oh for fuck's sake Sparks, you've drunk all the milk again! There's not even enough for tea!"

"I got up first. Why shouldn't I eat the milk?"

"You can't eat the milk. You drink the milk."

"Bollocks. I'm eating it with these Cheerios and a spoon. How can I be drinking it?"

"What are you watching?" I ask him with a sigh, one eye on our new *Sony* flat screen TV, which I'm paying for in instalments.

"The Olympic Flame. It's going through Derbyshire. Look, that bloke is taking it into a cable car. The Heights of Abraham? Where the fuck is that? Israel?"

"Right, so now, I'll have to go to *Starbucks* on the way to the office. I've got a big interview today. Pandora Poste."

"No way! Really?" Suddenly Sparky is interested. "What, the woman that wrote that dirty book for women? What do they call it, 'mummy porn' or something?"

"I don't know," I answer. "I have no idea who she is and I've got to get to the office early to do some research."

"Don't know who she is? You cock! She's the new JK Rowling! She is minted, mate!"

"What, have you read her book then, tosspot?"

"Yeah, a bit. On-line. Page 174, that's all you need to read. It's shit. It's not proper porno".

"Well, you'd be the expert there, Sparks. You want to watch out mate, porn messes up your attitude towards women, and it's addictive. We did a unit on 'porn in the media' at uni. For instance, would you like to see your sister in one of those magazines under your bed?" From the shifty look on Sparky's face I see that he wouldn't mind at all seeing his sister in *Jazzler* (or whatever his favourite whack-off magazine is called).

"Ash sher if she gray". He's slurping at his chipped blue-stripy bowl again, and I can't hear what he says properly because his mouth is full of Cheerios. One is sticking to his chin.

"What?"

"Ask her if she's gay! Pandora Poste! There's lesbo action in her book. *Black Heart*, it's called. So I reckon she's gay, or 'bi' at the least."

"I thought my boss told me she was married? To Noel…no, Neil, I think? She dedicates her books to him apparently."

"*Was* married, Mil, *was* married. On the market again now, pal. Not bad looking either. Massive jugs."

I always get nervous when Sparky starts talking dirty, so I shuffle out to the front door and put on my red Glenmuir jacket and pick up the golf brolly my Dad gave me. Dad is a businessman but he seems to spend most of his time playing golf, so he gives me a lot of stuff from his 'Golf Days'. Brollies. Golf balls. Waterproof jackets. Metal things that look like those wooden forks you eat shrimps with in polystyrene pots at the seaside (I like mine with vinegar and white pepper). Golf shoes. I don't play golf myself, so I don't wear the golf shoes; whilst they do look pretty cool, they have spikes in the sole and mark the floor. Finally, my trusty rucksack with my journo stuff; laptop, iPad, iPod, journo pads and loads of sharpened pencils. They taught me well at Bolton University, where I did my degree in Journalism, and the *West Sussex County Times* is giving me my first break. I am determined not to blow it. When I think I might blow it, I recite these words to myself, out loud:

"*You only get one shot, do not miss your chance to blow, this opportunity comes once in a lifetime, yo!*"

It doesn't sound as good as Eminem when I say it, but it fires me up anyway. Also out loud, I say my 'leaving the flat mantra' when I leave the flat. "Keys, wallet, phone." Sometimes I say the mantra but forget to actually check I have all these items and leave one or more of them behind. Today, I'm on the ball though, and I pat my pockets as I say my 'leaving the flat thing'. Popping my head back in the main room (that's what we call it, the main room, it feels a bit too empty to be called a lounge, plus it also has the kitchen in it) I smile wryly at Sparky who has his eyes closed and seems to be going back to sleep.

I have one more leaving ritual, I nearly forgot. Hanging on the outside of my bedroom door handle is a sign; it's one of those 'Do Not Disturb' cards you get in hotels'? Only this one also has a 'people icon' design thing on it which is a bit different, and it's a bit rude. It's like, a stick man icon lying on his back and a stick lady icon straddling him. On the flip-side of the sign it says, "Maid, Please Make Up The Room" and this time the stick man is sitting up in bed on his own wearing a cheesy smile. Sparky gave it to me, and though it's sexist and chambermaid-ist and not even that funny, I use it to indicate to Sparky when he can and can't come in to my room, so it is useful. I don't know where Sparky finds this sort of stuff, but I guess it's the same place he finds his crap T-shirts. He has too much time on his hands, and he spends the day surfing for the worst mail order T-shirts he can find. It's like a double bluff…he finds them funny because they are so bad. So he has those ones with icon people doing obscene things to each other, he has loads of 'beer jokes' ones and a comprehensive collection of what he calls his 'Do It' T-shirt range, like the one he is currently slumping about in and spilling Cheerios down. It features a line drawing of a woman perched on The Periodic Table. It says "Chemists Do It on the Table… Periodically." The trouble is, he wears these things in the street and down the pub, which can get embarrassing, but the more crass the T-shirt, the more he seems to like it. I flip the dodgy sign on my bedroom door to "Do Not Disturb" and I'm ready to leave.

"See you later, Sparks." He doesn't answer, so I conclude he has fallen asleep. He's my dearest friend, and a complete twat.

IT'S RAINING AS I hit West Street and walk past the bus station. My destination is the Horsham office of the West Sussex County Times. We cover the Horsham area (which is where I'm from - my Dad helped me get my first job through his mates at the golf club) which includes villages like Warnham and Itchingfield. My Mum and Dad live in Nuthurst (which is about five miles away) with my younger sister Naz who is doing her A-Levels. Me and Sparky rent a flat because we needed our independence. I tend to go home every weekend though, to get my washing done, plus Mum's cooking is the best.

Time ticking on, I give *Starbucks* a miss, avoid the puddles on Market Square, past the bandstand, and into the office. Our office is made of brick. I think it was built in the sixties. Eight fifty-five hundred hours, I stride into the office - only Nathalie who works on the front desk is here - I went to school with her and she was in the year below me. She worked in *Boots* for a bit before she too got her big break. She smiles at me, I think she likes me a bit. Sometimes I bring her sweets, like a sherbet dib dab or something like that? Not that often though, 'cos I don't want her to think I'm coming onto her or anything, because frankly, I'm not.

"Do you want your coffee yet, Mil?" she asks me sweetly, and I give her my big smile and do the 'OK sign' with my thumb and forefinger making an 'O'. Bruce Willis does that in a really cool way, so now, I do it.

I unpack my bag onto my desk with my usual routine, but, ah…oh shit… not so cool. My red Glenmuir jacket is one of those that you pull off over your head, and I forgot to lower the zip before I did so, and it is stuck under my chin. I'm like Houdini in a straightjacket, wriggling to get free. At last, I feel the zip slide roughly over my nose, dislodging my glasses (today I'm wearing my Clooneys from *Specsavers*) and Nathalie is standing there having helped me out of my cagoule. Dammit. Not cool at all. Bruce Willis would never get his head stuck in his cagoule.

"Ah, thanks Nat, got a bit stuck there," I gibber, stating the perfectly obvious. I feel my face burning with embarrassment. My complexion is quite dark, because my Mum is from Iran, but my Dad is from Bootle and he is quite ruddy. So due to his contribution to my genetics, I can go quite red, just as I am going right now.

"Here's your coffee, Mila," Nat is smiling that nice smile of hers again, but before I get chance to thank her, my boss Ray breezes in, stinking of the fag he was smoking on his way in.

"Morning Milan," he croaks. Ray always croaks first thing, and coughs a lot. He always gets my name wrong too, he calls me Milan instead of Milad, but I don't like to correct him, he's my boss after all. I like Ray, he is nice to me and reminds me of a cartoon hack. "Double expresso from the machine please Nat, pronto. Big day for you today, young feller. This could be your big scoop, boy!" Ray slaps me on the back, really hard. He doesn't seem to know how hard his encouraging slaps are. "Where are you meeting her - and what time?"

"Er…I thought you were arranging the interview, Ray? Sorry, I…"

"What? You little prat! Pandora Poste's big home-coming and you haven't arranged a meet? Fuck's sake. Well she is staying at *The Mercure*, hang on, I'll sort this out."

Ray didn't ask me to arrange a time and a place and I know he forgot to do it, but I don't mind him blaming me, because he's my boss and even if he says rude stuff to me, I know he doesn't really mean it. He storms into his office, smacks the fluorescent light on, slumps into his big leather swivel chair, grabs the phone and puts his feet up on the desk. I notice he hasn't taken his mac off yet and it's soaked.

I settle down at my desktop computer and get into *Google*. "Pandora Poste", I type in. "Images", I click. Wow. She has got big, erm, whammers, just like Sparky said. And lovely eyebrows. Threaded they are, my sis can thread eyebrows. Big brown eyes. Scarlet mouth. Little ears. She is quite a -what does Sparky say? A fox?

"Right Milan, I've saved yer bacon. Half ten. Mercure Hotel, lobby. Grab some petty cash off Nat for a taxi and buy Pandora some brunch or whatever she wants. Oh, and take this with you." Ray goes back into his office and rifles through his ancient leather briefcase, removing a very dog-eared paperback book. "The missus wants Pandora to sign her copy. "To Cynthia", Milan. And don't fuck up the interview…check your Dictaphone has batteries and take notes. I don't have time to prep you, I have to get to the council planning committee. Breaking news…new Tesco's Extra in for planning permission. The fogeys won't like it. Best of luck, young man."

"Thank you, Ray, I'll need it. I can't believe that you're trusting me with this one."

"Neither can I!" shouts Ray, slurping down his 'expresso' in one and dashing out of the office again. He always says 'expresso' rather than 'espresso', but I don't like to correct him, because he is my boss.

OK, I have about forty minutes to prep this interview. I inspect the dog-eared book on my desk. On the cover, the knot of a tie. (I think Americans call them neckties). But not like my tie, an expensive one, probably silk, with a complicated pattern. On the back, I'm expecting a picture of Pandora arching one of her threaded eyebrows, but nope, no piccie. Just blurb. I read it out loud to myself:

"*Passionate, naughty and completely absorbing, this is a novel that will grab you, keep you, and stay with you for the rest of your days.*" A bold claim, methinks! The only novel that has done that is *The Hobbit*. And possibly *The Gormenghast Trilogy*. The back-blurb continues:

"*When history student Gemma Ironside meets successful entrepreneur Barnabas Black, she finds him very handsome and deeply compelling. Convinced that he hardly noticed her, she tries to forget him – until he turns up at the campus coffee shop and invites her out.*

"Naive and innocent, Gemma is astonished to find she wants this man. And, when he tells her to keep her distance, it only makes her more determined. But Black is a control freak, and damaged by his many demons. As they become embroiled in a tempestuous love affair, Gemma goes on a journey of self-discovery, as Black's dark secrets emerge..."

This just sounds like Mills and Boon, I think to myself. My Mum reads them now and again. We looked at a few of them in A-level lit. Sort of escapism for women, cornball romantic fiction. Like a rom-com. Naz watches a lot of rom-coms. Usually they have the actors from *Friends* or Colin Firth. I like action films. Spiderman. Marvel Superheroes. That sort of stuff. I thumb through Pandora's book.

As I expected, all Mills and Boon, really. Hang on, what's this? *"Holy fuck..it hurts?"* Aha, it is quite rude in places, this is. *"Now I'm going to fuck you"*. Blimey, so not quite what I thought...OH, NATHALIE?!!"

Nathalie has crept up on me and surprised me, so much that I have dropped the book on the floor and knocked my coffee over after it, which seeps into the pages of the splayed book. I fall to my knees, rescuing it from the creeping brown pool.

"Nathalie, what were you doing creeping up on me like that? This is Ray's wife's copy of *Black Heart*! He wants me to get Mrs Poste to sign it. Oh man, it's all gone soggy!"

"Sorry, Mil!" squeaks Nathalie, also falling to her knees to help me mop up. I can't help a quick peek down her dress at her bra, which I notice is black today, but I look away before she can notice I'm looking. I've noticed that Nathalie wears different colour bras. Sometimes you can see the strap quite clearly; other times she wears tops you can see the bra through. To be honest I think that's a bit too risqué for the office, but I don't say anything and Ray seems to be OK with it, and he's the boss.

"I was just bringing *my* copy of *Black Heart* over when I made you jump. I was hoping that Mrs Poste could sign my copy as well, you know - after you've finished the interview with her?"

"What, you've read *Black Heart* too? What is it with this book?! I can see how *The Harry Potter* books became legend…and Dan Brown, of course. And what was his name, Stieg Larson, to some extent…the Girl With… what was it?"

"The Dragon Tattoo! Loved that movie. Daniel Craig was in it. Love Daniel Craig." Nathalie acts out all gooey-eyed and like she's swooning.

"OK, fair enough, that book was OK, but what's going on with this one?" I brandish in the air Nathalie's non-coffee stained but also very battered copy of *Black Heart.*

"It's a turn-on, darlin'!" Sheila, the experienced journalist I work opposite (also arriving reeking of fags) flings her bag onto her chair and she is shaking her brolly out (dangerously near to the extension lead that houses both our computer mains lead plugs). "We've all read it, ain't we, Nat!" she cackles, throatily.

"It's racy!" giggles Nathalie, blushing.

"Is it racy?" I ask stupidly.

"IT'S RACY!" they both agree simultaneously, and then start laughing.

"You mean you haven't read it, Mil?" Sheila makes a gawping expression in my direction as she wriggles out of her coat and straightens down her skirt (too short, in my opinion). "How are you going to interview Pandora properly? Perhaps I should do it instead?"

I respond firmly. "No thanks, Sheila. Ray has asked me to do it, and I will do it. I've got half an hour to speed-read this book and I can do my questions in the taxi."

"Suit yerself. Get me a latté sweetheart. Two sugars this morning, Nat. But watch out, Mila…they say she is quite the cougar now she's single! I know her from the old days…she was a year below me in school. Not much, she wasn't. She never won no writing prizes, like I done. But she *did* have a rich husband in publishing, I expect that helps a tiny bit? She won't remember me, but tell her I barged her over at netball once. That's a claim to fame, barging Pandora Poste over. *And* she wasn't Pandora then. Her name was Susan."

I put in my earphones, and get ma hip-hop bangin' on ma Pod. Oh yeah. It's *Melody* by *MF Doom*. This is a sign to Sheila and the rest of the office that I don't want to be disturbed. But I have to take them out of my ears, because I can see Sheila is mouthing something at me.

"Be a darlin' and get 'Suse' to sign my copy would you? To 'Sheelz'. Ta, Milad."

I try the earphone 'do-not-disturb' thing again and go back to ma man Doom. I read in concentration about Mrs Poste on Wikipedia. *"Rapidly becoming Horsham's best known person after Shelley (poet) and Holly Willoughby ('cleavage of the year, 2012'), she was born in Horsham in 1967".* I sometimes wonder who writes the stuff on Wikipedia. But it is usually true. So, I note on my pad…she is 45 years old and 46 on November the Fourth. She is about the same age as my Mum, though I can't ever remember exactly how old Mum is. It doesn't matter does it? It's just my lovely Mum! Now, back to Mrs Poste - three teenage kids, married 20-plus years, divorced last year from Neil, the same year that her husband's publishing company published *Black Heart*. Formerly in PR. Good old Wiki, everything you need to know about anything and anyone at the click of a button. Right, time to go, Nat calls me a taxi (Horsham Cabs 333333 - a nice easy one to remember), and we decide that I'll take her copy of *Black Heart* to sign for Ray's wife as both copies look identically battered, and Nat keeps the coffee-stained and unsigned one, as she agrees with me that it was her fault that the book got damaged, for creeping up on me. I reluctantly take Sheila's book as well, though I don't really want my in-depth interview turning into a book signing.

I ZOOM OUT OF TOWN, indicating that I do not wish to talk to my cabbie, by ignoring his prattle. I need to write down my interview questions, but it isn't easy in the back of a stop-starting cab, and in addition to feeling queasy, my writing is all over the place. I pay the cabbie off, who is annoyed with me that he didn't get to talk, and I don't tip him after asking for a receipt, which makes him even more annoyed. Too bad. Ray is really rude to cabbies and I'm following his lead.

Into The Mercure Hotel. I've only been here twice before, once for my cousin's wedding and once for a High School Prom long ago when I was

16. I shoot a glance at the laurel bushes where I was copiously sick on the former occasion, and the 'Highgate Room' adjacent to the lobby where I was copiously sick on the latter occasion, behind a rack of chairs. I secure myself a position to the left of the huge chandelier in a circular booth set off the main lobby, and get my interview stuff set up. I catch the eye of some waiter dude, and as instructed by Ray, ask him to inform the front desk that Mr Brown is waiting for Mrs Poste.

"And a glass of sparkling water please. With ice and lemon." This was a tip from my Dad, who does a lot of business meetings. He's told me what to order, and what not to order. Problem with tea and coffee cups in saucers is that they can rattle about, and make your hand look shaky if you're nervous. *Coca-Cola* can look a bit chavvy, but sparkling water…cool and classy. Never order pastry, he told me. It goes all over you when you eat it. My Dad lets me into the mind games he plays in meetings. He might order crumbly pastry for people he wants to out-do, and not touch his, so they get full of pastry crumbs, this giving him the psychological upper hand. "That is called 'pastry-ing' someone, Milad," he told me. He also showed me how to use the Rolex watch he gave me for my eighteenth to distract people by reflecting sunlight in their eyes. I practise this as I sip my water; not because I want to use this trick on Mrs Poste, but because I want to keep in practice for when I do need it, like in office staff meetings when I want to try to end some long-winded speech by Eric, the office bore. OK, Dictaphone check. "Hello, hello, testing 1,2,3. Mercure Hotel, Horsham, it is 10.35 anti-meridian, and awaiting to interview, I mean waiting to interview, Mrs Pandora Poste." I play the test message back…I sound less than authoritative. I decide to lower my voice when my interviewee arrives. I suck one of the ice cubes bobbing about in my tall glass, to cool the palate of my mouth. I like doing that.

"Mr Brown?" A guy with slick-back hair, a foreign accent and *Police* sunglasses is standing over me in a dark suit like one of the agents in *The Matrix*. I reckon he's Italian.

"Si. Signori Brown," I reply, with a flourish of my hand, which is kind of Italian, like Al Pacino does sometimes. And I am a *big* Pacino fan. My Mum says I look like him a bit, but a taller version.

"Huh? Sorry?" The agent looks puzzled. "I am looking for Mr Brown. My client Ms Poste is expecting an interview with him. Are you Mr Brown?"

I can't hear him. There is white noise in my head. There is a woman of extravagant curvature tottering towards me on very high platform shoes across the lobby. She is wearing a green dress, chiffon I think. Everything about her is in motion. She is beaming bewitchingly and bits of her are bouncing up and down in syncopated rhythm. A cloud of expensive perfume envelops me. The ice cube slips from my slack jaw and bounces off the table in front of me. All the words have slowed down to ultra-slow motion.

"Miiiiiiiiiissssterrrr Beeeroowwwwnnn?" the Italian guy is mawing at me. Suddenly, all the sound comes back on and I start one of my occasional coughing fits, during which I attempt to confirm that I am Mr. Brown. The dude is pushed out of the way by the vision in green, who is patting me gently but firmly on the back. Her dress reminds me of the one that everyone made a fuss of on Keira Knightley in the movie *Atonement*, except this dress is on a proper woman and I am staring down a canyon of cleavage contained by an exotic dark green Paisley patterned bra with black webbing on top. Holly Willoughby - Cleavage of the Year 2012? Not anymore she isn't. Now I'm shaking her hand, it's firm, it's soft, it's nails are ridiculously ornate, expensive rings glittering at the base of her tanned fingers and silver bracelets clanking at her powerful wrist. I'm swallowed by her large brown eyes, her brilliant metallic red hair shining iridescently in the light of the chandelier. And what's this? She is saying something to me!! Fortunately, the slo-mo ends and we are in real time again.

"Are you going to be OK to do the interview, Mr Brown?" That is what she is saying to me.

"Aha! Yes of course, Mrs Poste…"

"Muzz Poste, Mr Brown. But you must call me Pandora. May I call you…?"

"Yes of course, you must call me!" I blurt, just as I realise she is asking my bloody name. "Ah, sorry, Milad, Mee-lad, it's Persian."

"Oh," she purrs, "a handsome Persian boy to interview me in my home town! How marvellous Mee-lad. Am I pronouncing it correctly? Meee-lad. And were you born in Persia?"

"No miss, I mean…Pandora, I was born here! In Horsham!"

"Ah, then we are connected by a sacred bond. The same home town, eh? That can be very important to the inter-twining of two lives. It is not a co-incidence that myself and Shelley were both born here, for instance. Oh, I am sorry, this is Arne, my marvellous driver and PA, from Oslo, Norway. You don't mind if he joins us do you?"

Arne lifts up his sunglasses to reveal mocking steel blue eyes in a very pale face topped by the slicked back hair which is clearly blonde. "Buongiorno, Signori Brown. Come sta?" I wish I knew some Norwegian to reply. But I don't.

"No, no of course not! Arne, good to meet you. How do you do?" I reach over to shake Arne's cool white hand and I hover over the Grand Canyon again, noting a glittering heart-shaped ruby nestling within.

"Righto," I go, trying to compose myself under the beam of Pandora's indulgent and supernaturally white smile. "So, I am going to turn this little device on…just get the volume right…"

"As long as it doesn't turn *me* on!" My interviewee has a throaty laugh at her own amusing innuendo. I smile back, it is funny. She is funny!

"Hehe, no indeed, Muzz Pandora, I mean Pandora, let us hope it does not…sooooo….first question…"

"Are you intending to offer Ms Poste morning coffee, Mr Brown? If not I will do so. Ms Poste likes to have a double shot skinny latté and a pastry at this hour." Arne frowns at me, most severely. My father's Bootle ruddiness chases my mother's dusky melanin from my face. How stupid and rude of me!

"I am SO sorry, Arne, Pandora. I expressly intended to do so. Please forgive me whilst I summon a waiter…" But Arne has clicked his fingers and a waiter is already taking his order.

"For you, Mr Brown?" he snaps.

"Err...I'm OK thanks. Arne."

"Oh *do-oo* join me, Mee-lad! I detest eating alone! And I don't think Arne eats at all! Do you, Arne?" That throaty laugh again. Infectious. I write the word down on my pad, which seems full of indecipherable scrawl from the taxi ride.

"As you insist, Pandora. I'll have the same then, waiter. Thank you. OK, so...thank you so much, Ms. Poste for agreeing to be interviewed by the West Sussex County Times, in this your home town. How does it feel to be back?"

"Well, I do return quite often actually, as my mother lives here. I live in London, in Holland Park, so it isn't far to travel. I had a wonderful childhood here, and a *very* good schooling."

I try what we journos call 'ad hoc'. It's sometimes a good technique for 'breaking the ice', and putting an interviewee at their ease. "Actually a colleague of mine on the paper knows you from school? Sheila Stanley? She never got married, so her name is the same."

The smile freezes on Pandora's face, and the layers of foundation on her cheek look like they might open out into jagged fissures. Arne shifts in his seat and his knuckles go white. Well, even whiter.

"I don't know anyone of that name, I'm afraid." Pandora has given me a withering look.

"Ah, I think she said she was in the year above you, and you may have played netball with her?"

"I SAID, Mr. Brown, that I do not *know* anyone of that name! Did you not *hear* me?"

Arne stares at me like a frozen fjord. "I think we had better move on from that question, Mr Brown".

Jesus, my ice-breaker has gone horribly wrong. There is tiny tumbleweed blowing across the glass table. And I can't read my second question.

Thank God, here is the waiter with the coffee, and a trolley heaving with pastries. Pandora is rubbing her hands together, and looking gleeful.

"Thank the Lord, I'm ravenous! Arne, get me two cinnamon twirls, and a Chelsea bun." Whew, she seems to be thawing a bit as she takes a chunk out of one of the twirls with her amazing white gnashers. Mental notes to self...don't do her school days. Seems to be sensitive about them. And don't give her Sheila's book to sign. I notice that Pandora isn't bothered about being 'pastried'...she lets the crumbs and flakes and bigger bits sit about her cheeks and fall unashamedly about her green dress. My Dad would never have been able to out-pastry *this* particular woman!

"Ash me aneur queshon, Mee-lad!" She seems to have recovered her smiling demeanour now, and I like her speaking with her mouth full, she carries it off, somehow. That's not something I could carry off, or actually anybody else I've ever met, especially Sparky, who disgusts me when he eats with his mouth open. But this vision of lady loveliness...she not only carries it off, I'm actively interested in the masticated mess in her mouth.

"Where did you get the inspiration to write *Black Heart*?" I ask. She loves that question. She is bouncing up and down on the leatherette, and her massive breasts rise and fall as she does so.

"Mainly from my domestic god, Neil. Even though we reached the end of our line, last year." Oh no, she is getting upset! There is a tear in her eye. Arne is leaning forward in concern and handing her an immaculately folded white handkerchief with which she dabs her eye and blows her nose with a loud blast. I've fucked up again! Two questions, two disasters. Jesus, ace reporter...not! But then, I remember my training in Bolton. I have pierced the skin! This isn't bad, it's good...I might get some copy here that more banal interviews wouldn't. You have to be crafty at this game, that's what Ray tells me.

"I'm so sorry to have upset you, Pandora." My eyes must be wide with sympathy, and possibly even a bit dewy, because she takes my hand in both of hers...it feels like my hand is in a tight embrace with her whole body.

"My darling boy, you haven't upset me. You *couldn't* upset me. But my wounds are still fresh. I had to leave Neil, you see. For...artistic reasons. I broke the poor man, I know I did. He hasn't left the house in months. But

I had to do it, Mee-lad, I had to do it. The caged bird inside me had to take flight. Arne has been such a support. Thank you, Arne." She hands the handkerchief, now mottled with her hot tears, mascara and bubbly phlegm back to the unsmiling Nordic, who I vaguely suspect could be her lover. Lucky bastard. I reckon I have cracked the interview now - her words are unstoppable. She speaks long and movingly about her life; how she wrote unsleeping through many nights to complete *Black Heart*; and how much white wine she and her close circle of reading group lady friends shipped in discussing and honing her prose. She weeps and laughs raucously as she describes her 'Bonkers Babes' and gets Arne to order her a glass of Cava.

"And are you working on a sequel to *Black Heart*, Pandora?" I interject as she immediately drains the fizzing champagne glass, which appears super-fast from the bar.

"Berp! Oooh, do excuse me! Darling, this must stay between us, but yes, I am well on the way with *Black Heart Darker*. Oh God, silly me. Mee-lad. Stop your little machine." What the fuck...Arne already has it in his white hands and he is rewinding it! This is bang out of order...

"Er, Arne, what are you doing, mate?" He looks at me for the flicker of an instant, but he has expertly deleted Pandora's last comment from my Dictaphone, before handing it back. "Please also erase any record in your notebook of the working title of Ms Poste's new novel, Mr Brown. We will assume that this will not appear in your copy, or I am afraid you will hear from our lawyers."

"Oh don't be so formal, Arne! I'm sure Mee-lad would never upset me so, and besides, it was my silly fault. I think the bubbles must have gone to my head! I don't usually drink so early, Mee-lad, it must have been the association I made when I was telling you about my Bonkers Babes. Actually, I'll have another, Arne, rather nice. You can turn your little machine on again now, my handsome boy! Another question, another question, I love being interviewed about my work!"

I am a bit pissed off. Not with her obviously, but with Arne. But as the true professional I aspire to be, I am not going to show it. I set the recorder off again, and try not to sound ruffled with my next question.

"So, your book signing tour begins in your home town tomorrow, Pandora…where next?"

"Oh, it is going to be such fun, but *such* hard work, Milad. All the major cities of course. But towns as well. I feel like I am the Olympic torch, travelling the length and breadth of the country to illuminate the lives of women…and men of course! "

"Ah, that's interesting, Pandora, your audience is intended to include men… as well as women?"

"Of course!" she looks shocked as she stares at me over her tilted wine glass. "Berp. Of course, darling. Have you not read my booky, Mee-lad?" Shit, cornered! What crappy research I've done. I'm not a good liar, but sometimes you have to be a professional liar to be a journalist. That's what Ray has taught me.

"Yes, yes, I have, I have! It's brilliant Pandora, it's really…good…stuff. Well, I have only speed-read it as research for this interview, but I'm looking forward to reading it properly in my own time!"

"Oh, good, good, Mee-lad." She has taken my hand in hers again, and gives me a very serious look, a bit like my headmistress used to when she was advising me on my career choices. "You should. It will…teach you things." She drops my hand and raises the crystal glass to her lips, her eyes sparkling with feminine mystery. Right, that's that settled then. Sheila will not be getting her copy of *Black Heart* back for a couple of days. Anyway, I need to manoeuvre off the subject of how little I know about her novel, and I inspect my pad for the next question. But the taxi-ride scrawl is utterly indecipherable. More table-tumbleweed among the lipstick-stained coffee cups and wine glasses. Arne is looking at his watch. Pandora is draining her glass. My time is nearly up. I go for it. It's the wild card. So help me - I'm going with Sparky.

I lean forward, and attempt an ironic smile. It may look like I'm leering. "Pandora, your novel contains love scenes between women. Is there a gay side to Pandora Poste?"

Arne starts, as if stung by a wasp on the back of his neck. So much so, that I am checking the air for wasps. Pandora stares at me, at first with an expression of sudden hatred (exactly the same one with which she greeted

24

my question about her schooldays. Or about Sheila, at least). My ironic smile/leer freezes on my face under her wintery gaze. And then melts into a thawed wavy line. She is suddenly laughing that lovely gravelly laugh. And then hooting, like the whistle of a steam train. In a good way.

"Ooooh, Mee-lad, you are a ONE!" And that is all the answer I get to Sparky's rubbish question. Arne is on his feet, my hand is icily and stiffly shaken, and the still-hooting authoress is led away waving at me…and blowing me a kiss! I watch her, spellbound, sashaying across the shiny lobby in her expensive green dress and high-rise shoes, hotel guests frozen in their tracks as they recognise who she is. She disappears into the lift, and as the sliding doors close…she blows me another kiss from afar…I catch it and hold it to my mouth. Shit, I suddenly remember! Ray's wife's copy of *Blackheart* unsigned!

I DON'T REMEMBER how I got back to the office, but I think I walked it, deep in wonder. Ray was quite pleased with my interview article. He edited it together with a gorgeous promo photo of Pandora. We ended the article with the date (the day after tomorrow), time (10.30) and place (Waterstones, Horsham) of Pandora's book signing. But he wasn't very pleased with me for forgetting to get his wife's book signed.

"Right, you can fucking well go to the book signing and get it signed there. 'To Cynthia', remember. And I don't care how long you have to queue *and* you can do it in your lunch hour."

No problem, Ray, I smile to myself. That gives me two nights to read *Black Heart* and a priceless excuse to see *her* again! I think she will like my article too. I go back to my desk and allow myself to swing my feet up on my desk just like Ray does, and stretch my arms behind my head, which contains my little secret with Pandora. Well, and Arne. I'll keep it safe, Pandora. *Black Heart Darker* will never pass my lips.

CHAPTER TWO

My heart is pounding. I'm in my room and I can hear Sparky's *Brian Jonestown Massacre* booming out from his Bose speakers. Sparky and some of my other mates are in a band called *The Orange Spangles*. It's quite a clever name. *Spangles* were tubes of boiled sweets in the Seventies, and according to Sparky's Dad, there were a mixture of flavours and you used to offer your mates one - but nobody liked the orange ones. So that gives the band a good retro name because they are into that, and also a kind of outcast image. They thought about *The Fruit Polos* for the same reasons, but thought it sounded a bit gay. Sometimes the lads practice at our flat, well, usually until Mr. Spellars downstairs comes up in his slippers, and complains. Mr. Spellars is a bit of an old fart but I guess drum kits and bass amps in the room above could get a bit annoying. I'm not in the band, I don't play anything really, but I help them move their kit about and sometimes they introduce me to people as their manager. I wrote one of their gigs up for the paper; it was in *The Tilted Wig* (that's our local pub, we call it *The Wilted Tig* - bit childish but it stuck after Sparky got his words wrong one night out). Good spoonerism there, Sparks. We love Spoonerisms, and sometimes we go and get pissed and make new ones up. We more or less talk in Spoonerisms. Poor old Reverend Spooner. Apparently he only ever uttered one Spoonerism and then his mates took the piss for the rest of his days. My Dad used to go on about an actor from his home town of Bootle called Charles Workman who used to get booed off stage for getting his words in a Spoonerist tangle. He became a comedian and his obituary said that he could "make an Englishman laugh at breakfast". My Dad really liked that, and used to see if he could make me laugh at breakfast before I went to school. Sometimes he did and sometimes he didn't.

Anyway, my heart is pounding, and it's nothing to do with the hi-fi in Sparky's room shaking the wall. I can't get her out of my head. I close my eyes and I can see her face, all concerned and bending over me as I have my coughing fit. I'm gazing down the canyon, the red ruby heart dangling before me in the dark. I can smell her perfume on my sleeve. My guts feel funny and I keep smiling for no reason. And I do what I always do when I'm feeling the love vibe. I write a poem.

OK, here's how I usually compose my poems. First job, random words and phrases, just get 'em down on a bit of paper. Then, cut 'em up with my trusty scissors, put the bits in a glass or something, give 'em a good shake and pour 'em onto the bed, or a table, it doesn't matter. See where they fall…that's important, yeah? It's the random chance element that makes a good poem. Rhyming is good, but it doesn't always work. It's the pattern and rhythm that's important. I had a great English teacher, called Mr Hennigan. He killed himself unfortunately, chucked himself off a train. Bit depressive, poor guy. I wrote a poem about him after he died, it was quite angry, a bit Bob Dylan.

Do people see my poems? No way. Well, yes way, if you include the ones I wrote for Lisa. Lisa was my girlfriend for a bit when I was doing my degree in Bolton, I met her in the campus bar one night. She took me to see The Wanderers play footie at The Reebok Stadium on Saturday afternoons. We had pies with brown sauce at half time and went to the pub after. I wrote a poem about going to the footie with her, called *It's More Important Than That*. There was a legend manager of Liverpool called Bill Shankly, and he once said *"Football isn't a matter of life and death…it's more important than that."* Lisa loved that quote. She is a football fanatic (in the true sense of the word – I am a Bolton fan, but she is a Bolton fanatic) and she used to get totally carried away during the matches. I just clapped a bit - I wanted to join in the songs and swearing at the ref, but well, just couldn't really. I wrote quite a bit of poetry for Lisa, but I don't think she got it. I'm not even sure that she appreciated it…she always seemed a bit embarrassed when I gave her one. Uh-ho, innuendo! That's another thing my gang likes to get bantering with down the pub. Rollo once came up with a Spoonerist innuendo, I can't remember it just now but we all pissed ourselves for ages. I was upset in May, because the Wanderers got relegated from the Premier League. Me and Lisa are still friends and I called her to see how she was, but she just cried. I'd never heard her cry before. I have to admit it made me feel quite horny, but I was quite ashamed of that and thought of Owen Coyle (Bolton's manager) and that soon calmed me down.

Right, so here we go, poem words. Or phrases. OK, 'canyon', obviously. 'Ruby heart'. 'Scent of magic and mystery'. 'Brilliant smile'. 'Infectious'. Not very inspiring so far. Sometimes it can take a long time, sometimes it comes quickly. You never know with poetry. Oh bollocks, it's Sparks rapping on my door. I check I've put the bolt on, sometimes he just walks in, even if the dodgy 'Do Not Disturb' sign is showing.

"What's up, mate?" I call through the door.

"The boys are coming round. It's England vee Sweden tonight, remember? I'm off to get the beers in."

"Ah, OK mate. I'll make a chilli, yeah?"

"Spot on, Mils."

My Mum taught me how to cook a few things, which is a few things more than most of the boys in our gang, so probably about twice a week I cook something. Otherwise Sparky seems to live off *Cheerios* and *Pot Noodle*. Of course, we have loads of takeaway like Pominos dizza, konner debabs, chish and fips (note Spoonerisms there). Right, the love poem is going to have to wait. I nip down to *Nisa* to buy mince and beans and rice, and I get cracking on the chilli.

THE LADS COME ROUND just before the game starts and the five of us sing the national anthem and crack open cans of *Carling*. There's me, Sparks, Rollo, Pottso and Dean. It's a funny thing, but we always sit and watch the telly in the same places. There's Sparks, Pottso and Dean on the battered old sofa, there's Rollo, who always sits in the chair at about ninety degrees to the telly, and he cranes his neck round to see the screen. We always ask him if he can see properly, but he says he's fine. I sit in my red beanbag on the floor, on the opposite side of the sofa to Rollo. This match is going to be wicked.

"Come on England!" I shout, and the lads join in. We are all really pleased that Andy Carroll is starting, Sparks reckons he will be the player of Euro 2012. We love the long-haired giant Geordie, well, apart from Rollo, who reckons he is a big clumsy carthorse.

"Oooooooh, Scotty Parker!!" shouts Dean, rising to his feet and sploshing lager on his trainers, as the gritty terrier of a midfielder sees his rising shot clawed away by 'keeper Isaksson.

"We are on top here!" says Rollo, creeping forward to the edge of his chair and clutching his can tightly. Rollo can be quite intense. We always talk all the way through the footie, well, not Pottso, he's the quiet man in the gang, but when he says something, man, you better watch out.

"OHHHH! Danny Welbeck! Chance!" shouts Sparks.

But it isn't long before we are all on our feet. Cross from Stevie G. Carroll is up like a gigantic salmon, Boom! What a header…unstoppable!!

We are hugging each other, jumping on and off the sofa, going mad.

"YOU WILL NEVER SEE A BETTER HEADER THAN THAT! YOU WILL NEVER SEE A BETTER HEADER THAN THAT!!" Dean is yelling. I hope Mr. Spellars downstairs likes football. It must sound like a herd of crazy mo-fo elephants got let loose above his ceiling.

"Who needs Rooney, Rollo, you big twat?" teases Sparky.

"One swallow does not a summer make, Sparks," grins Rollo, who can say some very clever things at times. But he's as happy as the rest of us to see the big lad score. Come on England. Sweden are our bogey team, and we have never beaten them in a competitive international. I like Swedes in general, though I don't know very much about them. They seem like nice people. There was a Swedish girl on the course in Bolton. But she wasn't blonde, and her eyes weren't blue. And she left after three months; I think she preferred Gothenburg to her digs with Mrs Shipperbottom in Kearsley.

Just before half time, I put a pan on the electric hob to boil some rice and I start reheating the chilli. The lads like it really hot so I put loads of dried chillies in (though I break them open first to remove the seeds. I always do that - not sure why). I use baked beans instead of kidney beans, but you have to remember to wash the sauce off them.

Half time and Flat 3 is buzzing. We are well on top, and starting to get carried away and talking about England winning the tournament. England's new manager is called Roy Hodgson, but we call him Woy as he can't say his

R's and I don't mean nearly. So all our R's have wecently been weplaced by Ws.

"Wew, Mila," goes Sparks, off into his vewy good Woy impwession, "Wooney is a bit wing wusty in twaining so we cannot expect him to weturn fow the Ukwaine match fully fit."

"I will put the wice on," I add, grinning. I can't do the Woy accent that well, so I just do the 'w' thing in my normal voice.

"Vewy good," goes Rollo, "I must say I am starving hungwy."

More beer, more banter. I am smiling, I am happy. I love my mates. I love my life! Everything about it - my family, my job, everything.

"Jesus H Christ. There's something amazing in the stweet, I mean, street." Dean has lifted up the corner of the massive England flag which dominates our window overlooking West Street and is doing some serious gawking. "Lads, come and look, quick!"

"Phwoooar!" goes Sparky.

"Look at the melons on that!" goes Rollo. "Mila, get over here…you have to see this!"

"Hang on guys, I'm just getting the rice on. What's the matter with you idiots?!" I tip the *Uncle Ben's* long grain into the boiling water and make a note of the time on the blue fluorescent clock below the hob. Ten minutes. Shit, I've forgotten the salt. I pick up the tub of *Saxa* and pour a good stream into the bubbling pan. I go over to the window to see what these fools are gawping at. Oh no. OMG. The white noise in my ears has returned. The *Saxa* tub crashes to the ground and spews salt all over the already filthy carpet. Must hoover up some time. My guts writhe like eels. My eyes I cannot believe and I pinch the skin at the top of my nose and look again. It's actually her. It is literally her. Pandora Poste is walking up and down West Street, Horsham. Arne is trailing behind her, glancing anxiously at his *Tag Heuer* watch.

"Wait a minute…that's Pandora fucking Poste!" shouts Sparky. "The woman you interviewed today, Milad! Sorry, buddy, I never asked you how it all went?"

"Er, yeah! It went…OK, thanks Sparks. Charming…charming woman…" I look down at myself uttering random words. I think I'm having an out-of-body experience.

"FUCK! She's looking up here! She's fucking seen us!" Dean drops the corner of the flag and for some reason dives behind Rollo's chair. "Hide, hide!" he's shouting.

"Come on lads, calm down, second half is starting," says Pottso. "Get the chill sorted, Mil?"

"Yeah yeah, 'course, chill. Chill. Take a chill pill, Till." Tilly is Pottso's lovely girlfriend. He is lucky Pottso is. I stir the rice and boil the kettle. Important to drain all that starchy shit they put on *Uncle Ben's* to stop it sticking. What is PM Poste doing in West Street? Maybe she is doing a kind of memory lane tour of her home town? Ah, that'll be it. You'd want to check out West Street, for sure. Or maybe her Mum lives around these parts. Maybe I even know her. I'm always polite and say hello to old ladies, just like my Mum taught me to be.

We just about have five plates, all chipped and most with a trace of fried egg on them. When I'm here on a Sunday (which is not that often, I'm usually at home), me and Sparks have a good old full English fry up. But we don't have a dishwasher so we don't wash up that much. We have five assorted forks, four assorted knives, and not enough spoons. One day, we might go to *Ikea* to buy more crockery and cutlery. But we hate *Ikea* – we get really confused in there. So that day may not come.

"Do some bread and butter, Sparks?"

"Fuck off, they've kicked off again."

"Do some bread and butter, Sparks, or you don't get any chilli. Mmmm, it's a good one too," I say, dunking a crust of bread into the bubbling red sauce. "Phew, it's more than a good one!"

Sparky knows that I don't make idle threats and to get Sparky to do stuff you have to blackmail him. I always hold out too. It's good for him. Like a sulky kid with malevolence in his eyes he slinks over to the kitchen counter and starts pasting *Countrylife* butter over *Warburton's* thick sliced white loaf (the one with the orange wrapper). I notice he is wearing a new crap T-shirt this evening, which I am presuming is intended to be worn by a certain sort of woman. It says *"Hands Off The Bumps"* with a pair of handprints where boobs should be. Or are, if you count Sparky's 'moobs' as boobs, which we have been giving him stick for recently. He is getting fat due to his take-away diet and total lack of exercise. As well as doing Woy Hodgson, Sparks does other impressions really well. Some of his impressions aren't so good though, and now he is doing one of his bad ones – 'Kevin the Teenager' off Harry Enfield.

"I 'ate you!" he is whining at me, but he really needs a baseball cap on back to front and a fringe. Sparks has a sort of curly Afro. Only not cool like an Afro. His hair is just naturally bushy and wiry and he's too lazy to get it cut, or to think of a style.

"I hate you too, Sparks." I smile. I dole out steaming piles of rice, and make a hole in the middle of each one. I try to find the big spoon to ladle out the chilli, but I can't find it, so I use a tablespoon instead, which takes ages.

"Here you go, boys. Chilli is served." The lads leap up and grab their plates and forks and a piece of bread and butter.

"Ah, genius, Milad. Top nosh this is," goes Sparks.

"You are Jamie Oliver, with better diction, mate." Rollo is getting tucked in.

"Cheers, buddy," go Pottso and Dean, shovelling in the rice.

"Right, everyone got a beer? Good!" I slump down in my bean bag and raise my fork. This is going to be a goddamn hot one.

"Oh, for fuck's sake. That beardy bloke who used to play for Villa… They've equalized!" Sparks is right. The Swedes have equalized.

"What a fucking mess. How did that not get cleared?" Rollo is angry. He doesn't like Glen Johnson at right back and says so.

We all stop eating for a moment and it's silent. Then there is a knock at the door.

"Oh, it's not that old bastard from downstairs is it?" Dean is up on his feet. "I'll get rid of him. If you can't make a bit of noise on a Friday night with your mates during Euro 2012, when can you?"

I shovel in another forkful of chilli. There are tears in my eyes. This is a really hot one. And I know that it is not Mr. Spellars at the door. I can hear Dean stammering. I can smell her perfume.

"Er, Milad. There's someone here for you."

I stumble to my feet. It's never easy getting out of a beanbag, especially with a plate of food.

She is there, at the threshold of Flat 3. At the threshold of my life. She is speaking to me.

"Milad, I'm so glad I've found you!" she is saying. The lads have frozen into their seats. They eat their tea, silently.

"Aho…Muzz Poste, erm, Pandora. How marvellous to see you again!" Stay cool, my brain is trying to tell me. Stay cool. But my eyes are watering from the chilli, and my face is the colour of my Dad's after he has drained a whole bottle of *Chateauneuf du Pape*; that is to say, a livid shade of red verging on purple.

"I hope I haven't called at an inconvenient time?" She proffers her fragrant cheek to be kissed. I'm conscious of having breadcrumbs all over my suddenly dry mouth, and give it a wipe with my sleeve, before mucking up my first peck and then doing little better on the other proffered cheek. There is a short silence. My legs are shaking. Sparky is starting to giggle, the fucking idiot.

"No, no, inconvenient? Never! Erm, would you like to come in? Er, it's a bit of a mess in here I'm afraid." What am I on about? Of course she doesn't want to come in! My brain is racing…did I pick up something of hers during the interview this morning that she needs back? I can't think of anything?

"I'd love to come in and join you! Now you're sure I haven't called at an inconvenient time? Arne, go and wait in the car. I will SMS you when I'm ready for you." Uneasily, Arne departs and uneasily, I show Pandora into the squalor of the main room.

"Oh, I am sorry, you boys are having your evening meal!" declares Pandora, lifting her hand to her mouth in apology. She did that a few times during our interview. Such poise - I love fine manners in a woman. "And these are your friends, are they?"

"Yes, erm, allow me to introduce...Sparky, my flatmate, Pottso..." It's like introducing these gimps to The Queen. They all rise to their feet in turn, putting down their plates of chilli on the sofa and shaking hands. I think Dean is actually bowing. Or curtseying.

"Guys, this is the famous Pandora Poste, author of the best-selling novel, *Black Heart*. And she is in our flat." I don't know why I say that last bit. It is a statement of fact, but there was no need to say it. I'm still racking my brains as to why she would want to be here. Maybe I got something badly wrong in the interview, and she wants the tape? That's it! She wants to tell me not to use something she said. Or everything she said! But she doesn't look displeased with me. She's smiling that big white smile at me again, the one after I recovered from my coughing fit.

"Erm, would you like to join us for something to eat, Muzz, I mean, Pandora. Erm...it isn't much obviously, but I have made a chilli for the boys. And it is quite a hot one."

"A very hot one," agrees Dean, perspiring heavily and blowing his nose.

"How lovely! I adore chilli, and I must say that I am ravenous!"

"Right. Erm..." This I did not expect. I was just being polite. Sparky is glowering at me, I know he had his eye on seconds. I act fast. "Rollo, get out of that chair and let Pandora sit down. Come on, squeeze up lads." Rollo darts onto the sofa, where he, Sparks, Potts, and Dean look like the four wise monkeys. Or the three wise monkeys with an extra one. I tip my own chilli into a cereal bowl and quickly wash my plate in the washing up bowl and dry it with the one clean-ish tea towel we have left and I do the same with my fork. There's a plastic one in the drawer left over from a Chinese takeaway that will do for me. I pour the rest of the rice onto a plate, and carefully arrange re-heated chilli on top of it, as artfully as I can. I grate some cheese, and sprinkle it on top. Finally I garnish it with thin slices of the remains of a red pepper that I find in the back of the fridge. It's hardly Gary Rhodes, but it will have to do. I carry it over, with the clean-ish tea towel for her lap.

"Here you are, Muzz, erm, Pandora. It isn't much, but…"

"How smashing!" She takes the plate from me, and taking the *Yogi Bear* cushion from behind her back, places it on her black velveteen skirt, her legs clad in exotically patterned black tights and boots which I think are called stilettos. She seems to be making herself at home! What easy grace she has.

"You never garnished *our* chilli with cheese and red pepper, Milad!" grins Sparky, wickedly. "OH FUCKING HELL. That beardy bloke who used to play for Villa has scored a-fucking-gain!"

"Sparks, mind your language, mate! We have a guest here now?" I take my bowl of chilli and lower myself as gracefully as I can back into my beanbag. "Oh, I'm so sorry, Muzz, I mean, Pandora, I haven't offered you a drink! I'm afraid we only have beer?"

"Beer and chilli, what could possibly be nicer!" she replies in a jolly way. I'm sure she'd rather be drinking a nice Shiraz, but what grace she has. I rise, trying to find a decent glass in this dump.

"Don't worry about a glass Milad, I can drink from a can as well as any of you men!" How empathic she is. Yet firm. I smile as I rip open a chilled can and hand it to her, ensuring the froth is not dripping over the edge.

"Cheers, gentlemen! Lovely to meet you all!"

"Cheers!" we all return. She must be very thirsty; she is gulping in *the* most ladylike way, half the contents of the can.

"Aaaah!" she gasps, followed by the most feminine exhalation of pressurised gas I have ever witnessed. And she is really tucking into her chilli. I love a woman with an appetite. "Now, how come these boys get bread and butter with theirs and I don't, Mee-lad?" she asks me in a kind of playful girlish whine.

"Oh, I never thought!" I say leaping to my feet. "One round or two?"

"Two would be marvellous, darling. Now, what is going on here gentlemen, is this football you are watching?"

"Erm, it is, it is England's second Group D match. We are playing our bogey team. Sweden." Sparky is good at explaining stuff.

"I see. And we're losing. We always lose to Sweden, do we? I'm sorry, what was your name again? Sparky? I'm very bad with names, but I never…forget a face." She is giving Sparky *that* look. I can't help but smile, he is all red now, like he is after a kick-around in the park.

"Well, we've never beaten 'em in a match that's worth anything. Oh, that's it Woy, get Milner off. Theo's on."

"Oh, I say, I like him! Theo, is it?! I do love mixed-race men. Such a beautiful, hybrid vigour about them. I notice we have several such players on our team." Shit, she's smiling at me. Mixed race. That's me! Holy crap, this chilli is hot. I glug my beer in embarrassment under her hot, brown-eyed stare.

"YAAAY!" The monkeys on the sofa can't help themselves. They are up on their feet, Sparks is bouncing on the sofa. Theo has scored! The celebration is a lot more muted in present company than it usually would be, and I try and stay cool on the bean bag, though Deano has ruffled up my hair.

"That was a super goal he's done, wasn't it? Lovely Theo!" purrs my football-loving queen, as she gracefully tucks a bolus of food into her cheek so she can speak. She looks like the cutest hamster when she does that… she did it loads with her pastries during our interview.

"Well, I think it was a bit of fluke, to be honest," says Deano. "But it doesn't matter how they go in, it's getting it in that matters." We are all suddenly aware of our precious innuendo, and Sparky is doing the worst possible thing. He is bottling up laughter. Bottled laughter is infectious. I try not to look at him. So don't the other lads. But Pandora is in control. She leans over towards Dean, and puts her hand on his knee, the cleavage canyon yawning to the hypnotised gaze of the four wise sofa monkeys.

"I do so agree, Dean. It *is* getting it in that matters." Dean gulps hard as he meets her gaze. We all stare at the footie, trying not to think of sex.

Pandora is smiling like the *Mona Lisa*. Or Nigella. There is silence for a while. Well, apart from the sound of masticating (Sparks always eats with his mouth open, really disgusting) gulping from lager cans, suppressed belches from the lads, and of course Alistair Bruce-Ball's slick commentary and Lawro's reflexive questions and lightning humour. We love Lawro.

"That was absolutely delicious, Mee-lad, thank you so much." I hurry over to take Pandora's plate to the galley kitchen, and she meets my eyes, coquettishly. "Another beer for a lady?" I think she just winked at me.

"More beer, anyone?" I ask the sofa-monkeys. They all put their hands up, like they all want to answer a question in the classroom when we were at school. Pandora joins in, and I smile at her raised arm. She has big arms. But shapely. Very womanly. I hand out the cans, making sure that Pandora's is open, so it doesn't spurt all over her.

"Come on England!" shouts Sparky at the TV. "We have to fucking totally go for it now! This match is for the taking! Turnips mash The Swedes...do I like that!"

"Sparks..." I try to admonish him once again for his language, the boy just has no breeding.

"Oh don't worry about me, gallant sir, I've heard all that language before, I can assure you. I think a good 'fucking' is highly appropriate on occasions, don't you, Milad?"

I had to be mid-lager gulp when our game gal quips this, don't I? Involuntarily, I cough it all down my red England shirt. Sparky can't contain himself. And suddenly we are all laughing. Raucously. Especially Pandora. She is slapping her voluminous thigh and emitting a high pitched whoop between gravelly gasps.

Then we are all in the air. I don't know how he's done it, but he's done it. Danny Wellbeck has back-heeled the winner. I am hugging Dean. I am hugging Pottso. And then...I am in the arms of Pandora. I am sinking... sinking into her, losing myself, I am a galactic speck in a fragrant universe of unimaginable softness. "Is there somewhere we can talk?" the universe is whispering. "Alone?"

I AM SITTING ON MY BED as I have sat many times before. It is properly my bed, my Dad moved it over here from home and I have slept on this double bed since I was about nine. Me and this bed go back a long way. But something truly epoch-making is happening here. I have sat on my bed with girls before, sure. Once, when Lisa came down to stay with me and my family in Nuthurst she slept in it (I was in the spare room obviously). Next day when my parents went to work and I was sure Naz was asleep, I crept in and snuggled up next to her, and I did snooze for a bit, so technically, I have slept with a girl in this very bed. But now we are talking about a whole new thing. I am sitting on my bed. And next to me – very, very near to me – is a woman. And by that, I don't mean any woman. I mean this astonishing embodiment of all woman-kind. This curvaceous goddess, this distillation of all that is desirably feminine. And she is holding my hand. Thank God I made my bed and tidied up a bit before I went chilli shopping. And took the dodgy "Do Not Disturb" sign off the door handle.

Whilst I bask like a rabbit in the glow of her headlights, I remember that she is here for one thing and one thing only. To admonish and reprove me for my incompetent interview. It seems odd though, that she would want to unzip and kick off her pointy black boots and wiggle the painted purple toe-nails imprisoned in her patterned tights (or are they stockings? – I'm not sure I know the difference), in order to do this.

"Mee-lad." She calls out my name in her husky voice (she seems to have a lot of different tones…I resolve to describe each one in my poem). The schoolboy in me wants to answer "Yes, Miss" but I am no longer a boy, I am a man, and I tell myself to be cooler. "As cool as Clooney" as me and the lads like to say.

"Pandora." I answer, trying to waggle my head like I've seen George do when he is seducing women.

"I like your style, Mee-lad," she purrs.

"Do you, miss?" Dang and blast! I've gone high pitched and soppy - where did George Clooney go? I sound more like George off *Rainbow*.

"I do. I do. Now, I have come to ask you something. How would you, my lad, like to join my… entourage?" My head is swimming. Has she punned on my name? I have heard that a thousand times…Milad, My Lad, it gets dull. But I don't think she did that. Anyway, never mind….she is asking me to do what??? Entourage - what is that? Doesn't that mean cleavage in French?

"I have a terribly exhausting book-signing tour ahead, and I need good people to look after me. To deal with the press. To protect me from the paparazzi. I do not wish to end like poor Diana, hounded to the end… extinguished like a candle in the wind. And then, darling, the Americans want a piece of me, it seems, and who knows *where* after that. My agent has thirty-seven countries on the radar. I'm going global, darling, and there's simply no stopping it."

Crikey. I'm not being told off. I'm being head-hunted! By Pandora! The woman I …admire. But hang on, what about Ray, and Nathalie, and the West Sussex County Times? I've only been there six months. That is my big break…but hang on…is this an even bigger break?

"Naturally, money is not an object, darling. I don't wish to have an extensive staff, but I do wish to have a loyal one. And loyal staff need to have commensurate remuneration. I will double your current salary Mee-lad, whatever it is. But be duly warned, my fine lad…you will earn it!"

This sounds too good to be true. I want to ask Sparks about it. And my Dad.

"But Arne…doesn't he look after you, yeah? He seems most…loyal."

"Ah, Arne is a good man. He is the muscle, the driver…but press? I don't think he can read. I can rely on Arne to get rid of anyone who bothers me - literally if necessary - I believe one of his many talents is as an assassin. But I need someone to charm the press, to organise my events…to influence my PR and my image. You see Mee-lad…" she is leaning her head lightly on my shoulder as she says these words, and moves her hand from my hand to the inside of my upper arm, and starts stroking it. I feel like I am starting to melt.

"It's a fact that not everyone likes my booky-wooky." She seems sad at this, and I immediately feel disloyal by thinking that I might just be one of those people.

"Oh, all the women in my office like your, erm, booky, Pandora. In fact, I was meant to ask you to sign two of them at the interview this morning, but I er, forgot. And you are zooming up the best-selling fiction charts I noticed today!"

"Oh, I know darling, I know. But you see, some of these critics are so horrible about me. These people that review the books for papers and magazines. They are very critical, nasty people. And I know we authors have always endured brickbats from these spiteful vipers…all failed writers, the pack of them. But you see, I want the youth of Britain to enjoy me. To truly understand me." She sits up, takes both my hands in her tanned hands, and fixes me imploringly with her bottomless brown eyes. "And I want you to be my ambassador. I am the Queen of Mummy Porn, yes, I accept that title, with honour. But I want the youth of the world to love me also. I want your youth, Mee-lad! And I so *do* want you."

I feel the heavy weight of destiny on me. I struggle for a reply, looking beyond Pandora's shoulder at my poster of Al Pacino in *Scarface*, thinking he might inspire me to a reply of gravitas equal to Pandora's earnest request. Instead of Little Al though, it is Jarvis Cocker who comes suddenly to my assistance. *Common People* is one of our sing-along-anthems - not that we are common people, (well, maybe Sparky is); I think we are all lower middle class people, though I've never been very sure what that meant. Anyway, my reply comes out pretty cool. Well, what else could I do? I say, "I'll see what I can do."

CHAPTER THREE

Nathalie is ecstatic. We are in a long queue in Waterstones and I can just about see Pandora's brilliant shiny red hair and I can hear her gravelly laughter as she delights her fawning public. I see her graceful hand sweep a copy of her novel from the top of an enormous stack piled beside her, and with a beautiful pen, she scrolls a message, no doubt individual to each soul that passes before her. I study the shuffling queue. The excited faces look like an adult version of the queue in front of Santa's Christmas Grotto (I hated going to see Santa in the shopping centre, it was the same guy every year and he stank of rolling tobacco and BO). Each bowing and scraping punter reluctantly leaves Pandora's company as Arne escorts them firmly away. Me and Nat have our own copies of *Black Heart*. Well, Nat has her coffee-stained one and Sheila's, and I have Ray's wife's.

Nat is practically squealing with excitement, and keeps jumping up and down. I'm playing it cool in my Ray Ban shades. Not that it's sunny, it's pissing it down outside again actually, but it's humid inside the shop and everybody is perspiring slightly. I watch a bead of sweat run down the nape of Nathalie's neck and disappear towards the strap of her bra (white today). We are getting closer to the glow of celebrity…I hope so too, because my lunch hour is nearly up and I am a punctual person, I want to be back at my desk for fourteen hundred hours sharp.

Arne notices me first. It's not difficult; I'm the only man in the queue. I see him lean over to Pandora, whisper in her ear, and point directly at me. Pandora explodes from her seat and beckons me (and I guess Nat?) to jump the queue. Why not! As my Dad often says, "it's not what you know, it's who you know!" I take Nat's thin arm and escort her to the signing table. Pandora envelops me and hugs me to her like a long-lost lover. I can feel her breath at my neck, her heart pounding through my newly-ironed white shirt. No 'Day 4' shirts for me anymore. She holds me at arms' length, and then plunges me back into a second embrace. I can hear the astonishment of the ladies behind me in the queue, one of whom is a friend of my Mum's. Well, some of the ladies are muttering about "queue jumping" as well as being astonished. During the second hug, Pandora is whispering in my ear.

41

"Mee-lad, my Mee-lad! You are going to join my entourage! Say you will, darling, say you will?"

I open my squeezed closed eyes, and over my shoulder I see Nathalie, whose gaping mouth seems to simultaneously encourage me and warn me. But I have already crossed the Rubik Cube. I have discussed it with Mum and Dad. And Sparky. I'm bloody well going for it.

"I will, I will!" I breathe in Pandora's shell-like ear. She doesn't reply. She doesn't need to. She merely hugs me tighter. So tight, I am unable to breathe. When she finally releases me (I think Arne assists) I am panting. And so is Pandora. She folds like a doll back onto her chair, lowered expertly by Arne, who places a silk cushion at her back, her eyes moist and fierce.

"And who is this young lady with you, Mee-lad?" Her expression and voice tone have dramatically changed. She is not smiling at Nat. She is quite frosty, in fact. Poor Nathalie is trembling slightly, and the fair hairs on her forearms are standing on end.

"This is Nathalie, my *colleague* from the West Sussex County Times, Pandora."

"Ah, your *colleague*, is she?" I detect Pandora's demeanour soften slightly. "Not your *girlfriend* then?"

"Oh God no! Ha ha!" Shit, I've gone Bootle-red again, and Nathalie's cheeks have flushed scarlet. "Lord no, Pandora. We are colleagues - aren't we, Nat?"

"We are Mil, we are," Nat agrees nervously. "I adore your book, Ms Poste. I have read it three times. I would love it if you would sign my copy."

Pandora leans back on her cushion, and runs her limpid brown eyes up and down Nathalie, with a very slight smile. She looks at her for what seems like quite a long time. Nathalie's face has gone beyond crimson.

"Three times, you say! You *have* had some fun with yourself, my girl! Well, if Mee-lad isn't your boyfriend, who *is* your boyfriend?"

Just when I thought Natalie could not get redder, she got redder.

"I….I…haven't got one, miss!" I understand why Nat calls Pandora "miss." It sort of comes to you, like you are in a classroom with a teacher that you are a bit scared of - and also quite fancy. That was Miss Leggett for me, when I was about ten.

Suddenly, Pandora isn't looking at Nat anymore, and doesn't seem very interested in her either. She pops on her glasses and starts writing with a fountain pen on the inside cover of a clean copy of her novel drawn from the top of the stack. "To Nathalie, is it? Is that with an 'H'?

"Er, yes, ma'am, with a 'haitch'. N-A-T-H-A-L-I-E."

"I think I can spell, girl, I am a best-selling author, you know!" Everyone in the queue laughs, including me - and Nat - as Pandora uses her biting wit to charm everyone. Pandora hands the signed copy to Nathalie. "Give your money to Mr. Bastad, please."

Bastad! Arne Bastad…ho, ho! Wait til the lads hear this one! I want to laugh out loud, but we have a bit of an embarrassing situation to deal with. Nat and I had no idea we'd have to buy new copies of *Black Heart*, and Nat has just spent her last tenner buying us both baked spuds at Wilda's. (I had beans and cheese filling, Nat had tuna mayo).

"What is that battered copy you have dragged in, my darling boy? I noticed *this girl* had one too. You don't expect me to sign *that* do you? I am a professional author, darling, I need to shift this stock next to me!"

"Ah, of course, Pandora, of course, actually, this is for my boss, Ray. Or rather for his wife, Cynthia. Well…" I stoop to whisper in her ear, capturing her scent as I do so, "I mean, my *ex-boss's wife*." She is cackling and happy again, as she winks deliciously at me.

"Just as a favour to you, Mee-lad, I shall sign this dog-eared and obviously much 'employed' volume of my erotic fiction. To "Cynthia", you say." She pouts her lovely extensive lips and puts on her sexy reading glasses, as her exquisite hand flows black ink across the page, ending in a 'kiss'. I noticed that she didn't 'kiss' Nathalie's new copy.

"Right, I'm so sorry, but I am completely exhausted now," Pandora announces to the twenty or so ladies behind us in the queue. "You will have to come to Chichester tomorrow. Arne, escort me to my resting room, if you please. And has that girl paid yet?"

The ladies behind me are not happy, mainly with me, it seems, as they are stating in no uncertain terms that they would have their signed copies by now had Nat and I not jumped the queue. Time to leave. I thrust a tenner in Arne's hand telling him to keep the change (signed copies of *Black Heart* are selling today at £7.99, one pound less than the rrp). Grateful and slightly less red in the face, Natalie smiles at me as we leave the shop, and as I turn to wave goodbye to Pandora, she blows me a kiss, which I swear I can visualise as a tiny red heart which floats through the air towards me and I catch it and hold to my chest. She also seems to be scowling at something in my direction – I think it is Nathalie. I swivel away from the angry ladies in the queue, and Nat and I walk swiftly across Carfax. Sometimes, Nathalie puts her arm through mine when we are walking, which I usually like, but not today. I let my arm go limp so she can't do it properly. She doesn't seem to mind, and checks out the barely dry signature "To N-a-t-h-a-l-i-e" on the inside cover of her new book. Ha-ha, Pandora did spell it out – how droll she is!

"Ah, thanks for paying for this, Mil. I didn't realise we'd have to pay again!"

"Neither did I! I think she did me a special favour by signing Ray's wife's copy. Authors don't make a lot of money, you know Nat, so it's only right we pay for signed copies. And she does have an exhausting schedule ahead of her."

"She is SCARY!" giggles Nat, suddenly seeming a lot younger than me. I stop her in our tracks, and give her one of my serious looks.

"Nat, Ms. Poste is not 'scary', as you put it. She is probably the most erm, what's the word, *charismatic* person that I have ever had the pleasure of encountering."

"You said that last year about Chris Tarrant, when he came and opened the new Arcade. You said that *he* was the most charismatic person that you have ever had the pleasure of encountering!" Nat saunters off with one of her cheeky smiles that make her cheeks dimple, still reading her book's signed inside cover, and I skip after her, having to reflect that I did think that Chris Tarrant was charismatic when I met him, but now I think he is a total nob. Well, I was twenty last year – perhaps now I'm twenty-one, the boy has become the man? Well, I'm going to need all my manhood when I tell Ray I'm quitting on a week's notice. He is going to go ballistic.

"YOU LITTLE TOSSER! I send you to do an interview and you come back with another bloody job?!" Ray is bawling me out in his office. I feel ashamed and stare down at the holes worn in the beige nylon carpet. Then he starts laughing, and he's up and giving me the hardest slap on the back yet. "Good on you, Milan. I'd do the same thing…double the money? No brainer, boy. Pandora Poste's media representative! Get you, Bigshot!" Then he's pinching my cheek between his thumb and forefinger and tugging it. Dead hard. "You must have made quite an impression on PM Poste, you fast talking little devil! Oh, it'll be great, lad. Nationwide tour - fantastic opportunity. Any advice you need, Milan, you call me. Now, I need you to work that weeks' notice, because …NAT! GET IN HERE!"

I am rubbing my aching pinched cheek, as Nat, all flushed in her tight pink T-shirt bounds in. I am distracted by her hard nipples poking at the flimsy floral bra beneath. I think Ray might be distracted too.

"Er, oh, Nat. Why did I call you in? Oh yeah, that's right. I guess you know Bigshot here is leaving to join Pamela Poste's publishing entourage?" She doesn't know. And she bursts into tears.

"Oh, Christ Almighty….TISSUES PLEASE, SHEILA!" Sheila rushes in to comfort Nat, looking daggers first at me and then at Ray.

"I don't know what you are looking at me like that for, Sheila," blusters Ray, "it's Alastair bloody Campbell here causing the upset. Though this will cheer you up, Nat…you are filling his boots! Far too good for the front desk, there's a journalist in you petal, and we'll get her scrawling!"

"Really?" Nat's mouth is buried in tissues, but her streaming eyes gaze incredulously at Ray. "Me? A journalist? I can't be…I'm…"

"Oh, shut off the waterworks Nat, there's enough water outside as it is. Shadow Bigshot for his final week and then work with Sheila. You're a natural. Right, I've had enough drama for one day, fuck off all of you and I want stories by five or nobody goes home."

We troop out of the office, and Sheila is giving me the inquisition about my new job. "I hope you've got it all in writing, Mil. 'Susan' was a right sneak at school. By the way, what happened to my signed copy of *Black Heart*?"

"Oh, you can have this one, Sheelz," says Nat, blowing her nose, piercing me with her reddened eyes and retrieving the book from her desk, "I can't stand PM Poste!"

I'm not really listening to Nat though, as I'm thinking about what Sheelz had said…I have resigned from the County Times but I do not have a new contract from Pandora…shit, that was exactly what my Dad told me not to do - "get it in writing, son!" His words are ringing in my ears now. OK, I'll ring Pandora and sort it out. Hang on, I don't even have a number for her. Double crap. I'll have to catch up with her in Chichester on Saturday. And that can only mean one thing. To the Sparkymobile!

SPARK'S CAR IS THE WORST CAR OF ALL TIME. Colour – shit brown (exterior and interior). Model - Skoda Estelle. Age - old as the hills. Condition - illegal. MOT - expired. Tires - bald. Brakes - shoeless. Windscreen - cracked. Exhaust - rattling and belching. Battery - usually flat. But at least he has a car, which is more than I do, I don't even have a license. And one really good thing is that it has a CD player and great speakers that Sparks recently put in himself. We are cranking up the hip-hop, mirror shades on, blazing south down the A29. Rick Ross is bossin' it with *9 Piece*, and we are doing the rappers' sway, helping Rick out with the chorus.

"I'm smokin' dope, I'm on my cell phone
I'm sellin' dope, straight off the iPhone
He wanna quote, he talkin' nine zones
He bought four, I front him five more!"

Chichester is a funny place. Posh round the Cathedral and quite run down in nearby streets. We leave 'Estelle' in one of those run-down streets. That's the advantage of a crap car…you actively hope it gets nicked. But Estelle never does get nicked, whether we leave her open or not. Sparks locks her up on this occasion; he doesn't want to lose his new sound system, that's for sure. As we pass a Wetherspoons pub on the way to the signing at Waterstones, I hear a familiar peal of laughter from inside. It is unmistakeably her!

"Oh, off in for a pint are we, Mil?" says Sparks in surprised delight, as I usher him into the warm beer smell and clamorous chatter. "Great stuff, pint of mild and a bag of porky scratchings, please mate."

"Meeeeeeee-laaaaaaad!!!" Pandora breaks off holding court with a group of baldies in jeans and denim shirts all balancing pints of lager on their belts and throws her arms about me - and half her vodka and tonic down my back.

"Shorry dahling, *do-ooo* get me another, would you! And Schh-parky is with you. Sccccccccchhhhh-parky!" She tries to throw her arms around him too, but he is too reluctant and too fast. Sparky isn't tactile like I am, he doesn't like physical contact much. To tease him I do something we call 'the crane fly landing,' which involves making your fingers into a daddy longlegs and making it really lightly – I mean almost imperceptibly – land on the back of your victim's neck or their forearm when they are not looking. Some people (like Dean) it doesn't bother; but some people shiver and writhe about and yell, like they've got St. Vitus ' Dance. And Sparky is one of those people. It would be quite interesting to do it to him when he has a full pint in his hand, because one of our gang's own Ten Commandments is… *Thou Shalt Not Spill The Beer'* (Commandment Number Seven). Beer is to be drunk and *definitely* not spilled. So it would be a good experiment with Sparky - could he control the crane fly landing and not spill his beer, or would he not be able to help himself and break a Commandment? I think that now isn't the best time to try this, but I do make a mental note to do it down *The Tig* one night.

"She's battered!" Sparks whispers to me as I queue at the bar and Pandora, admittedly slightly uneasy on her legs, totters back to the gallery of appreciative red-faced men.

"Just a bit of 'Dutch courage' before the signing, I expect Sparks. You know, some ladies get a bit squiffy on a spritzer. Women can't drink as much as men, it's a biological fact. Yes, thanks mate, a pint of mild, a pint of lager, a packet of porky scratchings and a double vodka and tonic, please."

"A TREBLE, MEE-LAD! A TREBLE V & T, DAHLING!" I smile and wave at her. Blimey, those little shell ears of hers must be good…I don't know how she heard my order to the barman over all this din. Still, I like a lady who knows what she wants, and if she wants a treble, she certainly gets a treble. She accepts the drink wordlessly (well-bred people often don't need to use 'please' and 'thank you') - I'm well happy that Pandora feels so comfortable around me already, and that there is no need for such formality. Me and Sparks sip our pints and watch in awe as she gives these imbeciles a lecture on "the quintessence of the feminine". They probably think 'quintessence' is a new perfume range by Kylie Minogue.

"Have one of you gentlemen got a fag?" she asks her spellbound audience in a commanding voice, one of the lag-types immediately proffering a Silk Cut from a packet drawn from the back pocket of his horrible jeans. Now, this is a bit of a surprise to me, as she totters outside with the guy and is puffing a plume of blue smoke into the grey sky (which yet again threatens rain). Not that I'm anti-smoking, by any means. Me and the lads like to get 'lean', especially when we camp out in the woods or go fishing. Oh yeah, we likes our weed, we do. And Rollo smokes fags, sometimes he carries ten Marlborough Lights or ten Bensons. But I didn't have Pandora down as a smoker. She seems like someone who would want to keep her body as a temple, as it were? But what the heck, all good things in moderation! I like a lass that can have a smoke and a joke with the lads, and boy is she doing that right now! She is slapping her thighs in uncontrollable laughter at something Baldy-red just said to her. (Probably from Oscar Wilde…er, not?). Oh no, her thigh-slapping has become a stumble! I watch in impotent horror as she slumps backwards towards the pavement, her fag rolling in the gutter and her glass smashing onto the flagstones. But just as she is about to have a nasty bump on her derrière…Arne.

In one movement, my goddess - what am I on about?! I mean, my future employer – is swept up against gravity by the well-tailored Norwegian, and hoisted back to regain her dignified poise, or at least most of it.

"Hahahahahahahahha!!" she laughs, as she is led away down the street by her frowning henchman. "My hero, Arne, my hero! You would never let me fall, would you, my dah-ling." Sparky can be quite cruel at times, and often laughs at the misfortunes of others, as he is doing now. I hand him my half-drunk pint. "Here, you can have this. I'd better help her get set up at Waterstones before I ask her about my contract. I'll be back in a bit."

Outside of Waterstones, there's a crowd which starts to applaud as Pandora staggers into the store, waving to her readership with regal acknowledgement and leaning hard on Arne. I'm starting to like Arne. He's a sound guy, as well as looking like an agent from *The Matrix*. Uh ho, the ladies from Horsham who were behind me and Nat in the queue have made the trip to Chichester – I'd better make sure they are at the front today. Now that is good, unpaid PR for the PM Poste Posse!

"Meee-laaaad, Meeeee---lad! How marvellous of you to come and support me, dah-ling. And I'm not even paying you yet. Such sweet loyalty, such…" A single teardrop rolls like a silver bead down her sophisticated make-up, intercepted by the crisp, clean handkerchief expertly position by Arne, who with the other hand is filling a fountain pen with black *Quink* ink. "Go and get me a black coffee from *Starbucks*, that's a dah-ling boy."

My heart swells with pride that I can be of service to her. "And will you see those ladies first, PM?" I ask her, gesturing to the Horsham Three, who are scrimmaging at the back of a disorderly queue at the signing table.

"Oh bugger them…they can take their chances with the rest of my fans. Arne, am I doing a reading today, darling?"

"Yes, PM. Four o'clock in the private room upstairs. Ticket only."

"Very well then, I shall finish here in half an hour, Arne. I shall need a further half an hour on my own to prepare for my performance. Milad, coffee." Sometimes (like now) she can change her tone to an immediate order, and I'm off to *Starbucks* in a flash. Well, after I remember to ask Arne if he wants anything, but he just shakes his head; though rotating his neck only about ten degrees, like you can barely see him shake his head. I am so going to copy that move.

DESPITE THE COFFEE, Pandora doesn't seem to be her usual fun self today, and she isn't speaking to her fans much. She is signing the books very quickly and dismissing people with a sweep of her imperious arm. Just as the Horsham ladies reach the front of the queue, she slumps back into her chair, and tosses her pen onto the table.

"Right, Arne, I have had enough now. Escort me to the private room. Milad, get rid of these people."

Suddenly, I am alone with an angry mob. Especially the three at the front. The Kaiser Chief lyrics are in my head. *"We are the angry mob. We read the papers everyday day. We like who like. We hate who we hate…"*

"It's you again!" one of the Horsham ladies is shouting in my face. "You are always trouble, you are! You buggered us up in Horsham! We've written some fan-fiction, we have!"

"Erm, so sorry, ladies, so sorry. Ms. Poste is in the middle of an exhausting international tour, and she has asked me to extend her apologies. However, I can tell you that on Monday, she will be innnnn…hang on a minute, I have her schedule here somewhere…yep, here it is…Bognor Regis! The Observatory Bookshop at 11 a.m. Hope to see you all there! With your fan-fiction perhaps, which I'm sure is most…interesting." A bare-faced lie, as I'm certain it's not interesting at all but I give them a disingenuous smile and attempt to sidle away. But the bookstore manager is approaching and he doesn't seem very happy either.

"Are you one of PM Poste's people? I thought she was signing until 4 o' clock? Until her reading? We are selling tickets for £5 each and I've ordered three hundred extra copies of *Heart* especially for this afternoon! Where has she gone?"

"For a lie down…" I peer at his store name badge "…Roger. I'm sure as a member of the publishing and bookselling community, that you can understand the schedule of a touring author is demanding and exhausting? You are very lucky to have such hot property here at all! "

"We're not going all the way to Bognor!" One of the Horsham Three is in my face, with breath like mouldy cheese.

"Bognor is a nice place," I lie, once more. "Sir Patrick Moore lives there," I add, admittedly rather desperately.

"He lives in Selsey Bill, you berk. And you wouldn't catch Sir Patrick abandoning a signing! Anyway, I think that PM was drunk!"

OK, I've had enough of this riff-raff. I'm walking away from the lot of them. Well, trotting, actually. I belt up the wide staircase, and at the top there's a room with a big sign outside it, on a kind of billboard. Wow, impressive marketing posters. *That* picture of Pandora again, the front cover of *Heart*, and "International Best Selling Author. PM Poste." That's all nicely printed, and then in black marker pen, no doubt written by the person with the best handwriting in Waterstones, Chichester, it says in block capitals "SIGNING AND READING, TODAY." Then in lovely upper and lower case italics : "Reading Tickets £5 from the counters." And then across that line in more block capitals, this time in red marker pen: "SOLD OUT". Wow, this tour is going to be massive. All the national papers are full of PM Poste today, and she is Number 17 in the paperback fiction charts! I feel like I'm about to be part of history.

Arne is leaning on the door of the 'reading room' like a dangerous security guard. Which is exactly what he is. "Is she OK?" I ask, with tender concern.

"She is having a nap. I will wake her in half of one hour."

"Right, understood. Erm…Arne, you know…you know that I'm joining the entourage next week? I'm going to be on your team, looking after the press and media…and that." Arne just nods, like he's not arsed one way or the other.

"Erm, could I ask, Arne, erm…do you have a contract?" Blimey, he nearly smiled then.

"What kind of a contract, Milad?"

"Well, you know, a contract of employment. Terms and Conditions, that sort of thing."

"No, I don't."

"Ah. Right. Erm, I see, sort of cash-in-hand job, is it?"

"Something like that. None of your business, though."

"No, indeed!" I laugh nervously and kind of hop around, "none of my business at all. At all! Sorry if I was being nosey, there. Not intended, I assure you." Arne just looks at me, impassively. Hard to know how old Arne is. Definitely thirty. But he could be older. Much older.

"It's just that, well, I'm leaving a good job, a very good job actually, where I do have a contract and finished my probation period as well, and I thought perhaps - Pandora's publishers, what are they called, *The Coffee Press*, is it... well, they might be paying my salary, and that maybe, erm, they would issue a contract?"

"If you want a contract, Milad, I'm sure that Ms Poste will draw one up for you. But not today, huh? I'll have a word with her later on. Meantime, it would be good if you could stick around to help. There's going to be a lot of people. We may need some crowd control. There could be hysteria. Can you handle one of these?"

From his suit pants, Arne whips out an object about six inches long. But with a flick of his wrist, it is sixteen inches long.

"Expandable three-part steel friction lock crowd control baton. Behind the knee, effective. To the ribs, painful. And to the neck...potentially lethal. Here." Arne tosses it to me. I'm not that good at catching, and after I've butter-fingered the baton, I'm crawling across the red carpet after it, as it rolls into the shiny shoes of Roger the store manager, who has come upstairs to see what is going on.

"You won't need microphone equipment, lads," he says, picking up and handing me my weapon, which I suppose could look like audio equipment to the uninitiated. "It's all wired up in there. What time can we start letting people in? And how long will there be for questions?"

"Let them in at 3.45. Ms Poste will read at 4pm for fifteen minutes. There will be fifteen minutes for questions. We will leave at 4.30. Exactly." Arne is well precise. When he doesn't need words, he doesn't use them. I am going to be more like him. Succinct.

"Blimey, that isn't long!" protests Roger. "For a fiver?"

Arne ignores Roger and looks at me. "Milad will chair the session. Any inappropriate questions - we will immediately leave."

Hehe. I watch Roger gulp. He obviously hasn't been involved with professionals like me and Arne before. I whack the baton into my palm a few times, like the tough guy I could be. No doubt these cake-shop part-timers usually waffle on for hours with their dull questions. Not us. We don't hang about. We are *The Matrix* publishing people. I'm going to get a suit just like Arne's. It won't be cheap, probably over £200. I'll ask him later on where he gets his suits, probably not off the peg, he looks well tailored. I already have cool shades, though my Ray Bans are a bit smeary. I don't know how Arne keeps his shades looking so clean and impenetrable. Maybe I will ask him...I think me and Arne are going to be bi-ig mates.

Roger turns and goes back downstairs scratching his balding bonce...totally fazed.

"Arne, do you mind if my mate Sparky helps with crowd control? He's just round the corner in the pub and he drove me down from Horsham."

"Sounds like a useful man. Here..." Crap, once again I drop the jangling object Arne chucks at me, and I bend to pick up some classy car keys from the floor.

"New Park Road Car Park. Bay B42. Blue Maserati Spyder. On the spare tyre in the boot under the carpet. Get your man Sparky one of those batons. But do not open the green plastic package. And under no account lift the spare wheel."

"Maser—whoah. Er, shall I bring you a baton as well, Arne?"

"Nah. I think I'll be OK with these today." Arne tugs back the cuffs of his jacket and cuff-linked shirt and brandishes the no doubt lethal weapons that are his snow white hands. Arne Barstad. What a cool guy.

"FUCKING HELL! IT'S A MASERATI! Come on, Mil, let's have a drive in it!" Sparks has managed to down three pints in Wetherspoons whilst I was on duty with Pandora and is acting daft.

"Sober up, Beavis, you great prick! Shit, you had to wear your Daffy Duck T-shirt today, didn't you? Come out of the way - look, this is for you. It's a crowd control baton. Though soon as Arne sees you, he'll probably send you packing."

"Whoa! That's well cool!" Sparks is dancing around New Park Road Car Park like Luke Skywalker with his light sabre. He is making those 'zumming' noises as he pretends to take on Darth Vader.

"Put it away, Sparks!" I hiss, as shoppers returning to their cars with bulging plastic bags watch him in mounting concern. "Look, you retract it like this, shove it in your pants, and nobody knows you are carrying a lethal weapon."

"I already gotta lethal weapon in ma pants, baby!" replies a grinning Sparks, highly predictably and doing his ghetto accent, which I have to say is pretty good. Crap, it's twenty to four, we need to be on duty!

AS WE ARRIVE BACK, Arne is opening the oaken doors of the reading room to a big crowd of people - including the Horsham Three, who make a mad dash for the front seats.

"Took your time, Milad."

"Yeah, sorry Arne, this is Sparky." I lower my voice and lean into Arne's ear. His cologne smells really exotic and expensive. "I was just showing him how to use the expandable three-part steel friction lock crowd control baton."

Arne is checking out The Sparkster. He nods. "OK, you look like a man who can handle himself, Sparky. Get these people in their seats. Without violence preferably, but do not hesitate to use it if PM is under threat of any kind, and that includes verbal." Sparks looks well chuffed. I thought there was a fifty per cent chance Arne would reject him, and send him back to Wetherspoons.

Me and Sparky patrol the aisles, getting people seated. We wink at each other…these people have no idea what is going to come out of our pants if trouble starts. The seats are soon full; people are standing at the edge of the room, perching on stone windowsills and squatting in the central aisle. When they are all crammed in, Arne closes the big doors at the back, and stands impassive, his hands locked in front of him. He nods at me, and I nod back to my mate Arne. But like, almost imperceptibly?

Pandora, regal and refreshed, wearing a figure-hugging black dress (which just exudes fashion designer class) suddenly appears on the raised stage at the back of the hall. There is a buzz of excitement in the throng as she sits, and I take my place next to her, and smile. My retracted baton has got caught in my underpants and is thrusting obscenely like a metallic erection, and before I can shift the damned thing, Pandora notices.

"Is that a gun in your pocket or are you just pleased to see me?" she whispers into my ear with a salacious smile, which adds to the confusion in my underpants. I think that's a quote from someone, but I don't know who it is…I will check on Wikipedia later on.

"Ladies and gentlemen of Chichester…" I start.

"And Horsham!" shouts Cheesebreath in the front row. I decide to put a stop to the crowd participation straight away. I want to show Pandora how authoritative I can be.

"And Horsham too, madam, but I must use your interjection to warn you all that…the lady that I am about to introduce to you is a very busy one indeed, and very much a rising star of our times. If you do choose to shout things out, I can assure you it is your time you are wasting and not ours." The mob is on my side, and an old chap with copious white ear hair, leaning forward on a shooting stick at the edge of the room, is their spokesman.

"Yes, do shut up, you. Get back to Horsham with your bad manners. Please do continue, young man." There is a spattering of applause, and Pandora is gazing at me with admiring eyes.

"Thank you, sir. It is my very great pleasure to introduce today a lady who actually needs no introduction. Hailing from these parts…"

"Horsham!"

I indicate to Sparky - with what could be taken as an obscene gesture - to withdraw his crowd control baton, and to go and stand next to Cheesebreath. What I would like to say is, "Madam, if you interrupt me and this erudite literary audience once more and waste any more of PM

Poste's time, I will have my henchman take your inconsequential head off your lumpy shoulders with his night stick." But I don't say it. I ignore her.

 "She is becoming one of the country's best known writers, and specialising as she does in erotic fiction with her best-selling novel *Black Heart* – which I know many of you have read and had signed today …" Out of the corner of my eye I see one of Cheesebreath's cronies rise from her seat apparently in protest, but whatever she wanted to say or do is quickly extinguished – Sparks has got his stick out - and she quickly sits down in alarm.

…and so without further ado, the wonderful…PM Poste!"

I half-stand to lead the applause, and the room resounds with clapping, whooping and cheering. The audience is mainly female, with a spread of age groups with a median around thirty-five, I reckon. But it is the men in the audience that interest me more. There are some who are quite clearly young camp gays, some appear to be boyfriends and husbands unwillingly dragged along by their girlfriends and wives. But the one that takes my eye is the old codger who shut Cheesebreath up. He is leaning forward with interest on his shooting stick, as Pandora rises imperiously from her chair, raising her arms and spreading them wide to receive the adulation of her fans. I watch her in awe, grateful for a legitimate opportunity to feast my eyes on her magnificent profile. She has closed her eyes, her smile beatific. I mentally trace a line down her back which curves in and then arches out into a luxuriously upholstered posterior, which in turn gives way to voluptuously bulging thighs and curvaceous, salacious calves. I like a woman with a decent behind. And this woman has a decent behind. Pandora opens her eyes wide and looks fondly over at me, and I try to look like I've not been staring at her ass. She expertly lets the audience settle, and her eyes close once more as her arms drop gently to her sides. If it was dropped, you would hear the proverbial pin, in the expectant hush. I watch many of the punters lean forward in their seats, as if drawn to Pandora like, well, pins to a magnet. Another pin analogy in my head there, for some reason. Pandora opens her eyes, sets her half-moon glasses onto the bridge of her nose, takes a huge breath…and her reading begins.

""Miss Kavalo?" He extends an elegantly-gloved hand to me. "I'm Barnabas Black. Are you all right? Would you like to repose?"

So young—and powerful, very powerful. He's tall, dressed in an expensive black suit, white shirt, and black tie with an unruly mane of dark hair and intense, coal-black eyes that undress me, and pierce me. It takes some time for me to speak.

"Um. Er...um." I blither. If this guy is over forty, then I'm a Dutchman's uncle. He reaches down to shake my hand, which I lift, trembling. As our fingers touch, I feel an ice-cold shiver run through me. I withdraw my hand as if bitten by a cobra. Must be my imagination, running away with me. My heart is beating fast and my eyelids flicker, like they do when you get an eye muscle spasm.

"Miss Kavalo is poorly, so she sent me to interview you. I am Candy Pergola. I hope you don't mind me, Mr. Black?""

Pandora's voice is commanding and compelling, with an actress's range from soprano to bass, and she even does accents! The male hero of her book is American, and she does his dialogue in a really good West Coast drawl. Her heroine is an English rose, and she does her in a squeaky cute voice.

What Pandora evidently enjoys getting her mouth around are the naughty bits of her novel, and I am a wee bit surprised that she has chosen to include these in her public reading. First she is the American bloke.

""Show me. Show me yourself. All of yourself. Now. That's it. Candy, you must show me how you pleasure yourself ... keep still ... we're going to have to work on keeping you still, Candy-baby, my Candy-floss. So sweet...and fluffy ... Let's see if we can make you come like this, oh my, you're so deliciously, soaking wet. God, I want you ... I'm going to fuck you now, Miss Pergola ... And I'm going to do it the hard way. Come for me, Candy. Do."

Then, she does her squeaky heroine.

"I pull his thing deeper into my mouth so I can feel him at the back of my throat...and then out to my slurping lips again. My tongue swirls around his man-end. He's my very own Barnabas Black-flavoured popsicle. I suck...harder and harder...hmm... my inner goddess is doing the rumba with some conga moves."

My instinct is to look at my feet during the rude bits, but I check out the audience, who seem to be blushing, and exchanging secret smiles with their friends and partners. I see Arne stop and press a button on what looks like a very expensive iPod speaker, and music pours out, it's beautiful, like choral music, I think. As Pandora's couple get down to the business, the music swells to accompany her urgent and panting voice. The old codger takes my eye - he seems to be having a coughing fit.

"Get him out, Milad," hisses Pandora from the corner of her mouth, "he's ruining the mood."

I give Arne the signal, and he is on it.

"This is all a bit much!" the coughing old codger is complaining. "I was told PM Poste was in the mould of AS Byatt or Iris Murdoch! They *can* do fruity, those ladies. But frankly, this is all a bit much!"

But those are the last words he has in this particular company – Arne has him by the arm in a gesture of *faux* concern – but I know he has applied an insistent arm lock and the old fool is being ushered swiftly out. Pandora, the consummate professional, ignores the commotion and continues with her rising crescendo, becoming Candy again.

""He leans down and kisses me passionately, his fingers playing a Mahler symphony inside the goddess, his thumb circling and pressing on my G-zone. His other hand twists and scoops my hair into a ponytail, and whirls my head around with it, like a merry-go-round with a pony tail. His tongue is not to be left out of the action, flickering like a snake's. My legs begin to wobble as I push against his hand, and I feel the onset of cramp. He gentles his hand, so I'm brought back from the brink of cramp and my climax, but not for long. I come instantly again and again and again and again and again…and finally, again. In my panting, I'm through, I'm finished, but no…not with this man, this, machine. I'm building again … I climax anew, calling out his name….Barnabas…Barnabas...Barnabas!!""

Pandora collapses back into her chair, flushed and spent as if having had one of Candy's climaxes herself. The audience is in raptures of clapping and whooping; some of the women are fanning themselves with open copies of *Heart*, others rise to their feet or even their chairs to deliver a resounding standing ovation. Somehow, and with my assistance, Pandora is able to rise to her feet once more to savour the hot appreciation she is deservedly receiving. She gives me one of her great all-consuming hugs, and releasing me, waves to her cheering fans, as she disappears through the door of a small ante-chamber behind the stage, which I hadn't noticed before. Blowing a final kiss to her audience, she whispers, "Come with me Mee-lad. Arne and Sparky can get rid of this lot."

She closes the door of the musty chamber behind us, and I can hear the clamour of Cheesebreath and her cronies trying to follow her in for yet another attempt to get their copies signed and their rubbish fan-fiction read, but I can hear the swish of a baton and their horrible voices quickly recede. I discern that Pandora has used the ante-chamber as a dressing room. There is loads of make-up and hairspray and perfume and stuff on a big table, and some clothes, immaculately cleaned and pressed, hang from shelves on coat hangers in filmy plastic bags.

"Unzip me, darling," she breathes, her back to me and her iridescent red hair drawn over one of her freckly shoulders, over which she looks at me, smouldering. I am trying to stay cool as I step towards her, but my hand is trembling as I lift the tiny black zip of her designer dress. She turns her head away and lowers her chin to her chest, and in a very low voice, commands me again. "Unzip me, darling."

How to do this? I could just do it really fast, and then she'll probably want me to leave so she can change. There's no-one else to help her do it, after all. (As me and the gang found on our surfing holiday last year, it's hard to do your own back zip. Our wetsuits had Lycra cord attached to the zips, so you could actually zip and unzip yourself, I remember thinking how clever that was.) Just as I am figuring out how to do a business-like unzip for Pandora without catching her orangey-brown skin, she gives me further instruction.

"Slo-owly darling. Slow-ly."

"Ahem, right you are, Pandora, slowly it is. Slow as she goes." My face has gone 'Bootle' and my whole arm is quivering now. I hold my right arm steady with my left and try to keep some semblance of control as I jaggedly lower the zip, the tight dress bursting open as it is lowered. Over the thick black back-strap of her bra, which has not one, not two, but three catches. I have never seen such an extravagant brassiere creation. Most of Lisa's bras opened up at the front, and I never look at my sister's when they come out of the washing, but I know they are not like these. The zip continues its descent. She is a woman of so many surprises. Towards the small of her back, where fine blonde hairs start to bloom, is the top half of a tattoo, which looks quite recent…the flesh around it is a bit red, and there are a few tiny scabs on the ink, which I want to pick off with my nail. At first, I think the tattoo is a goldfish. But as the zip is lowered further, it is revealed as a splendid Japanese carp, swirling its powerful tail in a load of pond weed. The fish is all kinds of colours, blue, red, gold. It is magnificent. Conscious that I have reached the level of her waist, I stop, assuming that she can wriggle out of her dress from here, and that my work is done. I am wrong. "Lower, darling. Over my bottom. And slowly. Do it properly. Onto your knees, Mee-lad."

My breathing is out of control as I obey and fall to my knees, my left arm still supporting my right. I think the word for my breathing is 'wheezing' as the zip jags lower. I hit a bit of a problem. As her ass swells, the zip sticks fast, like when your suitcase is too full and you have to work hard to close it, but like the other way round? This becomes a two handed job. To shift the stuck zip, I have no choice. My left hand is on her left buttock and I press on it to release pressure on the zip, which thankfully resumes its descent.

"Mee-lad, you are cheeky!" she admonishes me. "Take your hand of my booty, immediately!" She doesn't sound very cross, but I withdraw my hand like her bum is red hot. Actually it is really quite hot. The zip reaches its limit, and Pandora's magnificent ass is my face in all its glory, captured by black tights with complex patterns of what I think are vines, and glowing beneath are the thin bands of a bright pink G-string.

"Stand, Mee-lad, and lower my dress from my shoulders." I am starting to get an urge. The urge to run. But I handle myself, and now with my legs shaking as well as my arms, my palms as clammy as as shellfish, my breathe an asthmatic rattle, I do as I'm told. She emits a strange sigh as I hitch the dress from her shoulders and it falls down her arms. I am shivering.

"Mee-lad, Mee-lad," she is whispering hoarsely, and she leans her weight back into me. I very nearly collapse backwards and no doubt she would have followed me. It would have been like one of those *Carry On* films that my Dad loves. *Carry On Authoress,* perhaps. But I oppose her womanly pressure with an equal and opposite force of my own (I was good at GCSE Physics), and she arches her head back onto my shoulder, her dress falling over her womanly hips to the floor, from which she nimbly steps in her gleaming black high heels.

Oh no. Her left hand is running up and down my left thigh, and now the same of the other side. Her breath is getting shorter. Then with her left hand, she is squeezing my nuts. I am gulping like the goldfish I thought was on her lower back. Suddenly she spins around, and with eyes like burning coals that meet mine, squats down, supported by the spikes of her shoes, and her beautiful nails are at my belt.

Holy crap. My giddy aunt. This cannot be happening. I respect this woman. She is my boss! And it seems highly likely she's about to give me a blow job. And I'm wearing my *Transformers* underpants. I know that I'm too old for wearing *Transformers* underpants. My sister Naz gave me them for Christmas as a joke after we went together to see *Transformers: Dark of the Moon*. Me and Naz love The Transformers. We used to have Transformers toys and I'd be Megatron and she'd be Optimus Prime. And though Transformers are cool, and these pants are really comfy, this is clearly not the moment to be wearing them.

My suit trousers are around my ankles, and my legs are visibly wobbling, as she runs her hands up and down the backs of my (very hairy) legs, and nestles her cheek against Optimus Prime and starts to lick him with her flickering pink tongue, her burning eyes still meeting mine. Her bosom, heaving below me, encased and squashed in enveloping cups is the most magnificent I have ever seen or even imagined. But I am 'not responding, Captain', as *Star Trek*'s chief engineer Scotty used to regularly report to Captain Kirk of the oft-stricken *Starship Enterprise*. I squeeze my eyes closed, my hands press on Pandora's muscular shoulders, and I will - nay command - my mast to rise. It does the fucking opposite. I can feel it shrivel to the size of a peanut, my nuts withering to the size of marbles… and that's the small marbles, not the big ones.

I consider some kind of intervention excuse, like "not now, Pandora, not here" or something equally desperate, but I can't speak as she attempts to massage life into my bloodless groin. Thank God for Sparky. He is rapping on the door with his crowd control baton.

"All clear Mrs Pandora. Safe to come out now. Arne says the Spyder will be out front in ten."

M M Gibbons

"Damn and blast!" hisses Pandora, grabbing my forearms and pulling herself up to meet my gaze. "Just as we were getting to *know* each other, Mee-lad!"

"Very well, Sparky," she calls confidently. "Wait by the car."

She is business-like once more. "Pull up you trousers, Milad. And never sport that underwear again. We must go shopping, my fine lad." I am Bootle-red and grinning like an idiot, as I obey her and as I do up my belt, I watch this magnificent creature button into a white silk chemise and a pair of very tight fitting designer jeans with lots of rips and tears in them.

"Go now, Milad, " she commands. "Wait outside of the door until I am ready."

"Yes, Pandora. Anything you say." Like a man reprieved from a firing squad, I draw the door bolt, and squeeze outside, grateful that Sparks has left the empty reading room. I lean back on the cloister door, sweating, gasping, incredulous at what just happened. I try to stop my head swimming and my legs wobbling.

A few minutes later, Pandora emerges with a beaming smile like nothing out of the ordinary just happened. She hands me her leather valise, takes my arm and leads me through Waterstones, ignoring residual gaggles of her fans, and a frowning Roger. Sparky is practically shoved out of the passenger seat of the revving Maserati by Arne, and Sparks has a go at courtesy by holding the door open as Pandora lowers herself in, and clips the seat belt between her enormous breasts. Arne snaps open the boot with a control on the dashboard and I place Pandora's valise next to the green carrier bag he told me not to open.

She is waving through the open passenger window as Arne launches the Spyder down Chapel Street, expertly and narrowly missing gormless shoppers who wave their fists and shout "oi!" Sparks and I stand and gawp at each other.

"Did you get to see her tits?" asks Sparks, distractedly, watching the Spyder rapidly disappear in a metallic blue blur.

Well at least I can extend one of my tools. I flick out my crowd control baton and whack Sparks behind the knees, just as Arne taught me. Sparks

62

folds like a broken marionette, and I turn and run whooping down the road, before he can catch and thump me.

CHAPTER FOUR

It's very quiet, apart from the curtain of rain pouring through the streets of Bognor. I sit in a sparse *Starbucks* doodling on my journo pad and sucking on a Frappuccino. Suddenly, a crowd of people with big brollies, macs and little sodden paper Union Jack flags troop past the window and I pull up the hood of my red golfing waterproof and join them on the street. A woman called Gabriella Broadhurst is carrying the Olympic Torch through gritted teeth, and I wonder how the flame in the giant golden cornet is staying alight in this downpour. A photographer from *The Guardian* who I met in the coffee shop is stooping in a huge puddle to take a picture of Gabriella that would make tomorrow's front page. I told Ray that I wanted to do a story on the passage of The Torch through the region, but I've started to tell several such lies lately. I will do a story of course, but guess who else is in town? I'm moonlighting for Pandora, and I have an appointment this afternoon at The Observatory Bookshop.

I spent Sunday (yesterday) in bed, but not at Mum and Dad's this weekend. First, I was trying to process the dramatic events of Chichester. Second, I was trying to get my willy to work. I spent much of the day with my eyes clenched, replaying in slow motion the downward journey of the black zip; the thick bra strap; the common carp tattoo (nothing common about it, that's just the species it was, according to my research on Wikipedia); the black patterned tights and the pink G-string; her hungry mouth, her blazing eyes, the bouncing bosom. But no matter how often nor how slowly I replayed the fantastical scene in my head, nor how vigorously I massaged the 'one-eyed wonder weasel', nothing could be stirred. Bastard thing. Now, what I think about when I have a crafty chub-slap is my business. OK yes, sometimes it involves Nat. But mainly it's Pamela Anderson. Or Gillian Anderson. Or Carol Vodermann when she was doing *Countdown*.

But I don't want to betray Pandora for Pamela or Gillian or Carol. I want to focus my sexual psyche on her, so if what happened in Chichester does happen again – and I'm very well aware that it might not – I won't let myself down again. But try as I might, the memory of her just wasn't hoisting the mainsail. I tried something drastic. Sparks was at a band rehearsal at Rollo's and I know his bedroom is a) unlocked and b) littered with pornography.

I crept, naked from the waist down wearing my Transformers T-shit that I wear at night (also bought for me for Christmas by Naz) like a thief in the day, into Sparks' room. I never go in there. It smells rank, mainly of the old socks that no doubt vie with the porn for majority occupation. Sure enough...issues of *Jazzler*, Spark's favourite gentleman's magazine, littered the carpet. I picked up a couple, and sneaked back to my room like the sex criminal I have become, my heart pounding.

I hopped into bed and set my pillows behind me. I have four...I like a lot of pillows. Not that I prop myself onto all four like The Elephant Man, I just like to have them there and I have to confess I've been sleeping with one in my arms, pretending it's Pandora. I thumbed through the pages of *Jazzler*, trying to forget that Sparky may have contaminated these pages. Ah. The centrefold on this issue is stuck fast together – it has definitely been contaminated. Yuk. Let's try another volume of *Jazzler*. I turned the pages, but none of the girls displayed in shameless gynaecological detail were doing it for me. I was about to give up, when I reached the plethora of ads for phone sex, and someone took my eye. Blimey, it could have been her, but it wasn't - thank goodness. I was drawn to the gigantic pink nipples on a busty red-headed stunner of about the same age as Pandora. Something below my *Avengers* duvet began to stir. I propped the page up on a pillow and used the image to assist my imagination. I'm transported back in the ante-room chamber of the reading room in Chichester. My underwear is transformed to grey silk boxer shorts and I am bending to unhook the gigantic clasp of Pandora's bra and her juicy whammers (here they are in front of me in the phone sex ad) tumble out, her enormous nipples hardened as I twirl them gently in my fingers. I am in her mouth...stiff as a flagpole, her moistened lips running up and down my eager gentleman. Oh yeah baby, this is working for me now. My right hand is pumping away, and my vision of the phone porn model is getting blurry. I don't need her any more. As I close my eyes, Pandora has me, deep, deep down. Here I go...I want to ask her, "do you swallow, Pandora?" but it's too late...I'm going to assume she does. And she has. I fall into a heavenly reverie.

"WHAT THE FUCK are you doing with my mags, Mil?"

"Wha…wha…SPARKY!! GET…GET OUT DAMN YOU! How many times have I told you not to walk into my room!"

"The sign on the door says 'Make up the Room', pervert. Anyway, it doesn't stop you walking into my room and helping yourself to my girls does it, you hypocrite? Get your own jazz mags, loser. And that's my favourite one on the floor, my special girlfriend is the centrefold! You better not have made a mess all over *her*! Oh, dear, you better keep that one - it's fucking stuck to you…I'm off!"

Sparky slams the bedroom door. *Jazzler* magazine is stuck fast to my genital region, and is going to need some careful extraction. There's got to be a whole month's worth of gentleman's relish all over Pandora's phone sex ad look-alike.

Once extricated from the magazine, I crept past Sparky in my blue towelling dressing gown and had a very long shower. We didn't speak for a quite a time, but during Germany vs. Italy, he started laughing. At me. And I joined in. Well, I had to, really.

BACK TO THE PRESENT, and the driving rain in Bognor. I have thrown away the *Transformers* underpants and this morning, I spent a king's ransom on new undercrackers in *Next*. Unbeknownst to the good people of Bognor, I am striding their sodden streets in silk grey boxer shorts. The boy is becoming the man, and he is heading for his woman.

Pandora waves as I enter The Observatory Bookshop, and Arne acknowledges me, in his subtle way. Some people would think he was ignoring me, but me and Arne have developed an almost telepathic way of greeting each other. *The Matrix* publishers are way to cool for saying 'hello'. Must ask him about his suits, this Moss Bros job has to go.

"Mee-lad! Good afternoon, my dahling. Mmmmm, and how wonderful you smell, is that Hugo Boss?"

Spot on! What a nose for classy aftershave this lady has. I have gone up-market from the Iceland Breeze that Naz bought me two Christmas's ago. I peck Pandora professionally on both cheeks, and help with building the book pile. No reading today, just a two-hour book signing.

Pandora is on great form, dressed in a tight red crew-neck lambswool top and grey trousers which hug her figure, before tucking into riding boots. She is lovely to everyone, and today she goes through the whole two hours of the signing, plus ten minutes extra, and every one of her south coast fans goes home happy. The bookshop owner is ecstatic…he has sold over three hundred copies of *Heart* and it's his best day's takings in years. She invites him for a drink at The Royal where we are staying.

We saunter down the Esplanade, and though there are ominous black clouds hovering above the grey evening, there is a pause in the continual rain. Pandora skips along like a schoolgirl, her left arm in mine and her right arm in the bookstore owner's (a black guy, whose name is Marvin). Arne hovers behind us, looking ever about him for possible assassins or unwanted autograph hunters. Pandora leans all her weight on me and Marvin, and gaily swings out her feet, like a carefree lass in the playground. But we can't support her womanly weight for long and after we haul her back to her feet, she goes back to playful skipping. Then she is doing some hopscotch, picking up a stone, rolling it and retrieving it with hops, skips and jumps. Me and Marvin applaud, laughing, and she curtseys low, her thumb in her mouth. Arne gazes out to sea, probably checking for signs of would-be pirate kidnappers from Somalia.

AT THE BAR AT THE ROYAL, Arne sorts out the drinks. Pandora has a G & T, followed by a glass of pink fizz, followed by a stiff V & T (treble). I have a couple of pints of lager with Marvin; Arne drinks nothing and spends the whole time texting on his Android phone. We (well, mainly Pandora) demolish two trays of mixed nuts kindly provided *gratis* by the white-coated barman.

"I am staa-a-aarving!" yawns Pandora, and I can't help staring down her throat as far as her tonsils, something twitching about in my new silky kecks. "Will you join Milad and I for dinner, Marvin? I don't suppose that Arne will be doing so. So boring, Arne." Arne responds by very slightly raising his blonde right eyebrow, in a gesture which means "no thanks, I have better things to do like go on a surveillance recce of our next destination."

Marvin stretches contentedly. "I had better say no, Pandora, though thanks so much for the invitation. I have to get back home and help with the kids' homework tonight, but such a pleasure to meet you and thank you once again for coming to my humble shop. I wonder if you would do me the honour of being in a photograph with me?"

Marvin withdraws a pocket digital camera from his tweed jacket pocket, holding it up hopefully. "Of course, darling, of course! How do you want me? Milad, go over by the bar. Arne, get out of the shot."

I take several photographs of Marvin with Pandora, in various poses. Most of them I thought Marvin would probably not want to show his wife, especially the one of Pandora straddling him and laughing over her shoulder, but I'll leave the editing to him.

"Book a table for two for eight, Mee-lad, I want to take a bath before I dine." Come and collect me from my room at ten-to, I do so hate coming down to dinner alone."

She breezes off, her magnificent rump sashaying behind her, and I have a bit more of a chat with Marvin, before he departs for home. I watch him walk slowly across the car park, deleting pictures from the digital camera as he goes.

I text with Sparks and Potts for a bit, and put another pint of lager on Pandora's slate. I fire up the old laptop, belting out my rubbish story about the Olympic Torch and E-mailing it to Ray. Only two more days to go at *The Times*, but my head isn't really there anymore. Sheelz has kindly organised a leaving do for me on Friday, and we are all going out for a curry. A bit more net-surfing, and before I know it, I look at my watch and it's already ten to eight…I swear that time goes faster on some days than others, and today it has really flown. I get my laptop and bag to my room, and then hasten to Room 364, Pandora's. I arrive breathless and a bit late. Her room door is slightly ajar, and I am expecting to be admonished by Pandora in yet another amazing outfit (I love her clothes sense) for being late, and I knock lightly and slightly nervously on the door with my fingertips. But there is no reply. I knock more firmly with my knuckles (is that rapping on the door?) but still, nothing stirs.

Irrationally paranoid, I wonder if someone has broken in and murdered the woman who is becoming so dear to me. Of course they have! I enter the room like a detective, vividly imagining my darling woman splayed on the bed with her throat cut, or shot through the temple in the bath. My theory proves one quarter right - but she is far from dead.

"Mee-lad! Oh, Mee-lad!" her voice is coming from the echo-y bathroom, along with the overpowering smell of a *Lush* bath bomb. I know that smell, I bought my sister Naz one for Christmas. I pad towards the steamy bathroom, the door of which is half open. Oh sweet Jesus, the vision. In a bubble bath of foam which rises in frothy peaks almost to the ceiling lies the recumbent goddess, her red hair piled above her head and roughly secured by various combs, pins and bands. She is giving me the unmistakeable 'come hither' sign with her long-nailed forefinger.

I enter the bathroom, breathing hard, partly because of the choking bath bomb, and partly because I am presuming she is not wearing a bathing suit under that colossal layer of foam. I am wondering how many of those little plastic bottles she tipped in, though I see the silver Jacuzzi pumps arrayed around the bath may well have contributed to the foam extravaganza. I am trying to prevent myself having another coughing fit, as she smiles at me like a sphinx.

"Undress, Mee-lad. Slowly. And then - join me."

"Erm, won't we be late for dinner, Pandora? We don't want you getting hungry?"

"Bugger dinner. That can wait. I said undress. Slowly."

I recall *The Full Monty*, the movie about male strippers, and this is surely my only inspiration. Very grateful of the three pints of lager that my writhing stomach eels are gently pickling in, I set about sort of unconvincingly gyrating my hips. I remove my jacket, which I whirl around my head and throw out of the bathroom. I remove my tie (making sure to preserve the knot) and then shimmy out of my trousers. Pandora seems delighted with my performance, and claps a rhythm which helps my little dance. Soon down to my new undies and socks, I hop about a bit trying to get the socks off (not easy to do that and stay sexy. However, since I wasn't very sexy at the start of the routine, this is not a major problem). Now the really nervous bit. The kecks.

"Off, off!" demands Pandora. Now, Pandora is surely a woman of the world, and I am very far from being a man of the world (as yet). When it comes to the business of a gentleman's wedding tackle, Pandora may be something of an expert. And women today seem to be obsessed with penis size, I like it's to do with feminism. According to Wikipedia, the average length of an extended trouser snake is 5.4 inches. If I really get Willy Wonka throbbing (rubbing in chilli powder works quite well), I am the magic number. But…the thing about the male member is that some blokes' johnsons shrink when 'at rest' more than others. And mine seems to shrink more than those others. Sometimes, say if I come out of the shower at the flat and the bathroom is really cold (like it always is in autumn, winter, spring and even sometimes is in summer), I can look in the bathroom mirror and wonder if I have a peanut for a penis. But then if I coax it out with my hairdryer, it looks like a pretty decent dong. But you never know if it's going to be peanut or priapic, it depends on a whole range of factors like temperature, my state of relaxation, how much beer I've drunk, and so on. I guess that means I could never be an underwear model for H & M, like David Beckham. On a bad day, instead of a manly bulge, I could be a Bangkok lady-boy. Maybe they use a hairdryer to get the swell on Becks when he is modelling underwear, or perhaps he has a fluffer. Posh Spice wouldn't like that. Unless she is the fluffer, I suppose. Anyway, I prefer to think about Becks the footballer. I had a 'Beckham' shirt when I was little, even though I don't support Man-U and my Dad is an Everton fan. My Dad reckons he was a 'good' player, but I reckon he was a 'great' player. But good player or great, I need to banish thoughts of Golden Balls, as just now, it's my own underpant-equipment that is under scrutiny.

I get the strong feeling that, despite the far from freezing temperature of this particular steaming bathroom, this could be a peanut moment. I slide my hand into my boxers in a gesture that is meant to be part of my routine, but is in fact a disguise to check the status of my resting tumescence. Yep, peanut it is. I have to think fast. I turn my back to her, still wiggling my non-existent hips and skinny bum, and slide my kecks down over my ankles. Pandora is wolf-whsitling and shouting "PHWOAR!", as I spin around, hands on the tackle and I'm in the bath like lighting and swallowed by foam. My feet slither around, trying to establish where my legs should go. As they do so, they slide over either her body, and yep - definitely no bathing suit. I am in a foam jacuzzi bath with PM Poste, and we are butt naked. I repeat, I am in a foam jacuzzi bath with PM Poste, and we are butt naked.

Pandora seems highly delighted. She is laughing like a very deep bell, and clapping her hands, a cone of foam on her nose which makes her look cute. I am laughing too.

"Oh Mee-lad, Mee-lad, you are such *fun*!" The lads all say that, especially when I am pissed. They called me Fun Milad for a bit, but it didn't stick for long. Look out, here's a big moment, my eyes are out on stalks. Pandora is rising and surfacing from the foam, and there is a scraping and whining sound of bum on ceramic as she does so. Her skin is a wonderful warmed pink, and as she sits and leans forward, the breasts I have been dreaming of reveal themselves as they bob up from the depths like submerged watermelons (only pink, not green). Her enormous pink nipples – a vast spread of aureoles with a bull's-eye nub like a turret, view me like huge, startled eyes.

"Do you like them, Mee-lad?" she purrs, massaging her orbs together and pinching the helicopter landing pads into long, hard cones.

"I…I…I love them…P-Pandora. They look really…great on you?" Crap, I must stop that stupid habit of turning everything into a question, like the Aussies do, and all young Brits.

"Would you like to fee-el them, Milad? Would you like to *touch* them?"

"I would Pandora, very much. In fact, there is nothing I would more rather do."

She leans forward, takes both my hands, and presses them firmly onto her watermelons. I knead them like the bread dough I occasionally make with my Mum. I roll the hardened nipples between thumb and forefinger… gently of course, I have read somewhere about how sensitive ladies nipples can be. But not Pandora's, apparently.

"Harder darling. Pinch them harder. Dig you nails in. Do it. Aaaaaaaaaah, yes." I'm pretty sure I must be hurting her, and I revert to a sudsy massage. I'm thinking about Sparky and the boys. If they only could see me now!

Milad Brown's hands are all over PM Poste's tits. Repeat, Milad Brown's hands are all over PM Poste's tits.

She throws off my hands in a sudden gesture, and foam flies everywhere.

"Now it's my turn!" she grins, with a piquant twist of evil. But I am praying she doesn't touch my nipples. I fucking hate that. Lisa started sucking them once and I had to ask her to stop. When she pinched them it made me feel quite sick. But Pandora's ringed hand does not extend to my chest. It plunges into the water and fishes about for my manhood. It takes her quite a long time to find it.

"Gosh, this is a bit of tiddler, isn't it, Milad?" The look of disappointment on her face is palpable. But soon she melts into a smile. "But let's see what we can do with it, shall we?"

I can testify that it is very hard for a man to gain an erection after the woman of his dreams has described his penis as a "tiddler". But somehow, this clever woman coaxes one out of me. It has something to do with her scrabbling around the floor of the bath to retrieve the still fizzing remains of the *Lush* bath bomb, which she deftly and cheekily places in my bum-zone. Something about the gentle emanation of bubbles relaxes my soul, and centimetre by gradual centimetre, my manhood expands in her insistent hand.

"Ooooh, now that's more like it, Milad. Mmmmm. Let's see how big I can make you. Stand up."

Grateful to eject the fizzing orb, I push myself with both arms to my feet, and since I have nothing more to hide, allow her to inspect me at the closest of quarters, as she rises to her knees.

"What super thighs you have Mee-lad. And the washboard of your stomach, quite simply marvellous. And this modest organ is swelling nicely. Mmm, how very cute you are." I open my eyes, and I am quite proud of what I see below. I can feel the weasel throbbing as it has never throbbed before, as she places it between her soapy breasts and presses them together, encasing my dude piston in them. Up and down she moves, the cheeky feller peeping out of her cleavage on every down-stroke. My hands move onto her shoulders just like in my fantasy, and she is purring as she glides up and down me.

"Are you enjoying my boob-pleasure, Milad?"

"Yes…yes…yes…yes..Pandora…I am enjoying it thoroughly," I reply through gritted teeth. "I am…I am…OHHHHHHHHHH GOOD LORD!"

My head is spinning, my temples crashing, I can see violent clashing colours in my retina as my eyes shut tight, I am panting like I've just run for the bus.

I want to bend down and kiss her mouth, but like the supine fish on her back, she has descended to the foamy deeps and is cleansing her mighty breasts. Rising to the surface once more, she gives my flaccid cock an almighty slap, which brings me right back down to Earth.

"Out and get me my towels. And re-book the table straightaway. I am famished!"

Our dinner passes in a heavenly haze, Pandora ordering for us both and I eat pasta and drink a glass of red in a blur. She keeps winking at me and rubbing my thighs under the table, arousing me once more. I am assuming that another course of our love will follow later in the bedroom. But I am wrong. After she has consumed a large portion of cheesecake with double cream with an espresso chaser, she rises imperiously, and stretches her arms to the ceiling.

"I'm tired and I'm going to sleep. Sign the bill and put it on my room. But check that it's right, won't you, dah-ling." She takes my head in both her hands, and kisses me hard on my forehead. "We'll always have Bognor, won't we, my bubbly bath-mate," she whispers in my ear before releasing my head and clicking away across the polished floor in her heels.

I wonder why the waiter is smirking at me as he brings a silver plate to the table. I discover later that I have a scarlet lipstick kiss in the middle of my forehead. As I run through the bill, having no clue whether we consumed the listed items or not, I wonder what the next amazing encounter with Pandora might bring. Slightly sadly, I remember that her goodnight words echo those of Rick in *Casablanca*, one of my favourite films. Perhaps that would be it, and she would revert to being solely my fabulous, amazing boss. If so, she was damned right. I'd always have Pandora's bath bomb boob-job in Bognor. Just wait til Sparky hears about this.

CHAPTER FIVE

Arne opens the passenger door to the iridescent blue Maserati, and I slide in. We exchange our now familiar ultra-cool non-greeting, and speed off down the A259 to Worthing. Arne is also too cool for speed cameras, and I give each one the finger as the flashlight goes off - in vain. Arne has rigged up a reflector on the registration plates, and all the fuzz will get is a blinding flash and a pang of envy.

Pandora was on Daybreak TV this morning, and in addition to completely overwhelming Dan and Kate, read an extract widely deemed inappropriate for pre-watershed broadcast and according to Sparky's texts, there is quite a media uproar about it. Which will do our sales no harm at all…hehe. I am officially Pandora's man now - I had my farewell curry from *The Times* on Friday, and they gave me a really nice card with a Photoshop picture of me and Pandora on the front, which I thought was a bit inappropriate, though it did exaggerate my manhood generously. Nat put fifty-three kisses after her nice words and cried after her third pint of Cobra. They also gave me a really cool engraved silver fountain pen in a leather case, which I am taking on tour, in case Pandora needs a spare signing pen.

But I'm still a bit worried…I sent Pandora a text message on her personal mobile about this contract business. I had to tell a white lie to my Dad that I did have a contract and well, the fact is that I don't. Though I do trust Pandora (and trust is better than any legal contract in my book) she hasn't replied to my text yet, despite I sent it on Friday and today is Tuesday. Anyway, enough of such petty concerns. The Spyder speedo hits one hundred (mph, not kph) and Arne hits the media centre. *Spem in Alium* by Thomas Tallis rings out. It's the music that Pandora uses during her readings and it features prominently in *Black Heart*. So cool, it's just like listening to the voices of angels. I don't believe in God that much, but maybe I should now after landing this awesome dream job with a dream lady. After a while, I get bored of listening to the choral stuff - I could use a hip-hop fix, and resolve to ask Arne later if he likes hip-hop or not. He doesn't really seem the hip-hop type, but you never know with hip-hop - all kinds of people like it, even really straight people sometimes.

As we arrive at Georgian Worthing, I am reminded of a Morrissey song. Lisa liked *The Smiths*, and she used to sing their songs loads. We used to exchange Morrissey quotes in the pub, and to keep up I had to do a lot of research and I-Tunes loading. I pay for my music, though Sparky is the king of illegal downloads, music, films, you name it. We row about it, sometimes. Even though he isn't a Communist he thinks music should be free. Well, free to him at least. I don't, I know how hard artists have to work and I think they deserve a few quid for their albums or books. Morrissey has had a few quid from me, I hope he appreciates it. Anyway, *"This is the seaside town, they forgot to close down"* is a line worth a tenner all by itself. I sing it to Arne, who gives me one of his sideways looks, which could mean he thinks I'm an imbecile, so I don't carry on. I try to make conversation instead.

"So…Arne, what's in the mysterious green bag in the boot that you told me not to open?"

"A gun."

That crisp answer stops me in my tracks. Fucking hell! I am riding with a killer. I nod and give it the staring ahead cool treatment.

"And under the spare wheel?" SHIT, WOOOOAH! I lurch forward as the car goes from fifty miles an hour to zero in six seconds. I am slumped forward, the seat belt biting into my ribs. Arne hasn't budged.

"Milad, I'll tell you this once and only once. Never look under that wheel. And never mention it again. To anyone." I am propelled back into my seat, as suddenly he hits the gas hard and we are roaring once more beyond the suburban speed limit.

"No problem, Arne," I croak, my guts in my oesophagus. Trouble is - I have mentioned it to someone. Someone inadvisable. Sparky. We debated the possible contents of the Maserati boot whilst driving Estelle back from Bognor. Sparky thought it must have been a grenade. I didn't have a clue. But now I'm thinking that if there's a gun in the green bag, it could well be a grenade! But why would anyone need a gun and a grenade on a book-signing tour of the south coast?

We pull up outside one of the many whitewashed Georgian hotels on Marine Parade, and from afar, I see Pandora waving, her hair redly iridescent in the glum grey evening light. Ah. Uh ho. She may not be waving, she may be shaking her fist. I can hear her yelling at us even with *Spem* ringing out and with the tinted windows closed. Now she is giving us the 'wanker' sign. Ooops, something is definitely up.

"WHO BOOKED ME INTO THIS FUCKING SHITHOLE!" she is shouting as we pulls up. "WHO?"

I press the super-cool window opener and she shouts it again, in my face. Her face is a rather fetching angry scarlet, and she is perspiring about her cute flared nose.

"Arne, who booked Ms. Poste into this fucking shithole?" I ask Arne coolly over my new aviator mirror shades I got from *Boots*. I know it wasn't me, so that's me out of the firing line. Arne has his super-cool flip-over mobile at his ear already.

"Fiona at Coffee. She said it was a value deal," Arne reports severely.

"RIGHT, I WANT FIONA GONE RIGHT NOW OR THE TOUR IS OFF!" Pandora is gasping with anger. It is a *total* turn-on. Arne is speaking very quietly into his mobile.

"Fiona is gone, Ms Poste. You are transferred to The Burlington. But only one room left. Milad and I will have to stay here, it seems. Milad, take our bags in, I will drive Ms Poste to her new hotel."

Still fuming, Pandora practically rips me out of the passenger seat by my jacket collar, and I nearly go sprawling into a pile of dog shit left by an irresponsible owner. She is surprisingly strong is Pandora, for a woman. I bet she could look after herself in a bitch-fight. My now familiar trouser stirrings react manfully to this thought.

I give her my sympathetic smile, and put my hand thoughtfully on her bare freckly shoulder which I adore. It's as well I have fast reflexes because she has slammed the door which was about one-tenth of a second from severing my wrist and leaving my sympathetic hand to comfort her on its own, like Thing in *The Addams Family*.

The Spyder blazes off, and I trudge up the cracked stone hotel steps with two bags (Arne's is leather Gucci, mine is a plastic Adidas sports bag) smiling at Pandora's class. That's the problem with us Brits…we're too polite to complain about poor service. I struggle through a broken revolving door into a damp-smelling reception area – what a dump. There are a lot of folk milling about - I see on a red board with gold clip-on lettering that tonight is "The Annual Conference of The Society of Udertakers." I presume that they've missed out the 'n', judging from the number of tail-coats and top hats with black silk bands round them.

The receptionist is quite cute, and I tell her there's been a serious mistake booking PM Poste into this down-market establishment, but that Mr Bastad (she smiles at this, bless her) and I would be OK with it, as blokes can rough it better than girls can. Then she hands me a key with a big wooden fob on it and I wait for the other room key. But there isn't another room key forthcoming.

"Er, where is the other key, erm, Sharon…for Mr Bastad?"

"Oh, I'm sorry, Mr Brown, we only have one room left. But it is a twin room, with a nice sea view?"

Huh? Sharing with Arne? As John McEnroe once said before I was born…"*You cannot be serious, man!*"

Leaving our bags with Sharon, I mount three flights of creaky, mouldy steps and check the room out. It's a high-ceilinged room, and when I attempt to open the immobile window, plumes of plaster fall from the peeling ceiling rose and coving. There are two twin beds separated by a bedside cabinet full of cup-rings. My Dad hates 'cup-ring' and goes ballistic if I forget to use a coaster on the coffee tables or mantelpiece. The bathroom smells like the pipework needs unblocking and lime scale covers the bath and sink. Black mould infests the yellowing tiles. I close the bathroom door, causing another dusting of plaster from the ceiling, and sit down on a battered sofa bed, which also smells funny. Lifting the cushion, there are small black droppings and a hole where a mouse has made a nest. I don't think someone as cool as Arne will want to stay here. I hope not, as I hate sharing rooms with other blokes. Me and the lads stay in a YMCA in London sometimes and I've shared a couple of Travelodge rooms with Sparko. Anybody snoring and farting (Sparks is an expert at the latter and dabbler in the former) and I just don't sleep. At all. That said, I don't have Arne down as a snorer, or a farter. He doesn't eat anything for starters (or at least he doesn't seem to) so there can't be much ruminating away in his guts. Anyway, this is all academic, because there is no way that Arne will want to share a room with *me*.

"OK, we will move one bed by the window, the other by the wall." Arne is suddenly in the room with both our bags, hanging up his jacket in the creaky, veneered wardrobe. "Lift."

"Arne! Er, are you sure you want to stay here, it is a proper dump…"

"No matter. I have stayed in worse. Much worse. Lift."

Blimey, I *am* going to share a room with Arne! The beds rearranged, Arne unpacks his clothes into a cheap white chest of drawers, puts a leather Gucci wash bag in the en suite bathroom and then, taking a leather-bound volume from the depths of his bag, lies back on his bed by the big window (which he has somehow opened) opens a page and starts reading from it. I play it cool. I lie in exactly the same posture as him (shoes still on) and text Sparks.

"Shring rm in Wthg with Arne ;0 The Matrix pblshers!".

Arne raises a blonde eyebrow as my iPhone makes its 'incoming text' bleep. I turn it to silent, and read Sparks' message with a grin.

"Cool as fck! Keep 1 eye opn, see if he hs any wpons on hm. [⚥]"

Out of the corner of my eye, I catch something move. It's the bloody mouse, emerging from the sofa bed! It creeps warily across the worn carpet, I don't think it knows that me and Arne are here. I'm not sure whether to inform Arne that there is vermin in the room…but suddenly there is no need. Without taking his eye from his book, Arne's white hand flashes to the carpet, scoops up the mouse, crushes it (it makes a kind of crackling noise) and chucks it out of the window.

"Arne just killd a mouse." I text Sparks.

"Wot, wiv a gun?" I get back immediately.

"No, bare hands" I reply.

"Er, would you like a cup of tea, Arne? Thought I'd have a brew."

He does his almost imperceptible head-shake thing and carries on reading. I creep about the creaking room filling a tiny lime scale-encrusted kettle with a four inch mains lead, and wait an age for it to boil. Jesus, *Lipton's* tea and those horrible plastic milk jiggers which my Dad reckons are carcinogenic. This is not going to be a good cuppa.

As I brew up, I peep over and see what Arne is reading. Blimey…Psalms, Old Testament Bible. Ah, that explains the suits and the look. He's some kind of Mormon Bible basher! I'm a bit disappointed to be honest - that's not so cool.

"Ah, looks like you are church-goer, Arne," I venture.

He looks up icily from the Good Book. "Not in the least. I just like the Old Testament language. I have no taste for the modern."

"So-oooo, you haven't read Ms. Poste's book, no?" Arne gives me the same look of disdain he would probably give the pile of dog shit outside on the pavement. He doesn't reply, and turns back to his reading, with a finality that says "this conversation is over". Man, I have to learn how to do that look. After my carcinogenic tea, I go into the bathroom to brush my teeth, and practise it.

Ambling in and out of the bathroom, I give him the casual, 'talking whilst brushing my teeth and walking about' thing. "Coming down for dinner, Arne? I'm getting a bit peckish and thought I might go in the restaurant before those funeral people start their dinner."

"No, I won't join you. I, er, may be out when you return. Until late. I won't disturb you though if you are asleep. I am, quite…quiet."

Unsociable Bastad! Oh well, just me and matey-text I suppose; I head for the empty dining room, which is full of kitsch decoration and crap muzak. I don't really like eating alone, but at least these days you are never alone with your iPhone. I text Dean what I'm ordering and eating…prawn cocktail…soggy. Sirloin steak – pub meat. Rhubarb crumble and custard – cindery and lumpy respectively. The bottle of house red is OK, and I use it to wash down the poor fare, finishing it before I know it. I order a brandy to take away the after-taste of the crumble. My Dad usually has one of those in hotels and I make sure it's *Remy Martin*. The undertaker people start drifting in for their dinner and I think to split, until an interesting looking girl with dark hair in long Victorian curls sits down at the table next to me, wearing a retro dress which looks like some kind of cut down vintage wedding dress. Her legs are bare, and I notice a tattoo of ivy that starts at her ankle, weaves around her calf, over her knee, around her thigh, and becomes thicker as it disappears up her short skirt. To my great embarrassment my eyes are clamped on the hem of her dress when she turns to meet my eyes.

"Are you in the funerals business?" she asks. "I haven't seen you before at The Society?"

"Ah no, actually, I am in the publishing business. I am the media advisor to PM Poste, the international authoress," I tell her with pride. God, how much better does that sound than 'local hack reporter on the *West Sussex County Times*? 'Ivy' looks impressed.

"Really? Isn't she the one who writes dirty books for women?" I'm used to fielding and returning this question already, my return throw flies low into the hands of the wicket keeper two centimetres above the bails. I love sporting analogies, though in fact I'm useless at cricket.

"Well, her current best seller is erotic fiction, we like to refer to it as erotographia. Though PM writes in a number of genres. Her poetry is especially sophisticated."

"Is that so? Oh, my name is Isabel, by the way…" she offers me a ghostly hand, and the ivy creeps down her skeletal wrist and onto the back of her brittle, blue-veiny hand.

"Very nice to meet you, Isabel. Milad. Mee-lad. It's Persian." I hold her hand lightly, lest it should crumble to dust in my grip.

"I can see that you like my tattoo, Milad. I'll show you where it goes later if you like?"

And I had to be mid brandy-gulp, didn't I? Yep, all down my shirt and over the table cloth it goes, in a fine Remy Martin spray-mist. And naturally, the coughing fit follows. I can taste rhubarb crumble regurgitating into my throat. And kind Ivy - I mean Isabel - is patting, nay, thumping me on the back. I wouldn't have thought that she would have such strength. And then I look up, and I see a ruby hovering in a canyon.

"Pandora! Where?…"

"I'm not having this on tour, Milad! Chatting up a different girl in a different hotel every night! Who do you think you are, Julio Iglesias?"

"Er, who…?" I splutter.

"Never mind 'who?' my lad, who is this…this…corpse?!"

"Er, this is Ivy, I mean, this is Isabel. Isabel, allow me to introduce you to PM Poste, the famous authoress."

"Yes, I saw you on TV this morning. A bit rude for kids eating their Shreddies, I thought."

Pandora's right fist clenches, and for one awful moment I imagine her right hook would explode Isabel's thin skull to chalk dust. Instead she leans forward and growls. "And what would you know about the written word, Corpse Bride?"

"Plenty actually. Read English Lit at Oxford. I'm an engraver now. For headstones. I'll do one for your literary career next year, if you like." Yowch! Bitch fight? No, surely only one winner? Much as I would like to see where Isabel's ivy tattoo rambles between wrist and thigh, I take a snarling Pandora by the arm and lead her away to the bar, where I snap my fingers like Arne does and the glass-cleaning barman roundly and insolently ignores me. But he doesn't ignore Pandora, who furiously orders two double brandies, and after swilling the first down in one, orders two more.

"I came to see Arne actually, not you, you dirty little whore-catcher. But he's already gone out. Gluuuug…aaaaah, that's better."

"Where has he…gone, Pandora? He told me he might be late," I say, fishing.

"Don't ask," she replies, curtly. "Barman, two more."

After drinking in sulky silence for a while, she suddenly takes my arm and with a girlish smile says, "Come along Mee-lad. Walk a girl along the prom. I have something for you." We walk in the cool evening air, and she has her hand on my bum. And she coquettishly places mine on hers.

"Now, Mee-lad, I have that contract that you've been pestering me about. There you are, you impudent boy!"

From her Armani handbag, she hands me not one white A4 envelope, but two. Probably one copy for keeping and one for signing and returning. "Oh, thanks Pandora, I hope I haven't been a nuisance over this business?"

"Well, you are a very naughty boy. I expect you'd like to take me under the pier and get my knockers out, wouldn't you!"

"Er, well…."

"Well, you are not going to!" she laughs, skittering down the prom, "and you needn't walk me home either! A girl needs her space, Mee-lad!"

Against my gentlemanly instincts, I obey and smile and wave as she recedes into the blue darkness, swirling around to wave occasionally. I head back to the hotel, where the undertaker's ball is in full swell. Knowing that it's more than my job is worth to see if Ivy/Isabel is still around. Feeling a bit pissed, I trudge up three flights of creaking steps to the darkened room and switch on the depressing glare of the 40 Watt tungsten light bulb under the dusty tasselled lightshade. Arne isn't here, and I turn on the TV, and open the first envelope rolled in my jacket pocket. Just what I wanted…and more! A formal-looking contract from Coffee Press, all the right numbers on it *and* paying me in advance instead of arrears. Happy days! I see there are two copies of the contract in the envelope. So what's in this other one then? I slide more formal-looking papers from the second envelope, sit back on my bed, rearrange the pillows a bit, and start to read.

CONTRACT

Made this day _____ of 2012
("The Commencement Date")

BETWEEN

MR. MILAD BROWN of Flat 3, West Street, Horsham, West Sussex

("The Submissive")

Ms. PANDORA POSTE of 36, Greveldon Terrace, Holland Park, London

("The Dominant")

What the f...? What's all this about? This contract is about ten pages long...and there are three Appendices as well! I scan it through and the following excerpts jump off the pages before my widening eyes:

"The fundamental purpose of this Contract is to allow the Submissive to explore his sensuality and his limits safely, with due respect and regard for his needs."

Eh? Who needs a contract to do that? And what does she mean by 'Submissive'? Is that a contractual term for an employee? I presume 'Dominant' means the boss...like Ray. Or in this case, Pandora.

"The Dominant shall take responsibility for the wellbeing and the proper training, guidance, and discipline of the Submissive. She shall decide the nature of such training, guidance, and discipline and the time and place of its administration. The Submissive is to serve and obey the Dominant in all things."

That all seems reasonable enough. We had a training and guidance programme at *The Times*. In fact, Nat texted me today to tell me that the paper is sponsoring her to do a course at Brighton University, which is really good. I think she puts too many x's on her txts though. Me and the lads call it the 'kiss barometer'. X = friends, your mum, you can even send one of these to your mates or your Dad without being too gay. Xx = never to other men, but OK to your Mum or sister, and par for the course for your girlfriend or boyfriend. When I got that from Lisa I knew everything was OK but when it dropped down to x...it was all over soon afterwards.

Xxx = something a bit special. Could be a birthday greeting from Sis, or when things were going really well with Lisa. Xxxx = you are entering the big love zone. Or you did or said something really, really good. Xxxxx = Five star lurve baby, you made it to the top. I never got a 5X from Lisa (or indeed a 4X), though I did send her a 5X once and in reply received a rebuff of a 2X. That calmed my ardour - I was depressed all weekend. Now, every now and again, you do get something to top the 5X. Potts got a 10X from Tils once. Nat gave me a 53X on my leaving card. And now she has probably gone into the Guinness Book of Records with what by my count under this dingy light bulb is... 57 text x's. 57X! But, I think that is way over the top, to be honest. For a day release course in Hove? Come on Nat, save it for your wedding day! Anyway, good to see that Pandora is looking after my CPD (Continuing Professional Development). I read on...

"The Submissive will make himself available to the Dominant from Friday evenings through to Sunday afternoons each week for a Term of Three Months ('The Term') at times to be specified by the Dominant ("the Allotted Times")."

Hang on a minute here, I know that I'm expected to work weekends, but this seems a bit specific?

"The following service provisions have been discussed and agreed and will be adhered to by both parties during the Term:

- *The Dominant shall make the Submissive's health and safety a priority at all times;*

- *The Dominant may restrain, handcuff, or bind the Submissive, and for extended periods of time;*

- *The Submissive accepts the Dominant as his mistress, with the understanding that he is now the property of the Dominant; and*

- *The Submissive shall accept without question any and all disciplinary actions without hesitation, enquiry or complaint.*

Aha. Oho. The penny is dropping. Pandora wants me to be her gimp! What does M & S stand for again...masochists (they like pain?) and sadists (they like giving pain?)...or is it the other way around? My eyes are swimming around the pages, each of which I flip on the bed in turn. Right, what are these bloody appendices all about? Appendix 1. First section, 'Obedience'. Hmmm…lots of quasi-legal shit…blah, blah, blah, OK basically, I have to obey her all the time. She's my boss, why wouldn't I? Next bit, 'Sleep'. Seems I have to get loads of sleep during the working week. OK, well, I always do that. I am the king of sleeping. Next bit, 'Food'. She gets to choose what I eat. Suits me…bring it on! Pandora is great at ordering in restaurants. Section 4, 'Clothes' - she gets to choose what I wear. OK, ditto…she can teach me a lot in that department. No more *Transformers* undercrackers for me! Section 5, 'Exercise' – yep OK, I could do with more of that, no quibbles there. Next, 'Personal Hygiene'. Hmmm, does she think I smell? I think I'm pretty good at the old PH, well, certainly compared to somebody like Sparky. OK, maybe a bad comparison to the lowest common denominator of personal hygiene, but I change my socks every day, I brush my teeth twice a day, I shower most days. However, I don't change my shirt every day, but I will start doing that from now on. Probably that's what she is getting at here. So, that's Appendix 1, and I don't really have any issues with it. In fact it could be really good for my CPD, and my personal development as well.

I fill a glass with water from the bathroom tap and take a good swig, my mouth is well dehydrated from too much brandy. Right, where were we? Appendix 2 is entitled 'Hard Limits' - what the heck are they, then? Blimey. *"No acts involving fire play?"* Fire play? Have to look that one up on Wikipedia. Eh? *"No acts involving urination or defecation"*? Jesus! Is it necessary to proscribe pissing and shitting on each other? Do these M & S people do that sometimes? Anyway, relieved to see that isn't happening. However, I am now imagining Pandora standing up in the bath to wee all over me, and I am not finding that thought unpleasant. Look out, I'm turning into one of those extreme fetishists. Better keep that particular fantasy right inside my head. Maybe that's where these things should stay. Definitely a hard limit that one. Another gulp of water.

Next, *"no acts involving children or animals."* Huh? For fuck's sake! Now I'm sweating again, that this should even be in a document like this…surely this is M & S is all meant to be a bit of fun, isn't it? Paedo? What the fuck. I remember when we did 'Personal Studies' in school (oh man, Sparky was a nightmare in that class…our teacher Mrs Honeyman chucked him out eventually) learning that Queen Victoria refused to believe that it was possible for two women to have lesbo sex, even though she was a bit of a goer herself and had her husband's cock pierced (yowch!). That's kind of how I feel about paedos. I just don't want to go there. Otherwise, I just get all *Daily Mail* about it, and want them all either rounded up and executed or better still, sent to a really hard prison forever where 'Big Vern' is going to send them to living Hell.

I remember my Mum warning me when I was about six about a "soft bloke" who hung around the playground with really thick glasses with Elastoplasts holding them together. She said that he was "harmless", but to never go anywhere with him or take sweets off him. Why do they always have bags of sweets, these weirdoes? I never told my Mum, but I did once take a sweet off 'Mister Retard' (that's what we called him, we didn't know his real name). It was a sherbet lemon, and I just really wanted one. He just smiled and he never asked me to go anywhere with him, though he probably would have done if I had taken another, say a strawberry bonbon or a flying saucer. What we used to like best was pelting Mr Retard with wet grass. Say it had been raining a lot, like it has been this summer, and the council guys comes with their big mower and cut the grass in the park, there'd be great, thick clods of wet grass all over the field. We would all have fights with them sometimes; Sparky usually started it (that's how long I've known Sparky, we go all the way back to the age of five). But what we liked best was creeping up on Mister Retard, and then someone would maybe pretend to want one of his stuck-together sweets, and whist he rummaged in his pockets, we would absolutely pelt him. Then we'd all run off killing ourselves laughing, though he never tried to chase us. He just sat there covered in wet grass. He used to sob a bit, and that made us laugh even more. I don't know what happened to him, Mister Retard. He just disappeared one day.

"No *acts involving animals*"?! Strewth, what do they call that…beastie-philia or something? I'm pretty 'Queen Victoria' about that one as well. Although…I have to say that me and the lads are not above an occasional joke about it. For example, there was this one lecturer at Bolton Uni, Miss Hover, complete nutcase, and she used to bring this slavering Boxer dog called Butch into lectures with her. And there was something a bit literal about her when it came to being a 'dog lover'. Butch used to sit under the desk, and we were not sure 'funny stuff' wasn't going on down there - her expression used to glaze over occasionally and she forgot where she was. One of the guys in the class, Kelvin, his name was, he was a really good cartoonist (and in fact I believe he has got a job as newspaper cartoonist in London- I must try and look him up) and he drew this belting cartoon of Miss Hover lying flat out on the big desk at the bottom of the lecture theatre, her legs up the air and splayed out, and old Butch, front paws up on the desk is giving her a right good seeing to. I remember it being passed around the class, and everyone absolutely killing themselves. Miss Hover didn't seem to notice or care though, she just went rattling on about linguistic form or something.

And then of course, there is the *Pet Shop Boys*. I really detest the *Pet Shop Boys* actually, not because they are gay or anything (I'm not 'Queen Victoria' about that) but because of their dreary, monotonal songs that go on forever with rubbish 80's percussion beats, and also, because they are called *The Pet Shop Boys*. My understanding here (and I could be wrong, though Sparky has the same impression) that this is a less than subtle joke about the alleged habit of some gay men (probably in the 80's) of allowing a live hamster to enter and explore their back passages. I am 100% 'Queen Victoria' on this one, and it is one of those things that I hope is an urban myth and doesn't happen, didn't happen and never happens. But every time I hear *West End Girls* or *It's a Sin*...I think of unfortunate hamsters. Anyway, I am making a note against this particular Hard Limit, to say I want it completely removed from the contract, on what I shall call 'The Queen Victoria Rule'.

What other 'Hard Limits' has Pandora proscribed then? *"No activity that involves the direct contact of electric current."* Whoopee-do. She isn't allowed to electrocute me. Seems to be a thin line between M & S and illegal torture, to me. Me and the lads have this weird game in the flat (we have a few games, like *Boggle, Scrabble, Subbuteo Football, Dizzy Bug* and our favourite, *Perudo*, or lie dice. I am the king of *Perudo*). I don't know where it came from, I think Sparky's mum gave it to him for Christmas, it's called *Shocking Roulette*. Four of you sit round this little disc thing, you stick your forefinger into holes, and then press a button which starts a sort of countdown bleeping sound. And then one of you (you don't know who) gets an electric shock! It's horrific, and we've only played it twice. Waiting to see if you are the one that gets shocked is bad enough, it's like being Christopher Walken in the Russian roulette scene in *The Deer Hunter*. But if you are the shocked one - fucking hell, yowch! And it's only a couple of AA batteries! Christ only knows what proper electrocution must be like. One of the charities I donate to by direct debit every year is *Freedom from Torture*. The others I donate to are *Greenpeace* and *Oxfam*.

OK, so much for the 'Hard Limits' Appendix. I don't get to be burned, electrocuted, pissed or shat on, or be forced to engage in acts with minors or Boxer dogs. Good to get that out of the way, then. To Appendix 3. Appendix 3 - 'Soft Limits'? What are these all about?

"Soft Limits. To be agreed and discussed between both parties.

1. *Does the Submissive consent to: cunnilingus/fellatio/masturbation/ intercourse/anal intercourse?*

Right, well I'm not entirely sure about which one is which between these weird Latin-sounding names. But it's oral, right? OK, can do. Masturbation. Commonly known as 'wanking'. (Or 'self abuse' as Mrs Honeyman used to refer to it in 'Personal Studies' - I don't think she was keen. She seemed very uncomfortable waving a 'Rabbit' vibrator about, and especially when Sparky insisted on asking dozens of questions about it, including whether men could use it or not.) Well, it's obviously OK to have a handy-shandy now and again. But what about ladies? Do they call it 'wanking' when they are pleasuring themselves? I'm not sure, but I'm pretty sure that Sheelz at work has used that expression in reference to her own private habits. Next - ah, good old-fashioned intercourse. Or in the vernacular, shagging. I freely consent to that Pandora, as often as you like! But bumming up the anal…that is a definite, definite, no thank you, madam. I cross that one out firmly with my pen.

2. *Does the Submissive consent to: bondage with rope; bondage with handcuffs; bondage with tape?*

Now my head is swimming with frantic and deranged imagery. I am not sure who is tying who up. Am I handcuffing Pandora, or is she trussing me up with parcel tape like a Christmas present from my Nana in Bootle? I did once playfully tie Lisa's hands together with her Bolton scarf, but she wriggled out of the knot pretty fast and strangled me with it. I mean, really strangled me with it? My face was as Bootle-red as it goes, and my eyes were bulging. My coughing fit afterwards went on for flipping ages. I didn't attempt any further 'bondage play' with Lisa after that. But what the heck, with Pandora at the helm, this all sounds like a lark. Tick, tick, tick.

3.   Does the Submissive consent to be blindfolded?

I get this daft image in my head of me pinning the tail on the donkey after Pandora has spun me around three times. I guess that isn't what she has in mind. Or maybe it is…a kind of nude kinky version? This also sounds like a bit of a laugh. Tick.

4.   Does the Submissive consent to be gagged?

I am really trying to get *Pulp Fiction* out of my head here. I'm the gimp with a billiard ball tethered into my mouth with a leather harness. I annotate this one. "Yes, but no billiard balls."

5.   How much pain is the Submissive willing to experience? (Where 1 is likes intensely and 5 dislikes intensely).

Yikes! Who *likes* pain? Well, actually, I can think of a few who do. We had to play rugby at school, and I remember hanging about on the wing freezing cold and watching some of my schoolmates piling into the scrum. One of the lads made it as a pro-rugby player, I think he plays for Bees or Wasps or Hornets or someone. Baz Hammond. He seemed to like getting hurt. And hurting. Baz was as hard as nails, but there was a rumour he was a transvestite. It wasn't a rumour you wanted to put to him. Sparky had a tattoo done on his forearm last winter, and I went to watch. It's a skull and crossbones with *No Fear* underneath, pretty cool. But he did seem quite fearful whilst he was having it done, in fact at one point I was pretty sure he was crying. Despite him trying to get me to have the same one, I didn't fancy the needles much. Plus, my Mum would have been cross.

When we were fishing last year, Potts cast out and somehow his hook got caught in my lip. Now that was painful. I 'manned up' pretty well whilst Potts took it out, even though Sparky was rolling about laughing on the canal bank. He recovered quickly enough to take a photo and posted it on Facebook with the sub-title 'hooked,' which got plenty of 'Likes' and humorous fish pun comments. Then of course, me and the boys went through our *Jackass/Dirty Sanchez* phase when we were about sixteen, leaping out of trees into hawthorn hedges, firing pellet guns into our bare backs, slapping each other in the face with wet fish, etcetera, etcetera. Potts turned out to be the 'Johnny Knoxsville' in the crew. He could put a staple through his own hand, and was totally the daredevil in a shopping trolley race down Prescott Hill. So Potts would probably take a 2 on this pain threshold scale, but me? I reckon I'm probably a 4? But maybe I could run to a 3 for Pandora. One for further discussion, I reckon.

6. *Does the Submissive consent to accept the following forms of pain/ punishment/ discipline?*

- *Spanking*

No bloody way. My Mum and Dad never had to spank me so why would Pandora?

- *Whipping*

That would be a definite no, then.

- *Biting*

Hmm. Depends how hard. Lisa used to nip my ear like a terrier sometimes, and I quite liked that.

- *Genital clamps*

What the f...? I'm thinking of metal clamp stands in chemistry class which you used to secure bottles and flasks and shit. You definitely wouldn't want one of those clamped to your bollocks. Another no, methinks.

- *Hot wax*

Ah, now, this I *can* do! After me and Lisa got pissed after a Bolton match we had a competition to see how much hot wax from a candle we could stand on the backs of our hands, and I won. Bring it on, Pandora, I can think of places I'd like to drip hot wax on you, baby!

- *Paddling*

What's that then? Doing it in a paddling pool or the shallows at the seaside? Pretty kinky, but put nothing past this hot, sexy lady.

- *Caning*

They didn't have the cane at our school, but Dad told me he'd get the cane loads and he suspected that his headmaster took fiendish pleasure in it.

Then again, Dad did go to school a very long time ago, like in the time of *Tom Brown's Schooldays?* Like whipping, caning gets a big 'no thanks' from me. Bu-uut...I wouldn't be averse to caning Pandora's shapely arse if she wanted it? Not too hard of course, perhaps just hard enough to leave some red marks...mmmmm!! But I don't think I get to do that if I am this Submissive Gimp she wants me to be. Perhaps you get to swap?

- *Nipple clamps*

That is a massive, fucking no.

- *Ice*

Aha, OK, ice. No problem. Standard prank with me and the boys, ice cube down the back of the shirt, or if you really want a laugh, the shorts. Sparky really hates it...watch him go mental and run for your life!

I lean back and look at the ceiling, sinking another good gulp of water. OK then, so I could sign up for hot wax, ice and a bit of biting. And I'll give her a bit of a caning. Her dressed as a schoolgirl and me as a headmaster! Phwoar! I bet she goes in for dressing up, big time. I've drunk too much brandy, and this second contract is, to say the least, a bit of head-fuck. I slither down the bed and put my hands over my eyes and grind them 'til I see loads of different colours and fractal patterns.

I AM DREAMING OF ARNE'S BIG WHITE FACE looming over me. Hang on, no dream. Arne's big white face *is* looming over me, and the light's still on.

"Alright, Arne?" I croak. The taste in my mouth tells me that I haven't brushed my teeth. "What time is it?"

"2am. Did you pass out? What are these papers all over you? Never leave official papers lying about like that, Milad. I have a portable shredder in my bag if you need one?"

I bolt up and scoop my 'contracts' together, and shove the papers in the bedside cabinet. "Er, no thanks, mate, maybe in the morning though?"

"You should get into bed properly. I am going to shower."

I get undressed, keeping my boxers on and putting on my white *Gap* T-shirt. Of course, at home I'd be in my *Transformers* T and no boxers, but when you are rooming with chaps, the kecks stay firmly on. I get into bed and pretend to be asleep.

By the moonlight reflected from the sea through the open curtains, Arne steps silently out of the bathroom wrapped in a towel, which he throws unselfconsciously onto the dresser, his muscular buttocks gleaming as if made from marble. But when he turns around, there's nothing Michelangelo's *David* about this guy. Jesus, what a schlong. That trouser snake is a lot more than 5.4 inches long...at rest! He is looking over at me and I close my half-opened eyes tight shut, and make sleeping sounds. I am dying to get up and brush my teeth, but that will have to wait 'til morning. I hear creaking and squeaking of rusty bed springs, and then...silence. I listen out for sounds of Arne's relaxing breathe, but none comes. The gentle waves hush me to sleep, and dreams of Corpse Brides dripping hot wax on the backs of my hands soon come.

"MILAD, IF YOU WANT BREAKFAST, you'd better get up." Arne, immaculately suited, booted and packed is standing by the half-opened room door.

"Uh...huh...what?" I bleat blearily, rays of morning sun belting of the sea and illuminating the room. The door clicks shut in answer, and Arne is the other side. Twenty minutes later, I am looking haggard in the breakfast room, Arne reading *The Times* and sipping a glass of water.

"Two full English!" announces a portly woman, slamming down two plates crammed with every conceivable fried breakfast ingredient, including some newly invented. Are these hash browns or chicken nuggets? So! *This* must be where Arne gets his energy...the most important meal of the day! I tuck into my black pudding and 'shrooms and shovel in the baked beans.

"I didn't order that, Milad, she must have misunderstood me. Have mine if you want. I will go and settle the bill."

I clear my plate, washed down with a pot of tea, and then make a decent go of Arne's bacon and eggs. Can't let good bacon and eggs go to waste, that's another of our Ten Commandments. As I eat, I remember my contract... not the one with the money, but the one with the spankings and the ice. I wonder how to broach the subject with Pandora?

"Come, Milad, time to leave. I'll get the car. You bring the bags." Arne is ready to rumble, but I feel a bit shit-faced, and could do with another hour in bed. But since that isn't going to happen, I swill down another cup of tea, and soon me and Arne are roaring down Marine Parade, me feeling a bit on the queasy side.

At the Worthing branch of Waterstones, Pandora is beaming and looking fresh as a daisy, already pleasing her queuing public by entertaining and flattering them. Arne sets up the signing table, and I skirt around Pandora, looking for signs that she might want to see what I made of the naughty contract.

"Milad, you haven't shaved," she admonishes me severely. "I hope you didn't spend the night with that Corpse Tart?"

"Er, no Miss Pandora, I mean Pandora, I went straight to my room. Erm, thanks for the contracts, I..." OMG. Fucking Hell! I've left the contracts in the bedside draw...panic!

"Never mind the blessed contracts, you have work to do, young man. Don't turn up for work like that again. And do your tie up, it's half way down your chest." With that she sweeps away from me and pushes herself close against Arne 'King Dong' Bastad and whispers something in his ear.

I'm partly ashamed about my dishevelled appearance, and despite my 1.5 fry ups I feel like I have a mild hangover. I need *Anadin Extra* and orange juice, our gang's sure-fire cure. Well, sometimes it's a sure fire for me, but it never works for Rollo, who has the worst hangovers possible, and he just writes the day off in bed. I'm not entirely sure what Rollo does except it's something to do with lawns, but his boss doesn't seem to mind him no-showing if we've been on the pop on 'school nights' as we call the evenings from Sunday to Thursday. But I'm less concerned about the hangover and my dishevelment than I am the hotel chambermaid finding my secret documents in the bedside drawer. I think fast.

"Pandora, may I get you some Starbucks' coffee?" I ask pleasantly, thinking there is just enough time to nip back to the hotel, grab the papers, buy coffee and *Anadin*, and return without undue suspicion.

"No, I'm good for coffee, Milad. You can go and get my elevenses later. Help with these books and get the local rag on the phone. I'm supposed to be doing an interview with them at eleven, but you can put them back an hour." Crap. My document recovery plan is scuppered.

IT IS LUNCHTIME before I can escape Waterstones and scuttle back down the promenade to the hotel. The room will certainly have been 'done' by now, and I'm hoping cute Sharon isn't on reception duty.

As I bound up the cracked and chipped stone steps and through the half-busted revolving door, I see that not only is cute Sharon on reception duty, but from her ill-concealed smile and averted glance that she (and therefore the whole hotel staff) know my dirty little secrets.

"Ahem, morning Sharon!" I bluster, attempting knowing laddishness and instead coming over like a total plonker. "I may have left some important papers in my room...erm, 307?"

She is trying not to laugh as she bends down to find an envelope under the front desk. Two other female receptionists, a porter, the portly breakfast woman and a cleaner appear as if from nowhere, all giving me the 'up and down' look. Bootle-red anyone? Sharon seems to take an age to hand me the envelope, by which time my dry mouth has cracked into a wavy line. I turn with my embarrassment papers, attempting an extremely rapid exit, but cute Sharon has exploded into a shriek and set the others off. A revolving door is not the quickest thing to exit from, especially this creaky, knackered thing and there *would* have to be two little old ladies trying to get in, wouldn't there? They attempt to squeeze themselves, along with two enormous suitcases held together with parcel tape, into one small quadrant and jam the whole damn thing up. The bell boy, an overgrown schoolboy of six foot seven comes bounding over looking like a model in a cheap mail order catalogue and bares his rat teeth, yellow against his sallow pock-marked skin. Though he looks like a complete cock, I have to assist him in the complex extrication of the ladies, in order to make my escape from his horrible tittering, and the chorus of laughter behind him.

Finally free, my burning face cooled by the sea breeze, I have the last laugh on this mediocre dump and its motley staff. The pile of dog shit is still there, hardened by the morning sun, and it sums the place up. Before I break into a sprint back to Waterstones (which might have kept me level with Usain Bolt for the first fifteen metres) I turn and give this reactionary conservative drag of an establishment 'the finger'. So what if I'm into M & S? So I'm a little bit crazy, huh? Sometimes you gotta live on the wild side a little. And that…is just what I'm a-gonna do.

CHAPTER SIX

I'M IN A HOTEL ROOM IN BRIGHTON. Brighton is a crazy place, London-by-the-sea, full of gay people. And weird people. It's alternative, it's risky, it's cool and it's edgy. And I'm sitting on the bed making annotations to my draft M & S contract, which I'm starting to think is very sexy indeed. I have one eye on the footie on the TV and one eye on my iPhone. That's the thing about my generation…we can totally multi-task, and that goes for men and well as women (in my Dad's generation, only the women can multi-task). It looks like England are heading out of the Euros as Italian midfield maestro Andrea Pirlo runs the game but Italy can't score, and we move into extra time. The lads are watching the game together back at the flat in Horsham and though I can't be there they are all texting me so it feels like I'm there in spirit. We all agree that Rooney is rubbish and Rollo is taking stick on that account, him being the big Rooney fan.

Somehow, we make it through both periods of extra time, so once more, it's the dreaded penalty shoot-out. The lads are confident, and a win will set up a semi against the auld enemy Germany. I can't multi-task now. I call Sparky and I put the iPhone on speaker so I can hear the lads' reaction to the penalties.

"YEUUUUUUS!!! Go on Stevie G, great pen, lad."

"WOOO!! WOOOO!! He's missed! Ha, haarr!"

"C'mon Rooney, you've done nothing all night….YEEEEEEEE-EEES! Two-one to the Engerland, two-one to the Engerland, Two-one to the Engerland, two-one to the Engerland!"

As Pirlo dinks in an equalizing penalty which is the epitome of Italian cool, there is a firm rap on my room door. I strongly consider ignoring it, but an even more insistent knock one follows. I know who it is, and I turn off the mobile, and open the door. Pandora is already in the middle of the room before I ask her in, and she hits the mute button on the TV remote. That wouldn't be so bad, but she is also standing right in front of the telly screen.

"Milad, I've just had an idea for the London launch. I could come down from the rafters dressed as an empowering arch-angel, you know, on one of those wires or whatever they use. What do you think? Could you arrange it for me, dah-ling? Wouldn't it be such fun?"

We're having a big party in London in two weeks' time at *The Café Royal* in Piccadilly and I'm helping the publishers to organise it. I kind of feel like I'm Danny Boyle, planning the Olympics Opening Ceremony, which is also happening next month. But right now Pandora's generous curves are forming a total eclipse of Ashley Young. My neck cranes over to one side to catch a glimpse of his penalty.

"MILAD!" shouts Pandora, banging her hand on the on/off button on the telly. The United striker, his foot about to strike the ball, disappears. "PAY ATTENTION AND STOP WATCHING THIS SILLY FOOTBALL!"

She seems genuinely angry with me and I feel a sort of weird quiver in my bowels. I haven't shat myself, have I? I think not thankfully, but I am gaping like the tattoo fish on Pandora's back, I can't quite believe she has turned the telly off at such a crucial moment. I keep it cool.

"Yes, yes, that sounds like a really good idea Pandora! I can see that, what a great entrance that would make!"

"Do you think so, Milad? Do you really, darling?" Suddenly she is kneeling before me, holding my hands in hers and with urgent fire in her eyes, her pupils darting this way and that as she studies my face anxiously. I reassure her, and squeeze her hands.

"I do, Pandora. It's a brilliant idea." She is on me, about me, kissing my face passionately, mussing up my hair, gasping into my ear. "I want to hear it again, my dah-ling. Say it. Say it."

"Er, it is a brilliant idea?" I think that's the bit she wants to hear again. Anyway, she is off me now and pacing around the room. Well, she can only do three paces before she hits the wall, but she sort of patrols like a sentry in a very small courtyard. Her fingers are bridged together at her chin as she walks, and she talks rapidly, a wild and transported look about her. I grab my journo pad and start scribbling.

"Yes, take this down Milad, capture my imagination before it flies from the window and hibernates to Africa forever. I see a chorus, in white and gold, below me, singing *Spem…*" Hehe, I write 'Spam' instead of 'Spem'. I went to see *Spamelot* in the West End with my Mum and sister Naz, it was brilliant. I love *Monty Python,* and so do the lads. Sparks is great as John Cleese, and he can do him in *Fawlty Towers* as well. I can do Manuel quite well, so we have a lot of fun with that routine.

"MEE-LAD!! Will you stop grinning like a fucking imbecile, dah-ling? It is putting me off my creative flow! Where was I? Yes, the chorus is in full voice, and I am lowered, dressed in a gold and pink gown, perhaps wearing some kind of tiara and holding a wand? What do you think Mee-lad?"

My iPhone, though on vibrate only, is going buzzing mental. Being good at multi-tasking, I craftily lean over as I scribble, to see if we have managed to scrape through for a date with Germany. If we have, I'm definitely not missing out on that one with the boys, I'll ask for an evening off. Oh, holy crap. No need for that then. We missed the next two penalties and we've gone out! Deano has texted something very rude about Ashley Cole. But that was the last text I ever received on this particular iPhone.

I am dimly aware of a blur of scarlet hair and the canyon, encased in a hugging black dress, sweeping down and scooping up my phone. With a piercing scream, she has chucked my mobile at the wall above the bed, like, really hard? I watch, totally gobsmacked, as it splinters into a thousand pieces. Well, that is a bit of a journalistic exaggeration - about ten pieces, in fact. I think I actually hear a roll of thunder as she stares at me (though the sky outside is reasonably clear) and she storms out of the room and slams the door. Wow, what passion! I sit a bit stunned for a while. It feels really odd to be suddenly incommunicado with the world, with the lads. I gather up the phone pieces and attempt to reassemble it, but it is Harry History. Perhaps I've just been fired. Alan Sugar doesn't throw anything at the poor saps he fires on *The Apprentice,* he just points at them, frowns even more than he does usually, and goes…"You're fired."

I've never used a hotel phone before. My Dad says they cost about £30 per minute and to use a phone box instead, but I don't think they do phone boxes any more. I need to talk to Sparks though, first to find out what happened to England, and second to see if he has any advice on the 'firing situation' for me. Sod it, it's the least Pandora can do to pay for a call home!

"Hello?"

"Sparks, it's me."

"Who?"

"Milad, you twat. I'm calling from the hotel phone."

"Why?"

"Because Pandora just chucked my iPhone at the wall."

"What?"

"Because Pandora just chucked my iPhone at the wall."

"Why did she do that?"

"I was meant to be taking notes and I did a bit of multi-tasking."

"And she chucked your iPhone at the wall?"

"Yes."

"Is it bust?"

"Yes."

I can hear Sparky telling the others what's gone on. "Mil's boss chucked his iPhone at the wall. It's bust." I can hear a murmur of outraged discussion. Though I think Dean is laughing. He sometimes does that in moments of crisis, I think it's like a nervous response? Sparky is back on.

"That's bullshit, dude. She needs to buy you a new one. In fact, a super-cool one, like Arne's. I think it's a Sony Ericsson."

"Yeah, yeah. She does, mate. Yeah, like Arne's. Anyway, what happened at the end, I missed the penalties."

"You what? He missed the penalties, lads. What, couldn't you bare to watch?"

"Something like that. We lost, right?"

"Yep, the curse of the penalties, yet again. Why don't we sodding practise them? Woy is vewy pwoud of the team vough, he weckons vey did us pwoud."

"Bullshit. We were second-best all match. I think the Italians deserved to win."

"Me too. Pirlo, what a player. We haven't got anybody in his class. He Panenka'd his penalty in."

"He what? Panenka'd it in? I saw that one. He chipped it! What do you mean, Panenka'd it in?"

"Panenka, you prat. He invented the penalty chip-in. Years ago. He was Czech. Had a big beard."

"You're making that up, you tosser!"

"Dean, Dean, come here, Mil hasn't heard of Panenka. Come and put him right, mate."

"Alright, Mil?"

"Yeah, alright, Deano."

"Your boss chucked your iPhone at the wall? Why?"

"She was a bit pissed off with me. I was trying to watch Ashley Young."

"What? Why the fuck *wouldn't* you be watching Ashley Young? Every other bloke in the country was! You want to watch that Pandora, mate. I think she's quite controlling, you know."

"Nah, she's great really. Sometimes it gets a bit stressy in the big-time, Deano. Anyway, what is this Panenka penalty bullshit? Sparky's making it up, right?"

I AM TURNING IN FOR THE NIGHT and brushing my teeth, when there is a very light knock at the door. I reckon I'm good at guessing folk by their knock and I reckon this is Arne. I'm thinking that Pandora has despatched him to straighten things out with me, maybe even to order me a new phone, just like his. So, I act all casual and carry on doing the tooth brushing thing as I open the door.

I reckon wrong, it isn't Arne. Oh my Lord. It's Pandora, looking unbelievably fantastic in a very flimsy see-through black nightie. She has some nerve, scampering down the stairs from her penthouse suite. She looks a bit cold, judging from her turrets, which jut provocatively forth. There is toothpaste dribbling down my chin, as she pushes past me and leaps (well, sort of 'Fosbury Flops' - but without the high jump bit?) into my bed. She wriggles into the sheets, her bare arms imploring me to join her.

"Come to me, Mee-lad!" she is beseeching. I notice she doesn't look ready to go to sleep, as she still has all her make up on. Lisa used to remove all hers carefully before she turned in, it could take ages. She looked like a denuded mouse, which I told her once, but she didn't like that much so I didn't tell her it again.

"Er, I'll just pop my toothbrush back, Pandora. Won't be a min!" Crap, this woman is full of holy surprises. I haven't had a shower today…I was going to have one first thing tomorrow. Right, quick - think fast. OK, I fill the sink with warm water, tip one of the little bottles in (no idea which one without my glasses, possibly the shampoo?) and slip my boxers off and give the old meat and two veg a bit of a splosh round. Towel dry, pants back on. Come on, hurry up - she may change her mind from whatever the heck she has in mind, and scamper off. Good, she's still there, and draping up the sheets for me to join her. And I do. OK boys back in Horsham. In the hallowed words of Norwegian football commentator Bjørge Lillelien on the occasion of Norway beating England some twenty years ago: "*Lord Nelson, Lord Beaverbrook, Sir Winston Churchill, Sir Anthony Eden, Clement Attlee, Henry Cooper, Lady Diana. Maggie Thatcher, can you hear me?*" I am in bed with PM Poste. I repeat; I am in bed with PM Poste.

She has her chunky though softly feminine arms around my neck, and she is pulling me to her. It feels like I am entering a soft, perfumed, feather-down pillow. She is breathing something low in my ear.

"I'm so sorry about your phone, my dah-ling. I will get you another one, a better one. Arne will take you to buy one tomorrow. I have such a temper sometimes. You must forgive your Pandora, my sweet boy. Fo-orgive...fo-orgive..." Uh ho, as she breathes these words in my ear, she is massaging me - down there. Thank God I had a bit of a wash. Oh my, she is descending like a submarine into a sea of bedding, mawing my chest and stomach with her lips, until she is...TOTALLY DOWN THERE!

I look down the bed, as she raises herself on her hands, and soon, the sheets are bobbing. And there are loud moaning, slurping noises from down below. I am not sure if I have a stiffy or not...my weasel seems to have melted away like an ice cream cornet on a very hot day. I reach down and take the liberty of helping myself to two great handfuls of Pandora's breasts, the weight of which I've been appreciating as they bounce and sway on my tensed thighs. Oh yeah, *we* got wood, OK! She's enthusiastically pumping her clenched hand, and I'm disappearing into her plump lips. I raise the sheet and blanket a bit, to watch her in action. BLIMEY! Where's the weasel gone? She stares at me from the depths of the sheets like a horny minx, shaking her red mane. This is a world's first lads, I am being deep-throated, and not by just any common tart! This is a celebrity deep-throating! The bobbing becomes more frantic. My hands grip the bed sheets, my eyes clenched shut, and I hear myself gasping involuntarily.

"AHOHAAAAHOOOOHAAAAAAHOOOOOOHAAAAAH....OH YEAH BABY!!!"

I am not especially a fan of Austin Powers and I have no idea why I have uttered his catch phrase at my moment of climax. Fluorescing blue and red rockets go off in the spinning black of my mind as Pandora suddenly surfaces like a naughty mermaid breaching the surface of the sea , flopping down on me and kissing my mouth, succulently, strongly, her tongue darting about my mouth. Suddenly she arches up and she opens her mouth wide. For one horrible moment, I think she is going to throw up all over me, like in *The Exorcist* or the '*Ladies*' in *Little Britain*. But of liquid there is none, though of gas there be a-plenty. I don't think I have ever heard a deeper, longer, more baritone belch than the one that is going off in my face, even down *The Tig* when the hardened pint drinkers see off their pints so they can get a last order re-fill. But the smell of this particular burp monster is quite entrancing...I think she probably had anchovies and scrambled egg for her room service dinner, together with a fruity Cabernet Sauvignon... and I distinctly smell sticky toffee pudding. Topped off with a lavish serving of my own double cream. I breathe it all in, the most contented man in Brighton...ph-ee-ew!

After her marathon belch, Pandora wriggles up to me, her mouth pouting at my neck, and I snake my arm round her. Man, that feels good. I've got my arm around my woman. In bed. Contentment hormones gush round my body and my brain, and I feel a kind of trancy reverie descend on me, as she squeezes me tight. But I don't have long to enjoy this blissful moment. She is clambering out of bed, grunting and snorking, in a cute kind of way.

"Right my dahling, since you've just experienced the best blowie you'll ever get, I expect you to be signing your contract in the morning. I have great plans for you, my boy."

My head is still swimming with pleasure, as I raise myself dazed to one elbow. Her cleavage and nightdress are caked in gentleman's relish, and I can't help thinking about Monica Lewinsky, who she does resemble a bit. "I have one or two caveats to discuss with you, Ms Poste, but I will be happy to enter into a contract of pleasure with you. I cannot wait."

"Oh Mee-lad!" she seems genuinely thrilled and clamps her hands to her enormous bosom. "We will have some fun together!" Giggling her girlish giggle, she turns to open the bedroom door, and I rise to drape her in a blanket, but she brushes me and it away.

"Breakfast at 8.30, Mee-lad. Don't be late, you know how I so hate to dine alone." With that I watch her sashay brazenly down the corridor, much like she did on the morning that I met her in *The Mercure* in Horsham. Unfortunately, before she can get to the lift, a businessman in his jeans and polo shirt carrying a newspaper comes out of it, probably having dined alone in the restaurant and en route to his room to call his wife. His eyes boing out on springs and go cross-eyed, his tongue lolls out of his mouth, his legs go bow-legged and start to judder, and his thinning hair stands on end. Well, that's quite a lot of journalistic license, but he is visibly shaken as he stands in his tracks to admire the Venus in a see-though, somewhat soiled Janet Reger nightie, her sex-hair wild and her make-up all over her face. She gives him one of her lovely smiles, and he actually runs away down the corridor. Boy, what would that geezer give to be in my shoes! I blow Pandora a kiss from the crack of open door I peer through, but I don't think she sees me as she is getting into the lift, joining and bidding a good evening to a young couple. What a gal! I dive back into the bed sheets, which are rather sticky but smell of her, and I pull them to my nose and resume my reverie.

PANDORA IS WEARING AN ASTONISHING white silk chemise as she comes down for breakfast, a great naughty smile on her scarlet lips and red chunky baubly jewellery at her neck and wrist. I got up early and spent over an hour on my ablutions according to Pandora's instructions - this really is a new me. I am shaved clean, moisturised, showered, powdered, aftershaved, suited, booted and I have for the first time in a long time re-tied my tie so it sits perfectly above my top shirt button.

"Get me some grapefruit juice, my darling. And muesli. And tea. And a plate of those mini pain au chocolat. And some yoghurt. And when you've done that, I want the papers. All of them."

I watch Pandora eating and reading with a mixture of awe and love. She is on her second plate of scrambled eggs with smoked salmon…breakfast is the most important meal of the day for Pandora, even if it isn't for Arne.

"So-ooo," she gives me a little half smile over her reading glasses as she crunches a piece of brown bread toast, "Soft Limits, Milad. What will you allow, dah-ling?" She winks mischievously and closes *The Daily Mail*. "Do-oo tell!" She has me off guard here, because I was not expecting to discuss this particular topic at a hotel breakfast table. In fact, I don't like to discuss any topic at this early hour if I can possibly help it. But hey, this is PM Poste…she writes her own rules! I try to stay cool.

"Yyyyyyyy….eah." I say quietly, leaning forward so our fellow breakfasters don't hear me. "Well…I'm good with the hot wax. Yep, no problem there. And the ice, whoah yeah, bring on the ice. And a bit of biting…" I do a strange thing here. I sort of mime biting with my teeth, turning my head from one side to another, a bit like Bugs Bunny eating a carrot.

"Uh huh." Pandora looks a bit puzzled with my biting mime, and I'm not surprised, I'm puzzled too. She leans forward and though her expression is business-like, her hand is running along the inside of my thigh under the tablecloth, and then she makes claws and rakes them, quite hard.

"But what level of pain, Milad? What can you stand?" she whispers urgently, ignoring the East European waiter who has arrived to top up her tea cup. "Are you a 2? Or even a 1? Tell me, tell me now!" I pause to let the waiter leave, but Pandora is looking him up and down, and I think she has to make a big physical effort to guide her free hand to her tea cup and not his crotch. He stands indulgently smiling down at us, and I am having none of it. I am learning a trick or two off my new, no nonsense *Matrix* posse.

"That'll be all thanks…Bartek!" I say, sarcastically reading out his name badge. He slinks off, and I think Pandora appreciates me for it.

"We-el, not a 2 or 1 Pandora! I mean, who *likes* pain? Y'know, I'm a game guy, I can do stuff, alright! All kinds of stuff! But on the 'liking pain scale'…I'm probably a 4? Or Four-and-a-half? Do you do halves on the pain scale, Pandora?"

Pandora eyes me coldly as she takes a sip, well, more a good swill really, of tea. Evidently, she doesn't do 'point-fives' on the pain scale. And it would appear that she is not impressed by 4.

"But, well, erm, I could probably stretch to a 3…for you?" I smile, feeling love for her. I don't know how she is doing this, but at the same time as sipping her tea with her left hand, with her right she has grabbed my bollocks and she is cradling them, a half-smile playing on her face.

"So *this* is a five, Mee-lad." Mmmm, five is nice. She is sort of strumming her thumb about the old weasel's nut sack. Quite nice, but not conducive to appetite and I don't think I will finish my Danish pastry.

"Four." Oooh, OK, four is firm, four is firm. My smile is turning into a grimace.

"Three." Ah, maybe I don't stretch to a three after all. I am beginning to feel sick, and I am perspiring from both temples.

"Two…." With a high pitched shriek I throw my chair backwards and I am immediately grateful for the floor-prowling Bartek. I would have gone clean over if he hadn't caught my chair. I check to see if my testicles have detached in Pandora's right hand rather than remain in my Austin Reeds. Though they do feel like they are in Pandora's possession, they nestle yet in their proper place, though throbbing - and not in a good way.

Pandora is shrieking with laughter. Just as well this is Brighton…our fellow diners in this establishment (which include last night's businessman in the corridor and the young couple in the lift) don't seem to mind our horseplay, but I daresay it would be a different story in Worthing or Chichester. I do a bit of humouring laughing myself, *a la* George Clooney, he is good at that sort of self-deprecating stuff, and I waggle my head about a bit, like he does.

I lean forward and almost touch noses with Pandora. She is beaming and has muesli all over her teeth, which looks really sweet.

"You know, you…are a bad girl!" I growl in a kind of husky way.

"Am I now?" She feigns innocence in that irresistible way of hers.

"Yes, you are…" I growl, sliding my hand along the fishnet of her inner thigh, and playing my nails back along the mesh.

"HOW DARE YOU! GET YOUR HAND OFF MY LEG IMMEDIATELY, MILAD!" she suddenly barks at me, at top volume. The chinking of cutlery on crockery in the breakfast room stops abruptly, as does the murmur of breakfast conversation. An icy wind blows tumbleweed across the polished wooden floor. My Clooney-jaw slackens and my body slumps, as she withdraws and rises abruptly from the table, bristling with offence and reproach, and spins on her heels and clacks away.

I sort of freeze, as my face assumes its' now familiar Bootle-red. He can't resist it can he? Bartek is in close attendance, no doubt with a supercilious grin on his Slavic face, and I must not meet his eyes.

"Anymore tea or coffee, sir?" he practically laughs.

"No, no thanks, Bartek, I'd better be getting on, thanks." I rise and meet the eyes of the young couple, who last night were probably more closely acquainted with at least one of my bodily fluids than they would normally have preferred in an ascending lift. I try to give them my 'normal/pleasant' smile as I nonchalantly pick up one of the papers to read, an action which sends all the rest of the papers crashing to the floor, and Bartek is in action once again, scooping them all up and handing them to me in a neat parcel. Me and the lads often argue in *The Tig* about exactly when teleportation will become a reality, as it surely one day will. We think probably in one hundred years' time (which I may be around to see, what with all this increased life expectancy). To quote Morrissey once again from his seaside classic *Everyday is Like Sunday; "How I dearly wish I was not here."* But since I do not yet carry a teleportation device with a red button, I slink a walk of shame from the dining room. Recalling that I have already checked out of my room, and noting it is raining hard outside, I have to sit with the papers in the hotel lobby to wait for Pandora, with only *The Independent* to hide behind. How that woman loves to humiliate me. Just as well my Dad made sure I had a tough hide and a good sense of humour.

THOUGH ME AND THE LADS ARE THRILLED to see Italy and the Mighty Balotelli knock out the Germans, and even more delighted to see Ronaldo cock up his penalty turn to let the Spanish through, my mates are disappointed and bit concerned that I won't be home for the final on Sunday. I had a really long chat with Pandora in Eastbourne on the subject, or indeed subjects, of bondage, discipline, sadism and masochism, which I now understand are contained in the acronym 'BDSM'. Pandora explained to me that this is something that she hasn't really been able to explore before, but in me, she senses someone who she can completely trust to help her explore and develop her erotic sensuality. Judging from my reading of *Black Heart* (I am about half way through) she must have a really good imagination, because some of the scenes I have to say, have got my willy waving wildly.

So, after we settled on a MAXIMUM pain threshold of 3 (but in general 5 and 4), I consented to everything but the clamps. I established that paddling had nothing to do with water at all but was yet another way of assaulting my buttocks, and so after we had a chuckle and a neckful of mojitos in a cocktail bar, I withdrew my silver pen, which before I signed my BDSM contract with it, disappeared like the fabled cigar in Miss

Lewinsky into what Pandora likes to call her 'inner goddess'. And with wet, black *Quink* drying on the paper, and goddess juice drying on the pen, I was invited to her home on Sunday, and more specifically to her 'dungeon', which she calls the 'Pink Room of Pain'.

I usually tell Sparko what is going on with me and Pandora (I blew his socks off with the bath bomb boob job and the deep blowie) but somehow, I can't tell him and the boys that instead of making my chilli and watching the Euro 2012 final with them, I'll be trussed up in West London getting a thrashing from Mistress P. Instead, I lie and tell him we are doing a signing gig, and then…I sort of have this voice in the back of my head that tells me to tell him exactly where I'll be on Sunday. And I do. And unlike Sparky, he actually writes it down…not in his phone but on an actual piece of paper with a biro.

"How are you spelling that, mate? G-R-E-V-E-L-D-O-N Terrace? Got it. Holland Park. Very posh." And then (and this is so not Sparky), "take care, mate."

CHAPTER SEVEN

For the first time in my life, I voluntarily go for a run. I am in a place called Rye, having crossed the border between Sussex and Kent, and this town is all twee and chocolate-boxy. The hotel room I'm in is tiny and crammed with junk ornaments, and the 'en suite' bathroom is half way into the bedroom so that if you sit on the toilet (like I have just done) you can't actually close the bathroom door and your feet are on the bedroom carpet. So I'm feeling all hemmed in, and I'm also feeling kind of nervous. I lace up the brand new white *Nike* trainers I have just bought from the local sports shop and do some toe-touching and other stretches, and then pound round Ypres Tower and the harbour. Rye is steep and it is hard work on the up-slog, and I'm happy that *Lil B* is with me on ma Pod, and I rap along with him to *Surrender to Me*.

Why am I nervous? Pandora now sends me little cards in a sealed envelope, containing instructions that must be followed. My first one was quite sweet…bring her tea in bed. That was in Bexhill. I thought I might get to join her in her bed but I was dismissed after leaving her a tea tray with four rounds of toast and several poached eggs. I was instructed to crawl out on all fours from her room, which was a bit embarrassing, as the maid came by to the linen cupboard in the corridor just as I was complying.

A second instruction card was shoved under my room door this morning (by Arne - I heard the squeak of highly polished shoe). During my frank conversation with Pandora in Eastbourne, I did ask if Arne was complicit with this whole BDSM game thing, and she assured me he was not, though she was quite coy on the issue of whether there was any 'thing' between them, or had been. I'm totally OK with it though either way. Hey, if I was gay, I would sleep with Arne - though I wouldn't fancy his trouser truncheon up my bum!) The second envelope contained an appointment card for *Amanda's Beauty Salon* down the road at 3pm. For a total body wax.

I pound up the steep hill, digging in as my soon-to-be baby smooth calves cramp up. I am quite a hairy guy, I guess it comes from the Iranian side. My uncles on my Mom's side are all hirsute, whereas my Dad and his brothers aren't very hairy. Lisa used to pull the hairs on my back when she wanted to be mean to me. I like my body hair, though my chest is oddly devoid of the wiry black stuff that covers most of the rest of me. I don't want to lose my body hair. But hey, it'll grow back. Or will it? Maybe it won't? Better check that factlet on line. I reckon a temporary loss of body hair will be well worth it for a romp with Miss Pandora…won't it? Anyway, I have signed her contract, with a pen dipped in her inner goddess; I have to honour this weird pact.

"GOOD AFTERNOON, SIR. Please go to Woom 7, take all your clothes off and put the green gown on. Julie will be with you shortly." What is it with people not saying their R's properly? The pretty receptionist can say 'green' perfectly well, but chooses to pronounces 'room' as 'woom'. Why do that? OK, some people, like Woy, never learned to say their R's pwoperly. Jonathon Woss made a whole career as a dodgy talk show host out of it. But why pretend to have a speech defect? For a split second, I think to reply, "sorry, did you mean *Rrrrrrrroom 7?*" with an exaggerated roll of my tongue, but then I remember I have more serious things to worry about than receptionists' diction. I head for Woom 7, in trepidation and fear.

Woom 7 is a cross between a surgery and a poodle parlour, and I'm not fooled by the whale song music…relaxing this will not be. I strip off (I had two consecutive showers after my run, so I am super-clean) and I put on the green gown, which has a load of slits down it like someone has vandalised it with a Stanley knife. I sit down and try to look casual, as 'Julie' walks in, and she is smirking, rather unprofessionally in my opinion.

"Roightyer'ereferthefullbodywaxoryer?"

"Er, sorry?" She has a very strong accent, possibly Brummie, and I didn't catch a word of what she is asking me, as her words all seem to run into one another. She simply repeats what she just said; possibly even more accented this time, and arches a rather aggressive sculpted eyebrow.

"Yer'ereferthefullbodywaxoryer?"

Definitely Brummie. And I just about caught 'body wax'. Just for the avoidance of doubt, I hand her my appointment card.

"Roightyer'ereferthefullbodystripwax. Yowadwunbefowar?"

"Pardon?"

"Yowadwunbefowar?"

"Erm…no. I haven't had one before. A brand new experience for me!"

"It'urtsabityernow?"

"Pardon?"

"It'urtsabityernow?"

"Ah, yes, I believe it does." Naz once put one of her waxing strips on my back and yanked it, so I have a fair idea what I'm in for. Except this is likely to be one hundred lashes rather than one.

"Roightoi'lldoyerbeckfurst. Loionyertummay." I must be getting my ear in to her deep Brummie; I lie on my stomach on the table and grip the sides, feeling like a lump of meat on a butcher's board. I hear the rasp of highly adhesive strips being withdrawn from their backing, and smoothed about my calves and thighs.

"Reddoy?"

"Ready as I'll ever be, Julie." There is a horrible ripping noise followed rapidly by a searing pain up the back of my leg, like the time I pulled my calf muscle during a kick-around with the lads in the park. I grip the legs of the table and my knuckles go white in my brown hands. I will not show pain. Just as well she can't see my eyes screwed up in discomfort. Then… scccchhhhhuuupp, scccchhhhhuuupp, scccchhhhhuuupp! Jesus, thighs are most def worse than calves. Definitely tears in my eyes.

"OroightMeesterBrawen?"

"Ah, yes, haha, no problem Julie."

"Oi'lljustroobsoomcreyumonyer."

"Pardon? Oh, cream, yes, right." Mmmm, cool cream feels good, my flesh feels like it's been burned with a wallpaper steam stripper.

"Roightoi'lldoyerboomnyow?"

"Bum. Righto, Julie." She flips the gown over my hairy arse and starts applying her torture strips. Jesus, this girl is shameless! She is wedging them right into my crack. Fuck! This is going to seriously hurt!

"Reddoy?"

I briefly consider telling Julie that I'm not 'reddoy' and that I'm calling off the whole thing and breaking my Pandora contract right now. But then I think - I have to get these strips off me somehow, and slow is probably worse than fast.

"Go for it, Julie. Do your worst."

Scccchhhhhuuupp, scccchhhhhuuupp! Ahhhhhhhhyayayayaya! The outer ass cheeks are stripped hair-bare first. I grip the table legs even harder, unwilling to show or articulate pain, but I brace myself as Julie nips the tops of the inner ass cheek strips and prepares to let them rip.

Scccchhhhhuuupp, scccchhhhhuuupp,
"YAAAAAAAAAAAAAAAHHHHHH!!!!" I articulate pain quite clearly and loudly.

"Yowhokaychuck?" I can't resist a line from one of my favourite films, *Pulp Fiction*. The scene where Marcellus is being rape-bummed by a couple of hilly billies, and Butch rescues him and asks him if he's OK.

"Nah, man. I'm pretty fucking far from okay." I think the reference may be wasted on Julie.

"Worsebeetsovah! Well, apawtfrumyerfruntsoide, acawse!"

After the agony of the inner buns, the flaying of my back, shoulders and upper arms seems pretty tame and I just lie there in denuding humiliation.

"Roightyerdoinreallywell. Aveadrinko'water and spin owver."

Inured to searing pain and only concerned with the groin experience to come, I surrender to Julie as she strips the front of my legs and arms, and my stomach. I am tremendously grateful for my natural lack of chest hair, as wax strips on my nips would certainly have me chundering and running naked and semi-waxed for the exit. But here we go. I have no further shame, and close my eyes. Julie unveils the peanut zone and I can hear her clipping with a small pair of shears at the pubic undergrowth. Then, the dreadful strips are applied. Surely not the nutsack? She reads my concerns.

"WedawntdoyeracchoalgenitawlsMeesterBrayawn." Small mercies. I suppose I'll have to do me plums myself with shaving foam and a razor. But this is going to be bad. I think of the pain scale. The inner bum area was a definite 2. This could so be your actual 1. I can feel cold sweat running in rivulets down my hairless body. She seems to be taking a long time, and for some peculiar reason, she is applying a cold eye mask to my fevered brow. The room turns into a gelatinous blue, and the cool prepares me for my short, sharp ordeal. Finally, I feel nail extensions creep into the top of the strips. Fucking do it, woman…get it over with! My legs are trembling.

Sccccchhhhhuuupp, sccccchhhhhuuupp!

"HOOOOOOOOOOOOOOOOOOOOOOOOOOO!!!!" It's a 1, OMGL (Oh My Good Lord, that stands for), it's a 1! I'm trying to think about the worst pain I have ever been in, and if anything beats this? I stood on a weaver fish on holiday in Cornwall with the lads (the same holiday we had the surf lessons), and that was seriously painful. Sparks took me to the hospital thinking I'd broken my foot. The nurse put my foot in a warm bath and the pain just melted away…apparently these fish inject a poison into you and it takes heat and alkalinity to break it down. OK, so if six - no, not six, *ten* weaver fish had scuttled out of the shallows and into my nether regions and done their poison fin thing…they would be less painful than Julie and her groin strips.

I am thinking about the weaver fish when Julie is surely taking things a little too intimately by rubbing cold cream into my shaven havens and massaging some size into the peanut…perhaps beauty parlours are simply fronts for brothels? I remove the translucent mask to inform this Brummie hand-whore that I will not be requiring extras thank you…and I find that it is no longer Julie administering pleasure after the pain…but a grinning Pandora!

"Oooooh, you are so smoooo-oooth, Mee-lad!" she beams, approvingly, no doubt having applied the *cup de groin* with her own fair hands!

My body appears to have gone Bootle pink in its entirety, and though the peanut has progressed to a chipolata, it appears to have been shocked into yielding no further erotic response.

"Er, Pandora, what a…surprise!" I say, understatedly.

"Did I hurt you, Mee-lad?" she coos, losing interest in my shrivelled member and tossing a towel over it.

"Oo-oh yeah! That was a definite 'double ouch', Pandora. A ten weaver fish experience!"

"Weaver fish? Aren't they those little things they put in my foot spa to eat off the dead skin?"

"Not exactly, PM, I think those are guppies, aren't they? But I'll do my best to find some weavers for you next time you do have a foot spa," I say grumpily, rising to a seated position. She is not going to do all the hurting and humiliating, I think to myself. I inspect my burning, hairless body, and do not like what I see.

"Oooh, it makes you look so much *bigger*, dahling!" she admires, as I get to my feet and the towel slides away. And so much…cleaner! But do get a Bic razor to your scrotum, dear. It looks like a little busby. And get dressed, you deserve a *stiff* drink!"

Stiff as in, unlike my chipolata, I suppose she means. This particular lady does have a 'wkd side' and no mistake.

HOLLAND PARK IS REALLY QUIET ON A SUNDAY. Even though I am in West London, it feels like I am Nuthurst, Sussex, where my family live, though the houses here are posher. I really need my Clooney reading glasses to decipher my *London A – Z*, but if I hold the pages at a certain focal length, I can work out roughly where Greveldon Terrace is. When I got back to my hotel in Rye after my de-nuding session and a skinful of booze, I opened the door to find a very nice surprise laid out on my bed, and I am wearing it. It is an 'Arne suit'…hand made in Jerome Street. It is amazing - lined with white silk, and made from fine black sheer wool, with a really subtle pinstripe. It must have cost a fortune. I went out and bought myself some new shirts from *Next* and I'm sporting a nice blue check-y one. Must get some new shoes. I have really big feet for my height, I'm size 12 but sometimes I try to squeeze into 11's so I don't look like Barney Rubble. I do polish my snub-toed black shoes from *Brantano* hard, but no way can I get them to look super-polished like Arne's. Wonder where he gets his shoes from. Probably Milan or somewhere like that. Also must get a new overnight bag, this *Adidas* bag looks shit. My new suit is chafing on the emerging stubble of my body hair, and I have a bit of a rash on my bum and inner thighs, for which the pharmacist gave me nappy rash cream. And some guys do this voluntarily?

I've reached Number 36, Pandora's house. I am nervous about a bunch of stuff. The first is that I'm not sure if Pandora's ex-husband Neil still lives with her. I remember her telling me in our first interview that Neil hadn't left the house in months after she dumped him, so perhaps he is still here? I saw a documentary about a lady called Hattie Jaques who my Dad likes in the *Carry On* films, and she was married to John Le Mesurier who was in the superb *Dad's Army* series that me, my family and all the lads love. Sparks does a brilliant Captain Mainwaring. And Corporal Jones. Anyway, she was a bit of a goer Hattie was, and Sergeant Wilson wasn't, so she only moved a young lover into their house! And poor old John sucked it up and stayed there! So maybe that's what is going on here…some drunk, washed up, chain smoking old clapper having to listen to Arne do his wife whilst he lives in the spare room. Wow, what an amazing house. It's a Victorian semi, which we have loads of in Nuthurst and Horsham, but because it is in West London…it just seems…well classier. The front garden is festooned with light pink Albertine roses (I know all about gardening from my Mum. My Mum is a brilliant gardener and I have always helped her do stuff like make compost and pot-on seedlings) and I walk up the sinuous cottage garden path and duck my head through trellises and pergolas, avoiding scratchy rose tendrils. The garden could do with a prune really, but where would PM Poste find the time?! Oh blimey, the door is opening as I arrive bang on time at 4pm, and it is indeed a husbandy-type bloke! But he doesn't look drunk or washed up, he looks quite happy and friendly! He's got a floppy grey fringe and he is wearing a mustard waistcoat and a blue shirt.

"Is it Milad?" he smiles, extending a palm, which is warm and genuine.

"Yes, yes sir, it is. How do you do? Lovely front garden."

"Very pleased to meet you - Neil. Pandora is expecting you. I am very well, thank you, do come inside, won't you?" His voice is rich and deep and sort of cultured.

I am ushered inside the house which expands like a Tardis, and smells… expensive.

"Please, come in." I walk into the front room, which looks like something from a catalogue. A very pretty slim forty-something woman with a sharp blonde bob and scarlet lipstick is sitting primly on the edge of a leather chair and is pouring tea into a china cup decorated with oriental blue dragons which match the pot. Next to her is an enormous vase with the biggest bunch of white lilies I have ever seen.

"Darling, this is Milad, Pandora's new press secretary. Milad, this is Susanna."

Susanna rises from her chair to offer me her hand, a bit like royalty might, the back of her hand towards the ceiling. I wonder if I should kiss this slender proffering, but settle for a slightly awkward and very light handshake.

"Would you like tea, my dear?" she asks me, I think her accent might be faintly Irish. "It's lapsang souchong."

"Erm…" I'm a bit confused. Am I supposed to take tea with Pandora's ex, and what could be his girlfriend? Neil comes to my rescue.

"Pandora told me to tell you that she is running a little bit late, so do join us for ten minutes. Please, sit down and take some tea." I obey of course, and Susanna is pouring, her tiny wrist wobbling a bit under the weight of the tea pot. A huge oil painting of a racehorse above the marble mantelpiece takes my eye.

"Lovely horse, Neil?"

"Oh thank you so much, yes, that's *Pandora's Pride* we put him out to stud last year. He did do rather well for us. Do you follow horse racing at all, Milad?" Come on, brain, remember something about horse racing, dimwit.

Dad took me to the Grand National at Aintree when I was 15. Ruby Walsh won it on Hedgehunter, 7-1 favourite. I had my money on Joly Bay but it came in 14th. I can hardly regurgitate that for Neil and Susanna can I? I'd sound like Statto! What about this year's race? All I can remember is that a horse called Sea Bass came third and it was ridden by a woman.

"Well, I follow the Grand National, that's all really. Good race this year wasn't it!" Oh, crap! Susanna has stopped pouring tea and is wearing an expression of intense pain. Neil goes over to comfort her with an arm at her shoulder.

"Oh, I'm sorry, Milad," she is half-whispering (definitely Irish) "I can't stand it when horses die during a race. I find the National such a cruel event." Fuckwit! Loads of horses died this year - that was the main story! Susanna does seem a very sensitive woman. Neil crouches into a tender posture, and holds her tiny elvish chin between thumb and forefinger. Neil doesn't seem very 'broken' by Pandora's well-publicised dumping of him. He turns to smile at me reassuringly, an expressive and complex smile which tells me that he loves this woman but that in no way am I to blame for upsetting her. He expertly changes the subject, whilst resuming the tea-pouring with his free hand.

"Yes, we prefer the flat racing, don't we darling. But Milad, when I was your age I wouldn't miss Aintree for the world. Such a spectacle. I went last in 2005. Ruby Walsh won it on Hedgehunter. There's your tea, dear boy."

Neil rises to his feet with a crunching sound from his knees, he winces and grimaces as he hobbles slightly to his armchair opposite Susanna. I muse that perhaps I brushed past this kindly man in the queue for the Tote at Aintree in 2005. Life is like that sometimes. Spooky.

"Are you enjoying yourself among Pandora's entourage, Milad? Though as I'm sure you know, Pandora and I have separated, we remain very good friends and we have three children together, after all. It is very exciting, this *Black Heart* phenomenon!"

"Yep, yep, so far so good." Damn this cup and saucer! It's rattling in my hand! Dad warned me about cups and saucers. OK, hold saucer in one hand, cup in other. "Yep, it's…alright, really." I take a glug of lapsang souchong (no milk or sugar offered, none requested) and it burns the roof of my mouth. God, what smoky tea. They wouldn't like this back in Flat 3. Oh, good reply, Milad, good reply, to Neil Poste, the king of publishing, the prince of words. "Yep, it's…alright, really." What an erudite fellow I must sound.

"That's smashing news, I know that Pandora works some of her people very ahem, hard. Anyway, Susanna and I are off to the Tate shortly, and we are staying in town tonight, so please make yourself completely at home, I see Arne has made up a room for you. It is lovely to meet you, Milad, and I am sure we will meet again, possibly at the London party?"

They are both smiling fondly at me, though possibly with a hint of something else, though I cannot fathom what it is. Perhaps he knows that I am Pandora's lover – but am I? Does a bathroom bonanza and a blowie make me Pandora's lover? Probably not! Maybe he knows that under this expensive suit, his ex-wife has personally shorn me of my intimate body hair! Even though they are separated, they may be one of those couples that tell each other everything? Like Hattie Jaques and John Le Mesurier. Anyway, they are exiting the room with such grace and charm that I am reminded of a pair of perfectly matched ballroom dancers and I am left alone to sip my souchong, which I briefly consider tipping into one of the enormous rubber plants or back in the antique tea pot. But I don't. I drink it up.

A few minutes later, I hear the front door close and I catch a glimpse of Neil and Susanna in expensive mackintoshes negotiating the rose foliage and ducking under overgrown thorny pergolas. I get up and walk around the room, and one painting on the wall takes my eye. It has a little card next to it, just like they do in galleries. My art teacher at school used to take us to The National Gallery on the train sometimes, and me and Lisa went to the Lowry Museum in Salford Quays a couple of times. I like Lowry. He painted match stalk men, and match stalk cats and dogs.

Anyway, this painting isn't by Lowry, it's by someone called Hieronymus Bosch, who I have never heard of, and it's called *The Seven Deadly Sins and the Four Last Things*. Eh, 1485? Blimey, it's ancient! I don't think this is the original, but you'd put nothing past these people with their racehorses and posh tea. I bet even these plants are in Ming vases! I am finding this painting very interesting. In the middle is a big circle, divided into seven compartments each illustrating a deadly sin. It looks like the *Trivial Pursuits* board…only it's not that trivial, I guess. Each sin has a little heading, but it's in a language I don't know - I'm thinking Latin? We don't do Latin in school any more, but my Dad is always driving me mad with it. Even though he left school at 16, he still seems to remember his "Latin declensions" from way back. There he is, buttering a piece of toast or something, and it's "amo, amas, amat, amamus, amatis, amant," or some such thing and I have no idea what it means and don't much care, really. But I do quite like his little Latin sayings, like "tempus fugit" which he says a lot, which means "time flies." Well, I could do with him now to translate these sin words.

The segment at the bottom, says "ira" and there are two dudes having a proper scrap, one of them has some kind of chair planted on his head which makes me laugh out loud. They seem to be fighting over a woman. I'm reckoning that 'ira' equals 'irate', so this section is 'anger'. I have to tilt my head a bit to try to work out the next compartment. I wish that I could turn it round like one of those old fashioned records that my mum used to have. If this was one of those vinyl discs, it would be on the 'Jesus' label, as there is a picture of the Son Of God in the middle looking crucified and pissed off. The next section round, I think reads "Invidia"? Hard to tell from this old-school writing. I remember Chaucer from school, he wrote like this, and he was probably around when this guy Bosch was about. Maybe they knew each other? Definitely one for old Wiki later on. 'Invidia' – invidious? But what does invidious mean, can't remember. Well, you are never far from knowledge with a smart phone and a decent tariff, so onto 'Online Dictionary' I go with my trusty touch screen. Hmm, 'likely to arouse resentment'. Envy? There are some poor-looking thin folk stuck in a little house, and outside there are well dressed fat folk with falcons and big bags of flour and shit, so that works. I can't remember what the seven deadly sins are, we didn't do a lot of religion at a school or at home, but I do remember a really cool old film with Brad Pitt called '*Seven*' which was about the deadly sins and was also quite creepy.

There are also seven virtues, but they weren't in that film. I do know them though, 'cos my mum made me learn them off by heart when I was little. They are: chastity, temperance, charity, diligence, patience, kindness, and humility. The first two aren't very popular these days (nor the last one, I reckon) but actually they mean more than not having sex or booze.

Outside the inner circle divided into the 'sin quadrants' are four smaller circles at the corners of the painting, and they are floating against a background, which is black and starry, and maybe, like, the universe? So these saucers must be the *Four Last Things*. These are pretty heavy. There is a dying guy getting the Last Rites, there is Jesus floating about surrounded by angels, there is some sort of court going on deciding who goes (as my Dad puts it) 'Upstairs' or 'Downstairs' and finally, one of 'Downstairs'. Downstairs is pretty creepy. There are these weird black beetly animals tormenting naked people - some are being boiled in oil, some thrown off high towers, some singled out for special chastisement. Right in the middle, this black wing-y critter is holding a sinner down bent over a chair or summat (Lisa used to say summat instead of 'something' and I've picked it up) and this woman is belting his bum with a big hammer. Yowch!

I am just working my way onto the next segment in which there seems to be a lot or arguing going on over books, when Pandora - looking flushed and excited - bounds into the room. When I use the word 'bound', I don't mean so figuratively. She literally bounds in. Like a woman on a pogo stick. There is lots of her still pogo-ing when her feet are planted before me. She is wearing a sweat shirt logoed with a big pair of red sequin-y lips and a pink tongue extending from them on it, which at first I think is the classic Rolling Stones *Hot Lips* thing, 'til I see the italic (also sequin-y) writing above and below it, which reads "Lick My Pussy". I don't think that Mick, Keef and the boys did a song called 'Lick My Pussy', but I will check on Wiki later on. She extends her arms, and raises her face heavenwards, her smile (almost literally, but this time figuratively) extending from ear to ear.

"Mee-lad, Mee-lad, Mee-lad," she exhales. "How ma-aaarvellous to have you in my home! Welcome, dear thing, welcome!" She is now (literally) smothering my face with kisses and then sort of shimmies her bosom in my face, a gesture I find brazen but fetching.

"Flanklou foll infliting me, Pandola," I manage, my cheeks immersed in her canyon.

"Ah, we shall have such fun! Such FUN! Now, you have met the ex - and that tart he calls his girlfriend. Lovely Neil. Poor man, broken, broken by his cru-el Pandora. He will never recover of course, the poor, poor man."

Neil seems to be doing a pretty good job of recovering to me, but I am more interested in the Hattie/John thing, and chance my arm.

"Does he still live with you then, Pandora? Not that it's any of my business, of course…"

"Oh yes, my smoothie, I simply couldn't put dear Neil out! Though I won't let that Irish whore stay under my roof! Oh no. Not even in the summer house, dah-ling. Besides, that is where Arne sleeps these days."

I never forgot my Dad telling me that in London, you are never more than18 metres from a rat. And I don't like rats. These days, I am never more than 18 metres from Arne. But I do like Arne.

"Now, let me show you around my lovely home!" Pandora is waving her fists about in excitement. There is something different about her. And she is trying to tell me what it is…she is waggling her hair about like a cute ragdoll. My Mum used to get annoyed with my Dad if she had her cut or fixed and he didn't notice, He said it was a man-thing not to notice, only gay gays notice haircuts. I think I'm doing pretty 'hetero' here, as I cannot fathom what has changed, but I do know there is something.

"Well, do you like it, Milad?!" Shit, her hair colour! It's bright blue! It was bright red, but now it's bright blue. Once when I was out with the lads chucking stones in the river, I saw a kingfisher flash by. None of the other lads saw it but Potts and me. It was the blue-est thing I have ever seen. I only saw it for a second, but I can still close my eyes and remember how blue it was. You see kingfishers on the telly of course like on *Springwatch* (me and the lads really hate that show and take the piss out of the nerdy presenters, but my Mum and Dad love it), but it isn't the same. Pandora's hair is not as blue as the kingfisher I saw in real life, but it is the next blue-est thing I've ever seen. It has the same sheen as when it was red, but now it is iridescent, kingfisher blue.

"I love it, Pandora!" I tell her, and I do love it. She appreciates that. Women love compliments and reassurance. That was good advice that Dad gave me when he used to drive me all the way up to Bolton Uni. We had some good old chats me and Dad when he picked me up and took me back, every term for three years. That's nine round trips of 500 miles, 4500 miles. That's like driving from London to Delhi. Of course, I was only in the car with him for half those journeys, so that's like driving to Iran, where my mum is from. We have been to Tehran several times, but we've never driven. My Dad used to drop me off at my digs in Bolton and give me a tenner and a big hug. He always had a tear in his eye, the big softie. I love my Dad to bits, but I never tell him, though I do give him the 1X on texts sometimes.

Pandora evidently likes my compliment about her hair because she looks exceptionally pleased with herself and squeezes my hand really hard. She leads me around her house, not letting go of my hand for one second. I reckon this must be the biggest house I've ever been in. Well, apart from stately homes, obviously. There are loads of rooms. The kitchen is massive, with a big oak dining table, but there is a separate dining room as well, with an enormous round dark wood table (mahogany, I reckon) and twelve really comfy looking chairs, that all match). Then, there is an actual library! With one of those moveable step ladders to get up to the high shelves. So many books. And I'll bet Neil has read them all, too. Downstairs bathroom, upstairs bathroom. Two studies (Neil's is locked, Pandora's a creative jumble of works in progress and her glowing laptop... no doubt with the latest page of *Black Heart Darker* freshly written!) Five bedrooms...most of the doors are closed and she doesn't show all the rooms to me, but ushers me into a nice room with a plumpy-looking single bed and loads of cartoon of cats in frames on the wall, and she tells me that's my room. Arne does a great chambermaid job...bathrobe and towels neatly folded on the bed, a pair of hotel slippers, and the bed smells of newly laundered linen. Even a little vase with beautifully arranged fresh flowers gathered from the garden on the bedside cabinet. I assume (wrongly) that Pandora has picked the flowers, as I thank her for my room and my posy.

"Oh, no need to thank me, dear. Arne is very good with things like that. He is doing a course in flower arrangement at the Royal Horticultural Society currently." Fucking Arne...what a guy, killer and flower arranger! Wait 'til I tell that to Sparks!

"Anyway, that's just about it for my little *chez moi* dah-ling!" pants Pandora, still out of breath from mounting the wide, slightly spirally staircase, with loads of different photos of Pandora in different poses on the wall, running from hall to landing. "Jump in the shower, Milad, and put on your robe. Meet me downstairs in half an hour. There is one more room to show you dah-ling!" She winks. I know what that room is. It's the Pink Room of Pain.

WHEN I WARILY DESCEND thirty minutes later, Pandora is on her mobile in the kitchen, barking (but in a good way) with laughter.

"Oh no, darling you didn't? OMG…OMG…OMG!! No, you didn't do that as well? GAGAGAGAGAGAHAHA! You wonderful slut, Angharad. OHHOHOHO! Ooooh, I've got to go, dah-ling, my delicious guest is here. GAGAGAGAGAGAHAHA! I will! I will, babes. You are naughtier than PM Poste is, I swear it. Hugs, darling. Love you too. Oh, Mee-lad, come here my dahling, I want to eat you all up."

As I am enveloped in her arms, she smells vaguely of piccalilli, and I see from the opened jar on the counter over her shoulder that she is halfway through a ham sandwich slathered in what me and the lads humorously call 'pickled willy'. (With our Spoonerist twisting though, this has mutated to 'wickled pilly'. I love wickled pilly, especially from *Asda,* and for that reason, a jar of the bright yellow stuff has reached Number 10 in the Flat 3 'Must Have in The Kitchen Top Ten Hit Parade'. This list is regularly updated and debated in *The Tig,* but it has reached a pretty steady state lately. Here goes, Pop Pickers.

Entering at number ten and kicking out *Branston's* pickle, it's *Asda's* 'own' wickled pilly. At nine, up one place from last week, it's a packet of sliced ham, from *Asda's* deli. At eight, a non-mover, *Cheerios.* Nuff said. At seven, down one from six, it's *McVitie's* milk chocolate digestives. At six, up two places, Costa Rican *Kenco* instant coffee…better than Nescafé and probably Fair Trade (when we can afford it, we like to keep an eye out for the world's poor). At five, a non-mover, *Anchor* butter (spreadable). At four, down one place, *Warburton's* thick toastie white loaf. Up two from five, *Silver Spoon*'s granulated sugar – me and Sparks both like sugar in our hot drinks and we won't have them without. A non-mover at two…a four-pinter of *Asda's* semi-skimmed fresh milk. We don't have a milkman, I don't think there are any in Horsham any more, but Mum and Dad still have one in Nuthurst. Milk is the biggest source of argument between me and Sparks. First, I do most of the buying, and second, he does most of the drinking. I really hate it when he uses the last of the milk and doesn't leave me a splash for tea in the mornings. And at Number One…for the sixth week running, Tetley's tea bags. Without tea there is no point in getting up in the morning, so there must always be tea. No tea, no getting up. So it is hard to see anything knocking Tetley's off the top spot. Though if there's no milk or sugar, there's also no tea worth calling tea, and you can't put tea bags on your Cheerios. So maybe the milk or sugar could make it to Number One, one day. For a while, *Lea and Perrins* Worcester Sauce was Number one, so you never know.

Now this is a pretty cunning top ten list. Me and Sparks reckon we could survive for a long time with these ten key items. We can have as much tea and coffee as we want (and we do want…we drink a lot of the stuff). Plus there's bikkies. We can have toast. We can have ham and wickled pilly sandwiches. And we can have Cheerios. We reckon we'd be OK in the event of a nuclear strike for quite a long time. I'm just thinking of what hovers above the Top Ten in the 12 and 11 spots when Pandora thrusts me to her arms' length.

"Let me show you…*downstairs,* darling," she smiles mysteriously, with a gleam of the actress in her wide brown eyes.

Not to my surprise, the Pink Room of Pain is in the basement, and she produces a key from the back pocket of her jeans, turns it in what looks like a pantry door, and beckons me down some stone steps, before following me, and turning to re-lock the door behind us.

Well, I can see why it's called the pink room, certainly. To say this room is pink does justice neither to the word 'pink' nor the colour 'pink'. It is a livid, lurid, brazen pink. Walls, ceiling, carpet. Bright, pussy pink. Nothing pale pink about it. This is *dark* pink. But in the Pink Room of Pain, your eyes don't dwell very long on the colour of the walls. There are a great many contraptions and paraphernalia which quickly distract.

To my complete surprise, I see that Pandora and I are not alone in this basement chamber, and that Arne, who is sort of whistling to himself (that's a new one, I haven't heard him whistle before) as he crouches with a spanner at the base of a sphere over ten metres in diameter. It looks like a huge globe made of wire mesh which is mounted on a complex plinth.

Arne seems to be performing some kind of routine maintenance, or possibly a repair.

"Alright, Arne?" I say, nonchalantly and mate-ily.

He looks up at me for an instant, and whilst he does not actually reply, he does smile. Briefly, but genuinely, I think.

"Arne, haven't you fixed The Gimbaler yet?" Pandora is puffing her cheeks out and giving him her frustrated look.

"It needs new bearings really, PM. I have oiled it, but it is a bit creaky still." Pandora whirls the huge globe around on its axis, and then tumbles it forward. It seems to have a little hatch in the top. If it had giant numbered balls inside and a handle on it, it would remind me of a bingo ball dispenser that my gran used to have in Bootle. Spinning in two planes, the sphere makes a whining, creaky sound.

"Oh, it will do, Arne. Leave Milad and I in peace. And lock the door behind you."

"Cheers, Arne!" I call after his clacking shiny feet. He turns and gives me another of his rapid smiles. Good old Arne.

"Oh Arne," Pandora calls after him, looking thoughtful with her index finger on her plump lower lip. "The Hamster's Wheel is functional, is it not?"

"Yes, Ms. Poste. Perfectly functional." Well, it doesn't take a lot of working out which of these contraptions is The Hamster's Wheel. We had a hamster when I was six, I called it Brownie (not very imaginative when you consider our surname is Brown) though my recollection is that it was more white than brown. It annoyed my Dad, because being a largely nocturnal creature, Brownie ran round his wheel at night when Dad was trying to do his Cost Sheets, or whatever it is that Dad does when he brings work home. Instead of the six inch diameter wheel that Brownie scrabbled round in, before me stands a six foot diameter version, that evidently Pandora is about to have Milad Brown scrabbling round in.

She takes me firmly by the hand with a distracted smile. "In The Pink Room of Pain, we have two changing areas, Mee-lad. Hers. And His." She leads me to two cubicles, similar to those you see in clothing stores like *Next*, with curtains across them. But as she sweeps back the curtain to 'His', I can see these cubicles are merely the ante-rooms to much larger chambers. I look around me in alarm at all the gimp-ware. A World War I gas mask takes my eye on a hook next to a deep sea trawlerman's yellow oilskin and sou'wester hat. It's great how all the old telly stuff is on *YouTube* now? My Dad introduced me to a kid's cartoon from his day called *Mr Benn*, which looks like it has been animated with a wax crayon. It's a weird story, this suburban bloke called Mr Benn who is always wearing a bowler hat and a suit (apparently back in those times all the civil servants wore bowler hats) goes in every episode to a fancy dress shop, picks a costume, and then walks through a secret door and has an adventure dressed as whatever he is. That's what this room reminds me of. The changing room in the fancy dress shop. But I don't think you'd see Mr Benn in the ensemble that Pandora is handing to me.

"Put these on, and then wait outside The Goddess Chamber." Her tone is icy and commanding. I think it's time to get into character.

"Yes Miss."

"You will call me Goddess during your internment in The Pink Room of Pain, Mee-lad. And I will call you anything I choose. Do you understand?"

"Yes Miss. I mean Goddess."

"Good, now get dressed." She sweeps away, no doubt not to be seen in jeans and T-shirt next time I see her! During our 'contract negotiations' I told Pandora that I wouldn't wear one of those classic gimp masks with the zip across the mouth like in *Pulp Fiction*, and I'm relieved to see that the head gear she has chosen is slightly simpler, in being a rubber hood that scuba divers wear. Then there is a black leather mankini like *Borat* wears; a pair of tight rubber boots that also come from a diving shop; a belt that looks like a weight belt but isn't that heavy; and then my accessories - a snorkel, a diving mask and a dog collar which matches the belt. Bit of a diving theme going on, then! I have my new Arne-phone in the pocket of my towelling robe, and as I change into my costume, I check that there is a signal, and I am relieved that there is one, albeit weak. I do trust Pandora, but there was something in Sparky's uncharacteristic concern for me that has put me on my guard.

I check myself out in the big mirror. I'm not one for theatrics or dressing up really, although me and the lads get invited to the odd fancy dress party and I went to the last one as Russell Crowe's Gladiator. I spent the whole night drinking some rubbish party punch and telling people *"my name is Maximus Decimus Meridius, Commander of the Armies of the North, General of the Felix Legions, loyal servant to the true emperor, Marcus Aurelius, father to a murdered son, husband to a murdered wife, and I will have my vengeance -- in this life or the next."* Sparky didn't make much of an effort and cut a couple of holes in a filthy old sheet and went as a grimy ghost.

So, I am standing in a very pink basement in West London looking like a kinky hairless diver. But I reckon this is all good for my personal development - Mum always says that I'm a bit too shy. So I flip back the curtain and stand next to The Goddess Chamber. I can hear sort of creaking and cursing noises within. A few minutes later, the pink curtain to The Goddess Chamber is flung open, and there stands Pandora. At least I hope it's Pandora!

"GET DOWN ON YOUR KNEES, BOY!" she commands, and I obey.

"Yes, Goddess." She is wearing thigh length leather boots with big spiky heels. From the waist up, who does she look like? That's it...Mr Benn! She is wearing a bowler hat with her shimmering blue hair pinned up inside, a dark pinstripe jacket which reaches the top of her boots, a white silk shirt buttoned to the top, and a black silk neck tie. In her left hand is a leather leash, which she attaches to my collar, and in the other is a very nasty looking bull whip.

"Get to your wheel, boy!" she commands. "And put on your mask and snorkel!"

She leads me on all fours across the pink carpeted floor as I breathe through the snorkel, the rubber mouthpiece clamped in my mouth.

"Now get on your wheel and run for your life, lad!" She unclips my leash. My mask has fogged up a bit, and my voice is muzzy up the snorkel tube.

"Yzzzzz Godezzz."

I clamber onto the big wheel, and get into a sort of crouching position. I try to remember how Brownie did this. Suddenly there is a crack in the air and a sensation at my bum like I have been stung by an enormous bee.

"YOWZZ!" I muzz through the snorkel. I hear another crack in the air - Pandora is standing legs akimbo like a demented circus ringmaster and (literally) cracking the whip.

"Move, you silly creature! I said move!" she is shouting.

I sort of scuttle around the wheel, which starts to revolve with a bit of a creaking sound, clutching and pawing the higher bars with my hands and making little peddling motions with my feet. I slip over quite a bit and slide down onto the bottom of the wheel. Every time I do that, the bee stings me smartly across the buttocks. It's hard work and I am sweating, blowing hard through my tube…but I am getting the knack of it, and getting up a lick of speed.

"THWAAAK!" OWWWWW! Pandora has exchanged her bull whip for a long cane, and she is goading me with it.

"Faster, faster, or I will thrash you boy!" She seems to be thrashing me anyway, and judging from the evil grin on her face, thoroughly enjoying doing so. As my legs pump harder and my hands scrabble, I smile that I am giving her pleasure. I want to give her pleasure. Even if it means running around like a rodent dressed like an aquatic Borat.

"Enough!" she commands. The lead is on again, and she peels off the snorkel and mask and kisses my panting mouth long and full. My bum is singing with pain, but at least she hasn't drawn blood.

"Now you will dance for me! Come over here, boy. Heel."

I am panting like the hound she wants me to be, as I crawl on all fours to the corner of the room. Yaay! A *Wii* Dance Mat and a huge screen in front of it. I love *Wii*! Me and Sparky don't have one (we have a PS4) but my sister Naz has a *Wii* and we play loads on it, the tennis one is my favourite. Pandora is squatting down to load a disc, and the round white moon of her derriere is exposed between boots and jacket. She is wearing no pants. Saucy.

"Stand. Dance. Dance for me, Milad." I am not much of a fan of Beyoncé, but she's OK and I know this track, *Party* (featuring André 3000). Like a bit of a *Wii* pro, I am grooving around the mat, my diving boots making a bit of squeaking sound on the mat. But whilst I am used to the Wii Dance Mat, what I am not used to is being whacked with a riding crop whilst doing 'ma thing'. Pandora parades around me, clapping in time to the beat, but every eighth beat, she gives me an almighty thwack about some part of my anatomy, and some of them are more like Pain 2 than Pain 3. Pandora has given me a code word (or rather phrase) to sing out if I am not happy with anything, and "Bubba Gump" plays at my lips as she leans into the mat to strike me across the front of my thighs. But I endure, singing along with André 3000, *"You a bad girl and yo' friends bad too!"*

As the track ends, my hands drop to my knees…it is knackering dancing to Beyoncé whilst being thrashed! Bad mistake to bend over. AAAAAAAHHHH! That was definitely a Pain 2 across the booty zone. The leash is back on, I am her dawg again, and she is leading me to the big mesh sphere she calls The Gimbaler.

"Get in!" she commands brusquely, as she opens the catches of the hatch, and I find myself inside the cage-ball, holding onto the mesh and peeping out through the six inch square gaps between the thin metal bars. She clips the hatch back into place, and starts spinning me about, first head-over-heels and then round-and round. Jesus! It goes round really fast…it's impossible to keep upright like you can on The Hamster's Wheel, and I just tumble about like laundry in a spin dryer. The inside of the mesh is padded a bit, but it's quite painful when the wire bites into you. She is revolving the globe, pushing hard with her womanly arms.

"Tell me you are a dirty boy, Mee-lad! She puffs. Tell me!"

"Er…waa-aaay, I…am a, whoaaa, dirty, aaaah..boy!" I obey, giving up any semblance of either balance or self-respect. I am getting all kinds of dizzy.

"LOUDER!"

"I….AM….WAAAAH!!….A DIRTY BOY!!"

"Right then, you dirty boy, I had better cleanse you, then!" Pandora allows The Gimbaler to spin me in ever more disorienting ways, as she pulls some screens down around the contraption, and unravels what looks like a fireman's hose. My washing machine analogy becomes even more apt, as one of the most powerful jets of water I've ever experienced presses me backwards against the revolving and tumbling mesh. My two thoughts are: a) that I can see why they use water cannon for crowd control in certain parts of the world; and b) that I wish I still had my diving mask on.

"I AM HOSING YOU DOWN, BOY!" Pandora is shouting, evidently very excited as she jumps up and down with the writing hose, and I can see she is getting quite a soaking herself, as the water ricochets back off the screens and The Gimbaler.

Suddenly, the gushing and spinning stops, and like a fish in a trawl net, I wriggle and drip, wiping my eyes with the back of my hands. I am totally dizzy, and can see about four Pandoras. And then, I see four Arnes. For fuck's sake, what's he doing back down here? And that is precisely what Pandora, hands on hips, is asking him too.

"I am really sorry to disturb you, PM, but there is quite an urgent fax from the US," he responds drily (literally).

Pandora is suddenly business-like in her dripping bowler hat, producing reading glasses from the top pocket of her jacket and she studies the fax in Arne's milky hands. It doesn't seem appropriate to greet my mate as I sit slumped at the bottom of The Gimbaler, water pouring away down some kind of drain chute below me. Plus, he doesn't look at me anyway.

"Very good, PM. I won't disturb you further," he is saying.

She is leading me out of The Gimbaler hatch, and I am lurching around like a drunken man. It looks like someone has drawn about two hundred 'noughts and crosses' boards on all parts of my body, where the wire has bitten into me.

"It's the US Publishers, dah-ling. Come and have a drink at Pussy Galore's Bar, I want to ask your opinion."

I stumble past the 'Alton Towers-like' curiosities of the Pink Room, avoiding something that looks like a man-trap in the 'set' position and gazing up in awe at a helter-skelter, the slide of which appears to be lined by raised (though mercifully blunt) metallic projections. Next to The Goddess Chamber is a fully equipped bar, and Pandora is bobbing up and down with a cocktail shaker that she has sploshed various spirits into, and some ice. I note that her shirt is wet through from her hosing, and that she is wearing no bra.

"He-re you are dah-ling. You have performed beautifully, Mee-lad. Cheers."

I am parched after my work-out violation, and I down my fruit and rum drink down in one. "Aaaaah. That's good, Goddess. What do you call that? Delicious!"

"Mmm, Arne invented that one, he calls it the Groovy Orgasm! Have another, dear, do, whilst I make you my favourite one...Sex in the Pink."

I don't mind if I do have another Groovy Orgasm, slipping down just a treat. As does the cranberry and mango Sex in the Pink. I'm feeling a bit pissed already.

"Kneel before the inner goddess," Pandora suddenly commands. "I will flavour myself for you." She swivels away from me on her pink barstool and grabs a couple of slices of mango from the bar. She swivels back around, and there before me is what Sparky disgustingly refers to as 'clunge'. She leans back on the bar on her two elbows.

"Taste me, Milad. Lick me." And I do. Mmmmm, mango-flavoured.

"Slowly, slowly, Mee-lad. Slower, that's it, perfect." She is scrabbling about in a metal tool box under the bar, which is bursting with gigantic sex toys.

"Shove this in me, boy. And do not on any account stop the tongue licking. Put it on level two and push it - in and out. Good boy, ye-es, that's it...go-ood boy." Needless to say, the vibrator she hands me is bright pink, and about twice the length and girth of my manhood, which is trying its humble best to bust its way out of its mankini pouch.

Pandora is groaning like a feral animal as she bucks and writhes around the barstool. Then she holds her breath for what seems like too long.

"AAAAAAH, AAAAAAH, AAAAAH, THE GODDESS IS APPEARING, THE GODDESS IS APPEARING, SEE HER, MEE-LAD, SEE HER... AAAAAAAAAAAAAAAAAAAAAAAAAAAAAAAAAAAAHHHHHH!!"

I gaze in awe at the dripping, yawning sight before me. Then suddenly, a stream of liquid bursts from her, and my face is running with it. There is barely time to wipe my eyes before another, even stronger spurt hits me right between the eyes. What the fuck is this? I thought we'd agreed no urinating?! Has she just pissed in my face at the point of climax? She is leaning back on the bar, her breasts heaving and her hands about them, her eyes screwed shut. She reaches down and massages my hair, pulling me to her and my nose disappears.

"Oh, Mee-lad, Mee-lad," she is purring. "You know *just* what to do to a girl!"

My throbbing mankini pouch is telling me quite firmly what to do next with this girl, but then I think, what's the deal with contraception here? Pandora probably does not want me to be the father of her fourth child, though I have to admit that the idea of fathering a child with Pandora is far from unthinkable…well, for me anyway. Should I have brought a three-pack of condoms with me?

But it doesn't look as though Uncle Thomas is going to get a look in just now, as Pandora is pouring herself another generous Sex in The Pink and glugging it down.

"Let me get you a bar towel, dah-ling. Didn't know I was squirter, did you, precious?"

She hands me a black Guinness bar towel and I swab myself down. A what? A squirter? What's all that about? I feel a phone call to Sparky coming on.

"Well, I think that is more than enough for one day, don't you, Milad?" she stands up and stretches in contentment. "You have performed very well. Do you like the Pink Room of Pain?"

"Er, yeah, it's alright, isn't it? There is certainly some interesting…stuff down here. A lot of work has gone into it, I'd say."

"Worth every penny, if it makes you happy, Mee-lad. Now, we have some real work to do. We have been offered a very interesting deal by a publisher in Chicago, and we need to talk to our lawyers. Arne is setting up a meeting at their offices next week. I need you to be there with us, my bright boy.

Arne is studying the fine print upstairs, and we must join him. You clear up this mess…there is a mop and bucket around somewhere. And wash these glasses up. I will have my shower down here, you use the bathroom at the top of the stairs."

With that, she is gone, her bare, sticky bottom sashaying past my nose.

As I clear up Pussy Galore's bar, feeling inebriated and slightly shell-shocked after my 'squirting', I return to Mr Benn's changing room and stand naked in front of the mirror. Jesus, I look as though I have been in a fight with an aikido expert and then dragged backwards through a hawthorn hedge. My ass looks like it's been fried in a griddle pan. I check my phone…two missed calls, both from Sparks. About ten text messages…half time in the Euro final and Spain are walking it. Hehe, I think of those boys huddled round the telly in Horsham eating *Doritos* and drinking *Carling*. I know where I'd rather be! I send a quick text to Sparks saying that all is well in the fast lane with the fast set, with an enigmatic ending: "*Learning loads about life. Pandora is an extraordinary woman. But man I miss ma dawgs!*" That's a reference to one of our fave anthems from *Lil Wayne*, I sing it to myself as I clear up Mr Benn's changing room and Pussy's Bar.

"*Man I miss my dawgs, many nights club poppin', many nights we were blowin' trees, many nights we were hustlin'. Man I miss my dawgs, me and you through thick and thin, me and you through the very end, for only you I was in the game.*" Love that song. A bleep as Sparks texts me back.

"Yo mutha. Yo dawgs missin you 2. Stay safe y'all. Word."

CHAPTER EIGHT

The following day, I call my Mum after I get home from work in London. I have a couple of days off, and I'm back in my bedroom in Horsham. Sparky is out with the band, and I am starting to find my *Avengers* duvet cover and wall posters a bit childish. I have brought back a roll of promo posters from the tour with Pandora on them, and I'm going to have a bit of a make-over. Pandora kindly gave me some baby oil for my 'wounds' and rubbed some in my bum for me before she tucked me into bed at her place after we had gone over some papers and Arne had cooked us a delicious dinner of shrimps and rice. Pandora turned the key in the lock from the outside after she shut my bedroom door, which I thought was a bit odd, but since there is a sink in the room I'd have to have had a pee in there if I needed one, but as it turned out I slept like a baby and the door was open the following morning.

"Are you OK, love?" My Mum sounds a bit anxious, and I waste no time reassuring her.

"Mum, I am more than alright. I am having the time of my life! What a waste of time the *County Times* was next to working with a world famous authoress! And they have paid me a month up front, and you want to see the suit Pandora bought me, it's totally lush."

"Are you eating properly?"

"All five star, ma. Whatever I want, all paid for. My mate Arne, you know the cool guy I told you about? He cooks stuff, but like, amazing stuff?"

"Well, you won't be wanting my lamb tagine any more then?"

"MUM! Don't talk crazy talk. You <u>know</u> your cooking is THE BEST!"

"Well, when are you coming for some home cooking, Milad? Dad says you are working weekends now?"

"Yeah, it's all happening for Pandora, mum, she is great you know. I am really close to her, really close. I stay at her house and everything."

"Well, she isn't very nice when she is on the telly, Milad. And that book of hers…have you read it?"

"MUM! I told you not to read *Black Heart* didn't I? And Naz the same! It isn't for you guys, it's for…it's for…other women than you!"

"No I haven't read it, thank you. But Molly next door has. And I think Naz has read it actually! I flipped through a copy in WH Smiths and I was quite shocked."

"Well don't look, Mum! It isn't for you! Pandora is writing for a… certain audience, you see. It's like..genre?"

"Well I don't like the look of her, Milad. Far too sure of herself. Just make sure you don't get carried away with her, that's what I am saying."

"Mum, it's fine, I am a man now. I am twenty-one! I can take care of myself, can't I? But listen, I have a day off next week, I will come and stay over then, I promise. And cook tagine! And don't worry about me, I'm fine. I'm having the time of my life. I'm learning so much, Mum, really!"

"OK well, if you say you are. Auntie Sara and Uncle Nersi are coming to stay soon, so you can see them too."

"No way?! Auntie Sara and Uncle Nersi! Wow, that will be so cool. They live in LA now, right?"

"Yes. I am so looking forward to see them again. Do come, Milad. Now, love from Dad, love from Naz and love from me. Take care, my darling son."

"Don't worry about me, Mum, and watch out for me on TV. Pandora is going to be on loads and you might see me in the background. I'll give you a wave. We are having a big party in London soon."

"Can't you invite your sister? She would love to go to a show-biz party like that!"

"Naz! No way, mum. She is way too young! And tell her not to read *Black Heart*. It's not for her!"

"I'll do my best. Love to you, Milad."

"Love you loads, mum. Call you soon. Bye. Bye."

Phew. Don't like the idea of Mum and Naz reading Pandora's book! But why not? OK, it's a bit rude and racy in places and a bit OTT. But nothing like what Pandora gets up to in real life! Blimey, I hope I'm not featuring in *Black Heart Darker*. My Mum seriously wouldn't like that.

EVERYBODY IN THE WORLD IS TALKING ABOUT PM POSTE, and Milad Brown of Horsham is getting a hefty slice of the action. The London book signings are mental, and Arne has had to draft in extra security guys who are two mean mo' fo's. One is calls himself Tank, the other has a knife scar down his face and therefore is called Scarface by Arne, though his real name is Bob. I'm getting to know the Coffee Press people pretty well and I'm on first name terms with the entertainment editor at *The London Standard*. But being a true pro, Pandora insists on having weekends to herself, and I am very much involved in her time off. Oh yeah. I've been on every device in The Pink Room of Pain (apart from the Man-Trap), and I can say without question that the 'Rough Rider' helter-skelter (down which I travelled in a kilt, sporran and Tam O' Shanter) was the toughest, especially when Pandora tipped a bucket of *Gloy* glue over my head when I reached the bottom, and then stuck me to the Human Fly Paper. Duly adhered, I was then hoisted six feet in the air and given the thrashing of my life with a giant fly-swatter. I was quite pleased in the aftermath to have no body hair, as it was tough enough getting the dried glue out of my head hair. All good fun though, and although I can't say I get a lot of pleasure from my painful humiliations, Pandora does, and so that makes it worthwhile.

Frustrating thing is though, after I get to 'perform' on Pandora and been drenched in her squirt-juice, she has a cocktail or four, and then retires to the Goddess Room. I get to clear up Pussy's bar, get spruced up and then and do some work upstairs with the team. Pretty early, I get packed off to bed on my own in the single room. Not that I am complaining, but I have bought a pack of *Durex* johnnies in the hope of getting it on properly with Pandora, but as yet, their seal is unbroken.

I bump into Neil around the house quite a bit, who is in and out of his study, and I heard him talking to Pandora on the landing one night after I was turned in, they seem quite chummy. Neil is really nice to me, and always making me cups of souchong, which I don't like, but I drink them anyway, because it would be rude not to. We talk quite a bit about Pandora's media strategy, which I don't direct 'cos Roz at Coffee does that, but I am already a pretty big cog in the PM publicity machine.

Arne and me get on super-well. He never mentions my escapades in the Pink Room, though I did catch him grinning a bit when he came down with another important fax during one of our 'sessions', when Pandora dressed me up as a flatfish (a plaice, I think) and she was dressed as a north sea trawler-woman in oilskins and sou'wester. She was on deck of HMS Pink, which has a winch on deck, which she was using to haul me aboard, having caught me in a metal trawl net. "FLAP FOR YOUR LIFE, BOY!" she was shouting when Arne interrupted us, and she taught me how to flap really well. I had to 'hang around' in the net for ages along with a load of other (non-human) rubber fish such as cod, haddock and tuna whilst my fisherwoman discussed the fax with Arne.

Arne even showed me his summerhouse quarters in the garden one evening, and I was able to text Sparky later to reveal the staple diet of the Norwegian hard man...*Pringles*. There were absolutely loads of canisters in his quarters, which are like no other 'summerhouse' I've ever seen. He has a sauna down there, as well as a separate bedroom and living area. He also has a dartboard, and after offering me a *Pringle* (Original Flavour), we had a game. He cheated a bit though...he had throwing-knives instead of darts.

Today, we are having another meeting about the 'London Party 'at the *Café Royal* in ten days. All the meetings are really professional - agendas, minutes, all that business - we never did that stuff at the *County Times;* everybody just said whatever trivial rubbish was on their mind. Pandora always chairs the meetings, and she does so with complete command. If anybody rattles on too long, she soon shuts them up, including me. Brilliant. She does most of the talking, in fact she does 93.7% of the talking, I have taken to timing and calculating that, it's good fun. I like statistics, especially sports ones. If it's nice weather, we have our meetings on the patio in the garden, but as it's always raining this summer, we usually meet in the front room where I first encountered Neil and Susanna.

Today, there are a couple of people from Coffee Press, a dude called Len, plus Neil, me, Arne and chairwoman Pandora. She is not in a very good mood today, on account of Len has evidently fucked up.

"Len, I am not going to tell you this again! I want a six metre marionette of me, I want her to walk round the *Eros* statue three times, before she walks slowly up Regent Street…"

"Pandora…I must…" Oh dear, this Len doesn't learn does he? You do NOT interrupt PM when she is in full flow. Arne looks like he might terminate Len with the pen he is using to take notes, which knowing Arne will have a poison dart in it or something. But Len gets something worse than a poison dart…the rough end of Pandora's tongue. I am shifting about in my armchair….mainly in anticipation of Len's tongue lashing, but also because of the bum-lashing I received from Pandora yesterday evening with a table tennis bat, surprisingly painful.

"LEN!!" she commands. "Do not interrupt my creative flow! If you do so again I must ask you to leave! Now, where was I? Ah yes, my marionette, in a flowing purple satin gown, she has thrice circumnavigated *Eros,* and she commences her journey up Regent Street, looking this way and that and waving at the astonished public, and then, now this is the bit you'll have to work out, Len. You might have to raise the entrance to the *Café Royal* or something…she makes her entrance, where I am suspended in the rafters to meet my giant alter ego. What fun it will be! Now…"

Pandora is astonished to hear Len clear his throat, in an "I want to say something" kind of way. She looks daggers at him. Uh-ho, Len won't be the first to be sacked from this campaign…nor the last! But Nice Neil attempts his rescue.

"Do let Len speak, Pandora dear, he does have a *very* important point to make!"

Exasperated, Pandora drums her Union Jack nail extensions on the coffee table. "Oh…alright then! What is it, Len? It better be worth it!"

Len is quite nervous under Pandora's withering and commanding stare.

"Well, it's just that…I think you need to know…that, well…" Len is red in the face as he gulps down some water from the glass before him.

"Spit it out, Len! We haven't all day!" Pandora is fiddling with a tress of her brilliant blue hair, which I've noticed is something she does when she is suffering fools not very gladly.

"It's just that, well, the *Café Royal*, Pandora…"

"Len. I am not going to listen to you telling me it's booked up! For some silly little pop star tart or some revolting, over-paid ignorant footballer. I am PM Poste! If I want the *Café Royal*, I will fucking well *have* the *Café Royal*!"

"It's not booked, Pandora, it's…"

"Well fucking well book it then, Len! If you are going to cheese-pare me on the costs of this important function, I will have no hesitation in leaving Coffee Press *and* your two bit event management company, *Twi-shite Productions,* or whatever you call yourselves!" Everybody laughs, me the loudest! We all know that Len's company is called *Twilight Productions* but Pandora always calls it *Twi-shite Productions*! Len has to laugh as well, even though it's obvious he doesn't find it funny.

"No, it's not booked up, Pandora, it's.."

"Well what is it, Len? What shitty excuse are you going to come up with? Tell me! I'm all ears!" She raises a sarcastic eyebrow at Arne, who nods back at her, gravely.

"It's closed, Pandora. The *Café Royal* closed in 2008." Len looks down at his scruffy cords, and reaches for his water again. There is silence for quite a time. Pandora's neck is going red.

"Neil! Did you know this? We went there on our wedding anniversary not two years ago. Are you sure, Len?"

"We dined there over five years ago, darling Pandora," replies Neil, placing a calming hand on his ex-wife's knee. "I'm afraid that Len is quite right…and to be honest, dear…it had gone to seed rather."

"Who closed it? WHO?" Pandora is trembling with rage. "Oscar Wilde was always there. George Bernard Shaw. Liz Taylor. The Al-Fayeds. Oh, Neil,

I *so* wanted my party to be at the *Café Royal*. Can't you open it again, or something? Just for one marvellous last night, before they knock it down?"

"I believe that it is to be turned into a luxury hotel, PM," contributes a woman called Renee, who I think is from Belgium. She is always nibbling the end of her pencil and wears thick designer specs, even though I suspect she doesn't need specs at all.

"Well, I want a night there. As soon as it opens. Make a note, girl."

"I have taken the liberty of inquiring after another venue, PM," trembles Len. "Which I think might be eminently suitable, given your desire for a giant marionette to be present."

"This had better be good, Len. I am *very* disappointed that the *Café Royal* has closed. I still don't believe it. OK, out with it. Where? *The Pig and Whistle* in Fulham, I expect!" Everybody laughs again, as Pandora makes a 'pooh-poohing' expression with her vermillion mouth.

"Ahaha, yes, no. Not a pub, PM, not a pub. He-har. But you see, for most venues, we would not be able to gain entrance for a six metre puppet! So, I thought…"

"What did you think, Len. What? Out with it, man!"

"St. Pancras Station." Oh fucking hell, Len. We all wince, audibly and loudly. Everyone, and I mean everyone, is inspecting their shoes, well aware of the impending storm that will blow Len away. Pandora rises to her feet.

"St. Pancras Station. You want to organise the soon-to-be world's best-selling authoress's London Party….AT A FUCKING RAILWAY STATION??!"

If Len was on a bike, he would be pedalling furiously backwards and be in Notting Hill in seconds. He has taken both hands off the handlebars and is cowering and waving them in submission before Pandora, who is towering above him, like an angry Boadicea. "Just an idea, PM, just an idea. It's the height you see…"

"WELL IT'S A FUCKING STUPID IDEA, LEN! OH I KNOW! WHY NOT CLAPHAM BUS STATION? OR LUTON AIRPORT? OR TILBURY DOCKS? OR…OR…A FUCKING SEWER!!"

Everyone is wreathed in Pandora's wrath. We are sort of doing a pathetic group simpering/tittering/grovelling combo. Len looks as though he may be about to get his coat. Taxi for Len, everyone!

"Actually, darling, Len may be on to something." It's Neil, sitting forward in thought, his elbows on his knees and his hands bridged together, forefingers at his nose. "Consider. St. Pancras isn't any old railway station these days. The gateway to Europe, Pandora, think of that as a sales metaphor. And a marvellous concourse. That lovely, huge statue. Then, there's a smaller one of Betjeman himself. And the great clock. Don't you remember, darling, when we took the boys on the ski train? There is a pub there, also *The Betjeman*, I think. And no problem with getting your puppet in, Pandora. Let's at least consider it, dear heart?"

Pandora slumps theatrically at Neil's feet, and puts her thumb in her mouth, resting her shimmering head on his bony knee. She has this really fetching little girl's voice that she does sometimes; she does it in the *Pink Room* for me every now and then, usually when she has exceeded my pain threshold agreement.

"Bwut Neewl, I *tho* wanted the Café Woyal!"

Neil strokes her bright blue head, consolingly. "I know you did, my darling, I know you did. But do you know, I think Len's idea will be even better than the Café Royal?"

"Doo yoo, dahling?" She is making big cow's eyes at her ex-husband.

"I do, dear."

Len has temporarily taken his hand off the grubby mackintosh hung on the back of his chair, and appears to be quietly hyperventilating.

"Arne, what doo yoo fink of vis wailway idea?" Her thumb his still stuck fetchingly fast between her luscious lips.

"Security may be a problem. Concourse will need an area to be sealed off. Surveillance required from above and the shopping concourse below. I can recce if you wish, PM."

"And Mee-lad, what doo yoo fink of vis wailway idea?" Dang it, got my souchong cup and saucer mid-lift and they start to rattle. Think fast. Don't think I've ever been to St. Pancras Station, not since it was re-developed anyway. Waterloo, that's my portal to London. That's a good station, why not there? Liverpool Street, that's pretty impressive. What are the other stations in *Monopoly*? I have a vague idea where Marylebone Station is. But where the Hell is Fenchurch Street Station?

"Perhaps we can have your marionette at *all* the London railway stations, PM? That would be really good publicity. You know, like Fenchurch Street Station, and er, like, Paddington?"

Pandora rises to her feet, and walks around the backs of her advisors, including mine. It sort of reminds me of that scene in *Once Upon a Time in America* when Robert Di Niro walks around a table of gangsters and then beats the fuck out them all with a baseball bat. With Pandora, that could *so-o* happen.

"Alright. Take me there. Now. I want to see St. Pancras Station. And if I don't like it Len, you are fucking fired."

THE PM POSTE ENTOURAGE are in the *Sir John Betjeman* pub, and Len is getting the drinks in. Len is a very relieved man, and he can't stop laughing nervously. Me and Arne go and help him carry the drinks, as it's obvious his trembling hands would spill them all over the place.

"I LOVE IT. I LOVE IT. I LOVE IT. I LOVE IT. I LOVE IT!!! Neil, you are such a clever man." Pandora is smiling radiantly in a very low-cut mustard coloured top, as she nestles up to her ex. "Sometimes, I don't know why I left you…oh thank you, Arne…oh, I just remembered why I left you, Neil! Hahahahahahahaha!!" Pandora is looking Arne's svelte figure up and down as she laughs at her quick joke, and even though it is at his expense, nice Neil seems to find it funny too. Arne doesn't find it funny, but then, Arne never finds anything funny. Well that's not strictly true. When we were playing darts together in his summer house, I went to pull my three arrows out of the board, and he chucked a throwing knife into the treble twenty which just missed my thumb. He bared his teeth and let out a sort of a howl. It was an unusual laugh, but definitely a laugh. Me and the lads reckon you can tell a lot about people from their laugh. Horrible people often have a horrible laugh, and beautiful people often have a beautiful laugh. Like Pandora - she has a really nice laugh, like quite a deep bell that can turn really high. Len has a sneaky laugh, he is quite sneaky. Renee has a false laugh, and she is quite false. You can change your laugh though, like a fashion laugh? Me and the lads have quite high-pitched ones at the moment, like hyenas. And you can copy laughs, you know, like someone's laugh you like. I have kind of adopted Muttley's laugh, off *Dastardly and Muttley*? But your natural laugh, when something really makes you laugh all of a sudden, that's like your unique laughter fingerprint. That's the one you need to properly suss out someone's character. So maybe I'm being harsh on Renee, maybe when she's home with her husband she might have a nice laugh, but probably I'll never hear it.

Anyway, fortunately for Len, Pandora likes his idea of using the concourse of St. Pancras as a venue for her big party, and so do I. What a great space. Pandora has told me to work closely with Len and *Twi-shite Productions* setting it all up, so I am going to be based with him in his office in Holborn for a bit, so that should be fun. What a brilliant party this is going to be! Maybe I will blag a ticket for my sister Naz, after all.

IT'S AMAZING WHAT YOU GET USED TO. My regular visits to the Pink Room of Pain get weirder each time, but somehow being issued with a uniform in Mr Benn's changing room, followed by some form of painful humiliation is becoming 'what we do'. I am sort of hoping Pandora gets bored and we revert to a more mainstream sexual relationship, but there is no sign of that happening. On my last visit, I thought there was a sign of that happening, when Pandora told me not to bother with a uniform and to get naked. But she did bother, and came out of The Goddess Chamber forty-five minutes later dressed up in game-shooting tweeds and wellington boots, with a toy rifle slung across her shoulder (at least I thought it was a toy). I then had to roll about in a paddling pool full of coconut body butter, which Pandora waded into to ensure that I was fully slathered, by rolling me about with the sole of her wellingtons. I was then leashed and led hound-like to a wire cage made of chicken wire, with a chute at the top, where I stood, wondering what might be about to pour down on me. I was quite surprised to soon discover that it was a great white cloud of chicken feathers, which stuck very effectively to the body butter. Pandora was mightily pleased with my 'butter and feathering' and she had to sit down for a while, as she was laughing at me so much. Then she released me from my coop, issued me with a plastic beak (with an elastic cord to hold it in place over my mouth and nose) and a pair of safety goggles for my eyes (she being contractually obliged to uphold my safety) - and then starting shooting at me.

The pellets she fired from the rifle smarted a bit as I ran about squawking with my hands over my tackle, but when she changed weapons to a paintball gun, the pain level shot from a '3' to a '2' and the chicken became a feathered commando, leaping and rolling to avoid the splattering paintballs. Me and the lads like a game of paintball, and if you get shot with one, they leave a bruise even through camo-gear. Naked, I discovered you *really* know about them. I was doing pretty well avoiding Pandora's aim, until I set off The Man-Trap, which mercifully did not sever my leg due to extensive foam padding, but it did hold me fast, putting the hunted at the mercy of the hunter.

"SQUAWK FOR MERCY, FOWL!" Pandora had commanded. My subsequent mercy-squawks were predictably in vain, as she shot me repeatedly in the bum from point-blank range, easily exceeding the previously most painful experience in the Pink Room (the Rough Rider helter-skelter). I was a pathetic sight as she released me from the jaws of the trap - a groaning, paint-spattered, dishevelled, half-dead chicken-man. I was grateful for my hosing down, which washed all the feathers away, to reveal measle-like spots from the pellet gun and boil-like welts all over my arse from the paintballs.

I managed to have a bit of a laugh about 'Chicken Shoot' in Pussy's Bar over a rum cocktail, though Pandora was doing most of the laughing. Before very long, she was thrusting my greasy face up her tweed skirt to perform my oral duty, which to be honest, is becoming a tiny bit dull. Still no sign of my eager gentleman seeing any 'Pink Room' action. Well, apart from last week, when he got a wooden clothes peg clipped to him, as part of a process whereby one hundred pegs were slowly attached to various parts of my anatomy. After that, I had to hang on tight to a clothes line in an extremely powerful wind-tunnel. It was interesting how the pegs pinged off one by one, and I had the vague sensation of weightlessness. Dressed ominously as a buxom washer-woman wearing *Marigold* gloves, Pandora then suspended me in 'The Trouser Press' where I endured the strange sensation of my lower half being lightly steamed and pressed, whilst my upper half, dangling vertically from the waist, was tickled with a peacock feather.

Whilst I can't claim to be actively enjoying my varied experiences in the Pink Room, they are more than compensated by my thoroughly hectic, well remunerated and enjoyable days at Len's office in Holborn followed by more work and leisure in the company of Pandora, Neil, Arne, and their many visitors at Greveldon Terrace. Sometimes one, two or even all three of Pandora's sons come over for dinner, they are all very posh and polite lads. I feel a bit weird being only three years older than the eldest one, Jasper. I wonder if he knows if I am his mother's love-gimp? If he does, he doesn't look as though he cares much, but then, he doesn't look as though he cares about much at all. He listens with glassy eyes and a sad smile and says unconvincingly that he is looking forward to going up to Cambridge next year. The youngest one is fourteen and is called Seth and he is hyperactive. Seth makes me laugh – he is always knocking things over and then apologising and then doing it again, driving Pandora nuts. She always seems pleased when she puts him in a taxi after dinner; I understand that their boys live with Neil's elderly mother in Hampstead these days, where they are all at private school. The middle one, Tyler, we don't see much, as he is a junior chess champion and travels all over the country winning chess matches. The first time I met him he challenged me to a game of chess and he won in six moves. Not that I'm any good at chess, but that was a complete embarrassment. Tyler didn't seem much interested in me after that, apart from telling me the room that I sleep in is "his" and that he thinks Arne is a vampire.

IT'S FRIDAY NIGHT, AND EVERYONE IS EXCITED about the Opening Ceremony for the Olympics just a few miles away from where Len and I are working round the clock on Pandora's party, which is happening tomorrow evening. Pandora and Neil are in fact attending the Opening

Ceremony this evening, but I am receiving a torrent of texts from her asking how the preparations are going. I tell her to relax and leave things to me and enjoy the evening, but she is ignoring me, and wants an update on the marionette. She may well ask, because we are having some problems. We have planned to do a dry run tonight around midnight when the station is quiet, but the people who have built 'Big Pandora' have been moaning that they were not given enough time or budget, and that they are behind schedule. I have been tough with them though, and fearing a long night, have booked me and Len into the St. Pancras Hotel.

It's a fantastic newly-refurbished hotel and they have upgraded me to a 'superior' room and I grab a nap for a couple of hours. My alarm goes off at 10pm, and I have a quick pint with Len in the *Betjeman Arms* which has become our local. The plan is to get 'Big Pandora' to walk through the big arch and for me to role-play 'Little Pandora'. The trapeze guys we've hired turn up on time, and start rigging up the wires, under the watchful eye of the station manager. These guys are brilliant and it all goes like clockwork. It's really good fun swinging about in a harness in front of the big clock. They gently lower me to the ground, and I reckon Pandora is going to be fine with the routine we've worked up. But when Big Pandora turns up, we are all in for a bit of a downer.

"What the fuck is that coming through the arch?" says one of the wire guys, looking spooked.

"My God," gasps Len. "That looks nothing like Pandora. Or any woman, come to that. It doesn't even look like a bloke!"

A kind of mutant robot creature, in half metal/half human form, comes lurching and scraping along with a bunch of guys in a sort of cycling car behind it. It looks like a zombie, or what does it remind me of? That's it… Robocop! An apologetic looking hippy type is shambling along backwards ten metres in front of it with some kind of remote control device, but he keeps shaking his long greasy hair in frustration.

"Dougal, what the heck! This is nowhere near ready! It's supposed to look like PM Poste, not a bleeding cyborg." Len is lighting up a fag, despite this is a no smoking station.

"Yeah man, look, we are having to use a base we just got back from a technology fair in Copenhagen, and I don't know what they've been doing with him, but he's totally fucked up. Look, every time I tell him to blink his eyes - well, his eye - he raises his hand. I press the hand control and he starts bobbing his head about. I mean, we are going to have to totally re-process this version."

"Never mind about his spastic twitching," I say, "How are you going to make this heap of shit resemble one of the most beautiful women in England by tomorrow?"

"Who is this dude, Len? Does he know anything about what we do? Or how we do what we do? Or how we…"

"Dougal, this is Milad Brown, PM Poste's media and events advisor, we have been working closely together on this gig. I have to say that we both expected Big Pandora to be more or less ready? Milad has all the big newspapers coming to this event, and you are going to look very bad indeed if your marionette isn't right."

"Oh, fucking hell, even his walking action is messed up. Look, he's dragging his back foot!" moans Dougal. The one-eyed cyborg man is limping along, looking like he's got a club foot. Perhaps he was dressed up as Lord Byron in Copenhagen.

"Look Dougal," I tell him sternly, "Stop this contraption right now." I've learned to be quite assertive under Pandora's excellent tutelage. Well, not assertive with her obviously, but with people like this bedraggled hippy. I get in his face, like Pandora taught me. I have to endure his garlic breath, but it's the only way.

"There is obviously no point in a dress rehearsal tonight, is there? You need to guarantee me that you will be back here in twenty-four hours with a functional and beautiful Big Pandora, or you won't get a fucking penny, mate. "

Dougal tries the laughing thing, but I am on his body language. I don't laugh. I don't smile. I am Arne. In an Arne suit.

"Hey, chill out, man…we do 'last minute' all the time. Our people are working round the clock on the Pandora shell and the robe is done. We are having to order a lot of extra silicone for her boobs and ass, but it is on its way by lorry tonight. She is a big girl, and no mistake!"

What? What? What's he saying about Pandora? My heroine, my mentor, my...? I don't have a temper usually, but I am kind of wigging out here! My ears are burning, I've probably gone Bootle red, and my instinct is to punch this insolent fucker in his dried up mouth. I settle for a two handed shove into his bony shoulders, and he reels back towards the one-eyed cyborg man and drops his remote control box. A he reels and totters, he is staring back me in shock, but I am on him again and shouting in his weasel face.

"FEELING LUCKY, PUNK? ARE YOU? FEELING LUCKY?" Why I go into *Dirty Harry* mode at this juncture, I am not altogether sure. Me and Sparks do it quite a lot when we have a bit of a scrap. We had a water pistol fight at the flat a while ago and I leapt over the sofa and grabbed him and then knelt on his shoulders and disarmed him. I was holding a 44 Magnum water pistol to his head, but unlike in the film, Sparks could clearly see that my gun was loaded, as it was made of see-through blue plastic. Anyway, I shot him in the hair before running for it down West Street.

I am shoving Dougal again, and I am really pumped up, shouting my Dirty Harry stuff into his creased up face. I push him so hard this time that he staggers back and kind of crumples onto his arse, and sits cross-legged in bewilderment. Len has come and thrown his arms around me, like a footie team member trying to get me away from trouble before I get a red card. I am the Mario Balotelli of St. Pancras.

"Jesus! All I said was that Big Pandora is big! How is that a problem, man?" It's not a bad point, really, that Dougal is making. But I still feel his comment was offensive and derogatory, and I'm not having it.

"You just do your job, mate! Keep your smutty obscene potty mouth out of it, right?"

"Obscene?" Dougal sits shaking his head, as if a great wrong has been done to him. Which it might have been. But he has bigger problems looming behind him. Len is going mental.

"ROLL, DOUGAL! DOUGAL, BLOODY WELL ROLL, MAN!! YOU ARE UNDER ITS' FEET!"

But the dozy hippy just sits looking baffled and wronged, just as the one-eyed cyborg man lurches onto him. He is quite lucky really. I think if the robot would have been fully operational, its left foot might have raked up Dougal's back and got all tangled in his hair, and it could have got very messy indeed. Maybe even squashed him flat. But Cyborg Man is doing a kind of crazy wobbly dance and he kicks Dougal in the arse with his swinging foot and in the same motion, lifts him to his feet. Dougal scampers forwards, picks up the remote and frantically hits a series of keys. This closes Cyborg Man down, who seems to sigh as he freezes, in a sort of disco dance position.

"You fucking mentalist! Who do you think you are, pushing me about like that? You should be ashamed of yourself! Right, I am off for a fat spliff, and then we can talk about this!"

I am ashamed of myself. In stark contrast to Clint in *Dirty Harry*, who has a right laugh at the 'punk' he fazes out and gets arrested - I burst into tears.

HALF AN HOUR LATER, we are all having a toke on Dougal's spliff as we sit on the steps below the St. Pancras Hotel. Len has done the diplomatic envoy routine, and I am apologising profusely.

"I can't say sorry enough times, Dougal. That's not me, it really isn't. It must be the stress, or something. I don't behave like that normally."

"It's cool, little brother," reassures Dougal, patting me on the shoulder and handing me the joint. "This is a pressure game we are in. People can behave in strange ways when they are under pressure. But out of adversity comes friendship. Out of negatives come positives. Out of chaos comes harmony. Out of..." I might be in apology mode, but I don't have to listen to his hippy-dippy clap trap as penance, surely?

"Well, I think I'll turn in, guys, I obviously need a good night's sleep." I rise and stretch in the chilly air. "Sorry once more...to both of you. It won't happen again, I can assure you of that."

I shake hands with Len, and Dougal gives me an unexpected hug. "Out of enmity comes friendship, man. Out of hate comes love. Out of..."

"Yes, well, goodnight gentlemen. See you both in the morning." I extricate myself from Dougal's patchouli embrace, and plod up the steps, feeling weary, slightly stoned, and baffled with myself. Under ten minutes later I am in bed, naked and asleep, too tired even to have brushed my teeth, thereby breaking one of my gang's Ten Commandments (Number Five) - *"No matter what thy state may be, nor how fatigued, thou shalt brush thy teeth before kip."*

I AM HAVING THIS AMAZING DREAM. One of those realistic ones, except it's ultra-real? 'Big Pandora' is ready; she is incredible. Hippy Dougal has done a fantastic job. She isn't wearing a purple gown, in fact she isn't wearing anything at all. Her amazing statuesque form is hovering above me, her breasts pendulous against my chest, her blue hair falling dark around my neck. She seems to be pushing me, urgently, insistently.

"Move up, darling. I'm knackered. And don't bother me for sex. I've just had a huge row with Neil and I cannot be in the same house as him. I came to see you, Mee-lad. And I need a big huggy buggy!"

"Huuuh….Pandora?" It's not a dream, it's bloody well real! We are in bed together again, at night, butt naked, and she is in my arms as I give her the 'huggy buggy' she needs.

"Oh alright, you can give me a quick fuck if you like. I know you men can't sleep without one. I can feel your pesky little man pressed hard up against me. But you'll have to be quick." Huh? Is this the moment I've been waiting for? The consummation of my…my feelings for Pandora? Certainly the pocket rocket down below is up for some. But hang on… what about contraceptionals? My unopened box of johnnies are in the bedside cabinet at Greveldon Terrace. How was I to expect hot Pandora action under the gothic eaves of the St. Pancras Hotel?

"Er, I would really love to, PM, but, erm, no condoms I'm afraid?"

"What! No condoms? Well, Arne always has some…but he is visiting friends in Finchley and I hesitate to have him bring us some. Call room service. They can usually help."

Room service? Aren't they for like, a sandwich…or when you need an iron? Is she joking with me? I know she has a wkd sense of humour! I look at her beautiful face in the reflected light of sleeping London and her eyes are closing. Maybe she isn't joking – and I don't have much time before she is slumbering!

"Hi, yes…Reception? Yeah, good evening to you, too. Yep, Room 652… Mr Brown? Erm, I have a slightly unusual request, erm, could you possibly supply me with a condom?" Dammit, the night porter guy is from Morocco or somewhere, and he isn't getting 'condom'. He thinks I'm saying 'condor'…no I don't want a giant bird of prey or a crap cigar, thanks.

"No, CONDOM. Condom. The popular contraceptive device. For the male member. You know, a happy hat, a jimmy cap, a nodder, a raincoat, erm…a rubber johnny?" Thank Christ. He knows rubber johnny, and he is emitting an inappropriate squealing laugh.

"You do? Ah, that's great. Erm…three? Great, thank you so much." OK, condominiums are on their way up. Now, just got to keep the sublime object of my desire awake.

"So, how was the Opening Ceremony, PM? The bits I caught on TV looked terrific!"

"It was awful, Milad." She yawns, but props herself up on one elbow. "That's what I had the big row with Neil about. It was all totally lefty. I knew when they appointed that communist, Jimmy Boyle, this would happen. You should have seen it, honestly. It started with sheer nonsense about the destruction of England's green and pleasant land, I mean, really. Just because he is from Burnley or somewhere up north - yes, we know it's horrid up there, but in the south, the beautiful countryside is still unspoiled. I don't know how dear Kenneth put up with that useless script. He was playing Abraham Lincoln, I think it had something to do with that marvellous vampire film. And then there were all these nurses bouncing around on beds, administering sick children. Shameless lefty NHS propaganda, Milad. Why should I support all these malingering people who can't afford to go private? The taxes I pay, all wasted on these scroungers. And his choice of music, honestly! The Jubilee Concert was so nice, wasn't it? Sir Elton John, Stevie Wonder, The Nutty Boys, Cheryl Cole, dear Robbie. Well, *this* was the opposite. All the horrid music from down the ages. And my God, you'd think the whole country was black. I mean, I am sorry, Milad, you know that I am the least racist person I know, well, I wouldn't be in be in this bed with you, would I, for a start. But all that rap hop music. It wasn't representative, at all. And there was this little horrid house playing annoying music and then inside was a computer programmer? Completely bonkers, dahling! And completely wrong! And to put the cap on it, well, I do not know how Her Maj got suckered into it. You can see how much power the lefties still have, at the BBC and trades unions and so on. They made Her Maj do this stupid film with James Bond - as if she would want to jump out of a helicopter at her age! Well, they made her do it. Heartless lefties. And she did not look happy, Milad. I was watching her through my little field glasses. Not happy. I'm very surprised she made it down in one piece. And just when you thought things could not get worse - they did! That idiotic Mr Bean *ruined* Chariots of Fire, and I was so looking forward to Sir Simon Rattle. To be honest, I think Sir Paul knew the game was up by the time he got on to sing *Jude*. He looked quite embarrassed. I was watching him through my little field glasses."

I am keeping one ear on Pandora's thoughtful critique and another on the room door. I am assuming they will discreetly push an envelope under the door. I am wrong. There is a hearty knock. And then another. I dash to the bathroom and wrap a towel around me; Pandora is still in full outrage mode.

"Neil actually *liked* it! No, *loved* it! Oh God, he was laughing away at Mr Bean, grooving around to Dozy Rascal or whatever the *fuck* he calls himself. He actually cried at one point! I mean, cried with emotion, rather than grief. Which I felt like doing, I can tell you. Now, I <u>know</u> why I left him, Milad. He's obviously unravelled completely, poor man. Oh God, I need a fag. The taxi man gave me one. Where's my bag?"

Pandora stands naked at the window she has just opened and she gazes magisterially down the Euston Road. However, I am conscious she is smoking in a non-smoking room, as I open the door a fraction, with the security chain in place. I see grinning long white teeth and big brown beady eyes through the crack in the door. It appears to be the front desk Moroccan himself.

"Thanks buddy," I whisper. "How much do I owe you?"

"Sign please, sir. Sign please." What? Sign?

"Er, can't I just give you some cash?"

"No, sir, sign. Please." Fuck's sake. I can't sign a chit though the security chain gap, so I close the door, take off the chain and open it again.

"What? No sorry, erm, Mohamed, you can't come in! My lady friend is erm…naked!" Cheeky bastard, he is on his way into our room as I shove him back! He is having a right beady look around as I manoeuvre him into the corridor and sign his blasted chit. Ten fucking quid? No way! For three assorted condoms in a St. Pancras Hotel envelope? Clearly, dressed in a bath towel which is about to give way in a hotel corridor, I am in no situation to argue, and I lean the chit against the wall and sign it. Mohamed (I know he is called Mohamed because of his name badge – unless he is wearing someone else's of course) is sniffing at the door, and I quickly close it.

"No smoking in room, sir. Big penalty fine." He is grinning still. "Two hundred. You give me fifty cash now, nothing said, sir." The red mist which rose when Dougal insulted Pandora's fine frame is rising before me again. I feel like grabbing this guy's scrawny chicken's neck and throttling him. But I don't. I am fucking well locked out now. And anyway, how is he going to prove the smoking thing? His word against mine. Likely illegal immigrant, against a British-born citizen of growing repute.

"Shall I get key, sir?"

"No you bloody won't. Now stand back." I knock lightly at the door, and again. As I wait, I inspect the condom packets in the unsealed envelope. These are not my usual brand. I usually go for *Durex Elite* (purple packet - ultra-fine with extra lube for heightened sensitivity). In here, we have two Durex ones, *Perfomax Intense* which according to the packet is *"designed for mutual climax"*; a banana flavour Durex *Fruit*; and a Trojan *Magnum XL*. And it looks like the Trojan has been partly opened.

"Where did these come from, Mohamed?"

"Left behind in rooms, sir. We keep for emergency supply. Like you. For emergency fucking." God, this guy is annoying, come on Pandora. Suddenly, the door opens wide, and Pandora is standing there in all her naked glory, reeking of fag smoke. I swear that Mohamed's eyes are boggling in his skull, and suddenly, he is no longer grinning.

"What is going on, dah-ling, I really must get some sleep, you know. Who is this little man?"

"Er, this is Mohamed, PM. He wouldn't know who you are. But he is just threatening me with a two hundred pound fine for smoking in the room."

"Oh, now, he wouldn't want to do that, I am sure. How do you do, Mohamed?" The dazed Moroccan is shaking her hand. "Now, you don't get many of these to the pound, do you? Do you like white women, Mohamed?" She has cupped her hands under the volume of her breasts and presses them together. Mohamed could not be more hypnotised if he was watching a dancing cobra in the market square in Marrakesh.

"Now I'd say an eyeful of these is worth well over two hundred measly pounds, wouldn't you darling?" The dazed Moroccan is nodding in agreement. "Jolly good, now off you trot you naughty little man. Not a word, darling, or I'll have you thrown out of the country, you peeping Tom!"

Mohamed obeys, and walks away as if in a sleeping trance, and we are back in the room, both of us laughing. I cannot believe how brazen Pandora can be, sometimes. Well why not? If you've got in, flaunt it! Fuck modesty! To Hell with humility!

"What are you going to do to me, you bad boy? Are you going to fuck me silly, darling? Is that what you are going to do? Well, we had better put one of these on you, because I don't want to spawn any little Milads, now do I?"

I am still not especially averse to the idea of little Milads (or little Pandoras?) but Pandora is on her knees working my eager gentleman to full attention, and she deftly opens one of the condom packets and furls it down my length. But the Trojan *Magnum XL* dangles like a bedraggled flag at half-mast.

"Ah, this one is a bit big for you. Let's try this one instead, shall we? Oooh, banana! How exotic." Amidst the reek of cigarette smoke and amyl acetate (I remember that is the principal active ingredient in bananas from GCSE biology) she leads me to the bed, and spreads her thighs, opening her inner goddess to me. I don't hang about, I plunge my banana rod right in up to his hilt. Hmmm, quite roomy in Pandora's IG! I pump away, our mouths meeting, and I suddenly wish I'd remembered to brush my teeth, I must have serious dragon's breath. She doesn't seem to mind, her acrid tongue working deep into my mouth.

"Do me dah-ling. Have your wicked way with me."

So here I am, lads. I am thrusting away at PM Poste. Milad Brown - super stud. She is yawning a bit, as you might expect, after the long day she has had.

"Come for me, Mee-lad. Fill me. Fill me to the brim." I feel like I may be some way from my ecstasy, but as she is looking at the chunky watch about her wrist, I try hard for her.

"Oooh, oooh!" I go. "So good, Pandora, so good." It's a funny thing, the male ejaculation. I find that I have to find something super-sexy to blow my load, and I focus on her rolling breasts and rhythmic hips. For no reason, Arne comes into my head, no doubt fast asleep in Finchley. Get the fuck out of my head, Arne - not now! I feel myself becoming flaccid. Maybe I should fake an orgasm, I'm not that bothered, really, I want to cuddle up next to her and stroke her hair. But she comes to my rescue, and starts talking dirty, I like it when she does that.

"Ride me, Mee-lad. Ride me hard. Do what you will with me, you dirty little man." I like this idea. I have often thought whilst she is hammering away at my buttocks with a table tennis bat or a riding crop, how I'd like to do the same to her. I give one of her buttocks, both of them wobbling under my thrusts, a little slap.

"Oh, you are so mean to me, Milad. Please don't hurt me, I am so defenceless and open to your every whim." Oh yeah, baby. I give her other cheek a good slap, harder than the first one. Arne is banished, and the flagpole is resumed under its banana sheath. I am getting there, one more slap, and my thrusts are urgent. "Uhuhuhuhuh," I moan involuntarily. Through my half-closed eyes, she is checking her watch again, and it is time…"ah…ah…ah….here we go…ah…ah….ahhhhhhhhhhhhhh!"

My passion is released and I fall, spent, to her bosom, my temples crashing and my breath panting. I feel her wriggling free of my shrinking gentleman, and she is inspecting the contents of the condom tip.

"Hmmm, not much, but well done. I don't like it when men pretend to come in me. They do you know, Milad, and it won't do. I see I have pleased you. Now *please* let me sleep. But go and brush your teeth first, your breath is quite rank."

I haul myself up, satisfied and stupefied, and by the time I return from the bathroom where I catch a silly smirk on my face reflected in the huge mirror, Pandora is blissfully asleep. I know this because she is making rasping sounds from the back of her nose. It's the same noise Sparks makes when he is snoring, but somehow it sounds sweet coming from her nostrils. I spoon myself into the rapture of her back and cup my hand around her breast. I don't sleep much during the night, but who would want to? I have Pandora Poste in the palm of my hand, and I have had her. I have *had* PM Poste. I think about texting Sparky but it's getting a bit late, and tomorrow…is going to be another long day.

IT'S THE DAY OF THE PARTY, and everyone is a mixture of nervousness and excitement. I am at the station concourse early, with Arne, Tank, and Scarface Bob. We parade our turf in our *Matrix* gear; I have permanently shiny shoes like Arne, now – my latest gift from Pandora and flown in from Milan. God only knows what they cost. We are looking good in our suits; apart from Tank who is a bit grunge and is wearing a faded *Nirvana* T-shirt which he often chews the collar of, cargo shorts and a pair of battered Converse basketball boots. Arne is checking the hoists and winches left by the trapeze guys - Tank is going to be Little Pandora later this morning and that should give them a real test. I grab a vanilla latté at my favourite coffee shop and sipping it, circle Betjeman's bronze with Bob, who reads aloud in his Norfolk accent the circular inscription around the statue base. Bob hails originally from Swaffham, which is cool because we are having a book-signing there soon, when *The Matrix* tour heads east.

"And-in-the-shadowless-unclouded-glare-deep-blue-above-us-fades-to-whiteness-where-a-misty-sea-line-meets-the-wash-of-air," he reads slowly.

"What does that mean, Mil?" He takes a considerable swig from his *Red Bull* can.

"Ah, it's just poetry, Bob. *Cornish Cliffs*, it's called. He was very keen on Cornwall was old Sir John. " I don't tell him I'm a poet too, as I don't want him to think of me as a softie. Word has gotten around about me shoving Dougal about (minus my tears) and I've noticed that Arne and the boys have been giving me a lot of extra rrrr-espec' as a result.

I inspect the portly poet who points skywards and I notice the detail of the fallen hem of Betjeman's right trouser leg, as does Bob. "He needs a tuck in the trouser. Nifty Needles could sort that out for 'im."

We amble back to the much larger bronze statue that stands beneath the lovely Dent clock and the vaulted brick ceiling of the renovated station hotel, where our event is going to take place this evening. We circle Paul Day's huge bronze *Meeting Place* in some contemplation. I love this statue. I note the angle of the man's hand on the woman's lower back, and the sinew of her ankle as she stretches to kiss her lover. This could me and Pandora, I think to myself, re-united after she has returned from Paris or somewhere.

"Do you know, Miw," drawls arch-Londoner Tank, "Or stayed at vis 'otel in sixtay-fowar, when aw wus liwle. It wus cawled ve Midland 'Otel back ven. Steam trains camin' in and art awl noight, noisy as fack it was. And gwimy." I wonder how old Tank is. He certainly is a grizzled specimen - he could be over sixty. But then, age is nothing, I've decided. So what if Pandora is 24 years older than me? Love isn't bounded by age. I mentally note to write a poem entitled just that, or some version of it. But my poetic thoughts are interrupted by the *Mission Impossible* theme tune on my ultra-cool Arne-phone.

"Brown." I go, in my *Matrix* agent monotone. It's Dougal. He wants to know what colour Pandora's eyes are. Boy, he is cutting it fine.

"Brown. Yes, I heard you Dougal. They are brown. Her eyes are brown. Yes, like my surname. Hair colour? Bright red…no hang on, what am I saying, bright blue. Yes, you heard me, brilliant blue. Like a kingfisher. Now, when are you going to be here? OK, well don't be later, huh?" I snap my phone shut. *The Matrix* boys don't have time for pleasantries like goodbyes. I am getting a lot of texts from the lads. I have got them all invited to the party, but I am insisting they come smart. They are scrabbling around trying to borrow suits and Dean has even bought one from *Next*. Naz is coming too, and I'm getting Sparky to chaperone her.

We have booked out Searcy's Champagne Bar just down the concourse for the evening, and it is going to be rammed. Pandora wanted Paul McCartney to play, but Len had to persuade her to settle for Nigel Kennedy, who is coming to play his fiddle. I check on Searcy's where all is well, and Arne has commandeered a station office which sits right above the *Meeting Place* statue. I go up to meet him; he seems edgy, and he can't get the window to open as far as he wants.

"It's not ideal," he keeps repeating. He is taking some tubes out of what looks like a snooker case. Fuck! It's a sniper rifle! He snaps the pieces expertly into place and peers down the barrel into the milling travellers below us on the station concourse.

"I can't get a full vision arc from up here. I need a man on the ground wired up to guide me. Is your friend Spark available this evening?"

"Er, Sparky? Well yeah, he is supposed to be minding my sister Naz though?"

"Someone else can do that. Get him here early. I will need to brief him."

"Er…" I am about to use my new-found assertiveness to tell him that's not possible, but frankly, some people you don't disagree with, and Arne is one of those people. "OK, Arne, I'll see what I can do."

"Do better than that, Milad. I want him here at 5, latest. And go and make sure PM's suite is acceptable."

Sparky is naturally delighted with the news of his promotion from sis-minder to security, and Tils and Potts are escorting Naz instead. I had to be really careful with invites for the *County Times*, because I didn't want Sheila coming to upset Pandora. So I told Ray that he and his wife were invited, and Nat, but not to tell anyone else. That's how it is sometimes in journalism; you have to be discreet, to protect your sources. Economical with the truth, we call it.

I make sure that Pandora's suite at the hotel is full of her favourite flowers (pink roses) and a full case of *Krug* in the chiller. I set all the cards from well-wishers (most trying to blag an invite, which most don't get) on a chest of drawers. She is resting up for most of today in Holland Park, in order to be on best form this evening. From the window of her suite, I see Tank dangling from the rafters in the circus harness - he looks scared shitless.

"Fack! Ow down loike 'oights, do oi!" he is shouting, much to the laughter of everyone below.

I AM STARTING TO GET A TENSION MIGRAINE, and I haven't got my migraine tablets. I am getting flustered as the Dent clock strikes seven - everyone needs a piece of me, especially Sparky.

"Fuck off Sparky, can't you see I'm maxed out? And why did you have to wear that T-shirt, you daft prannet?"

"You said to come smart, fuck-face. Anyway get off your high horse, you're only a runner...*I* am security...you know what I've got in my pants. I could take you out just for fun, fartknocker." Sparky is wearing one of those T-shirts with a dinner jacket and bow tie printed on it - what a tosser. He is extending his expandable three-part steel friction lock crowd control baton and thrashing the air with it, nearly decapitating a Japanese tourist. He is especially excited about his hi-tech earpiece and microphone, with a hot link to the ghostly sniper above.

"Arne, take out the loser next to me in the expensive suit and purple silk tie. Shoot to kill. Repeat. Shoot to kill." For some odd reason, Arne seems to like Sparks, and I can see him above doing his sneer-howl laugh. I hope Arne doesn't really have to shoot anyone tonight. I have carefully chosen my tie from *Tie Rack* to match the amazing purple frock that Pandora will be wearing - she is currently in her suite with her 'Bonkers Babes' and having a really good time the last time I checked in.

"Aye-aye, look at the suit on this lad, Cynthia!" It's Ray, who does the cheek-pinching thing and then slaps me rally hard on the back. Since my various ordeals with Pandora, it doesn't hurt like it used to. "Eh, I'll bet you miss your old job on the West Sex Times, don't you, Milan?"

"Ray, Mrs…" I am struggling to remember Ray's surname, "Erm, Mrs Ray. Great to see you both. I see you've got a drink, let's get you some lobster canapés. Oi you! Over here, pronto!"

The canapé tray waiter either doesn't hear me or ignores me and glides by. "Ah never mind canapés, Milan. Cynthia wants to meet PM…any chance of an introduction later?"

"I'll do my best, Ray…oh, Nat! You look amazing!" Nat throws her long thin arms around my neck and gives me a big hug. Girls don't kiss when they have lipstick on. And she really does look amazing, she has one of those little things they wear at Ascot clipped in her hair, which is all tied up, fascinatings, they are called. And a long evening dress made of yellow silk, which matches her hair.

"Oh, Mil, I am so proud of you!! You are so…important, now!" She gives a little squeal and gives me another hug. She smells of delicate flowers, like freesias or night-scented stock.

"Thanks for coming Nat, but me, important? Nah, you know I'm just one of the team. And what about you…ace reporter? How is the training going?"

"Milan, I have to thank you for vacating your seat, boy," Ray answers for her. "We have a proper journalist on our books now," He winks. "Seriously, though, she is going to be good. And any time you fall on hard times, Milan, we can probably find a spot for you making her coffee."

"Oh Ray, you know I'll never be as good as Milad!" smiles Nat, reddening a bit.

"Don't you do yourself down, young lady. But alright, I might trust Milan with the Births and Deaths column!"

I smile…I do miss the banter of the office a bit. There is no bantering in Pandora's entourage - well, unless it is Pandora doing the bantering, of course. "Right, I've got to sort out the show, guys, have fun and see you later!"

The Big Pandora guys have thrown a huge sheet over the mannequin, and the idea is to uncover her, whilst we sneak Pandora into the harness and raise her aloft, without too many people noticing.

"Hey, Naz! I didn't recognise you, sis! Man, you look great…but that skirt is a bit high, can't you lower it a bit?!" I give my little sis a big hug, she seems very small in this huge city. "Hey, Potts, very smart mate, good effort!" I think Potts is wearing his dad's suit, which is a wee bit big for him, but he carries it off. Tils is looking fantastic as always, and I know I can trust her to look after my sis. "Right, see you later guys…are Dean and Rollo here yet?"

"They are running a bit late - as ever," goes Potts. "They were trying to sort Rollo out with a tuxedo from a charity shop."

"Uh huh, right. Oh Naz…don't drink too much fizz, or Mum will kill me!"

Tank appears from the growing throng of London's rich and influential, and takes my arm. "Miss Pandora wants to see you in 'er suite, Mil. Pwonto."

IN PANDORA'S SUITE, the Bonkers Babes are part-aying hard. Rihanna is booming out of an i-Block amp, and around eight ladies in tight dresses are shaking some serious booty. The fizz is flowing, and one of the Babes in a dangerously bulging red dress is scooping lines of coke on a dresser with a credit card, and she beckons me over.

"You're Milad incha? Orm Rebekkah, wiv two k's and un aich. Orve 'eard al about choo, I 'ave."

"Pleased to meet you, Rebekk-ah. The famous Bonkers Babes! I've heard a lot about you gals as well!"

"'ave yer?? Nar, watchoo 'eard, ven?" Rebekkah seems to be entering the paranoid stage of a coke bender, and I decline the line she offers me. It's not my drug, really. Me and the lads pick up a gram or two sometimes before we go on the lash, but we don't reckon it much. Evidently the Bonkers Babes do though, because they are jostling each other like pigs in a trough to get the fiver stuck up each of their noses on a line. It's quite a sight actually; seven derrieres of the curvaceous colourful kind bending over a table…it looks like seven beach balls of various colours bobbing about in a paddling pool.

"Ah, Mee-lad, my Mee-lad!" Wow. Pandora looks magnificent in her purple robe, but what's this…her hair has changed colour again…it's livid shiny green! But the marionette has blue hair! What to do?

"Well, how do I look, dear heart? You haven't said?"

"Ah, you look green, Pandora. I mean great - you look great! Erm, you changed your hair colour I see, nice, really nice. Just excuse me, I need to make a really quick call?"

"You can make your silly call in a moment. I want to introduce you to my Babes. BABES! Your attention please!"

The beach ball bums each swivel a head around, some still with rolled up fivers up one nostril. The odd thing is that all these ladies look like some kind of farm animal – I don't mean that in a nasty way, because some are quite good-looking – it's just that they do resemble seven different farm animals. There's a horse, a pig, a cow, a chicken, a goat, a goose, and a ferret. The paranoid coke woman looks like the ferret, only her eyes are bright purple instead of pink. The pig woman is extremely red in the face and leers at me.

"Coh! E's bit of awlright Pand. As 'e gotta a bravva?"

I'm thinking of the funniest thing I've ever heard, maybe it was when Rollo came up with the Spoonerist innuendo that I can never remember. Or more probably, something that my Dad said, trying to make me laugh at breakfast. But these ladies have, courtesy of the porcine wit with a fiver up her nose, just heard the funniest thing they have ever heard. In the current words of the chicken lady, they are all "wetting themselves". I am thinking of all the vernacular phrases to describe extreme laughter and they all (literally) apply here. One is 'laughing until she cries', another is 'splitting her sides' as the growing rent at the side of her bright blue dress attests; one is 'rolling around or ROFL-ing'; and they are all 'howling'. But things are getting surreal, as each woman's laugh matches her animal! I've never taken acid, but Sparky has, and he said it was the weirdest experience. He reckons time travels backwards and your mind rearranges. I feel like I'm on acid now, as the horse woman neighs, the pig snorts, the cow woman moos, the chicken woman clucks, the goat woman bleats, the goose woman honks, and the ferret woman kind of...hisses?

Pandora smiles indulgently, but does not join her flock in the laughing cacophony, but merely raises her hand like the conductor of a mad farmyard orchestra and lowers it, to quiet them. The laughter stops, leaving a residue of throaty coughing.

"You are awfully mischievous, Danee! This is my lovely Mee-lad, he is Persian, you see. And I am so-oo lucky to have found this beautiful young man. He is my press agent, and...so-oo much more!"

The lady animals are whooping, clapping and shouting what sounds to me like abuse, but I'm sure it might not be. Whooping never sounds right to me in Britain, I think the Americans invented it, but it hasn't imported very well. Sparky started doing it for a bit, but we stopped him, it didn't sound good at all.

"Er, hello! Nice to meet you all, ladies!" I have gone pretty Bootle-red, but I'm getting over the being too bashful these days, thanks to Pandora; I give the Bonkers Babes a presidential wave, and my George Clooney mock self-deprecating head-waggle. "Just a slight correction though, my Mum is from Persia, well, Iran, but I am British. Actually, I was born in the same town as PM...Horsham, West Sussex!"

Much to my surprise, the ladies are laughing again, certainly less raucously than after Danee's *bon mot*, but definitely laughing. I want to tell them - that wasn't actually a joke? Perhaps they simply laugh at everything? They have certainly knocked back a lot of fizz and white lines judging from the empty bottles and traces of powder everywhere. I want to try an experiment, and announce "Bradley Wiggins won the gold medal in the cycling time-trial this afternoon!" to see if they think that is funny too, but before I can contemplate doing so, my phone is buzzing, and it's Len, who I need to talk to about green hair.

"Do excuse me, ladies; lovely to meet you all, and see you all later on, I hope you enjoy yourselves!"

"OH, WE WILL!" they chorus, and the scary laughter begins again.

Pandora throws both her arms around me; I can see she has been at the coke too, as there is a spot of white powder at the end of her nose. She is whispering in my ear. "See you downstairs, dah-ling. Just give me the call when to descend. I love you, my dah-ling boy!"

Momentarily, I am frozen to the spot. OK, she is a bit pissed and wired, but she just said the magic words. PM Poste loves Milad Brown. Repeat, PM Poste loves Milad Brown. I feel like my insides are melting.

"I love you too, Pandora," I whisper back, like a love-reflex, and I extend my arms around her waist and give her a loving squeeze. She pushes me playfully away…my legs are no longer that steady and I bump into the goose woman, who is wearing bright orange lipstick on her bill.

"Oh, I am sorry, er…?"

"Giselle. I'm from Luton."

"Nice to meet you Giselle. Look forward to honking to you - I mean speaking to you – properly, later on. Bye, ladies!" I wave as I take my leave, but as ever, Pandora has the last word as I reach the door.

"Actually, Mee-lad, *do-oo* you have a brother? A twin would be abso-loootely marvellous!"

I am about to inform her that I don't have a bother, nor a twin, but I do have my sister Naz, who is actually here at the party tonight. But before I can do that, the farm laughter cacophony rises to full volume again, and I quickly take my leave of Pandora's suite, wearing as gracious a smile as I can muster. And it spreads as I walk down the corridor, my phone at my ear. I love her…and she loves me!

LEN SAID THAT OBVIOUSLY THEY couldn't change Big Pandora's hair colour at this notice, but that he could rig up a green spotlight from the lighting gallery and that his technician would follow the slow march of Big Pandora, and that should do the trick. Big Pandora is looking pretty cool, as Dougal's men unveil her to the applauding crowd.

"Wow, they are the biggest knockers I've ever seen!" shouts Sparky standing next to me, applauding and grinning.

"Shouldn't you be mingling or something, Sparks?" I look up to see the anxious pale-faced assassin above us.

"I'm keeping 'em well peeled, mate, don't you worry about that. Arne - all clear down here, man." Sparky looks like the most ridiculous security guy I've ever seen, as he leans into his hidden microphone.

Hippy Dougal is wearing a suit, but that's a big mistake for the hippy with his lank thin hair tied in a miserable ponytail, as he looks even scruffier than when he is wearing his ultra-faded *Fairport Convention* T-shirts and jeans from Christ knows where or when. He is pacing slowly backwards, and Tank, chewing the collar of his T-shirt, ensures his passage through the throng. The crowd gasps and applauds as Big Pandora takes her first step, and bends her neck forward to wink at her Lilliputian public. Happy that the machine is working, I slip through the crowd to where Arne and the Bonkers Babes have managed to smuggle the real Pandora (who is having a giggling fit) to where the harness is lowered, and she is hardly noticed as we strap her in, her legs slightly akimbo as they brace on the trapeze, and with the Babes all drunkenly stage-shushing, Bob and Arne haul her up above *Meeting Place,* and I get a photographer to take some shots of her silhouetted against the Dent clock…a beautiful image which reminds me a bit of *Mary Poppins,* though without the brolly.

The crowd parts as Big Pandora becomes more animated on her slow sojourn across the concourse. I smile as her gestures do actually remind me of Pandora! I have to hand it to Hippy Doug - he has studied the video shots I made of Pandora, and the six metre high version glides gracefully in her flowing purple robe, raising both arms, looking this way and that, fluttering her eyelashes, winking and smiling broadly. As Big Pandora approaches the *Meeting Place* statue, a murmur goes through the crowd, just as Pandora brilliantly conceived.

"She's up there!" gasps someone in wonder. "It's the real PM Poste!" exclaims another. Suddenly all the crowd are pointing, as a white floodlight swings madly about, illuminating the goddess above and the eyes of Big Pandora and Little Pandora meet. Below them, a large choir dressed in pink and gold surplices strike up the *Hallelujah Chorus.* Both Pandoras reach out their arms, and in one of the most beautiful moments in the history of art…they are wrapped in each other's embrace. The crowd go mad with whooping applause…the Babes are (literally) screaming in delight. Flash bulbs pop, glasses are raised…this is a bloody media triumph! These images will be all over the dailies tomorrow and be on a thousand Facebook sites in about ten minutes.

Pandora waves in delight to the throng below, and showers kisses on her huge alter-ego. I am standing next to Doug, who now needs to withdraw Big Pandora a bit, to give PM the spotlight. But he is doing his frustrated head-waggling thing, and shaking his remote control box violently.

"Is there a problem?" I hiss out of the side of my mouth.

"Come on, baby, come back to me!" he hisses back. "We have a power malfunction, Milad. She isn't responding."

Sparky is nudging me in the back, probably with his baton. "Arne says - what is the problem, Mil?" He is also hissing. We are all hissing, like a nest of worried vipers.

"Power malfunction."

"Sparky to Control. There has been a power malfunction. Repeat, power malfunction."

All animated life seeps from Big Pandora, as I hear the strange sighing sound these machines make when they are switched off. Problem is that Pandora is trapped - wrapped in the arms of her big twin, and I can see that she is becoming agitated, as she tries in vain to wriggle free. Her anxiety is starting to spread through the crowd. "Is she trapped?" enquires a journalist next to me.

Just as I am attempting to lie to him that Pandora isn't trapped, she is suddenly and spectacularly un-trapped. A gasp rises from the crowd, as Arne swings from his observation window on a rope (he reminds me of *Tarzan* on a vine, only he doesn't do that yodelling noise, and he is wearing his suit rather than a loin cloth), and he karate-kicks first Big Pandora's right arm, and then on his second swing out, her left arm, clean off their sprockets, and they hang limp and obscene, like a cruel torturer has torn them from their sockets.

"Blimey, it's James Bond!" shouts someone, as Arne disappears back through his window. "A brilliant reference to the Opening Ceremony of the Olympics," notes the journalist next to me, scribbling on his pad and nodding approvingly at me. Freed of her shackled embrace, Pandora is beaming again, and waving and blowing kisses to her adoring public below.

The only person who isn't smiling is Dougal, who is storming off, no doubt for a spliff. He is waving his arms around at his entourage. "There was no need to kick her fucking arms off, was there?!" I can hear him bleating. "Turn the coolers on guys, I think she has overheated. I'm off to roll a fat one."

Sparky is doubled up in delight next to me. "Ho, ho, did you see that Mil? Did you? What a fucking hero that man is! And Mil!…"

"What, Sparks?"

"Big Pandora looks pretty armless now!!" He is creasing up at his own daft joke, as Rollo and Dean arrive, breathless.

"Yo, Mil, Sparks! Did we miss much?" puffs a perspiring Dean.

"Oh yeah!" confirms Sparky. "You missed it alright, boys!"

"What did we miss?" asks Rollo, wearing a white tuxedo two sizes too big and reeking of mould. In fact, not just reeking of mould, I can see green blotches at the back hem, possibly a *Fusarium* species if I recall my GCSE Biology correctly. "What did we miss? Jesus, why are the robot's arms hanging off?"

"Don't worry boys," I say cockily, "You'll see it all again in the papers tomorrow."

Dougal's boys are scrabbling away under Big Pandora, and have activated some kind of whirring fan, which is annoying, because it is going to drown out Pandora's greeting message, and the acoustics in the station are bad enough. I go over to tell them to turn it off, but once again, there is whooping from the crowd. OMG. Make that a Double OMG.

There is a famous film that my Dad likes called *The Seven Year Itch* starring Marilyn Monroe, who my Dad loves and I have to say she is one of the hottest women in cinema history, and it's a shame what happened to her. My Dad blames the Kennedy family, whom he detests, which is funny because my history teacher told me that JF Kennedy was one of his heroes before he was shot by someone. Anyway, in that film, there is a famous scene where Marilyn stands on a subway grate and her white dress is blown above her knees by a passing train, and sort of billows round her thighs… very racy for 1955! Well folks, here is 2012's answer to that scene.

The cooling fan that hums at the base of Big Pandora has sent an up-draft of air through the giant puppet, and it is as if the lips of Big Pandora are blowing air up the purple dress of Little Pandora, the skirt of which flaps upwards to cover her upper body and head. And she doesn't appear to be wearing any pants.

The lads around me are looking incredulously skywards, and Sparky is pushing his earpiece deeper into his ear. "I hear you Arne. I hear you. Wardrobe malfunction. Milad, Wardrobe malfunction!"

"I can see that, you berk!" Pandora is fighting like a ferret caught in a sack to correct the wardrobe malfunction, but the stream of air is too strong. Down below, the ferret woman and the other Bonkers Babes are pointing and screeching.

"Pand, cover your bits, you old slapper!" shouts Ferret Woman.

"We can see your fanny!" adds Cow Woman.

"I 'ope she don't need a piss!" cackles The Goose.

In fairness to the decorum of most assembled, there is very little flash photography going on, and many of the gentlemen and ladies present are looking elsewhere, suddenly very interested in the *Eurostar* trains. That number does not include Sparky, Dean and Rollo, who are having a right good gawp; and I can see an especially disreputable photographer of my recent acquaintance shoving through the crowd and fitting a long lens as he does so, to assume a position directly below Pandora and starts reeling off shots.

I act fast. I dive under Big Pandora and just hit as many switches and buttons as I can. I was told by Dean afterwards that at first the draft became stronger and nearly ripped Pandora's whole dress off, but mercifully I hit all the right buttons, and the gale and Pandora's skirt subsides.

I emerge to see the goddess above restored to modesty, but of course, this chick cannot be fazed. She is roaring with laughter, and so is her audience!

"Oh, I say, that was fun!" she is calling down, her grass-green hair looking like it did when she climbed out of bed the morning after our 'session' in the hotel the other day. She calls it her 'mussed up sex hair'.

"You can say that again!" responds the lewd photographer, no doubt already en route to *The Daily Star* or some other gutter press. But he has a big come-uppance. As he ploughs out through the choir and crowd, fag in mouth (despite the many no-smoking signs that we have been asked to put up by the station management), he walks straight into Arne, and bounces off him, like Arne is made of titanium (which he might well be). Quick as a flashbulb, Arne has the camera, has taken the memory card out of the slot, removes the long lens and tosses it to the mawing snapper sitting dazed on the floor, and then coolly and calmly smashes the camera body to pieces on the granite plinth of *Meeting Place*.

The stricken paparazzo is a big beardy unit, and is up on his feet, looking mighty aggrieved and aggressive. Arne just gives him a 'what are you planning on doing about that, then?' smirk. This totally faces Beardy down and he wisely - very wisely - slinks off. But Arne's work is not done... somehow he has noticed every flash that may have recorded Pandora's wardrobe malfunction, and he is instructing Tank and Bob to intercept various snappers and guests, and between them, they are confiscating or deleting the evidence. I note with some embarrassment that one of those inspected is Ray, and I see Tank deleting a number of shots from his pocket Olympus.

Pandora has already completely recovered her composure, fantastic and amazing woman that she is, and is now doing her speech to a crowd shushed up by the Animal Farm Bonkers Babes. The microphone system is working well, and her voice booms out of the many speakers. I give a thumbs- up to the PA boys up in a scaffolding gantry.

"My friends, thank you so much for attending my little party tonight!" Whoops and cheers ring out. "You have seen *slightly* more of me than I had planned, but perhaps a 'snatch' of my goddess is rather appropriate under the literary circumstances!" There is raucous laughter, although I catch Neil and his three teenage sons looking somewhat uncomfortable, though Neil continues to smile his patient smile, as ever.

"Now, many of you will have read my runaway successful novel, *Black Heart?*" Huge cheers, whistles, whoops and clapping. Some people are whirling copies around their heads. Pandora quells the crowed with her arms.

"Well, my darlings, tonight, I can reveal two more things about myself! The first is that you can be the first people to know, that my darling ex-husband Neil…"

Neil is smiling nervously amid further raucous applause, "…has told me that sales of *Black Heart* have today overtaken five million, ladies and gentleman. Five million! And that's before we embark on the US market, and the Europe one, you know France and so on! So even though you might be only one in five million people who have bought my booky, I want to thank you as if you were the only one who has bought it!" This brings "aaahs" from the crowd and more applause.

"And the second thing I can reveal this evening - well make that the third, haha! - Is that I will be later on giving you all a world premiere reading from my new book…the sequel to *Black Heart* and …which I can now reveal to you for the very first time will be entitled…"

Pandora allows a long, theatrical pause, like on *X-Factor* or *The Apprentice*, and it all goes quiet. "…*Black Heart Darker*!!" There is more or less hysteria on this announcement. I can hear journalists on their mobiles imploring their editors to hold the presses, and some of them are demanding a Press Release from me, which I have ready about me and I begin to distribute the photocopies.

"Right, gentlemen, bring me back to Earth please - and not with a bump…I think we've all had enough surprises for one night! Thank you and please make your way to Searcy's Champagne Bar! Please have a lovely evening…at my expense. Thank you. I love you all!"

As she is lowered, the choir dressed in pink and gold surplices begin to sing *Spem*, like a chorus of gaudy angels.

Arne and I supervise the lowering process as Pandora blows a profusion of kisses to the adoring crowd. We quickly and expertly release her from her harness and a hyper-excited Pandora, her heart throbbing into my own chest, is embracing me tightly, and whispering into my ear. "Tell Len that his puppet people won't receive a fucking penny, Milad. And whoever was responsible for that fan fuck-up, I want them in Len's office at nine o' clock sharp tomorrow. I haven't even waxed for a week. And not a smear of body butter on my bum."

"Don't worry, PM. Arne and the boys confiscated all the paparazzi pics. And you looked like a modern day Marilyn Monroe. If you've got it, flaunt it, I say!"

"Ah, dear Mee-lad, you are so good for me. So reassuring. They may all have seen my outer goddess, but only the privileged few may enter her, Mee-lad. And you, my boy are *most* privileged."

"Put him down, Pandora! Come here, babe!" Animal Farm has gathered, and each in turn grab her and hug her and shake her. Pig Woman lifts Pandora clean off her feet, which is no mean lifting feat at all. Then they lead her rapidly off to Searcy's, like a herd of tottering, primary-coloured, screeching beasts.

As we clear the concourse, I see Dougal and his crew shoving the stricken marionette towards an awaiting lorry, and I call after him.

"Dougal, Pandora wants to see you at Len's offices at nine sharp tomorrow. I'd bring some good gear for after she finishes with you, mate!"

Dougal wanders over and starts his pathetic remonstrations. "It wasn't my fault, Milad. We've never done that manoeuvre before, the hugging gesture. It must have totally overheated things. How was I to know the fan would… do what it did…as it were?"

"Tell it to the judge, Doug. I ain't got time, mate," I sneer, leaving him drooping and forlorn. As I usher folk alongside Arne with a security cord held between us, I quietly congratulate him.

"Awesome work on Big Pandora's arms, Arne. Awesome."

"Just doing my job, Milad. You didn't do so bad yourself, switching that fan off. I was about to blow its head off with a shotgun."

I smirk to myself. Wow. It would almost have been worth it to see that happen! But Pandora wouldn't have liked it. And it would have ruined tomorrow's press...which is going to be seriously spectacular. Milad Brown, Spin Doctor...give yourself a pat on the back, mate.

SEARCY'S IS SARDINE-PACKED AND well-oiled folk are spilling out onto the concourse. Arne, Tank, Scarface Bob and Sparks are heavily occupied in turning away would-be gate crashers and keeping some kind of order inside the party. I like London on Saturday evening for the sheer crescendo of noise that pours out of the pubs and bars. But the noise in Searcy's is close to pandemonium. All the booze is free, so there is no bar queuing, and these hacks and London's literati can surely put it away. The celebrity entertainment arrives in the form of a spiky-haired fellow in an Aston Villa shirt carrying a violin case. Sparky, who has no idea who he is, is trying to deny him entry to the party.

"I'm sorry mate. This function is invite-only I'm afraid. And in any case you are not getting in with a footie shirt. Especially the Villa!"

"Fack you, san!" goes Kennedy. "You are wearin' a fackin'T-shirt yersewf!"

"Yes, but mine has a dinner jacket on it. Your shirt has '*Twitter*' on it. I thought Villa were lucky to stay up last season anyway."

"Bollocks. 'Oo do you support ven?"

"Fulham."

"Wew, we beat you lot. Wan niw. And dwew ay yaw pwace. Niw niw."

Sparky is beginning to recognise Kennedy, and is starting to grin. "Wait a minute I know you, don't I?"

"Wew oi don't know you san, wiv yer kinky awfo bawnet! You gonna let me in or wot? 'Cos if not, or'll fack off."

"You are Johnny Rotten! You advertise butter, right? Used to be in a band, way back?"

"I'm really sorry Mr Kennedy," I finally intervene. "Just ignore this person. You can't get the staff these days. Please come through, the PA guys have set everything up for you."

"Fanks mate. Ow, 'e's awight…part from 'e supports the fackin' Cottagers!"

TWENTY MINUTES LATER the joint is rocking to Kennedy's Polish jazz and Jimi Hendrix Beethoven.

"This guy is super-cool!" shouts Dean. "What a brilliant party, Mil, you are a star, mate!"

"Thanks dude, I am so happy you guys are here!" I look along the line at my mates, Dean, Sparks, Potts, Tils with my little sis Naz, Rollo and…" Blimey! What's this? Rollo has his arm around Nathalie's waist, and they are canoodling, their eyes flash at each other like silver fishes in a dark sea. I get a funny feeling in my chest and my stomach flips over.

"Hey, are they an item?" I nudge Dean, feeling a bit shivery despite the mass of body heat around me.

"Yeah, 'bout a week!" Dean confirms. "Nat's doing well at the paper, isn't she?"

"She is mate, she is." I am cool. Nat and Rollo, why not? I clap along to Kennedy's electric violin, but I realise to my annoyance that I am experiencing a pang of jealousy. Nat is laughing and clapping, and she radiates vibrancy and happiness. It looks like Rollo, in his mouldy and moth-eaten tux, can't believe his luck. Well, best of luck to them both…I have my Pandora, who is (with the assistance of two of the Animal Babes) climbing onto the tiny stage and…pulling Kennedy's lead out of the PA! Kennedy is still inaudibly fiddling, as her breathy voice takes over at the microphone.

"Nigel, thank you so very much. The incomparable Nigel Kennedy, everyone!" Pandora leans away and starts the applause. The virtuoso seems a bit annoyed as he is cut-off mid flow, but bows his spiky head anyway.

"Now, it is the moment you have been waiting for. I am about to read to you - for the first time anywhere at any time - an excerpt from my sequel to my best-selling *Black Heart…Black Heart Darker*!" Utter tumult breaks out. Something is barging against the backs of my legs, and I look down, to see something bright yellow scrabbling about on all fours.

"Are you OK? Giselle, is it?"

"Nah, orm Lewcy. Or've lawst wan a me contacts, en aw. Cam an 'ewp me, Miw."

"Ah, right, OK." As Pandora quietens the excited throng, I drop to my knees and start patting the already soaking floor, in search of Pig Woman's bright purple contact lens.

It's slightly muffled from where we are scrabbling, but I hear PM clear her throat, and her voice rings out. It sounds from the accents she is doing (West Coast American and little girl English) that the characters from *Black Heart* have returned! I can also hear some rather rude words, and I am looking protectively up at Naz…and see Rollo's hand squeezing Nat's firm little ass. Rollo, please! I feel something under my palm, and suspecting it is broken glass, pull my palm away, but I can see it is a tinted contact lens.

"Is this it, Lucy?" I whisper.

"Aw yoo dawl!" she responds in not so whispery delight, and people look down in disapproval….especially when the next thing I know, Lucy has thrown her arms around me and is actually snogging me full on the mouth. Jesus H Christ! Tongue as well! Her grip around my neck is so tight it's like being snogged by an anaconda. My eyes swivel round…to be met by Nat's and Naz's. They look down with a mixture of disgust and shock, and quickly look away. Though Naz looks back again – and I am still in deep suction. Lucy tastes strongly of cheesy puffs.

"Hehehehehehe!" she mawls, finally releasing me, and tipping her head back to restore her violet eye tint. "Yoo wittle tawt! Or wawont tew Pandawa if yew dowant!"

I get to my feet and help Lucy to hers, and quickly shimmy through the throng away from her. Sparks has seen all of course, and is shaking with silent laughter.

"Fuck off, Sparks," I murmur in his ear as I pass him, and head off to stand next to Arne by the exit. I feel I need protection. He nods almost imperceptibly as I reverse into a little space between him and Tank.

Pandora, as ever, is really getting into her reading, and she writhes about on the barstool she is perched upon. Man, this is steamy stuff, even more than *Black Heart*. The audience is starting to perspire. Rollo's hand is moving up and down Nat's ass. Lucy is touching herself…intimately.

Barnabas Black is back…and he's baaad-assing!

"Candy. Listen to me. I need to ask you something. Before I spank the living delights out of you. Do you want a relationship with no finky kuckery at all? Because if you do, that's not who Barnabas Black, is, was, nor ever can be."

Candy is also back as first person narrator in *Darker*, and even squeakier than in *Heart*.

"My mouth drops open. "Finky kuckery? What games are playing with me, Barnabas? Is that a Spoonerism or are you just glad to see me? I can't believe you said that." He is playing games with me again. And not just spank fantasy games this time…word games."

Pandora takes a swig of fizz to lower her voice back into Black's baritone.

"This is not a game, Candy. Inky blackberry. Slinky kukri. Finky kuckery. It all adds up to the same thing. Answer me now girl. Do you want it? Or do you want it not?"

Pandora is back into Candy-mode.

"I feel suddenly that the rest of my days and the future of my happiness depend on my reply to his question. Do I? Do I want it? Or do I want it not? I gaze into the black pools of his eyes, which search me like searchlights, undress me, and roughly frisk my

bared girl-soul. I flush. My inner ladyship is down on bended knees and egging me, begging me. I give into her demands. "I like your finky kuckery," I whisper."

There is silence as Pandora smiles, folds up her paper, takes off her reading glasses and slides off the bar stool.

"Wow!" booms one guy, as the applause and whooping starts.

"Bravo, Pandora, bravo!" shouts another.

"Is she doing Spoonerism there, Mil?" asks a confused Sparky, leaning in my ear. "You haven't helped her write this one, have you?"

"Nope. Just as in the 'Darker' as you, Sparks."

"Finky kuckery? I mean…what is that, man?"

"I have no idea, mate. But these guys seem to appreciate it!"

Pandora bows deeply to her adoring, cheering audience and scribbling hacks, and suddenly Rihanna is over-crooning through the PA and The Babes are shaking their booty, knocking people clean out of their way with their swivelling hips, pulling Pandora off the stage to join their gyrations on the dance floor. Now the party really gets started, as the lights dim. It's like an orgiastic scene from a tiny club in Ibiza, as people have no choice but to move their bodies to the groove as they are so tightly jammed together. Champagne bottles are passed overhead, men remove their jackets and ties, and everyone is getting down. Kennedy is grooving on the tiny stage with Renee and the Coffee girls, and my posse has formed a tight gaggle. Potts has grabbed a bottle of Krug which we all take a swill from. Pandora's reading has set of shockwaves of sensuality through the throng, and weird stuff is going on. One of The Babes seems to be on her knees, her hands on some bloke's suited bum, and her head is bobbing back and forth. And I do not think that this is simulation, either! I nudge Arne, and discretely point, my eyebrow raised, but Arne just shrugs, and Tank has a big grin on his face. Oh Lord, another of The Bonkers Babes has her tits out, and she is staggering up onto the stage. She cups her hands under her udders and waves them about…to the leering cheers of the crowd. And who the holy fuck is that bloke gyrating himself up against my sister's ass! Well, if Arne won't intervene, I most certainly will!

I push my way through the gyrating bodies, and grab this guy by the collar. He stinks of cologne and is wearing foundation make up.

"Get the fuck away from my little sister, asshole!"

But suddenly, I cannot breathe. Oh no, not the anaconda again? Nope, something a lot more dangerous in the forest. I am in some kind of choke-hold, and I can sense that no blood is getting to my brain. My lights are going out…then suddenly come on again. I am panting and holding my neck, gasping out on the concourse for air. Arne has my arm.

"Sorry Milad, you can't be causing trouble at PM's party." What? I have been restrained by my own security? I go into one of my coughing fits.

"Kaaaah! Arne, you don't….kahhaaha!…get it mate, my little sister… koooooharrrrra!…is getting pestered in there. Kahahahahahahahaha!!"

"Tiny dark girl, black dress?"

"Y-y-y-kahahahahahahahaha!!"

"I'm on it." He whisks off to deal with the problem guy, but Tils and Potts are already escorting Naz out of the champagne bar, and she evidently *has* drunk too much champagne. They are followed by Dean, Rollo, Nat, and Sparks.

"I think it's probably time we headed home, Milad," says Tils, trying to keep Naz in a straight line. "Are you OK?"

"Huuuuh… Kahahahahahahahaha!!" Sparks is belting me on the back.

"Yyyyyeah, yeah, thanks Sparks, kah, that's better."

"That looked like a wicked strangle-hold Arne put you in!" beams Sparks. "I am totally going to get him to teach me that move and then - I will eternally kick your ass, bro."

"Woah, yeah, it was pretty full on! Kahaaa! I nearly passed out! Naz, I *told* you not to drink more than two glasses, come here!"

I give her a big hug, and she smiles up at me and hiccups, her deep brown eyes swimming in their huge white pools.

"Yep, get this one home, guys. So good to see you all, thanks for coming to support me. And you all look so fantastic!" I give them a big hug each, and finally, Nat.

"Look at you two, holding hands! Quite the mover, Rollo!" Rollo blushes a bit and looks down fondly at Nat, who reddens and giggles, and then jumps up at me like a fish leaping out of the water to give me a kiss on my cheek. It feels like a single drop of rain falling from the sky.

"We are so proud of you, Milad," she is saying, and they all are patting me on my back, before they head towards The Underground. I watch them with a pang of sadness as they disappear into the distance, all of us still waving and smiling at each other.

"AH!!!! *There* you are, my lad!" Pandora is giving me the 'come hither' with her index finger, a very naughty smile on her face. "Come and dance with me dah-ling. Come and dance."

Back inside, it's all going a bit Pete Tong, although the DJ isn't Pete Tong, it's a friend of Pandora's who is called Pete and calls himself Pete Bong. There are now several topless Bonkers Babes gyrating around, and my former editor Ray is doing some 'dad dancing' in front of the stage with a big grin on his face. His wife, whose name I can never remember apart from it begins with 'C' looks a bit uncomfortable, so I decide to make her day by introducing her personally to Pandora.

"Erm, Mrs Ray, I know you have been dying to meet PM Poste in person? Pandora, meet Mrs. Ray! She is married to that guy over there, who used to be my boss."

"Yes, he seems rather pre-occupied by my busty babes, doesn't he, dear!" She has to shout to be heard over DJ Bong's master re-mix. Mrs Ray is looking star-struck and in awe. She just stares up at Pandora with a slack jaw. Pandora, as ever takes the initiative. Instead of shaking hands with her admirer, or exchanging small talk (which would be fairly impossible at the current music volume) she simply grabs Mrs Ray's waist in both hands and starts grinding their pelvises together to the bass rhythm, gyrating up and down her, gazing all the time into her dancing partner's startled eyes.

I catch Neil's eye who is standing at the edge of the heaving gaggle of London's finest scrawlers, tapping text messages into his phone, no doubt to Susanna. I squeeze myself over towards him.

"DID YOUR LADS ENJOY THE SHOW, NEIL?" I shout through cupped hands into his ear, and I realise that his teenage sons probably didn't enjoy the sight of their mother naked from the waist down whilst suspended from the rafters of a railway station.

"YES, VERY GOOD!" he shouts back. "ACTUALLY, MILAD, I WAS GOING TO ASK YOU A FAVOUR? SHALL WE GO OUT, IT IS RATHER...LOUD IN HERE?"

It feels good to be out of the heaving bar on the concourse again, and we take a walk outside the station to the steps beyond the hotel. I don't really like nightclubs and dancing that much, I am more of a pubs kind of a guy.

"Pandora will need a break from London this weekend, Milad. She does exhaust herself, and we have a little retreat out in Suffolk. Well, it's a little island actually. Perfect for relaxing and as it were, getting away from it all? Quite literally, in fact. I wonder if you would do me a favour and take Pandora there at the weekend? You can borrow one of the cars if you wish."

"Er, yeah, well, I'll see what I can do, Neil!" I am a bit embarrassed, as evidently Neil now sees me as his replacement as Pandora's partner, but as ever he is being awfully kind and generous about it.

"That's very good of you, are you sure you don't mind? Dear boy, you'd be doing me a big favour. For some unearthly reason, Pandora doesn't like my Susanna, and I do so love to spend the weekend with her. I would be greatly appreciative, Milad."

"Righto, well...consider me in then! Erm, minor problem on the car front though - I can't drive." My Dad told me I would regret giving up the driving lessons, and now I seriously do. "But I do have a driver...he could take us and pick us up?"

"Splendid! Well look, take the Jag, the weather is going to be nice, and you can get the roof off. I'll call the cleaners and they will spruce Belle Island up for you. You have to row out to the island from a little boat house, but

I'll get Arne to make the arrangements. He could have accompanied you, but I understand he is attending some kind of convention this weekend. Right, I suppose we'd better get back inside, I'm off soon. I'll give you a tinkle in the morning."

The dance floor is heaving and bilging with coked up, pissed up literati dancing badly to Salsa beats and I am accosted by a long face with a long nose and long arms. The Horse Woman leads me in something I reckon is more tango than salsa as she keeps swooning and it's hard work holding up her long body. The party rages on, and there is always a full glass of fizz in my hands, and finally I am in Pandora's arms, seeing stars and getting one of those awful head spins where you have to grab something really hard to get through the slow spin, and I'm grabbing two handfuls of Pandora's hips.

"Yes, take my flesh and hold me close, Mee-lad," she is breathing in my ear, as I feel giddy and then actually sick. Thankfully, the feeling subsides, and I vow to drink no more. I would like to be in bed in this woman's embrace, very, very soon, in my room in the hotel above us. I nestle my head into her neck and she has her raking nails in my damp hair. But my hopes are immediately dashed.

"I'm moving on with my Babes, dah-ling. Please stay back with Arne to see all is well, and I want all the newspapers in Len's office before I have to carpet whoever was responsible for embarrassing me. Goodnight, my dah-ling!"

With that, she sort of snogs my lips off, rounds up the baying Babes, and the last I see of them is them staggering away in various states of sartorial disarray, demanding taxis. With the hostess departed, our crew and Searcy's staff encourage things to a halt, and half an hour later the last guests are on their way, though I am alarmed to see Tank haul a Paul Smith-suited unconscious body from under a table by his Gucci shoes. The guy looks quite dead, and Arne is taking his pulse.

"Alive. Barely. Tank, prop him up by the ticket office."

"Shouldn't we call a doctor or something?" I ask Arne as Tank slithers the man across the shiny concourse, heaves him into a slumped sitting position, and with a humorous twist, sticks an opened battered copy of *Black Heart* in his hands, so it looks like he is reading in rapt concentration. This makes Arne do his rare 'laugh howl' and I laugh too, sort of also doing a bit of an 'Arne howl'. I don't ask about a doctor again. We thank Searcy's people and Pete Bong, who has his stuff packed up and ready to go. Job done, *The Matrix* publishers put on their shades (well, me Arne and Bob, Tank doesn't seem to wear sunglasses) and we head off to various parts of London Town.

"Good job, Milad," says Arne stalking fast ahead of me. "You can pick up the papers from the stand at Kings Cross right now. See you tomorrow." With that, Arne spins hard right to the taxi rank and is gone. I look at my watch and it's coming up for 2am, and the bundles of Sunday's papers are arriving at the kiosk at the top of the Underground. I buy a bunch of them and take them back to my room, where I am too tired to scan them properly, though I can see there are plenty of pictures of Big Pandora, and so far, none of any wardrobe malfunctions. A very quick shower, and I don't remember getting into bed, but I do remember a weird, twitchy dream featuring Rollo and Nat standing at an altar at the top of a church aisle. I am trying to shout something, but it's one of those dreams where your words can't come out?

NEXT MORNING, I'M AT THE OFFICES OF TWILIGHT PRODUCTIONS in Holborn, and me and Len are going properly through the papers, and the publicity is sensationally good. Pandora hasn't been to bed, but looks remarkably fresh in her white summer skirt, blue polka dot blouse and *Chanel* sunglasses, and she has commandeered Len's office. She is really pleased with us, but poor old Dougal, who by contrast to Pandora, does look as though he has been up all night, is here for a major bollocking. He looks wretched as he hunches over, muttering to himself about the mannequin malfunction, as Pandora keeps him waiting.

The door to the office swings open, and Arne, looking as ever immaculate and efficient, addresses Dougal severely.

"Ms Poste will see you now, Mr Towke." Ha ha! Dougal Towke! That's even better than Arne Bastad! Brilliant, I'll tell the lads that, stoner hippy called Dougal Towke! I am grinning, but poor old Doug can hardly get to his feet, and he shambles pitifully into Pandora's office, Arne closing the door behind him and remaining outside.

"Mr Poste tells me you are escorting PM to Belle Island this weekend, Milad, is that correct?"

"Ah, yep, it is Arne. Sparks is driving us there on Friday and then picking us up Sunday."

"Fine. However, I will be arriving on Sunday morning, so there will be no need for him to pick you up. I will have the boatman take you over. Be there for 7pm on Friday evening."

Arne whisks off before I can ask him any more about Belle Island, and Len goes to get us breakfast from the coffee shop opposite. Left alone in the reception area, I can't see into Len's office as the blinds are drawn, but I cannot resist putting my ear to the door to hear Towke getting the bollocking of his life. I can't make out Dougal's bleating, but though slightly muffled, Pandora's voice is clear.

"I said I do not want to hear it, Mr Towke! " Now get on your knees! Did you not hear me? On your hands and knees! I do not want to hear another word! Now crawl, you silly little man. Crawl. Under the desk. Further. Now take these off. You heard what I said! Take them off!" Eh? What is going on in there?? My heart is pumping a bit…this isn't quite the carpeting I was looking forward to over-hearing.

"Now lick, for all you are worth, you pathetic creature. Ask forgiveness from the goddess with your tongue. Do it, you piece of shit!" Then I hear a sort of lapping noise, like a cat with a saucer of cream.

"Faster…and deeper! You are fucking hopeless, you really are. You have no idea where it is, do you you? Do you?" I hear a very muffled "No, Miss Poste" followed by more fervent lapping.

"Aaah, aaah, that' better, Mr Towke, much better. Now do not stop or I will brain you with this paperweight. Aaaaah, ahhhh, keep going, that's it, ahhhhh…"

I recoil from the door in shock. I have to be mistaken, surely. Surely? I am thinking of ways that Dougal isn't performing oral on Pandora. Could he be licking envelopes in a submissive way under the desk? Len returns with coffee and muffins, by which time I am taking deep breaths in my chair and pretending to scan the papers.

"Got you a vanilla latté, Mil, OK? Has she killed him yet? "

"Er, not exactly Len. Erm, yeah sugar, thanks." I try to get back to cutting out excerpts from the paper with Len, but the action in the office is getting louder.

"AHHHHHHHHH, OHHHHHH, HOH, HOH, AAAH!" Len looks at me in puzzlement. I look up at the door. The envelope theory isn't holding up. But now, there is a different ruckus emerging…it sounds like furniture is going over.

"CRAWL FOR YOU LIFE, YOU PITIFUL, HOPELESS BASTARD!"

"AAAAAH, PM, NO, PLEASE….AGGGHHHHH!"

"TRY MY LEFT BOOT AS WELL, MR. TOWKE…"

"AGGGHHHHH! NO, PLEASE, NO… NO, PLEASE… AGGGHHHHH!""

Len is on his feet in concern, and looks like he may be about to enter his office, but I grab his wrist.

"I wouldn't, Len. I seriously wouldn't."

He takes my advice, but as a second best, he is craning his eye like a man peering through a key hole through a space where one of the blinds has gone a bit crooked. I join him to peer as well, and behold an extraordinary sight. Doug is crawling madly like a terrified baby around the office in wild circles, pursued by a flushed Pandora, who is, in a pair of very pointy boots, kicking him hard in the arse, or more accurately, swinging her boot (like a rugby player taking a conversion from near the halfway line) between his crawling legs and making very effective contact with the testiculating area. Chairs and coffee tables are going over as she makes repeated contact with her target, and Doug sprawls away.

We see Douglas leap like a desperate salmon towards us for the door handle, and as we recoil from our spying positions, his head and shoulders emerge from the door, but his mottled eyes nearly pop from his head as he receives another nad-crunching boot in his derriere region.

"BLERRRRRRRRR….GET ME OUT, GET ME OUT, LEN, THE WOMAN'S BARMY!!"

But Len doesn't need to help him out, as Pandora kicks him clean out of the office like an over-sized *Gilbert* rugby ball, and he rolls, wincing onto his side.

"OUT! OUT! NO MONEY FOR YOU, YOU HOPELESS LITTLE MAN!"

She picks up one of the newspapers, rolls it up, and like an Amazon woman swatting a big beetle, lays into the rolling and screeching Dougal, belting him about the head and arms, as he rolls about in the foetal position. I don't quite know whether to enjoy the show or try to calm Pandora down, but there isn't much time to think, as unwisely, Doug has rolled away to the top of the stairs, to try to evade his newspaper bashing. Like a gladiator standing over a defeated combatant, Pandora chucks away her weapon, and turning to give me and Len the sweetest and most coquettish of smiles, simply applies her boot to Doug's back…and rolls him down the stairs. There is a horrible bumping and bashing and yelping sound as he descends to the door below.

Len scampers after him in concern. I'm relieved to see below that Dougal is at least able to stand and leave the office on his own legs, as he remonstrates wildly with Len. Pandora comes over to me, spreading her arms around my neck, in a surprisingly tender gesture.

"Aaaah, dealing with difficult people, Mee-lad. It is a difficult HR skill these days, isn't it? I need a big huggy-wuggy. Mmmmmm, thank you dah-ling. Now let's have a look at this mah-vellous press

work you are doing! Oooh, is that vanilla latté? And a bluberry muffin? Yummy!"

CHAPTER NINE

Sparky bursts through the wooden door of the boathouse, and pauses to flick on light switches.

"Not tho-ose wuns ye little prick…them wuns!" The face of an old codger - actually a very old codger, is suddenly illuminated by the flickering fluorescent tube bulb above his head, and I am reminded as I peer over Sparky's shoulder of a strobe effect, as the craggy face of the man with the hooked nose and red woollen hat with a white lobster knitted into it flashes in and out of the darkness. As the light blinks and clinks and finally settles down to a phosphorescent glow and dozens of moths flit clumsily about, I am drawn to the ugliness of the man's features. He is entirely bald, with many pulsing veins riddling the dome of his scalp, which he has removed his woolly hat to scratch.

"Wha-at kept yer?" he demands rubbing a considerable amount of rheum from his eyes and then eating it. "Oi mussa fawlyn 'sleep!"

"Sorry guv," says Sparky, "you'd be Mr Glossop, would you?"

"Mebbe oi arm, and mebbe oi aren't. Pends on oo arsks."

"Good evening, Glossop. Yes, the M25 was horrid and the A12 was worse. It has taken us five hours to do ninety miles. I hope Mrs Glossop has prepared supper, I am completely famished." On the appearance of Pandora, the codger's demeanour changes from bullish to entirely subservient. If he had any forelocks to tug, he would be yanking at them, but since he does have a cap to doff, he doffs it, deferentially.

"Roight yoo arr, Missus Poste. Byun, thass a lung rood to Lundun and no mistake it. Is these gentlemen be comin ovver wi' yer ma'am, cus awl eff ter mek two trips? And Mrs Glossop is all waitin' for yuz, she mayde er stargazy poi what yer loikes."

 "Oooh, stargazy pie, how lovely!" Pandora claps. "No. Only one of my companions will join me. Boys, go and get the luggage."

"What, the black 'un or the wun wi' the frizzy 'air miss? Juss the wun wi the frizzy 'air looks loike 'e may weigh us doon, and oi moight mayke another trip fur 'im."

"Well then, you'll be pleased to know that the slimmer gentleman will be coming over and the other one returning to London. I do wish you would be persuaded to have the gift from Neil and I of a mobile telephone, Mr. Glossop, and then I could have let you know that we were running so late."

"Don't wunt one, ma'am, though bless you fer worritin'. Oi down't wunt wun o' them blamed things trillin' away and wastin' good toime on drivel talk. Oi'm 'appy waitin' in me boat until the Lord thinks fit ter deliver ye to Belle Oirland."

Me and Sparks go back to the silver blue Jaguar XK, and take Pandora's two Burberry cases and my new Prada bag from the boot. The journey was long, but since Sparks got to drive a class car and I got to canoodle with a class bird in the cramped back seats, we are both happy. We drove through London with the roof down, folk spotting Pandora as we drove through Queensway and Paddington, and when we reached the M25 Pandora let us put our hip hop on, Earl Sweatshirt's *Molliwopped* sounding especially fine. We put the roof down when she decided it was time for Michael Bublé though. Sparks is going to stay with his aunt in Southend tonight, and Nice Neil says he can keep the car until Sunday, so he is going to take the gang out in it tomorrow night.

"Just don't crap the car up, Sparks. You've already got *Ginster's Peppered Slice* all over it."

"Me crapped it up? Pandora had three peppered slices...and a Scotch egg! Look it's loads dirtier in the back than it is in the front. And that's just the food! I saw you with your hand up her skirt, you filthy perve."

"Well...just get it valeted before you return it," I smile, smelling my hands that smell of her, "and don't get dents in it, either."

"Ah shut up, Bigshot. Tell you what, that's the easiest and most enjoyable hundred quid I've ever earned. Sure you don't want picking up Sunday?"

"Nope, Arne-boy will be here Sunday. Thanks mate, I'll take those, you get yourself on the road." We give each other a big hug, and Sparky isn't letting go.

"Look mate, I'm a bit worried about you and that woman," he is murmuring. "You might be infatuated with her, but she is way too old for you and way more controlling. If you need out of there, dude, you just call old Sparky and I'll come a-running. And a-rowing, if necessary."

"Don't *worry*, Sparks!" I smile, pushing him off. "You are worse than my Mum! This is all working for me man, I am having a ball with Pandora. Now get behind the wheel, you big wuss!"

Sparky shrugs and grimaces, tells me to take care yet again and then is roaring up the track, full throttle.

"THERE'S A GOOD CURRENT A-RUNNIN' A-NOIGHT, MA'AM!" Poor old Glossop is straining away at his rollocks, and we seem to have hardly left the bank despite having left the boat house a good fifteen minutes ago. Pandora, wrapped in a silk pashmina and my right arm, trails her hand artistically in the black summer water and looks distractedly at the deep blue night sky, ignoring her heaving minion.

"DO YOU WANT ME TO TAKE AN OAR?" I shout into the slightly salty wind as we move further out into the wide river mouth. I have been on a couple of boating lakes, and I reckon I'd be a good rower, it looks pretty easy to me judging from the guys in the Olympics.

"DOWN'T YOU SHIFT AROUND, MASTER! THERE'S PLENNY DROONED IN 'ERE WHAT TROIED THAT TRICK!" Glossop stares malevolently at me. He doesn't seem to like me much, but then, I don't care what he thinks.

As we slowly make our way across and down the current, I can make out a building on an island taking black shape in mid-river. It is circular, with a dome on the top, and as we get closer there is an entrance with stone columns about it. Blimey, I was expecting some kind of wooden lodge, but this is a serious building. Glossop looks like he might expire before he rows us to the jetty looming ahead of us, where I see the figure of a bent old lady wearing an apron and what appears to be a mob cap.

"Throw the rope to Missus Glossop, boy!" gasps the geriatric rower. I am glad that he doesn't have to make another trip across the river because I am pretty sure he wouldn't make it. Mooring ropes lashed about the jetty, we disembark from the rolling, pitching boat, Pandora out last, helped by all three of us.

Mrs Glossop squeezes Pandora's right hand with both hers, her eyes squinting in the lantern she has handed me, and like her husband, she exudes deference.

"It 'as been too long, Mrs Poste, far too long! But you 'ave got so famous now, more famous than Mr Neil, even! Now, get you'self inside, do. The summer is wearing on and it is getting a mite chilly. Come along, these two men will bring the bags."

Evidently, Mrs Glossop regards me as another manservant who is beneath even her greeting, but like her husband's, I'm not interested in her views on me. Well, at least I get a kind of a welcome from the bag of bones who insists on carrying both of Pandora's bags himself.

"Well, wherever you are from, welcome to the 'Ouse o' Correction," he puffs, as he waddles up the steps of the grand entrance, which I think from my GCSE Art days is called a portico…anyway it has four columns with those stone rams' horns at the top (Doric, Ionic or Corinthian? I'm not sure which one), supporting a triangular roof with a sundial or crest or something on the front of it.

"What do you mean, wherever I am from, Mr Glossop? I am from the same place Pandora is from. Horsham in West Sussex. Where did you think I was from?"

"I dunno. Peru?" I decide to ignore this.

"And what do you mean, House of Correction? Did this used to be a prison, or something?"

"Nope. Nut 'ouse. Well, koind of a prison oi s'pose. Fer nutters."

Crossing the threshold, I find myself at the foot of a central stair case, off which there is a seating area with a roaring log fire, a dining area with a large oak table and a dozen chairs, and beyond that a kitchen.

"I'll take bags to your roow-em, Missus. Where'll 'e be?" Surely Glossop is not going to attempt the stairs with the two bags, as he hoists them upwards once more.

"I'm just popping to the loo, Glossop. Milad is in with me." Pandora clacks away across the stone floor slabs. As if winded, Glossop drops the bags and starts coughing. I hear a soup ladle in the kitchen clatter to the floor. Ha ha, not just a manservant then! I don't like these two very much, but my Mum and Dad always taught me to have respect and manners for older people, so I don't gloat. I simply pick up my bag, and the heavier of Pandora's and then mount the stairs. Though there are three floors, I can see immediately that the next storey up is Pandora's floor...a bedroom on one side of the arc with a huge four-poster double bed, and on the other side a large bathroom, with a bath on legs and a separate shower. I drop both bags at the end of the bed, and take the other off Glossop, as soon as he wobbles up to the top of the stair. He stands and eyes me up. I want to say "that will be all, Glossop," and dismiss him from my presence, but I don't do that. I just ignore him and start to unpack my stuff. Eventually he shuffles off, still giving me the evil eye. Pandora bounds up the stairs, her eyes shining.

"Do you like it, dahling? Do you like our little Belle Island House?"

"Very much, Pandora, very much." We throw our arms around each other and fall onto the bed, like the lovers that we are. "Though I'm not sure about Hinge and Brackett down there. They don't live in, do they?"

"Oh, never mind about them. They are just part of the furniture, dear. They live in a little house on the shore but stay here when we want them to. Not in the house, *of course*. They have a hut thing down the island." That's good news. I wouldn't want to bump into either of them in the night, and they are the kind of fogeys who stand about in corners and lurk in shady alcoves, just waiting to make unsuspecting people jump.

"I gather it used to be called The House of Correction, did it, in the olden times?" I am eyeing a pair of iron manacles pinioned into the brickwork, and dangling from the ceiling are a great number of dark chains.

"Oh yes, until about 1930, darling. I'm afraid they treated mental illness rather differently than they do nowadays. Many poor souls died here. And many wish that they had died here. Well, on that macabre note, I smell Mrs Glossop's fish pie! Do come downstairs, dear!"

We descend hand-in-hand to the table, where Glossop has reluctantly set two places, and Mrs Glossop delivers a huge golden pie with several fish heads jutting out from the pastry crust.

"Ah, Mrs Glossop's stargazy pie! How marvellous, dah-ling, simply mah-vellous."

"Is this not a Cornish dish, Mrs Glossop? Are you from Cornwall?" My attempts at small talk with the mob-capped creature, scraping and bowing as she returns to the table with a steaming truckle of vegetables, are made more difficult by her complete inability to look me in the eye. He husband, who is attempting to uncork a bottle of Chablis with trembling hands, replies for her.

"Missus Glossop is not frim Cornywall! She's frim 'ere! And 'er stargazy don't 'ave pilchards frim the sea, 'er's 'as eels frim owr river. Gahhhhh, blast this ne-uw-fangled woine opener!"

Glossop is making a right mess of opening the wine with a 'waiter's friend'. I offer to help him out, but he's not having it. He scuttles off to the kitchen and I can hear him bashing the cork in with what sound like a hammer. Eel pie, eh? Not sure I like the sound of that. I think I tried jellied eels once and definitely didn't like it. But Pandora is loving the eel pie, she is piling up her plate up with it - plus broccoli, carrots, the lot, and getting well stuck in.

"Mmm…mah-vellous, Mrs G, simply mah-vellous. Where's the wine, Glossop, ah, here we are. A toast, Milad. To a restful weekend - away from it all. We have all worked so hard together, dah-ling, haven't we? Cheers."

Pandora and I discuss the hectic work of the last few days, and the tremendous publicity generated by the party. But with sales of *Black Heart* rocketing, Pandora is no longer feeling the need to do readings or signings, and wants to concentrate on the US and overseas launch of her first novel, as well as completing and negotiating the publishing rights for *Black Heart Darker*.

"I mean, *Coffee* are going to have to work *a lot* harder on the deal if they are going to publish *Darker*, darling, despite what I might have said at the party. Yes, more pie please, Glossop. And open another bottle of wine - but don't bodge it this time, there was cork all over this bottle. Ooooh, fruit flan for pudding, lovely."

I suggest to Pandora that Belle Island might be a good place to hole up and complete *Darker*, but she (literally) shudders at the thought.

"Oh no dear, I need to be around people, around my Babes. I need to write in coffee shops, pubs, parks, places that are vibrant with the energy of real people. How else can my characters breathe life? My God, I'd probably end up writing about hobbits or wizards or something if I was incarcerated here! Do you like Mrs G.'s eel pie, dear?"

Fact is, I don't like Mrs G.'s eel pie, and I'm picking out the egg and potatoes and pastry, and kind of leaving out the eel.

"It's OK, Pandora, but I prefer *your* cooking, to be honest." OK, it's shameless flattery, I know it, she knows it…she's only made me scrambled egg on toast so far (twice) – but it was the best scrambled egg on toast I've ever had. Anyway, her hand is on my knee and she kisses my cheek.

After fruit flan with squirty cream, Pandora dismisses the Glossops with an imperious wave of her hand, and they disappear without a word. I watch them out of the window from my seat at the dining table, his arm around her waist as they shamble down a sinuous path into a small wood of Scots pine and some other trees. (My Mum is good at identifying trees and plants, and you can't mistake Scots pine, especially its silhouette against the evening sky). It must be nice to be old and still care for each other, I think to myself, as I hold Pandora's hand under the table as she helps herself to another slice of flan, and laughs at the noise the squirty cream makes. I am lucky that my parents are not only still together, but that they actually like each other still, I can tell that. All my mate's parents are either separated or divorced – Sparky's, Dean's, Potts', Til's…not sure about Rollo's, I'm not sure Rollo even has parents, 'cos if he does, he never talks about them.

Pandora rises with one of her posh peoples' belches and she takes me to the sofa before the fire, which is low and crackling and smells deliciously wood-smoky. She leans on the arm of the sofa, kicks off her shoes and plants her feet in my lap.

"Give my tired footsies a massage, Mee-lad. And read me my party gossip reviews again." She shuts her eyes and I lean over for the bundle of crumpled newspapers and magazines. She actually purrs as I push my thumbs into the base of her toes and read *The Evening Standard* Entertainments page. She is soon asleep, there is no mistaking when Pandora is asleep. I lift her legs off me and pitch the papers to the floor, swinging my own legs up, and nestle into her bosom. I listen to the steady boom of her heart and the spit of heartwood from the fire, and my eyes too are closing.

I DON'T RECALL HOW I GOT TO BED, and I have a horrible feeling that I have broken the Toothbrush Commandment again. Our clothes are in a jumbled trail from the bedroom door and the room is full of candlelight from a dozen aromatic tea lights. Pandora, her hair in a messy ponytail, is idly playing with my gentleman whilst her other hand rasps with its' long nails the returning stubble around my crotch. She is whispering something in my ear.

"I think that you are about ready for something special, Mee-lad. Would you like me to sit on your face, my dah-ling?"

"Oh well, yes…that sounds delightful. Erm….mmmmmmwwwhhhah…."

Pandora can be very spritely, and before I am fully awake she has jumped up into a kneeling position, and splayed her knees either side of my ribcage, her face towards my feet. Then suddenly she leans forward, her breasts brushing my thighs and my face disappears between her buttocks. Initially I can't breathe too well, as I explore the smooth contours of her bum with my hands, and the bumpy fish tattoo on her lower back. She flops downwards holding my feet, and I hear her gasping as I work my tongue magic sex action. She pushes herself up by her arms, and I feel her lips about my one-eyed wonder weasel, which is soon deep inside her throat as she works it up and down.

This is a new one on me, I believe they call this the '69' position? So called, Sparky once informed me, on account of the year it was invented, 1969. It is kinky, and good. She is really enjoying it, I can tell by the muffled contentment down below, and the way her hips are jutting back and forth into my face. Uh ho, I think there could be a mutual climax here…I am getting near and so is she.

"OH, OH, OMG, MILAD, OH MY GOD, OH…OH… THHAAAAAAAAAAARRRRRRPP!"

Jesus H Christ, she has farted in my face. I briefly wonder if this is part of the '69' process of enjoyment/fulfilment, or indeed an analogue of the 'squirting' action from Pandora's usual climaxing, in which case there may be more than gas effluent to contend with. Actually Pandora's farts are quite pleasant, and she isn't shy of breaking wind if she needs to, I've noticed. This one I'm getting at very close quarters has more than a hint of eel about it, and the broccoli odour is intense.

"Oh, I am so sorry, dah-ling, I hope I haven't put you off?" She is kneeling up across me and her hips and neck turned, an actual girlish blush on her face and a guilty smirk. I don't think I have ever seen her genuinely blush before. It does things to me.

"You are a bad girl for farting in my face!" I say to her, lifting her knee and sliding out the other side, and rising to my own knees. "Now bend over, I am going to punish you!"

She puts her forefinger in her pouted mouth and does her little girl act.

"Oooh, punish mwe? For wun ikkle fart? You awr a cwuel man." Then she drops forward and I smack her bum – both cheeks, quite hard.

"Oooh, you smacked me, you cwuel man. But you make me weally wet too." My weasel is throbbing hard, and I rip open a condom packet and equip him with a raincoat, and before I know, he is pounding away at Pandora, as hard as I have ever felt him and going deep into her and almost out again before plunging back in, faster, faster, faster. A couple more slaps on her behind, and my lips are pursed, my eyes are rolling and I'm trying not to say "Oh yeah, baby!" I succeed in not saying it, in fact I am blowing so hard and dripping with so much sweat that all I can do, as I pump inside her, is to sink my head and chest to her back, and to pant her name as I close my eyes.

I DREAM OF BEING AT SEA. I am lying face down on a lilo on the gentle swell of a wine-coloured ocean and I am aware that I am being swept away on a riptide. I am at peace though, as the shore recedes to a thin grey line. A friendly seal bobs its black domed head from the waters and lets out a great snort of welcome to its domain. I wake up. Gosh, it looks like I have been sleeping on top of Pandora all night, and it wasn't the seal snorting after all. I'm no massive weight, but it can't have been comfortable for her having me on top of her. But her sleeping face seems contented, and I peel my moist skin gently from hers, and wrap a fallen sheet about her curves and arches. She snorts again, rolls over onto her side into a foetal position and puts her thumb in her mouth. So sweet! I walk silently to the bedroom door, closing it softly behind me as I go into the stairwell, where you kind of have to hop across the spiral stair to get to the bathroom. There is a little window next to the bathroom door at the top of the stairs, and I stand naked and gaze across the river to the coast, where the morning sun is shimmering among long, flat, white clouds. I stretch my arms high in contentment of the world, the warm oak floorboards beneath my feet feeling good, and my body glowing in reverie from the night before.

"YER WANTIN' YER TEA YET?" What the f…? Glossop, sporting his lobster hat and blue overalls with profuse white chest hair billowing from the open neck, is crouching below me on the spiral stair, mending a long wooden trap which I imagine is what they use to catch their eels in these parts.

"Glossop, you made me jump! What the heck are you doing in here? I… was just about to come down and make a pot of tea myself!" My hands swing together to bring modesty to my glowing manhood.

"Cawl that a dick, do yer?!" What? What did he just say? The Bootle blood is rushing to my face. I am trying to figure out what he might just have said in his broad Suffolk accent that was not "cawl that a dick, do yer?"…but I cannot fathom an alternative. Indeed, affirmation is on its way, in the most ghastly way. Glossop puts down his eel trap, descends the three stairs to the grey flagstones, pops open two stud buttons at the crotch of his overalls, flops out his member, puts his hands on his hips, and stares up at me with a slit of a grin on his battered old face with what I am imagining is pride.

"Now *that* is what yer cawl a dick!" he caws like a rook with a smoker's cough. I stand, appalled, frozen to the spot. I have an uncle, my dad's brother, who lives in Frankfurt, and we go over there to stay with him sometimes. I love German beer and sausage, especially currywurst. There is one sausage I don't especially like though; one they call the weisswurst, or the white sausage. And that is precisely what is hanging out of Glossop's overalls. A great white sausage.

"Put your horrible nob away Glossop, and put the kettle on." Pandora is standing naked and leaning over the stairwell, wagging her finger at him in admonishment. "Have you finished in there, dah-ling, my tummy is swirling a bit?"

"Ah, yeah, yeah, morning Pandora. Yep, sure, all yours."

Glossop puts himself away and slinks off to the kitchen bay, muttering. I skip back to the bedroom and rustle about for some boxers, shorts and a vest top. The House of Correction is wonderful, but it is one of those places that you can hear just about everything, wherever you are? So I can hear Glossop filling the big kettle and putting it on the Aga, which is fine, but I can also hear Pandora pissing into the toilet and making further gas. I am learning that perhaps I am a bit too 'buttoned up' for this very permissive and relaxed new world in which I find myself. Sparky can walk into our bathroom in Horsham and start pissing, and not only does he not shut the door, he carries on his conversation with me. I have to shout at him to shut the bastard door. Anyhow, he needs to concentrate more on his stream as it usually spatters the bowl, and it is always me that ends up cleaning the toilet every month. OK, change may come. I am cool with the little sploshes emanating from the bathroom and Pandora's satisfied groans. I am OK with Glossop getting his sausage out. I am going to embrace the naked biology of people, and celebrate it. But not my stinking armpits... where is my *Lynx*?

The sound of Mrs Glossop shuffling into the house like a small animal is soon followed by wafts of bacon in the sizzle of a frying pan. I descend into the kitchen where she completely ignores my cheerful good morning, and scurries about cracking eggs and slicing mushrooms. Glossop slams a huge pot of tea on the dining table and is muttering something about eels.

Pandora comes down in a blue cotton dressing gown, through which her enormous nipples are quite visible, but she doesn't seem to notice Glossop staring at them and rubbing his sausage. It is wonderful how posh people like Pandora can simply ignore the servant class. Ah, perhaps she has seen him. Ladies can see things without seeming to look.

"Glossop, row over the river and bring as many of the papers as they have in Carradine's would you? There's a good chap. Oh, lovely, thank you, Mrs G you are a wonder. And two rounds of white toast with some of that delicious butter you make?"

Mrs G. smiles and nods without eye contact, and we tuck into the most amazing fry up. I take a picture of my plate with my Arne-Phone to send to Sparky, who has already texted me to say he has left his aunt's and needs to know I'm OK. I send him an MMS of my plate and text that I'm very OK.

"Mrs G, I wonder if you will make Milad and I a picnic basket for lunch? We will explore the other little islands in the canoe today."

This sounds like a fantastic day ahead. Mrs G. just nods and brings Pandora's toast, which my goddess slathers with the yellowest butter I've ever seen.

"FLOATING, FLOATING DOWN THE RIVER IN MY DUG OUT CANOE". This is an obscure song by a band called *King Trigger* which happens to be on the jukebox at *The Tig*. One of our faves. I feel like singing it out loud, as I kneel at the back of a prospector canoe, a picnic hamper between me and Pandora, who is sitting with her feet out in front of her, braced on a wooden strut. But I don't sing out loud much - it takes a bit of nerve, really, so I just leave the song singing away in my head. I have a long single paddle, which I alternate from left to right of the stern, whilst Pandora has one of those double paddles which she expertly propels, and we are zooming along up-river against the current. I watch the muscles in her back flex as she lifts up one side of the oar and then the other, then draws the immersed side through the foaming water in a curve. I am feeling something greater than affection as she paddles, and I have to admit that this might just be a love I've never previously felt.

"To starboard, you scurvy dog!" she calls over her shoulder laughing, pointing with her oar to a small island ahead and to our right. I always get port and starboard mixed up, and I try to remember the mnemonics my Dad taught me. "The sailor left port with a red nose?" And what is it? "Star light, star bright, starboard to the right?" Something like that, anyway.

"Aye aye, Cap'n Pandora!" I am plunging my oar to the left and smiling, and feeling the warm sum on my face and the cool spray and splash of water on my arms.

We zoom towards a small curving pebbly beach on the island ahead, and I can see from Pandora's quickening strokes that she wants to hit the shore as hard as possible in order to beach the boat, so I bend my back to propel as much hard water as I can, my triceps burning as we hurtle on, and blisters forming on my thumb. I hear the scraping of stone on boat bottom (is that the hull?) as my captain raises her oar above her head, and half the boat is successfully beached as it lilts slightly over to port...no, starboard, no dammit, as you were. Port.

I paddle ashore as Pandora hauls the canoe well clear of the water and I lift out the wicker picnic hamper. She sits cross-legged, perspiring gently in the midday sun, her eyes closed in contentment. Some minutes later, she leans over to the boat to lift out a floppy straw sunhat which she fits around her green locks, which resemble the glittering weed waving in the shallows before us.

"In the hamper, Mee-lad, you will find a little pipe. And a blue pouch. Bring it to me."

I find a clay pipe with a long stem, reminding me of the Pilgrim Fathers, for no very good reason. And a blue velvet tobacco pouch. Wordlessly, Pandora stuffs the pipe with some rolling tobacco, and a pinch of what looks to me like weed into the bowl. She swirls and tamps the contents, before running a lighter over them. She reclines like the goddess of the river on one elbow, puffing clouds of exotic fragrance into the brackish air. After a while, she hands it to me. Uh huh, this is good shit. This is better than the stuff Deano gets when we go fishing. I usually go into one of my coughing fits when I smoke dope, but I am trying to be cool as I hand the pipe of peace back to her, but I have to clear my throat quite loudly. "Mellow. Ahhehemmm! Very mellow!"

Pandora smiles like a contented cat, her eyes turning smokier with each inhalation and exhalation.

"Do you knoooowww, Meeeee-lad?" she purrs.

"Do I know what, Pandora?" I feel as though I am smiling very broadly, as I take the pipe again.

"I am feeling ve-ry horny. Indeed." Whilst it doesn't seem very rare that Pandora is feeling horny, this may be a different species of horny than I have previously encountered? She rises, and slowly and sensuously removes her espadrilles and sets off barefoot into the tiny island - so slowly it is barely a walk, her hips slinging from side to side. She looks over her shoulder, casts off her hat, and shakes down her hair, gazing back at me like a jungle temptress, beckoning me to follow. At each slow stride, she is peeling off an item of clothing, and holds each aloft before letting it fall to the carpet of soft brown pine needles. She is soon walking in only her pants, and since these are a black G-string, she is effectively naked as he continues her carefree way. A heady combination of weed, nature and desire takes over in my cargo shorts. I follow. I reckon I am turning into a total stud.

In mid-island, we reach a glade towards the edge of which is a great oak tree and she stops and spins round. She leans back brazenly against its' enormous girth, her arms above her head and her eyes gently closed. It's a sight I'll never forget, or want to forget. I stop dead in my tracks, ten metres away, breathless with her beauty, with the beauty of the glade. It's a conker-wonking scene to remember. I close my eyes and open them again, like I'm opening and closing a camera shutter. I do that sometimes if there's something before my eyes I especially want to store in the memory card of my brain. One of the details my brain camera records is that there are a pair of leather gloves tucked into the front of her G-string. Hmmm. Interesting.

"Come here, Mee-lad." I need no second invitation, or I'll be arriving early in my cargo pants. She kisses me full on the mouth, the taste of the marijuana on her tongue, and then she spins me around so I face the mighty tree. "Hug the great oak, dah-ling. Feel his energy!" I do, and...I genuinely can! I don't usually go in for this tree-hugging malarkey, but perhaps I've been wrong...it's like a great pulse of life entering my body! And entering something deeper...my soul, maybe? As Sparks would say..."heavy, this is heavy!"

Pandora disappears behind the tree - probably a bit of 'hide and seek' on the cards here? Well, if it is hide and seek, it is going to be with a twist...I feel a rope around my left wrist, which tightens, then loops around my right wrist, and my arms are jagged in tight embrace around the tree! My right cheek is green with the moss and lichen on the rough bark as my face is pulled close to the trunk and my arm sockets are stretched. I am well tethered to this ancient tree! Pandora's face is suddenly pressed to my available left cheek and she is whispering something in my ear as she snaps open the button to my shorts, and they fall to the woodland carpet.

"Now, *you* were a very naughty boy, last night, Milad, weren't you?" she says in a sing-song teas-y kind of voice.

"Woj I Panndorra?" This comes out a bit slurred, not because I am especially stoned, but because it's funny how your voice changes when one side of your face is compressed into a tree trunk.

"Yes, you were. And it's not Pandora, to you boy. It's Goddess. Remember?" Uh-ho, her voice is turning severe, and it looks like The Pink Room of Pain is coming to a tiny island in the middle of the River Orwell. It's like the M & S summer road show.

"Yesh, Goddesh."

"Yes, very naughty indeed. I think you must have forgotten *all* about your contract. Who ever heard of the Sub smacking the Dom's botty? Well, she didn't appreciate it, Milad. And now you are going to pay."

I feel like protesting that she seemed to be OK with my command performance of last night, and that she had farted in my face, but a combination of the stuck jaw thing and the contractually-required compliance mitigates otherwise. She yanks down my boxers to expose my bum to the dappled sunlight. I am still half erect, and my eager weasel brushes the craggy bark.

"Yesh, Goddesh." I watch her one-eyed, as she withdraws the gloves from her G-string and peels them on. I have a jelly feeling in my solar plexus, readying myself for a leather-gloved spanking. But instead, she picks her way barefoot out of the glade and disappears down the woodland path. I hear the cracks of her footsteps from some way away, and I think to myself that I am vaguely needing a pee. Weed always seems to act as a bit of a diuretic on me. I am wondering where she has gone, when suddenly she re-appears like a bare-breasted savage from the forest, brandishing a great deal of foliage.

"Did you wonder where I'd gone, boy?"

"Erm, yep, I dl-id. Goddesh." I am drooling a bit, it feels like my right cheek has gone to sleep. Oh, fucking hell. The foliage she carries is a massive bunch of nettles. A mixture of those evil drooping flower heads; tiny bright sharp green new leaves (the worst stingers); and big floppy, hairy, mature leaves. My bollocks start to retract in fear.

"Yes, you were such a bad boy last night that I have had to bring you to The Glade of Pain. Let's see if these stingers will bring you to your senses, shall we?"

She is very lightly teasing my left buttock with one of the nettle flower heads, and I feel that weird, cool singeing and prickling feeling. It isn't a pain I feel too uncomfortable with. But not for long. Pandora plants her bare legs wide apart, and gripping the base of the stems of the nettle bunch, she begins thrashing me about my bum and legs with all her considerable might.

I am not sure who is howling louder - me or her.

"YOO-BAD-AND-WUDE-BOY!! YOU-WILL-BE-STINGY-THRASHED!!" she is yelling, and then whooping, like she does when her Babes are around. I am less articulate.

"YEEEEE-YEEEE-YAHAHA….YEEEE…..YOOOOO!!" But it is when she stops thrashing me that the trouble really starts. I remember blundering through a patch of nettles higher than my head when I went fishing with my Dad once when I was little. I was wearing my school shorts, and the whole of my legs and arms went red and were covered in irritating white lumps. But that, as they say…'was nuthin'. I feel - actually, I don't feel - my bum, or the backs of my stubbly legs. They tingle for a bit and then go numb, like they are actually anaesthetised. Which is just as well. She has in her hand a switch of silver birch which could not look more like a circus ringmasters' whip, unless it was painted black.

"Now, I am going to add some stripes to your spots, boy. Would you like that?"

"Yesh, goddesh." I would not really like the stripes which are about to be administered, but there is clearly little point in protest, or the stripes may become even more vivid and numerous.

"How many stripes would you like…you very bad tiger?"

 "Er…shree, goddesh?"

"Three? Three is it, my lad? Well, let us see how three stripes will suit you, then!"

"YEE-OWCH!!" OK, two more, you can take it, Milad.

"OWWWWW!" That was mean, that was right in the same place as the first one, I am reckoning. That's gonna be one vivid stripe.

"AHHHHHH!" Even meaner, right across the back of my fucking legs.

"I do apologise, naughty tiger. I have only given you two stripes. And three isn't nearly enough. Actually, I would say, six of the best stripes for you. How does that sound?"

That isn't sounding good to me at all. I am trying to figure out several things. I am wondering if this is genuinely a revenge attack for me taking on some 'dom' on last night, or if it was on the cards in any case? But more importantly, my pain threshold quotient is fast approaching during this birching, definitely leaving the 3's for the 2's. I don't know why or how, but this is more painful that the bull whip she was goading me with as I span around the Hamster's Wheel in The Pink Room of Pain. Maybe she is just whacking me a lot harder today.

"YOOOOOOOWWWW!!" Yikes, surely they heard that thwack against my bum on the mainland, and if not that, then my involuntary cry of pain.

"ANSWER ME, YOU IMPUDENT BOY!" Pandora roars. "I asked you quite clearly if six of the best would suit you Milad? And that one didn't count!"

"Yesh goddesh, shix shounds perfect."

"Ah, you want six do you?"

"Yesh goddesh, shix please."

"Right well, then that's better, you shall have them. You have four good stripes already, bad tiger. You need another across your manly thighs." I can see her out of the corner of my one functional eye, aiming a vicious swish. Right, I am not calling out any pain on these last two…

"AAAAAAAAAAAAAAAAAAHHHHH! " I lose my cool a bit here. "That was a fucking 2 Pandora! I am not signed up to Pain Level 2!! My limit is Pain Level 3…that is what the contract says. I am going to say the code word for release now. I've had enough of this shit!" I mean it…but the trouble is, I can't remember the code word, can I, or rather, the code phrase? What is it, dammit? Something like Gimp, no, I know, whew, I remembered.

"Bungee Jump, Pandora. Bungee Jump. Please untie me now."

Pandora's face is suddenly right in mine, mocking. "What are you talking about, boy? You want to go for a bungee jump? Well, that will have to be in your own time, not mine! And that certainly is no code word *I* have ever agreed to!" What?! Is she taking the piss? Hang on, no, she's right, it isn't Bungee Jump, is it? Crap, it's like that though, what the hell is it is it?

"Well, whilst you are having a think about escape words, you cowardly little maggot…let's have this shirt of your back shall we?" There is a terribly wild look about Pandora before she disappears behind me, and I feel both her hands yanking at the back neck of my vest top. It being a *Gap* top, she tears it easily in two. The work is shoddy, sometimes at *Gap*. She eases the two halves of the top over my shoulders, and is rubbing her hands up and down my back.

"Mmmm, such a brown back, Mee-lad. Such a smooth back. And such a stripey, well-muscled bottom. No more room for any stripes there. I shall need to flog your broad shoulders, won't I?"

"Look Pandora, this is going too far. I can't remember the code word, is it Bubble and Squeak? No? Anyway, it doesn't matter, because I didn't sign up for a flogging."

"Well I'm going to flog you anyway! What are you going to fucking do about it? I don't see anybody around here that can help you, do you?" She is reaching between my legs and cups my nutsack in her gloved hands and slowly clenches her fist.

"No miss, I mean, goddess, I don't. Ah…ooh…hah…"

"Well, I could carry on squeezing until you squeal like a *castrato*, or alternatively, you give me special consent to flog you, boy!"

Just like in many cowboy movies I have seen, I am making a bit of progress releasing one hand from the noose it is secured in. The trick seems to be to relax both hands whilst wiggling the fingers of one of them. I can feel my right hand is half way out. Play for time, play for time.

"Er, yes, please goddess; a flogging would be just the ticket. Thank you. Very much." There is a blessed release of the crown jewels, and I can extend my left arm just a little bit further to give my right hand a tiny bit more slack to work in. She is pacing around the glade, running the birch whip lightly over my back, and lays it across my shoulder blades where she is aiming to strike.

"Er, I don't suppose I could have a drink before my enjoyable flogging, goddess? I'm a bit parched after my nettling and striping?" The birch is allayed, and she inspects my visible eye, quizzically.

"A drink, wretch? You can have a plastic cup of my warm wee, if you would like?"

Huh? This contract isn't worth the paper it's written on! Urine is specifically written out! But…hang on. If she has to nip back to the beach to wee in a plastic cup – he, he, that is all the time I will need! By the time she comes back, I will be pretending to be straddled around this tree, and then…ha ha, well <u>then</u> we will see what happens!

"Yes, goddess, a cup of your warm wee would be marvellous. Just the job. Thank you."

Her eyes are upon my eye again, and they narrow, suspiciously. "Very well, you dirty little pervert. I will get you what you ask. But, I think I had better check your bonds before I go. Don't you?" No, no, do not check the bonds! I am nearly free! My fingers wriggle frantically, but it's too late…she is circling the tree.

"HA! I SEE YOUR GAME, VILLAIN!"

Shit! She has trussed my hands tight again, and I am once again defenceless against the birch whip -and for that matter, the warm wee.

"Mee-lad, Mee-lad," she purrs on her return to my half of the tree. "I don't think you want your flogging, at all."

"Don't you, goddesh?" I reply in vague disinterest, resigned to my fate, my face pulled hard against the tree trunk again.

"No, I don't." Her voice is suddenly warmer again, and she is massaging my shoulders. "And I have a large bunch of dock leaves to apply to your stingy legs. And do you know how I like to apply the dock juice to wounded soldiers?"

"No, goddesh."

"I like to do this." She rises, and crumpling a ball of dock leaves in her hands, she rubs them vigorously into her enormous jugs. I find the site of her green-smeared breasts strangely arousing. She is becoming a sort of green version of the blue jungle creatures in *Avatar*. Me and the boys love *Avatar*. We are planning to have an *Avatar* party but never seem to get around to it.

This busty, shorter, stockier version of a Na'vi Princess is grinding her green melons into my mottled and enflamed buttocks. I have never been convinced of the efficacious qualities of dock leaves, preferring a good dose of Calamine Lotion, personally. But hey, this surely beats a flogging.

Pandora is curiously gentle and tender during our remaining time of the island. She soothes my wounds, we smoke more grass; my head is in her skirted lap as she leans against the side of the boat and reads a novel called *The Devil Wears Prada*, occasionally reading bits out loud to me, as she runs her fingers through my hair. Yes, my stripes are singing, my spots are livid, but the island and its flora and fauna and lapping water all seem to confirm what I am thinking. I do believe that I am truly in love, for the very first time. There is another song in my head, something 'old school' that my Mum used to play. It's Jo Stafford, singing *You Belong to Me*.

"OOOH, PUT THE TELLY ON MEE-LAD! MY MO IS RUNNING!" I am watching the Glossops shuffle off down the woodland path into the summer evening darkness, Mrs G having prepared a buffet supper for us, of some lavishness. The kitchen table is heaving with local produce, and I am stealing shards of local ham and popping raw peas from their shells, something that reminds me of helping Mum make Sunday lunch when I was little. My specialist job was making the mint sauce out of mint leaves from the herb garden, with vinegar and sugar, in a glass trifle dish. But only when we had lamb, obviously. Pandora is calling from upstairs in the shower, the bathroom door wide open, and I have just descended having ogled her whilst I leaned casually in the door frame. She was standing under the huge drench shower head, her eyes closed and her mouth smiling as she was deluged with cool water, her green hair drenched, her light pink nipples contracted into dripping turrets, and as she turned, her bum was glowing peachy pink and running with the suds she bent to massage into her thighs. Turning towards me, and stepping away from the gushing flow, she had cupped up her breasts and pressed them into the glass of the shower cubicle, and bounced back and forth, like she was getting a good 'seeing to' from behind, smouldering at me as if to invite me to do so. As the orbs squashed into the glass and bounded back to their huge ovals, my pocket rocket had leapt back into life...but she was just teasing me. She had turned with a dismissive shrug, and returned to her intimate ablutions. With a pout and a wag of her index finger, she admonished me over the noise of the gushing water.

"Be off with you, you naughty Peeping Tom! And get rid of the Glossops if they haven't already left. Send them off to their little shack!"

Downstairs, I turn on the TV. Jess Ennis has won Gold, and as she weeps with joy in her post-race interview, I well up too, and a tear (I guess of pride?) trickles down my face. Mo Farah is up next in the 10,000 metres and some ginger bloke is doing well in the long jump. Pandora comes skipping down the stairs wrapped in numerous towels about her head and body, and she hands me a large comb. She plonks herself down on the floor, her back against the sofa, and reaches for a cushion which she wriggles under her bum.

"Comb my hair, dah-ling. But first get me a *huge* bowl of *Doritos* and Mrs G's delightful hummus. Oh, here comes Mo! Isn't he mah-vellous!"

I sit behind her on the sofa and run the comb through her wet hair, patiently easing out knots so as not to yank her roots, and I continue to comb it long after it is a shiny damp knot-free mat, my shorts soaked with the moisture which drips from the immaculately cut ends. We plunge *Doritos* into the thick chickpea and oil mix, and it tastes like the best hummus ever. Pandora is purring in pleasure as the comb gently rakes her scalp, and I lean over to kiss her damp neck.

Mo is doing well after the first ten laps, and I stand to remove my sodden *Reebok* shorts, and I pad about the House of Correction in my new Bjorn Borg's Suns of Energy stretch trunks that Pandora has bought for me. My legs and bum are tingling from the nettling, so I don't know if the 'boob-docking' did any good. The red wheals on my legs and bum are livid, and I still feel a bit livid about them, too.

I wander over to the kitchen area to pile two plates high with salad and local cut meats, and ply both plates with the unbeatable *Heinz* salad cream. It is high time that salad cream put in an appearance in the Flat 3 Top Ten. I do prefer the glass pots though, where you have to pat the bottom and it comes out in great gobs. With these plastic bottles, it just oozes out of the nozzle accompanied by an embarrassing farting sound. I am feeling a bit troubled. I am discovering that this masochism stuff is not for me, and though I love Pandora, I don't think I can do much more of it. If anything, I want to be the one disciplining her, though not in any kinky way. I think I just want to be her man.

"Come on, Mo!" Pandora is shouting and pumping the air with her fist. "Don't let that fucking Moroccan trip you up!"

I put our plates of food on the floor besides Pandora, and return to the kitchen area to pour two glasses of Cava, and when I sit down on the floor next to her, I hear the bell for the final lap. Mo kicks out in front.

"COOOOOM ARRRNNN!!!!" Pandora is bellowing like a she-bull. I smile at her enthusiasm, and recall Lisa when Kevin Davies (Lisa's hero) knocks one in for Bolton. "YES, YES, YES, HE'S DOING IT, YES, YES, COME ON MO, YES, OMG, I think I shall have an inner goddess ecstasy if he wins, Milad, pass me that Cava, mmm…
YES…..YES…..YEEEEEEEEEEE…..EEEEEEEEEEESSSSSSSSSSS!!"

Mo has collapsed victorious, panting and spread-eagled to the track, and so has Pandora. I think she may actually have had an orgasm (though one of her less messy ones). But she is soon back up and on the sofa, positively devouring her salad. And it isn't long before Team GB has yet another gold medal in the bag…the ginger guy has won the long jump!

Although I find the TV coverage a bit over-hyped (my media training at Bolton Uni always useful to spot hyperbole), I do feel so proud to be British on this night that somebody on the commentary team just called the best night for Britain in Olympic history. But my doubts about Pandora's kinkery continue to nag me as she tops up the fizz, and helps herself to another plate of meat. My doubts about kinkery are right to bother me.

"Take off your shirt, MIlad, and get on all fours. I am going to make you into my buffet bar!"

I am vaguely considering disobeying her. What is that crackpot contract worth anyway? But…my other contract…that is worth dollar, man, and I am suspecting that the two contracts may be interlinked. Great, I'm a male prostitute then? Nah, what am I on about? I know she has strong feeling for me too, and I remember that this is all just a fascinating game.

So, shirtless and down on all fours it is. I position myself so that I can see the telly, and grab a slurp of fizz, and then feel discs of salami and pepperoni slapping in a line up my spine, from tailbone to neck bone. I use my keen nose to ascertain the next buffet ingredients - she has a chopping board on my back slicing tomatoes, boiled eggs and spring onions, which she layers in a line adjacent to the cured meat. She is giggling a bit, and evidently enjoying herself. There is the dampness of washed lettuce leaves from a colander, and then she is off back to the kitchen - from where there are the sounds of the pop of the cork from a bottle of Prosecco; whisking in a metal bowl and the slicing of crusty bread.

She returns to drizzle the vinaigrette she has whisked up all over the lettuce, which dribbles over my ribs, and I think she is arranging slices of mozzarella cheese among the sliced tomato. Uh huh, I didn't think it would be long. She is sliding my Bjorn Borg's Suns of Energy stretch trunks over my stripy bum and down my table legs. She seasons her salad buffet from salt and pepper grinders, and then sits down to dine. Her table knife and fork are mercifully quite blunt, though they prick and glide, actually in quite an interesting way.

"Mmmmm, you make such a delightful light oak table, Mee-lad. Keep very still, I am putting my wine glass on you." It is surprisingly hard work being a dining table, especially when you are as fully laden as I am.

"Bee-RRP! Delicious! But I can't possibly manage all of it. Here, let's move it all to one side, so I can have my dessert." I feel the back of the knife scrape the salad to the shoulder end of my back, and I have a slice of salami on the back of my neck. Pandora removes her wine glass from me, and I hear her rise to potter about in the kitchen once more. I hear the kettle being filled and hissing on one of the Aga hobs. Hmm, bit ominous. Yo! I just remembered the code word - I mean code phrase. It's not Bungee Jump or Bugger Gimp…it's Bubba Gump! Funny how things come back to you at odd times. Right, I can keep that up my sleeve…well, if I was wearing any.

Aha, Pandora is making herself a cup of coffee (I'm kind of hoping there is a saucer involved?) and placing a dessert bowl containing what smells like Mrs G's chocolate cake and double cream. Wouldn't mind some myself. Aahahaahah…OK, there isn't a saucer, but it feels like a small espresso cup, so the heat isn't too bad. I attempt a table joke. As my Dad always says, never lose your sense of humour.

"I see you don't use coasters, goddess. You will leave a nasty ring on your coffee table, you know!" This goes down well, Pandora is hooting and clapping here hands.

"Oh you are such a funny table! A funny, sexy table! Oh, look here is Jess Ennis...isn't she wonderful? Turn the sound up, table."

Carefully, I reach for the TV remote (me and Sparky call ours Joey. Joey Remote. It's clever - a pun on Joey Ramone. We love *The Ramones*). I wonder if Joey Ramone has ever been a food table in his wild rock n' roll life? I lift one of my 'legs' (actually right arm) and push the 'volume up' button on the Joey to better hear what Jess is saying. Which of course (like all the athletes) is never very much - "unbelievable"; "crowd were amazing"; "incredible"; "coaches fantastic", etc., etc., and naturally what The Beeb really want is her in tears and the audience in tears, and it isn't long coming. I do wonder why they have to interview these sporting heroes – who really wants to see Andy Murray blubbering or Sir Chris Hoy weeping? My incisive media thoughts are interrupted.

"I think it would be so much more romantic if we dined by candlelight? Don't you, Mr Table?"

"Er, yes?" Must stop doing that question for an answer thing. I notice the Aussies do it all the time, like that swimmer that Gary Lineker has on his sofa. Gary Lineker. My Dad says that he was a brilliant striker, but I don't reckon him as front man for the Olympics coverage. Me and the lads think it should have been Adrian Chiles (who looks like Sparky a bit, but older). Now he is a funny guy he is...*and* he knows his stuff. Though he probably is rubbish at football. You can't have it all, as my Mum wisely says.

I can feel several tea lights cold on my skin in the available gaps between salad remains, chocolate cake and coffee, and I hear the rasp and click of a lighter. Mercifully, heat rises (GCSE Physics, useful once more) and the little metal dishes containing the tea lights warm but don't burn. Pandora is tucking into her chocolate cake with gusto, and the coffee cup is cooling down a bit. I'm keeping very still though, because I do not want it spilling! I can smell it is a black coffee, and likely to scald.

As she chomps and sighs with pleasure, I am reminded of the two New Zealander guys who call themselves *The Flight of The Conchords*. Me and the lads especially love Jemaine (though Bret is cool too and so is their manager). One of their comedy songs is called *If You're Into It* and has the fantastic line "*being rude, with the food, if that's what you are into.*" Me and the lads know all the lines and sing it loads. I am grinning as I sing it in my head. But I'm not grinning long!

"Ah…ah…ohhhh..aaaaaah!" Not unexpectedly, it's the hot wax treatment. Pandora is giggling as she tips candle wax on various areas of my back, and it sears slightly before quickly congealing. Wax, I can deal with. I am experienced with Lisa in the hot wax department. Plus I do not want to spill that coffee. But now, I can sense Pandora hovering over my bare bum.

"Hang on, Pandora. No. NO? YAAAAAAAAAAAAAH!" Her giggle turns to a guttural chuckle as she dribbles hot wax down my bum cleft. This is a weird sensation, as it reaches my clenched bum hole and is caking on my dangling tackle. Man, she is a bad girl. But I can take the wax. But not the hot coffee scalding my back The Milad Table stays steadfast. She is off to the kitchen area again, I hear her bare soles slapping on the stone flags. She is gone some time, and she is giggling again as she returns.

She is parting my bum cheeks, and I'm glad I'm hairless in there, because she is peeling off strips of set wax from my glory hole. Hang on a cotton-pickin' mo'?

"Pandora, no. I said NO! Remember the contract…remember? Uuuuuuuuuhhhhh? Noooooooooooo!"

By the smell of it, she has slathered Mrs G.'s homemade mayo onto some kind of vegetable…and she is shoving it up my arse!!!

"Pandora! No sodomy!" I protest. "Remember, we agreed that??!! Bubba Gump! Bubba bloody Gump!! Pandora, that's enough!"

I am still mindful of the hot coffee cup - even though I reckon I now have a courgette sticking out of my arse. Then, I hear the click of her camera phone. I can picture the photo only too well. It is Milad Brown, on all fours, underpants around his knees, back laden with a supper table, and a summer squash sticking out of his bum.

"Do not put that onto your Facebook page, Pandora! You are a wicked girl. I am getting up right now, I don't care about all this stuff on my back! Do you hear me, woman??!!"

"Oh, I wouldn't put in on Facebook, my dah-ling. But you do look so cute with a little tail. I simply *must* MMS this to the Babes!"

Right, that's it. Fuck this for a game of Arne-darts. I rise up to my knees, and there is an almighty cascade of food, crockery, cups and candles. The coffee and candle wax splash my calves as I eject the greasy courgette, hoist up my Bjorns and I am on my feet, as she runs squealing to the downstairs toilet and locks herself in.

"Pandora, come out! You are a wicked woman, and this contract is bloody well broken. I am going to give you the spanking that *you* deserve!"

"Ah, ah, you thcaring me oo big bwute! Ooo big bully!" she is whining in her little girl's voice.

"The longer you stay in there, the harder it will be for you! I am staying right here, *and* I'm eating the rest of the chocolate cake!"

I cut myself a decent wedge and spool double cream over it, before sitting against the wooden toilet door.

"Mmmm, delicious. You will stay in there all night whilst I stuff myself and watch the telly."

"Booo-hooo, booo-hooo. Oo awr a cwuel man. I want chocolate cake! I want CHOCOLATE CAKE!!" she is drumming her fists on the inside of the wooden door.

"Well then come out, take your spanking and *then* you can have as much cake as you want." I hear the bolt in the door slide cautiously back, and my Bjorn's are getting suddenly tighter. I put down my bowl and stand, as a mischievous brown eye peeps out of the opening door.

"Come out. It'll be harder if you don't!"

Little girl Pandora steps wide-eyed and timorous from her hidey-hole, and though the towel around her midriff remains fastened, the one tucked under her arms has fallen, and she seems suddenly smaller in stature and her huge knockers stiff in fear at the nipples. I take her wrist firmly.

"Come over here, right away. Now bend over that kitchen table. That's it. Now, for a taste of your own medicine."

I lift the towel to expose her quivering bottom, and I grab a fish slice from a metal rail.

"You are a very bad girl, and I am going to punish you!" My throbbing gentleman seems no longer very gentlemanly, as he rises to eagerly witness me pushing down with my left hand on her fish tattoo, and thrashing her wriggling arse, with resounding thwaps of the fish-slice. It leaves behind satisfying pink fish slice marks on both her bum-cheeks.

"Ow! Ow! Ow! Ow! Ow! Ow! Vat herts! Ow! Ow! Ow! Ow! Ow! Ow!"

I am slightly ashamed to admit to myself that I am enjoying this. Maybe it's a bit of revenge, or maybe I am the Dom-guy after all? My head is swimming, and my peeping weasel longs to join the action. I know I should run upstairs and grab a condom, but the moment would be gone, so you know what, fuck it. Down with the fish slice, off with the Bjorns, a step to the right, part her legs and I am in there giving her what for, my belly slapping against her collaged bum.

"AH…OH…AHH…NO…NO…NOT LIKE…NOT LIKE…" she protests in vain, her hands reaching out to grab the chair on the other side of the table, her breasts squashed and splayed out either side of her, as I pummel her harder than I've ever pummelled. Very soon, I feel myself ready to explode - right, gotta get the timing right here…uh..uh…uh…ah! Just before I feel myself coming to fruition, I withdraw from her and spurt my protein shake all over her carp tattoo and into its gaping mouth. The spattered fish gazes balefully at me, like I'm an abusive fish porno pervert. I quickly avert my eyes.

Pandora lies gasping, eyes tight shut, but I haven't finished with her yet. Revenge is truly mine. I speedily collect the greasy bum courgette from the lounge area, dash back, and I stick the rude vegetable right up her asshole, twisting and turning it, before withdrawing it and tossing it on the floor. She is writhing and squealing, and as the obscure object is removed, she lies, panting, pink and silent.

Righto. What to do now? Cup of tea, perhaps? Or should I make a run for it myself - maybe all the wrath of Hell will befall me?! The answer soon comes.

She peels herself off the table, naked now, and steps towards me. She throws her arms around my waist, her head is on my chest, in a gesture that I take to be submission. I have broken this wild horse…just like they do in cowboy movies! I stroke her hair, softly, and wrap my arm tenderly around her naked waist. And then - she bites my right nipple…really-fucking-hard. It is the worst pain that I can conceive.

"YAAAAAAAAHAAAAAHAAAAAAAHOOOOOOOOOOOYAAAAA AAHHH!" I think it not an exaggeration to say I scream. She looks up at me with dark devil eyes, my right nip still between her teeth (thank God, 'cos I thought she might have bitten it off). I feel sick with pain as she releases it, and she pads away with a mean look in her eye to collect a Cath Kidston apron from a kitchen peg. She pops it over her head, and wraps the string around her waist before securing it with a determined bow.

"Sit down at the table, Mee-lad. I shall make mew-angues." Hmmm, she isn't the Little Girl Pandora anymore, but she isn't Goddess Pandora either. She has affected a slight 'lithp'. I do sit down, partly intrigued, partly in severe pain, and partly knackered. I sit naked on the wooden kitchen chair and knock back a glass of Prosecco.

She is breaking eggs into a cup and pouring the whites into a mixing bowl, and then turns to pre-heat the Aga oven.

"Now, it's important you don't make a mess, here. I want none of that nasty yellow yolk in my bowl. So-oo, in goes the sugar…"

She grabs a balloon whisk from the same rack as the fish slice, and her boobs wobble under the apron as her strong wrist sets about the glass bowl.

"I want to make tall, stiff, shining peaks." As the mixture thickens, she dips her forefinger in and sucks it into her mouth. It pops out of her puckered lips with a wet pop, to be replaced by a provocative smile. She leans over the bowl, the orbs of her breasts jiggling as she resumes her whisking. She stops briefly to meet my eyes.

"It *is* hard work…but the end wesult is well worth it."

I get it! She is Nigella! And me and the boys fucking well love Nigella! We all go very quiet when she is teasing us with her obvious innuendo. Sparks does a Nigella impwession, but it is rubbish. My love wand returns from his satisfied slumber to keen interest in the cookery show.

Content with her stiff peaks, Pandora spoons white blobs onto a baking tray, which she has made all greasy with butter, and pops the loaded tray into the oven. She returns coquettishly to the long table, and slips the halter of the apron over her neck and ravels the apron over her boobs. She dips the spoon in the remaining mixture, and applies two further meringues to her huge pink nipples.

"Would you like to taste my mew-angue mixture, Mee-lad?" She sallies over to me, her boobs near my face, and I do try her mew-angue mixture, my tongue lapping it from her hardening pegs. I slip my hand under her apron skirt and play the lute in her inner goddess. She is gasping and raking her nails into my hair, and then panting.

"Huh..huh…och..och, do you…och…like my ooooh…mixture…Mee… Mee..Mee…AAAAAAAAAHHHH!"

Warm love liquid is gushing over my lute-hand, splashing onto the stone floor. She pushes her breasts into my face and I can heat her heart thumping like a mad drum. I wriggle out of my Bjorns and she plants herself onto my throbbing pole, and she is arching and revolving her hips, pleasuring herself on my stiff peak. I am about to reach peak pleasure again.

"Pandora..ah..oh..I'm..ah…not wearing a con…" But in her delirium, she isn't listening. She is whirling around on me like a Cath Kidston-patterned Kitchen Aid and I can't hold on. I fill her with white icing from my piping bags.

We are clasped to each other - throbbing, sweating, sticky with meringue, my face lodged in her cleavage canyon.

"Ooooh, my mew-angues! I don't want them to burn, do I!" She hoists herself off me with a wet slurp and pads over to the oven, squatting down to lower the oven door.

"A few more minutes, yet!" she declares with a satisfied smile, and hitches herself back into her apron.

"Dah-ling boy!" she returns to squeeze me tight. "You do please me so. But you are so naughty! You *must* use protection, dear. I think I'm safe today, though. But you are *such* a bad boy."

Then she takes the dinner plate with the huge two-thirds eaten chocolate cake on it, and balances it on her palm, a mighty great grin spreading across her face.

"Pandora, what, no…meehhhhhhhhhgnnnnuuuuh." She has placed the cake right in my face - clown custard pie fashion - and she is revolving the plate and squashing it in my nose, as much of the destroyed cake falls down my chest and piles on my meat and two veg. When she removes the plate, laughing her gravelly laugh, I can't see much, and I rub my eyes like the plaintiff clown I have become.

"RIGGHHHT!" I bellow, rising to my feet. "If that's how you want it, miss! FOOD FIGHT!"

We are soon scampering around like giggling school kids, throwing all the stuff we can find at each other. Pandora finds a bag of flour, my aim at her with the egg yolks is spot on. The kitchen table goes crashing over as she tries to run away from me and I slip over on a mixture of bodily fluids and double cream, slapping down onto my bum. Covered in flour and chocolate cake, I sit there, gasping with laughter as Pandora pours a pint of milk over my head and pelts me with grapes. I am back on my feet, half blinded, but catch her and push her onto the sofa, which catapults backwards, her parted legs kicking wildly as I hold her wrists together with one hand and grind *Nutella* into her goddess. She bucks and wriggles, escaping my clutches as my hands are so greasy I can't hold her, and next thing I know, a whole bowl of fruit is thudding down onto my head. I never realised oranges could be so heavy. Slightly dazed, I am up and after her again, kicking over chairs and footstools to rip open the freezer and grab a pack of frozen peas.

I catch her again as she flees shrieking for the stairs, but I grab her ankle, pull her back down the steps as she struggles, and wrest her around to face me. I rip off her apron, and pin back her arms.

"AH, NO, MILAD, NO…NOT THE FROZEN PEAS, NO, PLEASE….EEEEEAAAAAAAAAAAHHHH, YOU LITTLE BAR-STARD!! NOOOOOO!!"

Oh yes, Pandora. The frozen pea treatment. The bag is applied to her belly, her breasts…and then I yank her forward and press it to her lower back. The fish gets another shock – a cold one this time. Then, I rip open the bag with my teeth and standing above her, I shower my shivering and squealing best-selling authoress with a cascade of frozen peas.

We are on the floor, laughing, rolling, kissing. Best food fight ever. Loads better than the time me and Sparks chucked raw eggs at each other. Now, they really do hurt.

The rest of the evening is a blur. There is more Prosecco, more giggling as we hose and clean each other in the shower, and we nibble delicious meringues in bed, sweet crumbs all over the sheets. As I pass out on her shoulder I know, despite all my misgivings, that I am in love with this amazing woman. My last thought before sleep is that I must do a poem called 'Food Fight'.

BEING A LIGHT SLEEPER, I am woken by the door of The House of Correction being unlocked. I put on my glasses and look at my watch. It is 08.20 hours. And it isn't the aged shufflers downstairs, there is no mistaking the clacking of Arne's Italian shoes. No trainers for him on a Sunday then, even if he has just rowed into mid-river. OMG. I have just remembered the serious carnage we left downstairs.

I peel myself from the snuggling Pandora (who smells of a heady mixture of musky sweat and stale cream, and is making cute piggy noises). I get up and rustle in my bag to find a pair of clean Calvin Kleins and my jeans. I wish I would have brought another *Gap* vest top, since yesterdays was ripped in two, but I find a bowling shirt with *'Mac's Alley, Baltimore'* written in large scrolled italics on the back. I didn't get it from Baltimore, I got it from *Next* in Horsham.

"Morning Arne!" I yawn down the stairs, trying to look casual. Arne doesn't look at all casual as he gives me a hint of a nod. He is wearing his usual suit and tie, and he is scurrying around cleaning up the hell-hole we left downstairs. With a wince I watch him pick up *that* courgette…with his bare hands. And my soiled Bjorns too. I reckon he needs a pair of *Marigolds* for this job.

"Mate, don't clear that mess up…I'll do it. Erm, I think me and Pandora got a bit pissed last night. Must have been the excitement of the Olympics."

Arne just shrugs like he's seen it all before and ignores my request, filling the kitchen sink with *Fairy Liquid* suds and hot water.

"Ah! Arne, dah-ling!" Pandora is standing shamelessly naked at the top of the stairs. I feel protective, like I want to drape something around her to save her modesty from Arne's stare, but the Nordic Iceman stares not. I do stare though; she looks tawdrily magnificent; drugged with sleep, her body lined as if by swirling henna tattoos from the imprint of knotted sheets and exposed mattress, her hair wild and stiff with egg white and gentleman's relish.

"Good morning, PM," he replies briskly, lifting up the collapsed sofa and taking broken plates to the bin. "We should leave around 11 if you are able. Coffee Press want a conference call this evening."

"Don't be such a bore, Arne. I am going back to bed, for as long as I like. We have had such fun, haven't we Mee-lad?" She drapes her sleepy arm about my shoulders and plants a smeary kiss on my cheek. Despite the perversions of the previous night, I can't help but feel like a bit of a sex god, as I stand there, soiled and sullied but red-blooded - looking down on what seems like a frigid and asexual albino darting about clearing up after us. Maybe I am more man than Arne after all!

"Right, Mee-lad dahling. I want another two hours sleep alone, after that *mauling* you gave me last night, you wild beast of the forest! Now, talking of the forest, I want you to go out after you have helped Arne to clear up, and I would like you to forage for wild mushrooms. I *so-ooo* want them for brunch! Pick them for me, dah-ling. There is a basket by the front door."

As Pandora flops back into bed, after I've been to the loo and brushed my teeth, I help Arne repair the wreckage downstairs. It looks like a tornado blew in during the night. Arne is absolutely not interested in my attempts at blokey repartee as he scurries around, so I take the wicker mushroom basket and leave him to it.

IT IS PEACEFUL WALKING IN THE LITTLE WOOD on this cool morning which has the slightest hint of autumn about it. I paddle in the cold lapping water, deep in thought about myself and the profound change in my life over the last month. Sparky has sent me an MMS of him and they guys in the Jag…they are cruising around and having a ball…I notice Nat is there with Rollo. I haven't seen many mushrooms yet, and I'm thinking that maybe it's a bit early for them? Me and Sparky picked magic mushrooms once when we were much younger, around seventeen, I reckon. He made tea with them and was really sick, though he said everything turned a bit blue-ish. I bottled it and didn't drink any, though I pretended I had, and then faked being spaced out. I've never told Sparky that - maybe I should 'fess up sometime.

My eye is caught by something white moving about in the water in front of me. Is it a manatee? Do they have manatees in Suffolk? I think they have beavers, so why not? Well, if it is a manatee, actually it is a pair of manatees. They swirl around each other, like they are mating, maybe? Then I hear them laugh, and I see that though there is indeed a pair of cavorting white mammals, they are in fact Mr and Mrs Glossop. 'Butt neked', as Sparks would put it. I don't want to let them see me, even though they don't seem in the least bit shy as they splash each other, and embrace whilst treading water. I withdraw a bit into the tree-fringed island. I have to smile as they troop out of the shallows holding hands, Glossop's nut brown head contrasting with his flopping great white sausage, whilst Mrs G's many pendulous folds and faintly grey colour remind me of the old wrinkly elephants in the *Babar* books.

They are laughing as he dries her with a towel, and they shuffle off into their little wooden cottage from which a thin stream of wood smoke emerges from a crooked metal-piped chimney. So I am twenty four and a half years younger than Pandora. So what? When I am sixty she will be eighty-four…we'll both be old! Maybe we will be swimming about in the River Orwell like this pair of manatees! And Pandora isn't too old to have kids. Say if she had one when she is 48 and another when she is 49…that's not too old! I might even have put a bun in the oven with the meringues last night. I am way ready to have kids with her, no worries. Right, I'd better concentrate on finding wild 'shrooms, or there'll be no kids for me... what am I thinking, no brunch for me, that is.

I search hard and find one or two odd-looking specimens...I am not very good on mushrooms, but obviously you don't want anything poisonous like toadstools. I am kind of hoping the great white manatee will appear, but Glossop strikes me as being one of those guys who is there when you don't want him, and isn't when you do. And on this particular occasion my theory holds - he isn't.

What I decide to do is, go and ask Pandora if these are the right ones, because there are a few about, but I don't want to pick them if they are wrong. I look at my watch and see her extra two hours in bed are almost up, another twenty minutes or so. I twist the iron ring of the great front door of The House of Correction, and inside all is quiet and phenomenally neat. Arne is like Harvey Keitel in *Pulp Fiction* – he's completely cleared up the big mess.

All is quiet...and I don't see Arne about. Hang on, all is not so quiet. Blood rushes to my cheeks and I am feeling slightly queasy. From above my head comes the sound of moaning. Pandora's unmistakeable sex-moaning. And there is the classic rhythmic squeak of bedsprings, and as the grunting gets more urgent, the scraping of the wooden bed legs on the wooden floor above. OK, breathe, do not panic, Milad! My heart seems to be in my neck (rather than in my mouth...I have never quite understood that expression?). OK, Pandora is not having sex with Arne. That is my null hypothesis, as my Science teacher used to say. Pandora is doing what she often does, which is enjoying herself with a peculiar sex toy. That is what is happening upstairs. Arne has gone for a walk. That is the situation here, so I am going to put on the kettle, be totally cool, and make myself a coffee. So I do.

The theory is going nicely. All I can hear from upstairs is Pandora moaning - well, screaming actually would be a better description - and it feels like she might come crashing through the ceiling at any moment, bed and all. But there is no hint of male enjoyment, none at all. So I sit on the sofa, and start to take a deal of excitement from Pandora's wild masturbational frolics. Then - I see Arne's shiny Italian shoes neatly arranged at the foot of the stair. OK. Continue to defend the hypothesis, Mr. Brown! Erm, Arne didn't want to get his natty shoes dirty when he went for a walk, and he has borrowed…Glossop's wellington boots? I have no evidence for the existence of wellington boots, Glossop's or anyone else's. And it would have been fairly likely, on this small island, that if Arne was out for a walk, then I would have caught sight of him during my fungal foray. Not impossible to have missed him, but reasonably unlikely. And if Arne is giving Pandora one, is he likely to be giving it the all-American 'whooppeee-yahoo-yeah-baby', shout-it-all-out routine? No, during sex, Arne is going to be as silent and cool as fjord at night, isn't he?

I am thinking *Inspector Morse,* here. My Mum loves *Inspector Morse.* Now, what would old 'Endeavour' make of this, eh? Well, he was a detective, right? He would go and see for himself what's going on upstairs. I wrestle with this for a bit. What if Arne is up there, giving Pandora a seeing to? What would I do? Run away? Bash him round the head with his shoe? Cry? I don't know. But suddenly, I have to know, and barefoot, I am creeping up the stairs.

The door is wide open. At first, I am hugely relieved. Pandora, her back to me is bucking and thrashing, her green hair wild and her big bum heaving up and down. She is evidently pleasuring herself as she straddles a huge white object. But then I see socks. With feet inside them. They weren't evident at first as they are white socks, like the bed sheets. As are the pale legs above them. I nearly retch, as it dawns on me with horror that Pandora is in fact riding Arne, who lies very still and silent as her goddess clasps his massive schlong. As if sensing my presence (though Lord knows how, as Pandora's wide body is blocking any possible vision of me from where he is lying and I am standing) a white-blonde head peeps out from the folds of Pandora's bucking hips and his expressionless ice blue eyes meet mine. OK, now I do understand that expression – my heart is now most assuredly in my mouth.

My next reaction is to note with some surprise that Arne is still wearing his shirt and tie, his jacket and suit trousers neatly folded and on a hanger on the wardrobe door. He taps Pandora's straddling thigh, and her head spin rounds, her wild green hair all about her. I have never seen a face more wild with lust. She looks at me insolently, insouciantly, shamelessly. And she beckons me to her.

Still straddling the tumescent Arne, she is kissing me hard on my lips, her tongue deep in my throat, as she rides the recumbent Norwegian with what I think the horsey people call a 'rise and fall' trot. I went riding with Lisa a couple of times on the moors around Bolton, and I remember my big brown beastie walking, trotting and finally cantering for a bit (when I nearly fell off) but I didn't do the galloping that Lisa could do. Pandora is moaning deep into my throat, and she is unbuttoning my bowling shirt and pulling it over my shoulders and arms. Don't look at Arne, my psyche is telling me. Focus on Pandora. Do not look at Arne.

I look down at Arne. He has his hands behind his head, like he is taking a nap, though his steely eyes are open, and despite being ridden by a demented horsewoman, there isn't a glow of colour in his cheeks. He catches me checking him out, and his eyes glare back, totally expressionless. No guilt, no shame, no pleasure, no nothing. Pandora's urgent hand is in my Calvins. She is gasping something in my ear, almost slavering as her temples press hard to mine.

"I want you to do-ooo something for me, Mee-lad. Something I want. Something I've always wanted. I want two men inside me. Front and back. I want dee-pee my dah-ling boy. I want you in my derriere."

Jesus H Christ. I am so not cut out for this. Milad Brown, porn star... don't think so. Arne Bastad, porn star...think so. So, what do I do? Endeavour is useless to me...he has already pissed off for a pint of bitter in Oxford. What would Sparky do? No, don't think about Sparky. OK, here is what I am going to do. I am just going to stop thinking. I am going feral. I am a wild fucking beast.

I return her pressing kiss with twice her force, and put both my hands on her magnificent jugs...they always get me going. And she is clever with her hands - I am not anxious in them anymore. I am getting big. Not as big as Arne, but big enough for this lady's other tunnel. She has her mouth about my swelling manhood; she rips open a *Durex* as I disappear into her gaping mouth. Now, I seriously must not look at Arne's face, or all wood will be fallen timber.

"Sluuuuuuurrrp. Gogh...now dahling, now! Put it in me, put it in me!" As my intrepid explorer emerges from her throat he is roll-hatted between her thumb and forefinger, and she slathers lube-stuff all over the condom. It's now or never, folks. I shuffle on my knees, having to part them over Arne's stiff white legs. Curiously, with Arne present, I am determined to do a professional job. Well, the courgette went in easy enough last night…let's see. Jesus, that is tight. I rock, back and forth and I note to my surprise and pleasure that Our Harry is disappearing nicely, and Pandora is absolutely squealing with pleasure.

"Ride me my fine boys! Fill me, fill me completely!" she is yelling.

Well, I am doing my job - but one weird, weird thing…I can feel Arne's coppice pole rubbing on the base of mine! I had no idea the separation between a ladies front and back bottom was so negligible! And I have to admit, Arne's mechanical in-and-out action is hitting the spot for me. Pandora is holding her breath, and screwing up her eyes in ecstasy. She better arrive soon, 'cos I am also in the home straight and the finishing post is in sight.

Suddenly Pandora's whole body tenses and spasms…she throws both her arms wildly into the air and her passages are contracting and throbbing, her nipples like granite rocks.

"Uhuhuhuhuhhuhuhuhuhhuhuhuhuhuhuhuhuhuhuhhu," she is quietly moaning, her eyes glazed and rolling. It's all mind blowing stuff, and I am there too, my arms clasped about her midriff. Poor old Arne is still hard as a log as she slips off him and I withdraw my sated, shrinking, bum-exploring bad boy.

"Hooooooooooooo! That was mighty good gentlemen!" Pandora is gasping and sweating like a basted pig roast. "Now bugger off the pair of you and make me a bacon sandwich. I am starving!" She clambers off the bed, making shooing gestures with both hands, and air emanating loudly from her two downstairs orifices.

I am still winded on all fours with the nodder hanging off my apparatus. Arne commando rolls off the bed and is back in his white trunks and trousers before you can say fjord. He flips the suit jacket nonchalantly over his shoulder and without so much as a glance at Pandora or me he is off down the stairs. I thought that might be a cue for Pandora to give me a hug or something, but she is wordlessly off to the bathroom. I stagger dazed into some clothes, tossing the greasy condom into a lined bin.

I am struggling with my emotions as I descend the stairwell, but it doesn't seem like Arne has any emotions to struggle with, as he fries up streaky bacon.

"Would you also like a sandwich, Milad?" he asks without turning his back.

Sandwich. Is he trying to make some kind of reference to what just happened? Nope, I don't believe he is.

"Yes please, Arne. Tomato sauce on mine."

"Very good. Make sure your stuff is packed up and on the jetty within one hour."

And there doesn't seem to be any more to say. I slump on the sofa, my eyes fixed on the one thawed pea that Arne has failed to hoover up. It sits in the fire grate, mocking me. Covered in wood ash, it looks as soiled and stupid as I feel.

WE ARE ZOOMING BACK DOWN THE A12. Not in the Spyder, which can't take three people, but in a steel-grey Porsche Panamera, a seriously lush car. It's not one of Neil's cars, all Arne says is it belongs to a friend of his. I settle out on the back seat pretending to be asleep, Arne drives at high speed in rapt concentration, and Pandora claps and sings along to the appalling Michael Bublé. She is in very high spirits, and is mainly on her mobile to her various Bonkers Babes, hinting broadly at her pornographic exploits of this morning and laughing openly about the photo of me with the courgette up my arse. Occasionally she turns around to wink at me, but I pretend I haven't seen her. I am fifty shades of fucked up, here. One minute I am planning to have her kids, the next minute I am the ass man in a scene out of one of Sparky's grainy 70's pornos.

She is leaning over the back seat, kind of poking me with her nail extensions, and proffering a round metal box at me. "Would you like a mint, Milad?"

I open my eyes and give her a look, which I am hoping is a wounded one. "No, Pandora, I'll pass on the mints, thanks. Look, would you mind if I have a couple of days off? I know we have a busy schedule coming, but I haven't seen my Mum and Dad in a while, and I…"

"Arne, can we spare Milad for a couple of days?" Pandora is asking Arne earnestly, also offering him a Mint Imperial, which to my surprise he accepts by popping one into his cheek. He checks his phone calendar, whilst simultaneously undertaking at high speed a fist-waving geriatric Rover driver.

"I suppose we don't really need him for Monday and Tuesday, PM. We have meetings with a number of publishing houses but your contract lawyers will be present."

"Right you are, Arne. Yes Milad, of course you can go off and see your Mummy and Daddy. But you will stay with Neil and I tonight, won't you dah-ling?"

"Thanks, but if it's all the same to you I'll get the train back to Horsham. I've got…quite a lot to sort out."

"Oh well, suit yourself. We can drop him at Victoria Station, can't we, Arne?" Pandora folds her arms and swivels to face front, going into one of her huffs.

"Bit out of our way, PM. But we are making good time and the traffic in London shouldn't be a problem."

"Thanks, Arne," I say, and pretend to go back to sleep again. My phone is on vibrate, and I am getting a number of txts from my mates. Sparky and Dean are on their way into London to drop Neil's Jag back at Holland Park, but they are mainly daft messages and I'm not in the mood.

Pandora is poking me again, and beginning to piss me right off. She is listening to bloody Coldplay now. I open one eye and she is pointing at her phone, winking at me. Oh, she's sent me a text message, has she?

"Dling, u wr awesm tdy my hansm stud. Thnk u for wndfl wknd. Xxx"

I really do not want to answer this, but Pandora is craning round, like an expectant spoiled child. I will play the employee.

"V. hpy to b of service, PM. Enjyed ur island. MB x"

Her phone bleeps and she is reading my msg, as I stare blankly out of the window. She is tapping a response.

"Only wun tiny kiss fr ur godss? I wl cry if u don't send mre ☒"

I am not playing this game, and as she looks around at me with a protruding lower lip, I take my phone and make it crystal clear to her, that I am turning it off. And then, I really do go to sleep.

I GIVE HER A FROSTY HUG when we reach Victoria Station in mid-afternoon, as Arne dumps my case on the pavement. I have nothing to say to her, and she looks quite angry with me. I turn away, and with the clunk of the passenger seat door she is aboard and the mean steely Porsche zooms away down Wilton Road in mad acceleration. It's a sunny late summer afternoon. I decide to take a walk, and deep in thought, I walk up Buckingham Palace Road and along Birdcage Walk, crossing the road to St James Park, where I stand on the bridge across the lake and stare into the water and at flocks of exotic-looking birds. There is an ice cream van, and I buy myself a '99' and sit on a park bench where not very long ago, my Dad was sitting next to me and buying '99's for me and Naz. There is a partly-deflated metallic helium balloon tied to the back of the bench with *Spongebob Squarepants* on it. At first, Spongebob's indefatigable gap-toothed smile makes me smile too. But then tears are flooding down my face and I am sobbing my bloody heart out.

"MILAD! MILAD! WHAT THE FUCK ARE YOU DOING HERE? Neil said you were staying the night at his place?! Are you alright, mate?"

I am on the concourse at Victoria Station, sitting on my Prada bag waiting for the platform to be called for the 17.15 to Horsham, and suddenly Sparks and Dean are pulling me to my feet. Sparks gives me a big hug, and this time, it's me who doesn't want to let go. And though I'm done blubbering, Dean and Sparks can see that I'm not in a good way.

"What's going on, mate? Has she fired you?" Sparks is looking at me in concern and has picked up my bag.

"No, no, man, I'm fine. It's all fine. Just been a bit of weird weekend, is all."

"Right, what you need is a Mac." That's generally what Dr. Sparks prescribes when things are low. A Big Mac. And you know what, that is just what the doctor ordered. We get takeaway and we are munching away and slurping from straws aboard our train, as it eases out of London.

"So, you got the Jag back in one piece alright then, boys?"

"Oh yeah, no problem. What a nice guy that Neil is," replies Sparks, his mouth full of onion rings and half-masticated Maccie. "He says I can borrow it again if I want. Me and Deano valeted it ourselves, didn't we, Deano."

"Sure did, clean as a whistle it was, Mil. What was this private island like, then? Sparks said some old sailor bloke rowed you there?"

"Yeah, Mr Glossop. I dunno guys, it was all a bit of a head-fuck really. I don't really get these people. Maybe they are too posh for me, or something."

The lads are quiet for a bit. I can tell they have been discussing me and the whole Pandora thing, but they munch solidly away at their burgers.

"Ah, delicious!" declares Sparky, with pickle all over his chin and cheese all over his cheeks, screwing up greasy paper. "Let's clear this crap up - here, Deano, put this lot in the bin. Whilst Dean is away, Sparks gives me one of his serious looks, which is quite hard to take seriously at the best of times, but when he is wearing a Mac it is impossible. "Look Mil, let's go to The Tig when we get back. Just me and you. We need to talk."

"I'd like that, Sparks. I'd like that very much. And I'll put the beers on Pandora's bloody expense account. Plus as many porky scratchings as you can eat."

Sparky sits back with a thoughtful smirk on his face, and it's obvious what he's thinking. How many bags of porky scratchings he reckons he can safely consume.

CHAPTER TEN

"Thanks…and six packets of Mr. Porky's. Could you do me a receipt, please? Oh, and stick the next round on there as well. Cheers."

Sparks and I have chosen a little booth in the corner of the public bar in *The Tig* for our private chat, and I already feel tonnes better for being back in Horsham, back at the flat and ensconced in the local. The IPA tastes good. We sit and sup in silence for a bit…well apart from Sparky crunching at dried pork crackling. He is wearing one of his better drinking T-shirts – it is shit brown in colour and carries the non-hilarious motif "I drink, therefore I am" with an image of the philosopher René Descartes with a pint in his hand.

"She has been in the papers a lot, you know," Sparky says suddenly, between crackling fragments.

"Who has?"

"Pandora. You know, PM Poste."

"Course she has. It's my job to get her in them, you prannet."

"Yeah, I know, but like, the gossip mags? Nat brought one up to the flat. *Celebrity Goss*, I think it's called."

"Who reads *Celebrity Goss*, Sparks? It's all shit. But I'm not surprised that Pandora is in it. She is pretty much famous now. You saw all those people gawping when we were driving up the Marylebone Road on Friday."

Sparks is rustling in his battered *Vans* rucksack, and produces a furled up copy of the magazine weekly in question. "Thing is Mil - you are in it, mate. Along with a whole bunch of other blokes. Here." He shifts our pints and spreads out a lurid double page spread with the bright yellow headline "*Pandora and her Toy Boys*", followed by "*Black Heart Best-Seller Beds Boy after Boy after Boy!*"

There are six numbered boxes with six paparazzi snaps, and Box Number 3 is bloody well me! I'm quite pleased with the picture, as I leave the St. Pancras Hotel with Pandora on my arm with Arne close behind, I am looking pretty cool in my dark suit, and I am smiling broadly. I read the bright red text box beneath.

"Pandy's Number Three is Milad Brown, her hot shot young PR man. Milad (21) lives in Horsham, Surrey, and was previously a journalist on the West Sussex County Times. Pandy's randy eye candy is never far from her side, whether at her home in West London, exclusive London hotels, or PM's private estate in Suffolk. Good Going Gal!"

We studied the tabloid journalistic format at Bolton Uni, and I can write it myself quite well, but they still need to get their facts right! Horsham... Surrey? Very poor. But who are these other blokes?

Number One is apparently Louis from *One Direction*, though it looks to me like Pandora is following him out of a night club, and he looks a bit shocked as Pandora grabs his arm and beams into the camera lens. Number Two is Robert Pattinson, next to whom Pandora is sitting in Virgin Atlantic Business Class, and she appears to have taken the photo herself at her arm's length. Numbers Four, Five and Six seem to be young nobodies; though she does seem to be well acquainted with all of them, especially Number Six, who she is snogging against a brick wall in an alley.

Sparky is inspecting my reaction over his nearly empty beer glass. He looks a bit nervous and shifty.

"I'd better get us another round in, mate," I say, a bit winded. "Same again?"

"Oh yes. And I reckon I can do two more packets of Mr. Porky's. And a whisky chaser please, Randy Eyecandy." Sparky smirks his incorrigible smirk.

As I stand at the bar waiting to be served, I am haunted by these other young tabloid bucks, and also by the thought of being some kind of paparazzi target myself. Will there be snappers hiding with their long lenses outside of Flat 3? Or even in the shrubbery at Mum and Dad's house in Nuthurst? I return to our table with the beers, just as Nat and Rollo walk in hand-in-hand, and the bags of scratchings I am carrying in my teeth fall to the ground as my jaw involuntarily slackens. Rollo swoops to pick up the packets.

"Mil!" he exclaims. "I didn't know you were back! Brilliant party the other night, and it's in all the papers! Sparky is in one of the pictures in *The Daily Mail*. And *The Horsham Times*, though I think that had something to do with our ace local reporter here!"

I put the pints down on the table and give them both a big hug. "Really? Not in his bloody dinner jacket T-shirt! Oh no! Right, what are you both having, Pandora is buying. Come, on Sparks, let's move to a bigger table, shall we?"

I get Rollo his usual pint of snakebite and black (also Lisa's favourite tipple, she used to call it a pint of sass, which they do in Lancashire) and Nathalie a V & T. She seems to be excited to see me, but it's like she is with somebody famous, not me. She keeps smiling at me in raptures and squeezing my hand, though her other hand is clasped in Rollo's.

"So what about you two!" I exclaim, with exaggerated surprise. "You make a really great couple, you do." Nathalie blushes and so does Rollo, and they look shyly at each other and then at the floor. I feel a bit choked for some reason, and go over to the jukebox. I put on *Video Games* by Lana Del Rey - I'm ready for some sad stuff.

"Oh, I love Lana!" Nathalie is bouncing and smiling on the leatherette.

"Oh no, not this!" sighs Sparky. "Bloody funeral music!"

We all laugh, and Rollo pecks Nat's cheek, almost involuntarily, like an impulse he can't resist.

"Well, what is the next stop on your rollercoaster ride to fame and fortune with Mrs Poste then, Mil?" asks Nat, her eyes shining as she sips with touching femininity her vodka and tonic.

"Oh, I don't know, Nat. It's a world I don't know…and I'm definitely not up for regular appearances in *Celebrity Goss* magazine!" I pick up the rolled-up mag, which I know they have all read, and toss it at Sparky. "She is finishing up the sequel to *Black Heart* and they are talking about a US publicity tour. All I know, is I'm going to see Mum and Dad and Naz for a couple of days. And my Uncle Nersi and Auntie Sara are over from LA. It will be good to see them. Anyway, never mind about me, you are the hot shot journo around these parts, Nat! What's this story you wrote up in *The Times*?"

"Oh, that was nothing, Mil. Ray wrote it mainly. But I did want to make sure you and Sparks were in the photo we published. Wasn't that embarrassing - when her dress blew up?!"

We are all laughing in lewd recollection, and Sparks is rolling around like a Weeble.

"Oh, man!" he is spluttering. "It was like a full moon over London Town! And when Arne kicked the puppet's arms off! Ho ho…classic! I love that guy!"

Arne. Despite me being about as intimately acquainted with Arne as a guy can get, I realise that I know very little about him. I remember his expressionless white face and ice blue eyes staring up at me from the bed at The House of Correction, and I actually shudder.

"Just got a text from Potts," reports a chuckling Rollo. "Him and Tils are coming over, I better txt Deano."

TWO HOURS LATER THE GANG have gathered in the otherwise sparsely populated Tig and we are all pissed. Nat and Tils are dancing to Jessie J on the jukie, and Sparks is doing his Tinie Tempah rapping, much to the amusement of us all.

My Arne-Phone lights up…it's a text from Pandora. I consider opening it for a moment, but you know what?

I switch off my phone, and I join the dancers and rapper on the postage stamp-sized dance floor. My arm is around Sparky Tempah, and we are all singing, and swaying our arms.

"Everybody look to their left, everybody look to their right, can you feel that? Yeah? We'll pay them with love tonight."

Rollo catches my eye as he shuffles up next to Nat, and he is asking me something with his sharp blue eyes. I lurch over and give him the biggest hug, and I pat his back with my assent. Then all of us are leaping around like mentalists on the sticky postage stamp, as Eric the landlord gives us the evil eye. Which makes us sing even louder.

"Ain't about the cha-ching, cha-ching! Ain't about the ba-bling, ba-bling! Wanna make the world dance - forget about the…price tag! Yeah, yeah oh, forget about the price tag!!"

Pandora's Inner Goddess Soundtrack

1. Eminem, *Lose Yourself*

2. MF Doom, *Melody*

3. Brian Jonestown Massacre, *Servo*

4. Pulp, *Common People*

5. Rick Ross, *9 Piece*

6. Kaiser Chiefs, *We Are The Angry Mob*

7. Thomas Tallis, *Spem in Alium*

8. The Smiths, *Everyday is Like Sunday*

9. The Addams Family, *Theme*

10. Pet Shop Boys, *It's A Sin*

11. Lil B, *Surrender to Me*

12. Beyoncé, *Party*

13. Nigel Kennedy, *Gypsy Csardas*

14. Rihanna, *Umbrella*

15. Earl Sweatshirt, *Molliwopped*

16. King Trigger, *The River*

17. Jo Stafford, *You Belong to Me*

18. Flight of The Conchords, *If That's What You are Into*

19. Lana Del Rey, *Video Games*

20. Jessie J, *Price Tag*

www.ingramcontent.com/pod-product-compliance
Lightning Source LLC
Chambersburg PA
CBHW050426260626
47156CB00003B/1172